THE ENIGMA CUBE

Douglas E. Richards

Paragon Press

Copyright © 2020 by Douglas E. Richards
Published by Paragon Press, 2020

Email the author at douglaserichards1@gmail.com

Friend him on Facebook at Douglas E. Richards Author

Visit the author's website at www.douglaserichards.com

First Edition

PROLOGUE

Berlin, Germany, 1941

Otto Richter scribbled equations into a notebook at a furious pace, as if he were possessed by a berserker demon. He was in hot pursuit of a sudden inspiration—that superfluidity could be used to model exotic matter, which in turn could lead to a mathematical bridge between general relativity and quantum mechanics.

A remarkable insight that might have come from the mind of Albert Einstein on his very best day, but beyond astonishing coming as it did from the mind of a wiry sixteen-year-old boy, still awaiting his growth spurt, who couldn't have weighed more than a hundred twenty pounds dripping wet.

Otto urged himself to write even faster, annoyed at having to delay his thoughts in order to record them, but was unable to coax any additional speed from his right hand as it flew over the page.

Three sharp raps on the door dislodged Otto's consciousness from the nearly transcendent plane it had been on, and he returned to the real world with a violent thud. He scowled at the audacity of this abrupt interruption, which had ripped his mind from a Nobel-prize worthy inspiration and had reinserted it into the mundane.

Or perhaps these raps at the door were *not* so mundane.

They had been sharp, decisive—*demanding* even. Not the knocks of a friend or colleague, but the knocks of someone who was impatient and used to being obeyed.

A chill ran up Otto's spine, for no reason he could pinpoint, and he glanced at his parents, who had been reading by the fireplace, to learn if this visit was expected. From the mystified, worried looks on their faces, it was anything but.

Otto pushed his chair back from his desk and rose to answer the door, but his father, Hans, shook his head and strode past him. The elder Richter turned the handle on the door, and it was immediately shoved open from outside, slamming painfully into his body and driving him backward as if he were weightless.

Four men stood before the threshold, three of them with machine guns slung around their necks, and they rushed inside, uninvited, as though they owned the place. As if the *Richter family* were the trespassers. All four wore impossibly crisp uniforms and bright red armbands containing a white circle with a black swastika inside— essentially a wearable Nazi flag.

Otto had studied the swastika symbol in school, and many others, as the Nazi party seemed to be obsessed with symbolism. One of their only obsessions that wasn't deadly—at least, not *directly*. The same couldn't be said of their obsession with power, conquest, and genocide.

In 1923, Hitler and his Nazi Party had attempted to seize Munich and use this city as a base of operations for a coup against Germany's Weimar Republic. The attempt had failed, and Hitler had been wounded in the process. Still, this bold action had brought him to the attention of the German nation and the world, as did his three-week trial.

Hitler was found guilty of treason and sentenced to five years in Landsberg Prison, but he only served nine months. And while he was incarcerated, he came to realize that his newfound celebrity gave him the means to obtain power after all—but this time *legally*. He wasted no time vigorously spreading Nazi propaganda, beginning with the work he had penned in prison, *Mein Kampf*—My Struggle— which included his description of the symbolism of the Nazi flag.

The *hakenkreuz*, or hooked cross, had been a popular symbol throughout history, but Hitler preferred the Sanskrit term, *swastika*, meaning "well-being," and described this symbol in his book as signifying the "struggle for the victory of Aryan mankind."

So much for symbolizing *well-being*.

The four intruders to the Richters' loving home exuded nothing but menace and cruelty, sneering at the panicked looks on the faces of Otto and his parents. His mother attempted to stifle a gasp, but couldn't, and his father looked to be paralyzed, as if he had turned a corner and found himself facing a pack of rabid wolves.

Otto knew that his father would have *preferred* the wolves.

The three men sporting swastika armbands and carrying machine guns could intimidate anyone, but they weren't nearly as troubling as the man who had led them inside. Based on the insignias on his uniform, this man was exceedingly high in rank, a *gruppenfuhrer*, the equivalent of a major general, and he wasn't with the German army. That would have been a blessing.

Instead, the pairs of stylized lightning bolts affixed to his lapels made it clear that he was near the very top of perhaps the cruelest, most ruthless organization mankind had ever known, the *Schutzstaffel*, which literally translated into The Protection Squadron, an absurd misnomer more generally abbreviated simply as the SS.

The SS was the ultimate paramilitary force, responsible for security, surveillance, terror, and ultimately, genocide. A malevolent collection of psychopaths and bullies who would go on to run all of the Reich's concentration and extermination camps, and who were responsible for the detection of actual or potential enemies of the Nazi state.

And the man in front of him wasn't just a member of the psychopathic SS, his rank suggested that he reported to Heinrich Himmler himself, who was rumored to be the personification of pure evil.

Otto suddenly found it hard to breathe. The Richter family had zero Jewish blood, but many years earlier, most of his parents' closest friends at the university, where Hans Richter taught higher mathematics, had been Jewish. Hans had known enough not to protest too loudly when they had been relieved of their positions, along with all other Jewish professors, and had fled into the diaspora.

Hans Richter knew that his Jewish friends had been lucky to get out of Germany, and he only wished that he could follow. But as much as he wanted to, his wife had too many close relatives in Berlin, and she had persuaded him to remain at his post and do what he could to safely and subtly undermine Nazi propaganda, minimal though this effort might be.

Otto wondered if his father's attempts to influence key university personnel had been less subtle than the elder Richter had thought, and had been responsible for this nightmarish visit. But he quickly thought better of it. Even if these activities *had* attracted the notice of the SS, his father would have never attracted the personal attention of a *general*.

The sick feeling in the pit of Otto's stomach intensified as he realized that they must be here for *him*.

All of these thoughts, musings, and analysis flashed across Otto's unparalleled mind in seconds—his speed of thought just as extraordinary as its quality.

"How can I help you, Herr Gruppenfuhrer?" croaked his father. His mouth had become so parched, and his throat so constricted in fear, the words barely made it past his lips.

"My name is Magnus Becker," said the general, "and I'm here to collect your son."

Hans Richter's eyes widened in alarm and he opened his mouth to protest, or demand clarification, but he bit his tongue. They were at this man's mercy, which was sure to be exceedingly limited, so discretion was the better part of valor. "Apologies for my ignorance, General Becker," he began, choosing his words with great care and fighting to keep the outrage from his voice, "but I would be grateful if you could explain."

"I should think the explanation is obvious," said Becker in contempt. "Your son has come to the attention of the esteemed leader of the SS, Heinrich Himmler. I'm told that little Otto was fluent in four languages, speaking them all without accent, by the age of four. That he taught himself calculus by the age of six. That at his current age of sixteen, he has already made several groundbreaking contributions to the field of mathematical physics."

"That is correct, Herr Gruppenfuhrer," said Hans. "But experts in the Nazi Party thought it best for him to continue his studies at home, believing him to be too young for the university environment. In short, General, they believe it best not to dislodge the goose that lays the golden eggs from its nest. Not when it's being so productive."

"I'm afraid that policy has come to an end," said Becker. "The Reich needs his services."

"Is there no way for him to render services from our home?" pleaded Hans.

Once again, the general glared at the elder Richter in contempt. "Your son is the perfect example of the superiority of the Aryan race. It's high time he was properly deployed. Because of your age, and because you are needed to train the next generation of mathematicians, you've been given a pass in the current conflict." His lip curled up into a sneer. "But surely, Herr Richter, you didn't think your family could shirk all contributions to the war effort indefinitely?"

"That was never our intent, Herr Gruppenfuhrer," said Hans Richter quickly. "Our loyalty to the Third Reich is absolute," he added, a lie that Otto knew to be truly extraordinary in its magnitude.

The general scowled. "I've heard rumors to the contrary."

Otto's father shrank back, but he was too afraid to even reply.

Otto had been sure that Hitler and his band of irrational psychopaths would quickly lose the war, but their very ferocity, their audacity, had the opposite effect, and it now wasn't hard to imagine Nazi ideology spreading over much of the globe.

Hitler's domain already included Austria, Poland, Czechoslovakia, Denmark, Norway, Yugoslavia, Greece, Belgium, and France, and at times the German army appeared unstoppable. Germany's *Blitzkrieg*, which translated to *Lightning War*, had proven successful beyond all expectations, as huge concentrations of tanks, planes, and artillery raced ahead at speeds previously unheard of in war. These forces quickly punched holes in enemy defenses, like an irresistible battering ram, allowing tank divisions to penetrate and operate freely behind enemy lines, sowing shock and chaos, while thousands of German bombers kept the slow, entrenched enemy from resupply or redeployment.

Worse, the Nazis turned the blitzkrieg soldiers into an army of supermen, plying them liberally with crystal meth—speed—in pill form, shipping thirty-five million tablets to their three million troops. This drug allowed soldiers to advance for days without sleep, dulled their sense of empathy, made them feel euphoric and invincible, and turned them into aggressive, reckless killing machines.

And now, apparently, it was Otto's turn to be violated in whatever fashion the Third Reich saw fit, all in furtherance of mindless conquest.

Elsa Richter maintained a strong bearing, but a single tear escaped from her right eye and rolled down her cheek, beyond her control. "How long will you need our son?" she whispered.

"Until we don't!" barked the general. "My patience is growing thin. I want him packed and ready in five minutes."

"Wouldn't he perform better if we went with him?" said his mother, desperately trying to avoid the unavoidable.

The general issued a cruel snort, not even bothering to answer.

"Can you at least tell us where he'll be going?" she asked as several more tears began running down her face.

Becker shook his head in disgust. "Enough!" he barked. "No more questions. I can't tell you where he'll be, or what he'll be doing. Only that he'll be part of a team of scientists, working on an important, top-secret project, and will be treated well. You'll have no further contact with him until he is finished, whenever that might be. He won't be writing any letters, nor will he be receiving any."

"What if I refuse to participate?" asked Otto, blinking back tears of his own.

The general stared at him in disbelief, stunned that the boy had the audacity to speak. "You're obviously not as bright as I've been led to believe," he spat. "I'm going to pretend I didn't hear that. Not only will you participate, you'll excel. If you don't live up to expectations, there will be consequences."

"Even if I try my best," said Otto, "I can't guarantee results. No one can."

An icy smile spread slowly across the general's face. "Let me put it this way," he said. "The project you'll be on will have the full attention of the Fuhrer himself, along with Reichsfuhrer Himmler. If you perform as expected, if you distinguish yourself, great honor will accrue to you and your family, and the rewards will be significant."

"And if I fail?" asked Otto.

Becker's disingenuous smile disappeared, to be replaced by a scowl. "Failure will not be tolerated. Even success will not be good enough, unless we judge you to be giving it your all. In short, we expect you to *dazzle* us. If not, I'll have no other choice but to explore the rumors I spoke of earlier. The ones suggesting your father is committing crimes against the state, however delicate he thinks he's being."

Otto glanced at his father, who shot him a defiant nod, too quickly and subtly for the SS general to see. A sharp nod that spoke volumes. A nod that gave him permission to use far less than his full brilliance on the project. A nod that told him that if the project was designed to help further the Nazis' cause—which it surely must be—his parents would rather die than see him provide any missing pieces of the puzzle.

Otto turned his gaze back to Becker. "In that case, Herr Gruppenfuhrer," the boy whispered, "I'll make sure that you're dazzled."

But as he stared further into the eyes of evil, tears began streaming quietly down his cheeks.

"Stop your blubbering this instant!" demanded the general, spittle flying from his mouth. "You're embarrassing yourself and the Reich," he continued, enraged, "and it's a disgusting display! You're weak, pathetic—*soft!* Our boys are dying on the battlefield, and you're here curled into a fetal position because you won't see your *mommy* for a while. You make me sick!"

The general stared at Otto Richter in utter contempt, and his tone changed from fire to ice. "If your goal is to dazzle," he said slowly, biting off each word as if it were acid, "know that you're off to a very bad start."

PART 1

Enigma (**noun**): A person or thing that is mysterious, puzzling, or difficult to understand.

1

The outskirts of Spokane, Washington, 2027

Dr. Kelly Connolly stood by the entrance to a small, single-story factory building and watched as a civilian SUV arrived at a guard gate and the driver stopped to show credentials. The fence around the facility was laughably benign, unable to deter even a modestly capable ten-year-old. No rolls of wicked razor wire crowning every inch of its perimeter, and no deadly levels of electricity coursing through its metal veins.

The gatehouse was also the very picture of innocence, as was the attendant. There wasn't a hint of weaponry or military presence, and there were no spikes embedded in the pavement that could be automatically lifted to shred the sturdiest of tires as easily as a pin could pop a child's balloon.

But, like the faux factory itself, built at the edge of a vast woods, the perimeter was a deception, and far more secure than it seemed. In fact, the site was ringed with enough hidden firepower and other deterrents to ward off a small attacking army. Not that any of it would ever need to be used. Military installations raised eyebrows, piqued curiosity, drew attention. Small factories, appearing to be only minimally secure, on the other hand, drew nothing but yawns.

Kelly sighed. "I don't suppose there's any way I can get out of this," she said to the lanky, balding man beside her.

Dr. Harry Salazar looked amused. "Trust me, Kelly," he said, "you'll enjoy this visit more than you think."

"That would almost *have* to be true," she replied wryly.

She and Harry Salazar, vaunted director of Project Uru, had gotten along famously since she had joined his team seven months earlier. Which in this instance was more of a curse than a blessing.

She was a department head, yes, but only one of six. And yet she alone had been assigned the duty to join Salazar as a Walmart greeter, to welcome Major Justin Boyd, a high-ranking black-operations officer, and give him a guided tour.

Kelly knew full well why she was now with her boss playing hostess while the other department heads were allowed to duck this odious duty. The director of Uru liked being around her more than the others. It was as simple as that. Salazar had confided in her that he found her to be the most polished of the departmental heads when it came to both social graces and personality.

She was also female, and while Salazar would never admit it, she suspected he was playing to the major's more primal instincts, hoping that if he were the typical military hard-ass, he would be less so in her presence. Or better yet, find her attractive. And while she didn't cause auto accidents when she strolled along streets full of male drivers, this latter hope wasn't out of the question. Her smooth skin, large emerald eyes, girl-next-door beauty, and athletic body never failed to attract male attention.

"Trust me, Kelly," repeated Salazar, as the corners of his mouth turned up into a knowing smile. "You're going to be pleasantly surprised."

"What don't I know about this?"

"You have very low expectations for this visit. I get that. You haven't dealt with anyone in the military before, have you?"

Kelly shook her head. "This would be the first."

"I figured," said Salazar. "Scientists tend to think that anyone able to rise through the ranks of the military almost has to be a small-minded, war-mongering hard-ass. But some are very good men and women. Intelligent. Compassionate even. Really."

Kelly sighed again. "I know I'm stereotyping," she said. "But while he might not be a bloodthirsty barbarian, there's no way he's a pacifist, either. Which is why you don't see a lot of Amish generals," she added with a grin.

Salazar laughed. "True, but let me tell you more about the major. You've never met his boss, Colonel Tom Osborne, either," he said, referring to the man in charge of all of America's black sites. "But he's also impressive. Not at all the power-hungry hawk you might imagine."

"You mean other than being responsible for every secret program in America designed to develop the next generation of WMD?"

"Right," said Salazar, in amusement. "Other than that. But let me get to the punchline. This major we'll be meeting—Boyd—is a member of a black ops program right out of the comics. Supersoldiers. Enhanced human fighters, souped-up in any way genetic engineering and technology will allow. Captain America wannabees." He grinned and gestured at Kelly. "Go ahead, say it. I'll wait."

"And that's supposed to make me feel *more* comfortable?" she asked, right on cue.

"In an ironic way, yes. This program is called EHO, for *Enhanced Human Operations*. And the military took a long, sober look at what they were doing. If you're determined to enhance a soldier, you'd better be sure the men and women you recruit to be your Frankensteins, your unstoppable killing machines, all have a heart of gold and the morality of a saint. They figured enhancement would amplify a person's underlying characteristics. Enhance someone with even a hint of villainy at their core, and you get a super villain. Enhance someone with heroism at their core, on the other hand . . ." he added, nodding at Kelly to finish.

"And you get a super-*hero*," she said dutifully. "Really, Harry? You do know this is the real world."

"Lines between what's real and what's science fiction are blurring more every year. But the bottom line is that the military put a lot of thought into their EHO recruiting effort. They began with very good people. For this Boyd to have made the cut, he couldn't have been a typical military grunt. Osborne, himself, is a very good man, and he tells me that Justin Boyd has distinguished himself, even in this rarified group. Apparently, he's exceedingly bright, moral, decisive, and heroic. He's only thirty-two, but seen as someone with limitless potential."

Kelly was about to ask Salazar a question, but the man in question had made it through the gate, parked his rental SUV, and was rapidly approaching.

Boyd was dressed in casual civilian clothing, and lugging a gray civilian duffel bag, a sizable version that was stuffed to the gills. He was on the handsome side, although physically unimposing, looking to be of average height, weight, and strength. His demeanor was friendly but businesslike, commanding, but not bombastic.

"Welcome to Project Uru, Major," said Salazar, shaking the man's hand.

"Director Harry Salazar, I presume?" said Justin Boyd.

"Yes, and this is Dr. Kelly Connolly," he added as Kelly shook his hand. "But everyone here goes by their first names."

"Understood," said Boyd.

"Kelly has been with us now for seven months, and is doing some fine work."

"Is she your second-in-command?"

"I don't really have a second-in-command, Major. She's one of six department heads. But she's very good at explaining science, so I thought she'd be an asset today."

"Excellent. I can't tell you how much I'm looking forward to learning all about your program, Director," said the major.

Salazar nodded and ushered the small group inside the factory, which was an empty building whose sole purpose was to house and hide a number of small, self-driving shuttle buses and the mouth of a thirty-foot-wide tunnel. The shuttles took scientists to and from Project Uru's main base of operations, a sophisticated, multistory research facility eight miles inside the dense woods that abutted the factory, and buried half a mile beneath it.

Salazar gestured for their guest to take a seat in one of the shuttles, and he and Kelly Connolly sat across from him. "Feel free to leave your duffel bag here, if you'd like," the director offered.

"Thanks, but I'll keep it with me. It contains a lot of specialty items I used to carry with me in various vests and compartments on commando operations. The stuff in here saved my life several times, so I tend to keep it close."

"Even though you aren't on a dangerous mission?" said Kelly.

"Old habits die hard," he replied simply.

Salazar ordered the vehicle's AI to begin the short journey, and the all-electric vehicle immediately complied, soundlessly entering the smooth, concrete tunnel. The small shuttle picked up speed until reaching its plodding cruising rate of twenty miles per hour. The tunnel was well lighted and bore a continuous but mild declination all the way to the Uru facility.

"So how much do you know about Project Uru?" asked the director pleasantly.

The major shot his two hosts a sheepish smile. "Absolutely nothing," he admitted. "All I know is that it's called Uru, and that you've chosen to base it in a part of the country where it rains or drizzles about half the time."

Salazar smiled. "Actually, you're thinking of the western parts of the state—like Seattle. Spokane is considerably drier."

"Then I guess I know even *less* than absolutely nothing."

Kelly laughed. Perhaps her boss was right about this guy. Charming, humble, self-deprecating even.

Or was this just an act? A guy this bright and accomplished, who knew nothing about their program, would at least Google the city he was headed to. Had he purposely made this error to put them at ease with his humility and aw-shucks charm? If so, she wasn't sure if this made her think less of him, or more.

Salazar studied the major carefully. "I'm surprised to hear that you're so uninformed about us," he said. "I've been sending monthly reports to Colonel Osborne since this program began. Is there a reason you chose not to even skim through them?"

"It wasn't my choice, Director . . . *Harry*," said Boyd. "As you know, the colonel is planning to retire, and he wants me to take over. So I've been coming up to speed on all black ops activities under our purview, and made a list of black sites I planned to visit. Colonel Osborne insisted that I save this one for last, and that I go in absolutely cold. Believe me, I wanted to read your reports. But the colonel said they couldn't possibly do your project justice. That I really needed to see this for myself."

"He's not wrong," said Salazar soberly.

"Do you always visit these sites by yourself?" asked Kelly. "And wear civilian clothing? I'd expect the future head of black ops to travel with more of a military entourage."

"Uniforms and military entourages attract unwanted attention," replied the major. "But I do pay extra for self-driving rental cars," he added with a smile. "You know, so I can pretend I have a chauffeur."

Kelly laughed, finding it difficult not to like this man. "I don't mean to be too forward," she said, "but Harry just told me you're in a top-secret program called EHO. Which would make you the ultimate combat soldier."

Boyd sighed. "The better the skills and capabilities, the less need to use them, right? I've had to at times, but only when the mission was just, and lives were on the line."

"Still, why would Colonel Osborne want to tap you for an admin position?" pressed Kelly. "Kind of boring, I would think."

"Not at all. Having the chance to oversee black sites like yours, scientific sites, is anything but boring. The work being done at these sites is mind-blowing, and vitally important. Radar, computers, GPS, and the internet all came out of the military. I've had to engage in violence on occasion, but because I've witnessed the horrors of it, I plan to support tech programs that can be used to *prevent* violence, rather than creating more of it."

"I see," said Kelly, surprised to receive such a well-reasoned and articulate answer. This guy couldn't possibly be for real, could he? She thought of the old adage, when something seemed too good to be true, it probably *was*.

So was Justin Boyd just a smooth politician, in addition to his other skills? His answer had seemed a bit canned—like a stump speech. On the other hand, why would he need to win them over? The head of black ops wasn't an elected position, and Boyd was already slated to take the reins, even if it were.

"Getting back to Uru," said Boyd, "I haven't read your reports, Harry, but I have heard rumors." He raised his eyebrows. "There are lots of them. But if I had to guess which one was true—if any—I'd tend to guess it's the one that involves *extraterrestrials*."

"Really?" said Harry Salazar. "And why would you guess that?"

"Because there have been so many UFO sightings over the past few decades. And the colonel's behavior when it comes to your group is very odd. The rumor that rings true to me is that you're in possession of some kind of . . . alien artifact."

The hint of a smile came over the director's face. "Then you've chosen the right rumor, Major," he said. "But while *artifact* is as good a term as any, the truth is it's much more than a mere artifact. Since you haven't read my reports, I can give you the key take-home message in two sentences."

The director of Project Uru leaned closer to his guest. "My group is in possession of a piece of extraterrestrial technology. I believe this technology is *so* advanced, *so* astonishing, that if we could unlock its mysteries, we'd reveal scientific insights that are as far beyond our current capabilities as ours are beyond those of the *Neanderthal.*"

The major's eyes widened. "Now that's what I call a take-home message."

2

The shuttle continued moving through the tunnel at a snail's pace, inching its way toward the greatest find in human history.

"Unfortunately," continued Salazar with a frown, "we've made exactly zero progress unlocking its mysteries."

"So you have the ultimate treasure chest," said the future head of black ops, "but can't find a way to open it."

"Not from lack of effort," said Salazar. "And we will find a way. I promise you. But let me start at the beginning. As I said, it isn't really an artifact, not in an archaeological sense. Artifacts are historical remnants of a culture. This appears to be an active, working bit of alien technology they seem to have inadvertently left behind here on Earth."

"And by *they*, you mean . . . ?"

"I have no idea. You have access to more secret information than I do, Major, so maybe you can tell *me*."

"When it comes to possible alien visitors, I don't know much more than the public does. Namely, that there have been a rash of UFO sightings, which have become so persistent and compelling it's impossible not to acknowledge something is going on that we don't understand. And alien visitation is the obvious answer, even for a public with no knowledge of . . . well, of whatever it is that you're hiding here."

Kelly nodded in agreement. Almost every day, military pilots and other trained observers around the world were having close encounters with objects that seemed to defy the laws of physics. As far back as 2018 the US government had finally come clean, admitting it maintained a secret program to research and investigate UFOs, and released several videos of UFO encounters to the public. In addition, the Defense Intelligence Agency had briefed Congress that it was sponsoring extensive research into warp drives, wormholes, and other means of interstellar travel, to better understand how alien visitors might have gotten to Earth, and the advanced weaponry they might have brought with them.

"So I'm not at all surprised that Earth is being visited," continued the major. "No one who's been paying attention would be. I'm just thrilled to learn that the aliens finally left tangible evidence behind."

"*Finally?*" said Kelly. "I always assumed the UFO Exploration Group had found evidence a long time ago."

"I'm afraid not," replied Boyd.

"And they don't even know that we have, do they?"

Boyd shook his head. "My understanding is that the Secretary of Defense has chosen to keep this project the most closely guarded secret in the entire country." He gestured to the Uru director. "But please, continue."

"Thank you," said Salazar. "The alien object in question was discovered inside a large cabin on private property. The very property we're now traveling under. We believe that both the cabin and the artifact within had been abandoned for some time. Almost three years ago, two hikers, Bethany Cummings and Terry McNally, got so hopelessly lost in these woods they began to panic. When they came across this cabin, which was padlocked, they used a sturdy tree branch as a lever to break in, hoping for a phone, a fire, or some food."

"And that's when they found the object," said Kelly, relating the obvious punchline.

"It was glowing so brightly," continued Salazar, "that it was impossible for them to miss. You'll see it for yourself in just a few minutes. It's cubic in shape, and only the size of a softball, but it's truly otherworldly. Eerie, really. It exudes so much pent-up power that it's totally mind-blowing. Glorious and menacing, both—at the same time."

Boyd listened in rapt attention.

"The two women did make it back out of the woods, of course," continued Salazar. "When they did, they contacted NASA to report the object they had stumbled across. NASA checked it out, and it wasn't long before it became the most classified find in history and put under the auspices of black ops."

"Who owned the cabin?" asked Boyd.

"A dead end, I'm afraid," said Salazar. "There was literally no record that it even existed, and the owner of the land couldn't be found. It was marked as private property, but whoever bought the land concealed the purchase well."

The small shuttle bus slowed to a crawl and stopped inside another large parking area, joining three other shuttles currently available for the return trip.

Harry Salazar and Kelly Connolly ushered the future head of black ops through the main entrance to the Uru research facility in silence. Inside, it was bright and spacious. So much so that if not for a lack of windows, it could easily have been an expensive corporate research facility in a science park on the surface. Over the past ten years, excavation machinery had undergone revolutionary improvements in cost, speed, and efficiency, making elaborate subterranean structures surprisingly achievable.

"Let me take you right to the center of the maze," said Salazar, "to see the beast. A tour of the rest of the facility can wait."

The major nodded. "I couldn't agree more."

"We aren't planning any tests today," added the director, "so we'll be able to see the object up close and personal."

He ushered Boyd and Kelly through a long corridor that led directly to the center of the facility. They passed through a pair of twenty-five-ton blast doors and entered a spacious room that resembled a hockey rink in several ways, although square instead of rectangular, and lacking any ice. The ceiling was fifteen feet high, with the entire space ringed with transparent, floor-to-ceiling windows, like the protective glass that surrounded a rink.

Instead of stands appearing beyond the glass, there were a series of rooms filled with elaborate instrumentation, computers, or serving as viewing galleries, none of which were elevated. The floor and ceiling appeared to be made of the same material as the windows that surrounded them, although not fully transparent.

And at the precise center of the room, resting on the floor, sat the alien object, tiny but mighty, making its presence known by sending out thick beams of brilliant light from every vertex, each beam so blindingly bright it could be easily seen in a well-lighted room.

"How close can we get to it?" asked Major Boyd.

"As close as we want," replied the director.

They approached the gleaming, pulsating, otherworldly object, which the major could now see was cubic in shape, as he had been told. He crouched down to get a better view.

The object had an outer shell of edges linked together to form an open, cubical cage, about the size of a softball, as Salazar had said, or, more aptly, a large Rubik's Cube. It didn't have a color, but it shined with such unearthly brightness it seemed almost to be made of pure light. Within this outer cage was cradled a smaller solid . . . shape, which seemed to change continuously. Now a cube. Now a tetrahedron. Now one of an eclectic array of geometric shapes, some of which resembled 3D snowflakes. Now an impossible shape that was indescribable and unsettling to even observe.

As if this wasn't trippy enough, the human mind flipped back and forth between seeing the shape inside as being perfectly motionless, or as spinning at incredible speed, like an optical illusion image that could be visualized in two different ways, but not both at once.

The cube pulsated with energy, which the human mind sensed as being immense, limitless, and its rhythmic throbbing made the cube seem alive, as if it had a beating heart.

The major was mesmerized, as was anyone who had ever seen it. It was almost perfectly hypnotic, drawing him in with its unearthly power. Yet, like everyone else, he was unable to study it for more than ten to fifteen seconds without looking away.

He rose and turned toward the director, breaking its spell. "It's breathtaking," he said. "And frightening."

Salazar nodded. "It has to be seen in person to be believed."

"Speaking of that, how am I able to see it?"

Kelly grinned. "I *know*," she said enthusiastically. "From a distance, the light is blinding. If you're close to it and give it a tangential glance, it's just as bright. But if you look *directly* at it, you can see it clearly, despite enough illumination beaming out of it to put a lighthouse out of business. That's yet another aspect of it we haven't begun to figure out."

The major bent to study the object for a second time and then stood, less than a minute later. "Absolutely extraordinary," he said simply, as he and his two hosts formed a circle with their backs to the blinding light. "Colonel Osborne definitely saved the best for last. And he was right. Your reports couldn't have possibly done this justice."

"No doubt," agreed Salazar. "And when he said that you have to see this in person, that wasn't just a figure of speech. You actually *have to see this in person.* An attempted photograph or video of the cube captures nothing but light. And even if this object *could* be videoed, no video could possibly get across what it does to the mind, the feeling of immense power it somehow projects."

"We call it the Enigma Cube," said Kelly. "For obvious reasons. And we call this containment chamber we're in the Enigma Room."

"This room is in the precise center of the facility," said Salazar. "The floors, ceiling, and windows surrounding us are all a foot thick, and made of the highest-grade transparent aluminum available."

Boyd nodded, impressed. Transparent aluminum was a revolutionary alloy that had first been created in 2016 by researchers at Oxford, although the concept had been introduced twenty years earlier in a *Star Trek* movie. It was much lighter than glass, and far stronger.

"The facility itself," continued Salazar, "is encased in a massive block of concrete, three feet thick. And this block is topped by over a thousand feet of natural rock, mostly granite."

The major nodded thoughtfully. "That's quite a protective cocoon you've created," he said. "Your Enigma Cube will survive here, even if the world goes nuclear."

Salazar winced. "The survival of the cube isn't really our goal," he said. "Our goal is to ensure that the *world* will survive, even if the *Enigma Cube* goes nuclear."

Boyd swallowed hard. "Any reason to believe it might?"

"Not any overt reason, Major, but you've seen it. Any doubt that it could unleash world-destroying amounts of power if we riled it up somehow?"

"None," admitted Boyd.

"We have reason to believe it can tap into a nearly limitless power source," continued Salazar. "It's been blasting out light and performing its mind-bending transformational choreography now for three years. Probably a lot longer than that before we got hold of it. Its intensity hasn't diminished one iota, and we haven't exactly been plugging it in or changing any batteries. We've done some calculations, and we believe the energy needed to power the rotations of the inner object, as well as its kaleidoscopic shape changes, is massive. Yet the thing's power seems inexhaustible."

The director of Project Uru blew out a long breath. "So while we have no reason to believe it's volatile, we can't afford to be wrong."

"And even if the Enigma Cube isn't meant to be malevolent in any way," added Kelly Connolly, "we could destroy ourselves out of sheer ignorance. Bring a primitive man into our time, and he might thrive inside one of our homes. Until the day he shoves his finger into an electrical outlet out of curiosity."

"Good call, then," said Boyd. "I applaud your caution. But why build it here? Why not inside a mountain? Or a location even more remote than this one?"

"We didn't have a choice," said Salazar.

"Why not?"

"The cabin it was found in is a half mile above us," explained the director. "And I mean *precisely* above us. We bought the land for miles around it, and then bored a two-foot diameter hole inside the cabin going about half a mile down. The cube came along for the ride. And then we built this facility around where the cube ended up."

The major blinked in confusion. "So you essentially lowered the cube a half mile, without moving it horizontally."

"Correct," said the director.

"Why? Were you worried that horizontal movement might somehow trigger it?"

Salazar sighed. "Not at all," he replied. "We were *unable* to move it horizontally. Along with the Enigma Cube's other seemingly impossible characteristics, it's basically an immovable object."

He paused to let this sink in.

"The cube only weighs about forty thousand pounds," he continued, and then shook his head with a lopsided smile, realizing just how ridiculous this must sound. "Perhaps the word *only* isn't the best choice," he added, "since no material on Earth forged into a cube of this size could possibly weigh this much. And yet, somehow, it resists lateral movement as if it weighs tens of millions of pounds—maybe more. We have no idea how. All we know is that before we lowered the cube and built this facility, we tried everything we could think of to displace it laterally, without success. We even dismantled the cabin, tried to move it with a two-hundred-ton bulldozer the size of a house, and then rebuilt the original structure."

"So even the gargantuan dozer failed?" said Boyd in disbelief. "Seriously?"

Salazar raised his eyebrows. "Didn't budge it so much as a nanometer," he replied somberly.

The major grinned like a giddy schoolboy. "I have to say that I'm really, really beginning to like this thing," he whispered.

3

Commander Shen Ning kicked his legs high as he finished the third mile of his five-mile run, driving up a steep incline to reach the top of the hill that afforded the most panoramic view of Mount Spokane in the entire county.

Not that he would allow himself to enjoy the view. Or the splendor of the Spokane River and Selkirk Mountains. Or any of the vanilla tranquility that the area offered, for that matter.

He wasn't here to sightsee. He was here on an assignment that brought with it more visibility to the rarified upper echelon of China's government and military than any other assignment ever could. Working out of a private, secluded home that he had chosen to be their base in Spokane.

It had all begun less than a year earlier. Chinese physicists had come up with a device they hoped could detect disturbances in the curvature of spacetime throughout the cosmos. While their new sensor failed to detect anything in space, it did detect the faintest of signals coming from Spokane, Washington.

At first the physicists were convinced it was a glitch. But Chinese military intelligence decreed that it was worth investigating further. What were the Americans up to this time?

After some brilliant intelligence work, the Chinese intel community discovered that the Americans had set up a black ops facility outside of Spokane, Washington, manned by scientists studying a mysterious alien object of immense power and even more immense promise. One that had triggered this new sensor, and one that had quickly drawn the personal attention of the president of China himself.

And Shen Ning had been selected to be the key operative on the ground, to provide intel on this all-important discovery. It had been the greatest day of his life, a demonstration that his distinguished service had attracted even more attention than he had known.

He had met with China's paramount leader, Shi Yu, himself, who had told him that getting solid intelligence on the precise goings-on within the Spokane facility was among the highest priorities of any mission in China's magnificent history. Its importance could not be overstated.

Shen knew exactly why China's leaders were so obsessed with Spokane. They had long made it clear that they intended for China to dominate the globe, if not through military campaigns of global conquest, then through every other means available.

And when it came to exerting power, to achieving the greatest global reach, technology was *everything*. Whoever controlled breakthrough technologies controlled the world. It was as simple as that. And the object at Spokane represented the ultimate concentration of super-advanced technology. If the Americans had a eureka moment, China was determined to be looking over their shoulder when it happened.

The mission was so important that Shen had been authorized to make use of a prototype surveillance device of astonishing complexity. A bug that masqueraded as an *actual* bug. A fly drone constructed to look exactly like a small housefly, which could fly short distances and attach itself to pants and shirts and shoes.

The drone used active camouflage that put a chameleon to shame, and possessed both video and audio capabilities, miraculous in such a tiny package. Most importantly, it made use of breakthrough transmission technology that couldn't be detected by conventional means, so it was immune to security sweeps.

The Achilles' heel of this tiny fake housefly was its thirst for juice. Its many features, and especially its novel transmission method, required significant power, and its power source needed to be minuscule. The current prototypes were powered by light, but this had proven inadequate. If these devices ran out of power and ceased to be mobile, they would inevitably be discovered, and reverse engineered.

So it was lucky that the very location China most wanted to surveil was the one location that was perfectly suited to this novel technology. The object the Americans were calling the Enigma Cube gave off enough light to keep a fly drone *drowning* in power. So much, in fact, that the drones could be confidently shuttled to darker parts of the facility temporarily, and then shuttled back to the vicinity of the cube for recharging, without fear that the source would ever dry up.

Shen had landed these tiny flies on several scientists on the Spokane team, who had acted as clueless mules, shuttling them inside. So far none had been detected.

With this completed, he had begun the recruitment of an army of in-country mercenaries who, for the right price, wouldn't ask any questions or shirk from any mission, no matter how bloody. A network with offshoots in a variety of geographic locations within the States, so they could become China's own version of colonial minutemen, able to arrive anywhere on the continent in short order.

Shen had seen to it that this network was established, while making sure it couldn't be traced back to China. Since he spoke unaccented English, this hadn't been a problem. And he had completed this assignment in record time, working through an American intermediary to identify and vet the best mercenary networks. An intermediary whom Shen had killed the moment his task was complete, to eliminate all loose ends.

"Commander Shen," said the voice of his colleague, Li Jin, through the tiny comm embedded in his cochlea, "I recommend that you return to home base immediately."

"Report," he barked back, breathing hard as he continued running.

"We have Priority One activity at the target site," she replied. "Harry Salazar and Kelly Connolly are meeting with a Major Justin Boyd and giving him a tour of the facility. The major arrived alone, in civilian clothing."

She paused for effect. "And based on their conversation, Commander, this visitor is slated to become the head of American black ops."

Shen slowed to a stop. Vigorous exercise could wait. Nothing of interest had happened in four months, but they had just hit the mother lode. Short of learning that the Americans had made progress with the cube, this was as good as it got.

"How long have they been meeting?" he asked.

"Just over nineteen minutes. I can pipe the audio through to you now while you make your way back to base."

"That's not necessary. I'll be back soon, and I want to watch the video and audio together."

"Understood, Commander."

"How much longer do you think the meeting will last?"

"I can't be sure, of course, but I'd estimate at least an hour. They don't seem to be in a hurry, and have engaged in any number of digressions."

"Good. I'll be there in fifteen minutes."

The commander began running again, now eager to get back to the large private home that served as his base of operations as quickly as possible. He would need to contact Beijing and get satellites assigned to watch this Major Justin Boyd when he left the Spokane facility.

Despite the major's civilian clothing, Shen Ning had no doubt that the man would head immediately to nearby Fairchild Air Force Base, and from there hop a military jet to his next destination, possibly his home base.

Chinese satellites could track the plane in flight and an AI could guess its likely destination with a high degree of accuracy after viewing its course. Assuming there were mercenaries relatively close to where the jet was expected to land, Shen could have them take over surveillance. Ever so discreetly.

Chinese intelligence could also hack into American traffic cameras, and he would authorize this as well, pulling out all stops to track the major to his lair.

The cube had been a complete bust so far, and Shen Ning was convinced this wouldn't change.

But that no longer mattered. Because he now had a tiger by the tail—one by the name of Justin Boyd—and he didn't intend to let it go.

4

Justin Boyd stared off into space inside the Enigma Room—or more accurately, stared off at the viewing galleries ringing the room—ignoring the ever-present alien cube pulsing away with pure light and energy behind him, taunting humanity with its secrets.

"The cube is astonishing," he said finally. "*More* than astonishing. There are no words."

"We're lucky it was finally rediscovered," said Salazar. "Since it's immovable, someone must have originally found it in the woods and built the cabin around it. One with no windows, so its light wouldn't attract attention. Whoever built the cabin kept it tightly locked up."

"Why not just bury it?" asked Boyd.

"That's not clear," replied Kelly. "But there was mostly granite under where it was found, so this might have been easier said than done. Besides, if you have a one-of-a-kind painting by Salvador Dali, you don't bury it, you admire it. And the Enigma Cube makes the most masterful of Dali paintings seem commonplace."

"No doubt," said Boyd.

"So now you know why Harry named this group Project Uru."

"Actually, I've never heard the term. I promised Colonel Osborne I wouldn't look it up. He said it might be a spoiler."

"Interesting," said Kelly. "So you must not be much of a Marvel fan."

"I wouldn't say that," replied Boyd. "I've probably seen about half the movies. And *all* the Captain America ones, since he was arguably the fictional father of Enhanced Human Operations."

"I see. Well, it turns out that Uru is the name of a metal. The metal that Thor's hammer is made from."

"Of course," said Boyd, his eyes sparkling in delight. "Because his hammer is also a small, immovable object. One that wields tremendous power."

"Exactly," said Kelly. "Immovable—unless you happen to be Thor."

"In that case, Uru is a great name. But wouldn't Thor's hammer have been even better?"

"There comes a time when a name is just too silly," said Salazar. "And too on the nose."

"The other important thing you need to know about Uru metal," said Kelly, "just to further the metaphor, is that it can only be produced by a forge powered by the heart of a dying star. One run by Dwarves."

"Well, yeah," said the major with a grin, "everyone knows that Dwarves make the best weapons."

His smile vanished, and he became serious once again. "But I see why you think this is so interesting," he added. "Because the only way the cube could weigh even forty thousand pounds is if it contains a sprinkling of neutron star matter, right? Which can only be found at the heart of a dying star."

Kelly's eyes narrowed, and she couldn't help but be impressed. "I thought I was going to have to explain that to you."

"Like I said, I dabble in science."

"I guess so," said Kelly. "What else do you know about neutron stars?"

"The basics," replied Boyd. "They begin as stars much bigger than Sol. Then they die, and their outer cores explode in a violent supernova. The inner core that's left behind collapses in on itself under the irresistible pull of gravity."

"Nicely put," said Kelly. "For extra credit, the force of gravity is always this strong at the core of a star. So why don't they *all* collapse?"

"I'd answer," said the major with a playful glint in his eye, "but I don't want to ruin my reputation as a badass."

"If there's a world where a badass, souped-up killing machine can't also be a closet science geek," said Kelly, "I don't want to live in it."

Boyd laughed. "Well, when you put it that way . . ." he said by way of surrender. "Okay, Kelly, here goes. Healthy stars are powered by nuclear reactions in their cores. And these produce enough outward pressure to counteract the inward force of gravity. But once the star runs out of hydrogen fuel, it's basically *screwed*—which I assume is the correct scientific term for it," he added wryly.

"Exactly right," said Kelly. "The collapse squeezes a core that was bigger than our sun down to a ball with about a twelve-mile diameter."

The major arched an eyebrow. "Which is some seriously dense and heavy matter," he said. "And I believe that if an even bigger star goes through this process, the collapse can't be stopped, leading to a black hole."

Salazar shot Kelly a smug, I-told-you-so look, knowing the major was surpassing her wildest expectations, as he had predicted might be the case. But she was too focused on Boyd to catch it.

"Impressive," she said to the major. "Aren't you full of surprises."

"You have no idea," said Boyd.

Kelly studied him for several long seconds. "Getting back to the cube," she said finally, "you guessed that it was made with a sprinkling of neutron star matter. Why just a sprinkling?"

"If the entire cube were made of it, the thing would weigh as much as a mountain range."

"Outstanding, Major," said Salazar. "Right in every particular. A single teaspoonful of neutron star matter would weigh a billion tons."

"So how would one go about acquiring this matter?" asked Boyd.

"It's pretty simple, really," said Kelly. "Just drive your starship to the nearest neutron star. Send a probe down to the surface, one that can withstand gravity billions of times greater than we have on Earth and temperatures of a million degrees. And one that can somehow scrape a few bits of material from the most tightly compacted matter in the universe. Then you'd just have to retrieve the probe, which is impossible, contain the neutron star matter within a cube, which is impossible, and power the entire thing, which is also impossible."

She shrugged. "Piece of cake."

Boyd whistled and turned to Salazar. "So your claim that this tech is as far above our level as we are above the Neanderthals isn't just hyperbole."

"If anything," replied Salazar, "it might be an *understatement*."

Boyd turned to study the cube one more time and was instantly captivated by its appearance, mesmerized by the pull of its throbbing energy field, which somehow triggered a primal feeling of awe and unease in a human brain.

He turned back to his hosts. "What powers it?" he asked. "Seems to me that it would almost have to be zero-point energy."

Kelly Connolly shook her head in disbelief. He might be ruining his reputation as a badass at that. "How would you know that?" she asked.

"There's a zero-point energy research group under our auspices."

"I see," said Kelly thoughtfully. "Which means you might know more about zero-point energy than we do."

"Not a chance," said Boyd. "I haven't had time to read more than a one-paragraph summary. I only know it's supposed to be nearly infinite, and pervade all of space."

"Is this zero-point energy group making any progress?" asked Salazar.

"Almost none. It's considered the longest of our long-shot projects. But still well worth the effort and investment. I don't need to tell you that success would revolutionize civilization, like fire, the wheel, or electricity."

"Very true," said Salazar. "Most scientists believe tapping it is impossible."

"But we don't," said Kelly, "because we have the cube, and this is just one of the miracles it packs into a tiny package. It's a real showoff. We're like human scientists a thousand years ago stumbling upon a cell phone. They'd be blown away by its stunning array of capabilities, and all of them would seem like magic. The equivalent of a tiny supercomputer for a brain. The ability to use electricity as a power source. The ability to take and play back photos and video. To communicate across great distances. To understand spoken words. To access billions of pages of information. And so on."

"So for these aliens," said Salazar, "tapping zero-point energy is likely as mundane as tapping electricity is for us."

"And is this energy source really limitless?" asked Boyd.

"Pretty much," replied Kelly. "Quantum-field theory tells us that even in the completely empty vacuum of space there is a seething froth of activity, as virtual particles pop into and out of existence, creating energy. This is called the zero-point field, and its existence has been proven experimentally. And the energy of the void, zero-point energy, exists everywhere. In the coldest reaches of interstellar space and in the empty spaces between atoms of your body. The exact amount of energy available is controversial, but it's immense by any measure. An early paper published by NASA estimated that there's enough energy in a cubic centimeter of empty vacuum to boil away all of Earth's oceans."

The major paused in thought. "So to recap," he said, "you believe this cube contains neutron star matter and is powered by zero-point energy."

"That's right," said the Uru director.

"Is there anything else about it that you've figured out?"

"Not a thing," replied Salazar miserably. "But again, that's not from lack of effort."

"What have you tried?" asked Boyd.

The Uru director sighed. "It'd be faster to tell you what we *haven't* tried," he replied with a frown.

5

Harry Salazar turned to the cube and shook his head, as if it were a strong-willed, defiant teenager whom he loved and hated at the same time. As if the maddening, magnificent object was being uncooperative out of simple spite, and nothing more.

"I can give you an executive summary right now," said the Uru director to his guest. "If you want the nitty-gritty details, they're all in my reports."

"Fair enough," said the major.

"We've been focused on determining the cube's composition," said Salazar. "Or affecting its behavior or output. Both have proven impossible. Whatever it's made from, it's resistant to our efforts to find out.

"We tried to take a small sample of it, both of the outer cage and whatever it is that lies inside. There's a force field we can't breach keeping the inside from being examined, and the outer cage—which we can at least touch—is as impenetrable as the cube is immovable. We haven't been able to scrape off a single atom to study. Our most powerful microscopes have failed to show us anything."

"More than that," he continued, "we can't affect the material in any way. We've thrown every kind of radiation known to science at it. Laser beams of incomprehensible ferocity. But no energy can affect it, excite it, or drain it.

"We've hit it with acid. Tried diamond drills. Even used a scaled-down particle accelerator to hit it with matter traveling at ludicrous speeds. We applied a magnetic field that would pull a paper clip from your pocket at fifty yards. We acquired a microscopic amount of anti-matter, stored in a magnetic field, and unleashed it, with no effect. We tried dousing it with fire, and heating it to tens of thousands of degrees. We tried extreme levels of electricity. We tried freezing it with liquid nitrogen." Salazar shook his head in frustration. "But you can pour liquid nitrogen over the thing all day long without lowering its temperature one iota."

"Your experiments sound pretty . . . comprehensive," said Boyd.

"Just the tip of the iceberg, Major," responded the Uru director. "We've tried acetone, vinegar, alcohol, along with an exhaustive list of other organic chemicals, simple and complex alike. And we've even tried the ridiculous. Absurd long past the point of embarrassment. Like barbeque sauce. I'm not kidding. Who knows what might be this thing's kryptonite."

Boyd nodded slowly, deep in thought. "What about dark energy?" he asked. "Have you ever hit it with that?"

"As far as I know," said Salazar, "dark energy is impossible to generate. At least for human science. And we don't have sensitive enough sensors to detect it if we did."

"We have a black site research group dedicated to its study," said the major. "They think they've made a breakthrough when it comes to generating small amounts of it, at least on theoretical grounds. They're working on better detection methods, so they can determine if they've been successful, or if they're deluding themselves."

Kelly frowned. "I hate to say it, but my guess is that they *are* deluding themselves. I'm an expert in this field, and it's almost a certainty." She paused. "This is your anti-gravity group, correct? And I assume they believe that dark energy is a form of anti-gravity?"

"Don't you?" asked the major.

"Not really. The universe is flying outward, and we've discovered that this expansion is accelerating. Science can't account for it. Given the mass of the universe, it should be *decelerating*, or even starting to slowly collapse inward. Some mysterious force has to be responsible, one previously unaccounted for. Since no one has seen it, measured it directly, or has any idea what it is, it's been dubbed *dark energy*." She rolled her eyes. "Might as well call it 'we have no fricking clue.'"

"Yeah," said Boyd with a grin, "but the term *dark energy* does seem to roll off the tongue slightly better."

"I'm sure they don't have what they think they do," said Kelly emphatically. "My reasoning is too technical to share, but trust me on this."

Boyd shrugged. "Even if you are right, why not give it a try? What have we got to lose? If you're throwing *barbecue sauce* on the damn thing, why not this?"

"Because barbecue sauce is at least real," said Kelly. "This isn't. Trust me. It's a giant waste of time and effort. And you can get barbecue sauce at the local store. I assume it would take some doing to take a top-secret prototype device out of their labs and bring it here."

"This is true. But it'll give me an excuse to get to know the members of this team a little better. So I'm happy to get the device and bring it here myself."

"Thank you," said Harry Salazar. "If you're willing, we're eager to give it a shot. It can't fail any harder than anything else has."

"Another of our groups is finalizing work on a laser a thousand times more powerful than anything that has come before," said the major. "In a few months, we should try this too."

"Fantastic," said the Uru director. "Thanks. We can use all of the help we can get."

"Yes, thanks," echoed Kelly Connolly, but her tone was far less enthusiastic.

Boyd turned to face her. "You know," he said, "since you are such a dark energy expert, and also a skeptic, I'd like for you to join me when I retrieve the device. I can set up a meeting with scientists there and have them give you a tour. Uru is too secret for *them*, but you have security clearance to spare in the opposite direction. I can introduce you as someone I'm considering as a potential outside consultant." He shrugged. "Your reasoning is too technical for me, but it won't be for them. Maybe you can convince them of your views."

"When would you want to do this?"

"How about next Tuesday. Early in the morning. They're located at a place called Haycock Township, Pennsylvania, so the flight will be fairly long. But scientific cross-pollination is good for all involved. We can meet with them for three or four hours and then fly the device here."

"I think that's a great idea," said Salazar.

Kelly sighed. "Well, if both of you think it's a worthwhile trip," she said, not looking at all happy about it, "then how can I refuse?"

6

A holographic image of the Minister of Chinese intelligence, Yang Delan, appeared before Commander Shen Ning in his basement operations center, so realistic that it almost appeared as if he were standing in the room, despite being thousands of miles distant. Yang was trim and handsome in his impeccably crisp uniform, with eyes that shined with a fierce intelligence and a deep familiarity with command.

"I received your priority-one-urgent footage, Commander Shen," he began.

"I am pleased, Minister Yang. I would be happy to play it now and walk you through it."

Yang shook his head. "No need. I was meeting with President Yu when the message came through, and we viewed it together. We found it self-explanatory. And a remarkable development. Well done, Commander."

"Thank you, Minister Yang, you do me a great honor."

"The footage is the perfect storm of intel. We get the identity of the future head of American black operations, which by itself is huge. But even better, he just happens to be an American EHO commando. The first we've ever identified. And our intel on this program is lacking. Finally, we also get wind of a possible breakthrough development in dark energy generation."

Yang paused. "I understand that you invoked my command codes to commandeer a satellite to help track this Major Boyd after he left the Spokane black site."

"Respectfully, Minister Yang, I believed that such emergency powers were warranted in this case. I humbly offer my sincerest apologies if I overstepped."

"Not at all, Commander, you did well. Can I assume that you still have this major in your sights?"

Shen swallowed hard. Losing him would be a career-limiting mistake. "We do," he replied. "I've deployed every resource available, even those typically above my level, like satellites and hacking American street cams. I've augmented this with extensive human assets."

"Good," said the minister simply. "Make sure you don't lose him."

"I won't. I'm well aware that if we can keep him in our sights, the intel he'll lead us to will be of enormous value."

"I'm afraid that following him around will not be the plan."

"What then?"

"I recommended to President Yu that we capture this major instead. He agreed."

"This is an extraordinary measure, Minister. Can I respectfully ask why you would want to take this step? The risk is very high. And we will lose an unprecedented opportunity to unravel American black operations."

"I said capture, not kill, Commander. A proper interrogation might give us more intelligence on American black sites than we could have gotten by an extended surveillance. And yes, I'm aware that he is likely conditioned against truth drugs and will be very tough to crack. Tough, but maybe not impossible."

He sighed. "I'm also aware of the risk. But look at what we gain by taking him alive. Even if he won't talk, he can't help but give us critical intelligence. We can probe every millimeter of his body, inside and out, and study his DNA. Learn what makes him tick. Catalog every last physical, technological, and genetic enhancement he carries. This will allow us to improve our own enhanced soldier program, and to develop methods to counter theirs. This is an unparalleled opportunity for us. He embodies a treasure trove of intelligence that he can't conceal."

The head of Chinese intelligence straightened his uniform. "And then there is the matter of dark energy," he continued. "The plan would be to capture him right after he takes possession of the generator. As he's preparing to bring it to Spokane to test on the cube.

We can directly detect dark energy very weakly but can't produce it. America can produce it but not detect it. The ability to do both represents a giant step forward, and will allow our anti-gravity group to leapfrog theirs. Short of solving the cube, which we believe is increasingly unlikely, anti-gravity represents the ultimate technological breakthrough. I can enumerate all the reasons why at another time."

"I understand," said Shen. "But while we could *kill* this major fairly readily, capturing him will be another story. *Especially* since we need to isolate him so there are no witnesses who can point to China. We don't know what surprise enhancements he might have. And we'll have a narrow window to act, from the time he collects the generator until the time he delivers it to the Uru group. And he'll be with Dr. Kelly Connolly the entire time."

"Well, if it simplifies the job," said Yang, "there's no need to keep *her* alive. We already know what's going on inside Uru. Just be sure to destroy her remains."

"Thank you for that, Minister Yang. But the logistics will still be a nightmare."

Yang actually smiled. "I'm well aware, Commander. Which is why I'm glad you're in charge. You will have whatever resources you need, and I will leave this operation entirely in your capable hands. This includes your choice of prototype methods and technologies."

A slow smile crossed Shen's face. China had a number of impressive toys coming out of its secret labs that had yet to be used in the field. Held back until their use was absolutely necessary. Why chance revealing advanced technology when conventional technology would suffice?

"I will also rush a team of our own enhanced commandos there," continued the minister, "who will be at your disposal. In this way, we match strength against strength, with our side having both the element of surprise and superior numbers."

Shen took a deep breath and let it out slowly. "An inspired plan, Minister, and I am grateful for your confidence in me. But I should respectfully point out that I just set up a network of mercenaries here so our more . . . high profile operations can never be traced back to China. Our enhanced soldiers, on the other hand, are native Chinese.

If they fail, or even if they succeed without perfect stealth, the op gets traced back to us. The tensions between our two countries are already high. Imagine the fallout from this."

"You make a valid point, Commander. So I'll send the team, but start by seeing if your mercenaries can do the job."

"I will do so, Minister. But I fear that even the most elite of my mercenary force will be no match for Major Boyd. Unless the limited knowledge we have of the EHO program is substantially exaggerated."

"One on one, this is undoubtedly true. But can he defeat ten men? Twenty? Especially if they're supported by advanced tech that has never been used in the field before."

"It's impossible to say. And impossible to even plan precisely. Because we'll be up against unknown capabilities."

"All plans of this type face the unknown, Commander," said Yang, his tone making it clear he had lost his patience. "Deal with it. Plan for every possibility. Introduce multiple redundancies."

"I will, Minister. I will not let China down."

"See to it that you don't," said Yang grimly.

PART 2

"When it comes to the existence of UFOs, we've reached a tipping point. The burden of proof used to be on the believers to prove that UFOs are real. Now the burden of proof has shifted to the government and military to prove that they're *not real*. Because the evidence is overwhelming."

—Michio Kaku, professor of theoretical physics,
City College of New York

7

Major Justin Boyd and Dr. Kelly Connolly exited a quaint red farmhouse in rural Pennsylvania and returned to Boyd's rental car, a black Lexus sedan, parked on a gravel lot outside.

"Annie," said the major as he took the driver's seat, addressing the car's limited AI, "retract the steering wheel and take us to McGuire Air Force Base."

McGuire, also known as Joint Base McGuire—Dix—Lakehurst, was located eighteen miles from Trenton, New Jersey, and was the only base in America that included units from all five armed forces branches.

"Beginning trip now," said the pleasant female voice of the car through the speakers as Boyd placed his ever-present gray duffel bag between him and his fellow passenger. At the same time, the steering wheel began to retract slowly into the dashboard and the seat slid back, maximizing the roominess of the compartment.

Boyd was consistent in naming his self-driving rental cars *Annie*, and in setting the voice to pleasant and female. He had long reserved the name *Sage* for his personal AI, also feminine, who was vastly superior to any electronic assistant that would be commercially available for a very long time.

"Annie, estimate trip duration," ordered the major.

"We should arrive in approximately seventy-two minutes," replied the car helpfully.

It was the beginning of autumn, and the numerous trees surrounding the property were thick with leaves that had turned a wide array of spectacular colors.

Boyd turned to his companion. "I've arranged for us to return to Uru in a fighter jet," he said happily. "You're going to love it."

"You *are* kidding, right?"

He laughed. "Yes, I'm kidding. But you should have seen the look on your face."

"What plane *are* we taking back to Uru?"

"I'm afraid it will only be a simple, boring transport," he said with a sigh. "With no ability to generate G-forces that make you feel like your entire body is being crushed."

"As much as I hate to miss out on all that fun," said Kelly, fighting back a smile, "I guess it's a sacrifice I'm willing to make."

She had insisted on taking a commercial red-eye to Philadelphia International, where Boyd had picked her up in the rental at the crack of dawn that morning. Even so, they would be flying military back to Uru. Boyd's duffel, packed with high-tech military gear, weapons, and medical supplies, would never make it through screening, and he wasn't about to put the dark energy generator, about the size of a mass-market paperback, through TSA screening.

After he had met her at the airport, they had driven for eighty minutes, passing dense, multicolored woods for as far as the eye could see most of the way, and Kelly had repeatedly commented on the surprisingly vast expanses of woodlands in the area and the breathtakingly beautiful fall pageantry they displayed.

When they had begun the drive, Boyd had urged her to call him Justin when he wasn't acting in an official capacity. She had found this awkward at first, but was beginning to get the hang of it.

The anti-gravity group's headquarters was completely buried underground, as were most secret sites now that tunneling and excavation had become so cheap and efficient. In the case of the anti-gravity group, the facility was twenty yards below a farm in Haycock Township, Pennsylvania, a site carefully chosen for its proximity to Princeton and its Institute for Advanced Study, only an hour's drive away across the Delaware River and into New Jersey.

The tour and meetings had begun at 7:30 in the morning and had concluded three hours later. Due to the red-eye Kelly had taken, and the three-hour time difference between Spokane and Pennsylvania, they had finished their day here before Kelly would have normally even awakened for her day at Uru. Boyd suspected she was exhausted, but she hadn't shown it or complained.

He studied the woman who was seat-belted in beside him. He found her an enigma. Not a capital-E enigma, like the cube, but interesting and unpredictable in her own right. She had seemed intent on killing his idea of bringing the dark energy generator to Spokane to test on the cube. She had insisted that the anti-gravity group was delusional in thinking they had produced such a generator in the first place.

Yet during her tour of the Haycock facility and subsequent in-depth conversation with the lead scientists there, she had failed to challenge their thinking at all. Why so adamant in Spokane and so compliant here?

"So what did you think of the anti-gravity people?" he asked her as the car picked up speed.

"An exceptional group."

"They thought the same about you. I am surprised, though. I invited you here so you could try to persuade them to your point of view. Remember? So why didn't you engage?"

She sighed. "I realized I had been wrong."

"Just like that?"

"Just like that. I've been wrong before, you know. Once when I was a little girl. Once about four years ago. And today." She arched an eyebrow. "So three times in total," she finished with a grin.

"Are you sure you don't mean *four* times?" said Boyd impishly. "Because you were wrong about me, weren't you? Admit it. I could tell from your body language that you expected me to be a total dick." He paused. "And I was only a *three-quarters* dick."

She laughed. "All right, Major—*Justin*—you got me. I have to admit, I got you a quarter-dick wrong."

"I'm glad you're a big enough woman to admit that."

"Of course."

"But back to the dark energy generator," said the major. "Are you saying that you're now totally convinced that the anti-gravity group's suppositions are completely right?"

"I am."

"*Sage,*" he said subvocally to his personal supercomputer AI, "*is she telling the truth?*"

EHO had perfected a subvocal system that allowed its commandos to hold private conversations with their onboard AIs in a crowd, without anyone being the wiser. Boyd was now expert in making tiny movements of the muscles of his mouth and throat, which were amplified by minuscule sensors and sent on to Sage, who deciphered them with perfect accuracy.

Her reply came to him through a tiny comm that had been surgically implanted in his inner ear, which couldn't be seen or heard by anyone else, no matter how close they were standing. All in all, his practiced ability to subvocalize in conjunction with his custom comm made his communications with Sage seem telepathic.

"Yes, her statement is true," replied Sage, *"at a confidence level of eighty-two percent."*

Interesting, he thought. Sage wasn't a perfect lie detector, but she could access advanced sensors hidden in his clothing that could measure the heart rate and respiration of anyone in sufficiently close proximity to him. The AI also had access to visual input from Boyd's smart contact lenses that could measure the microexpressions of anyone he was watching. A complex algorithm crunched the data these sources provided and produced a verdict as to the veracity of any statement, one that was usually quite accurate.

"I notice that you never glance at the road ahead when we're in self-driving mode," said Kelly. "You trust the AI autopilot that much?"

"I do."

"I can see why you like self-driving cars. If you're able to really trust them, you can work, watch a movie, or sightsee while on long drives."

"The middle console even retracts if you want, so you can lie across the entire front seat to sleep," he said. He ordered the autopilot to retract the console to show her, as the extra room wouldn't hurt in any event. "Not that I've ever gone that far," he added.

Kelly smiled. "Yeah, I get that. It just doesn't seem *adult* to be sleeping across the seats of a car. But next time I need a rental, I think I'll give a self-driving model a try."

"There aren't many rentals available, and they cost several times as much. But you know," he added raising his eyebrows, "for the busy enhanced soldier on the go, they're very convenient."

"Very," she agreed. "And speaking of Enhanced Human Operations, Justin, how, exactly, are you, ah . . . *enhanced*? I mean, you've already admitted that your dick is only . . . well, only *three-quarters*."

Boyd laughed out loud. "Wow! You know full well I meant my *behavior* was three-quarters dickish. Not my . . . anything else. It was meant to be a self-deprecating joke," he added in amusement, "but not *that* self-deprecating." His smile remained as he considered her playful, sophomoric banter, which had been entirely unexpected.

"Sorry," she said, wincing. "I couldn't resist. I hope I didn't cross a line."

"Not at all."

"Good. But, really, I am curious to know what you have going on under the hood. You know, enhancement-wise."

"I wish I could tell you," he said, "but I'm afraid I can't."

"You know I have the highest security clearance there is."

"I do. But this is still on a need-to-know basis."

Boyd couldn't help but like this Dr. Connolly, warts and all. She was brilliant, but straightforward. Confident, even arrogant at times, but mostly down-to-earth and unassuming. She was still only thirty, just a few years younger than him. And the fact that she was quite pleasant to look at was also a nice bonus.

He hadn't allowed himself emotional entanglements, but he was naturally attracted to women who were smart and assertive, with a good sense of humor, and Kelly Connolly seemed to possess all of these qualities.

And something more, although he couldn't quite put his finger on what this something more might be. All he knew was that she had surprised him on several occasions, which was both rare and appreciated.

"What about your background?" she pressed. "Is that a *need-to-know* secret, also? How did you end up in the military?"

"Good question," he said, deciding there was no reason not to tell her. "The truth is I had absolutely no interest in it. None. So I didn't find *them*. They found me."

"How?"

"EHO was initiated when I was a junior in high school, although the first enhancements didn't happen until several years later. It was founded by Colonel Tom Osborne, the current head of black ops. Have you had the chance to meet him?"

"Not yet."

"That's a shame, because he's an exceptional human being. Smart, modest, and incorruptible."

"I've heard good things," said Kelly.

"Anyway," continued Boyd, "when he started the group up, he was looking for what he called *extraordinary* recruits. His words, not mine."

"And how did that put you on his radar?"

"I grew up an only child in Nebraska, and, well . . . with all due modesty, I guess I was both the number one athlete and the number one student in the region. Did well on standardized tests, was the captain of my school's basketball and soccer teams—with the soccer team winning the state championships twice. That sort of thing."

"With all due modesty?" she chided him with a wry smile.

"You asked," he replied good-naturedly. "Anyway, Osborne was looking for exceptional recruits for EHO, and he wanted them young. Just out of high school. He sought raw potential, which he could shape. So he had a team scour the country, looking at IQ tests, SATs, college essays, sports, academics, and citizenship. Apparently, they identified me as one of thousands of promising candidates."

"And then whittled these candidates down."

"Yes. I was given an array of extra tests, which I was told were for a special college scholarship I was likely to get. They put me through more mazes than a lab rat. These included extensive tests of personality, personal philosophy, morality, ethics, decision-making, and so on.

"Then, after I made it through their initial cuts, Osborne and his team began to surveil me, although I had no idea I was being watched, and wasn't told until years later. Every once in a while they would stage events to see how I'd react. Giving me the chance to be cowardly or heroic. Upright or greedy."

"So you passed their Good Samaritan and heroism field tests as well."

"Apparently," he said. "The thing of it was that Osborne wasn't looking for soldiers. He wanted young men and women who were comfortable in their own skin, had good athleticism, and in fact, wanted anything but a life in the military. He and his team began with the entire population of seventeen-year-olds in America, and ended by recruiting just fourteen of these when we graduated high school."

"So how did Osborne get you to join if you had no interest in the military?"

"He made me an offer I couldn't refuse," replied Boyd. "I was very much into tech, and the tech he described was pretty jaw-dropping. He promised to train me and enhance me. He disclosed top-secret intelligence, demonstrating the wide array of threats the average man was blissfully unaware of. Threats that people like me, properly trained and enhanced, would be in an ideal position to counter."

He paused, remembering. "He convinced me he only wanted me to use the skills and tech he would give me for good, not evil. That I could help protect the world. Change it. And I would be a guinea pig. Eventually, the enhancements that worked the best would be released to the public. Like GPS and the internet were.

"Finally, he assured me I would be in total control of my own destiny. He insisted that I could, and *should*, refuse any assignments that I didn't believe in. He appealed to my ego, my pride, and gave me a chance to lead a very unique and special life."

"Ever regret joining up?"

Boyd shook his head. "Not really, no. Everything Osborne told me turned out to be accurate. And I *have* been able to make a difference. In ways, and in magnitude, that only a few will ever know. And now I'm hanging up my combat spurs to make sure that black ops stays focused and accountable.

"Well, I'm mostly hanging up my spurs," he corrected. "My training, tech, and skills are too valuable to never use again. So, if the emergency is great enough, I might go back into the field for a rare mission or two."

"But only if you agree that the mission is worthy, right?"

"I couldn't have said it better myself."

Boyd wondered if he had told her too much, but decided he didn't care. He hadn't shared his origin story with anyone else for a long time—mostly because there were precious few authorized to even know he was in EHO—and it felt good. There was too much secrecy in his life, and too little sharing.

They drove in silence for some time as Kelly digested what he had said. She turned to him to ask another question when her phone chimed. It was her boss in Spokane. She kept it on audio-only and raised it to her ear.

"Kelly, it's me," blurted out Salazar, sounding panicked. "Is the major there with you?"

"Harry, what's wrong?"

"Is Major Boyd there with you?" he repeated urgently.

"Yes."

"Put me on speaker so I can talk to you both," he said, sounding worse with every word he uttered.

Seconds later a one-foot-tall holographic version of Dr. Harry Salazar was floating in the air near the center of the windshield. Boyd had instructed Annie to project him there, since holograms were permitted in cars that were operating in full self-driving mode.

The look on Salazar's projected face said it all. He was shocked. *Horrified.* As if the world were coming to an end. "I'm glad you're already sitting down," he began, visibly fighting to hold himself together.

"Spit it out, Harry," said Kelly. "What is going on? You're white as a ghost."

"I got in less than a half hour ago," he said, "just before eight. After some preliminary work, I went to the Enigma Room to prepare for your arrival. So everything would be ready for our experiment tomorrow morning. I wanted the major to be able to get the dark energy generator back to Haycock as soon as possible."

He paused, looking as if his head might explode.

"Go on," urged Kelly.

"I don't really know how to tell you this," continued Salazar. "I can't believe what I'm about to say—or even that it's *real*. But it's about the Enigma Cube. It seems to be . . . ."

He paused again, as if desperately not wanting to continue. Finally, he blew out a long breath. "Well, I'll just say it. The Enigma Cube seems to be . . . *gone*."

Kelly shrank back in confusion. "What do you mean, *gone*?" she demanded. "That isn't funny, Harry."

"Do I look like I'm *joking*?" he shouted, almost hysterically. "*Do you think I would make this up*? The cube is immovable. We all know that. Yet it's *gone*. As if it was never here."

"That's impossible," she said.

"Apparently not," replied Salazar, looking decidedly ill.

8

As the Lexus rental car raced along the highway on a self-guided journey to McGuire Air Force Base, Justin Boyd's mouth hung open. He continued to stare at the holographic image of Dr. Harry Salazar in dismay, reeling.

And if *he* was reeling from news of the cube's disappearance, Salazar was coming apart at the seams.

And for good reason, Boyd knew. Salazar was not only in charge of the Enigma Cube, but solving it was his passion. It was a riddle that consumed his every waking moment. And Salazar had vowed, to himself and to others, that he would eventually find a way to unlock its secrets.

But now it had shown that it had more secrets than anyone had even known, in mind-blowing fashion.

Just like that, it was gone. An object that represented absolute proof of alien visitation. An object that was a demonstration of god-like technology. The most important artifact ever found.

And now, the most important artifact ever *lost*.

Lost by Dr. Harry Salazar, who was now visibly shaking.

"Slow down, Harry," said the major as calmly as he could, noting that Kelly had become speechless, wrestling with news that she wasn't able to emotionally accept. "Let's take this one step at a time."

"One step at a time!" barked Salazar, still nearly hysterical. "There *is* only one step! I entered the Enigma Room and it wasn't there. Simple as that. No brilliant light, no mind-blowing little cube. Nothing in its place. No sign of anything in the room being otherwise disturbed. Hell, no sign of anything else in the entire *facility* being disturbed."

"As you know, Harry," said the major, "I have a dedicated super-computer AI that I've named Sage. I'm going to put her on speaker."

"What do you mean *dedicated*?" said Kelly. "Isn't she just a super-computer you access through the web?"

"No," said Boyd. "I've been issued a personal computer that I carry with me. So there's no time lag when I communicate with her, and no wireless connection needed that can go wrong. This also allows her to constantly perform deep scans of my surroundings for mics and listening devices, and alert me if any are found."

"So you have a supercomputer in your duffel bag?" said Kelly.

"Not exactly," said the major. "I'll explain later."

Boyd couldn't blame her for her incorrect assumption. Who could possibly guess that a twenty-million-dollar prototype supercomputer, Sage's home, was affixed to his upper leg by what appeared to be a four-by-two-inch bandage. The computer was bendable enough to contour to the curve of Boyd's thigh, and was constructed of carbon nanotubes, allowing its architecture to be built in three dimensions. This dramatically increased both its processing power and memory, while substantially decreasing its size and need for power.

The bandages that EHO had developed to conceal these computers were miraculous in their own right. The adhesive bond was unbreakable, and the material it was made from was all but impenetrable. The material allowed air to flow through, but its pores would slam shut in the presence of any moisture, including sweat, and it was absolutely waterproof. If the bandage was about to be seen by an enemy, the AI could release a small amount of blood-red dye onto its surface, allaying any suspicions as to its true purpose.

The supercomputer was hundreds of times more powerful than the best available smartphone, and significantly smaller. In fact, the majority of the area under the bandage wasn't even computer, but batteries, antennas, and a wide array of sensors.

It could either be charged electrically, or it could draw power from the heat and motion of Boyd's leg. Together, this ensured it could stay powered for a full two weeks, provided normal usage.

"Sage," called out the major after she was tied into the car's speaker, "were there any reports of UFO sightings in or around Spokane last night?"

"Nice," said Kelly, genuinely impressed. "You're thinking the only way it could be gone is if the alien owners returned to retrieve it."

Boyd nodded. "Exactly."

"Checking all civilian and commercial communications," reported Sage for all to hear. "Tying into Nessie now," she added, referring to the NSA's supercomputer AI, which had access to every call, text, and email in the country. "Not a single indication of a sighting," she finished immediately.

"Expand the search, then," said Boyd. "Check for sightings within a five-hundred-mile radius of the Uru site."

"No UFO sightings reported," came the quick reply. "Not for at least a week."

Boyd frowned deeply. It had been worth a try. "Harry," he said, "tell me what Uru surveillance cameras showed."

"The outside cameras showed nothing at all unusual. No unauthorized vehicles anywhere near the site. No UFOs. For that matter, no jets, cars, or even *skateboards*. No unauthorized entrances or exits to or from the facility. Nothing but the usual comings and goings of Uru personnel. No locks were breached. The whole thing is *insane*."

"What about the cameras *inside* the facility?" said Boyd.

"There *are* no cameras inside," whispered Salazar in disgust. "If this were a standard facility, we'd have dozens of them pointed at the Enigma Cube. But in this case, we didn't see the point of it, as all cameras get blinded by the light."

Boyd cursed to himself. Of course there were no cameras inside. Wouldn't want to make this too easy, he thought sarcastically. "We went through vault doors to reach the Enigma Room," he said. "How many people know the combination for these doors?"

"If you remember," said the tiny hologram floating in the air, "the doors were open when we got there. There is no combination. They're basically blast doors, there to protect the world from the cube. Not to protect the cube from theft. We never imagined we needed *security*. After all, an entire army couldn't steal the thing. It's a fricking immovable object."

"I think you got your tense wrong," said Boyd in frustration. "It *was* a fricking immovable object. That seems to no longer be the case."

Salazar blew out a long breath. "My people have been taking readings since just before I called," he said. "But so far, everything looks normal. *Perfectly* normal. No unusual energy signatures of any kind. We've confirmed the cube didn't turn itself invisible. If it somehow surged in power and punched a hole in the fabric of spacetime, or managed to teleport out of here, there was no local energy surge."

There was silence in the car for almost a full minute as everyone racked their brains for additional ideas, but none were forthcoming.

"Look . . . Harry," said the major, "I'll make sure we get to the bottom of this. The planned experiment is off, of course, but I'm still coming there with Kelly. We have to understand what just happened. No priority could possibly be higher. Call me immediately with any updates," he added unnecessarily.

He and Kelly rode in silence for several minutes after the call had ended, alone with their thoughts.

"Justin, all electronic connections are down," said Sage's feminine voice through the car speaker, startling both passengers who had all but forgotten she was still tied in.

"Your AI calls you by your first name?" said Kelly.

Boyd ignored her. "What do you mean, all electronic connections are down?" he said, his voice showing signs of strain.

"Wi-Fi, phone, military bands—all electromagnetic signals are being blocked."

"That's odd," said Kelly.

"More than odd," said Boyd urgently. "Wi-Fi and cell phones are too reliable nowadays, and we're in the middle of Pennsylvania, not on the Moon. Can't just be a coincidence. My instincts tell me this is the beginning of an attack. And if Sage hadn't volunteered this information, we wouldn't have had any idea that signals were being blocked until we tried to use our phones again."

Kelly didn't look convinced.

"The timing suggests that this is related to the dark energy generator," added Boyd.

"Look, Justin," she said, "don't you think you might be overreacting a bit? Why would anyone even *want* the generator? Its effect is so minuscule that we can't be certain it's even doing anything. And how would anyone even know we had one? Or who we are? Or where we are?"

"I have no idea. What I do know is that this is happening now, right after our visit to the Haycock site. And as I just said, I don't believe in coincidences."

Kelly frowned, deep in thought. "If all remote signaling is down," she continued, "then how are we still on auto-pilot? I thought the system needed to communicate with traffic cams, other cars, and so on. Shouldn't Annie either be pulling us off to the side of the road so you can take manual control, or at least warning us that all Wi-Fi is down?"

"Excellent point," said Boyd. Had someone hacked the self-driving feature, which was supposed to be unhackable? "Annie," he called out, "cancel our destination. Slow to thirty miles per hour and then take the next off-ramp."

There was no reply, and the car's speed didn't slow. If anything, it continued a very gradual acceleration, and was now traveling at sixty-five.

Boyd's eyes widened in alarm. What were they up against here? Whoever had done this must have attached a signal-jamming device to the Lexus, so that when the hostiles triggered it remotely, a cloud of *no reception* would hover over them as they moved. And these same hostiles seem to have hacked an unhackable autopilot.

His alarm grew as he realized something else. If this were true, they would need to be controlling Annie remotely—and this shouldn't be possible given that all incoming and outgoing signals were being blocked. Which meant that they had to be using a revolutionary method of remote signal transmission, one currently unknown to the US military.

The sophistication of the operation was off-the-charts high, which narrowed down the list of suspects to rogue elements within the US itself, or to China, Israel, Japan, Russia, and maybe a dozen other major powers.

They also must have known who Boyd was and where he would be. They knew of his habit of renting self-driving cars, and must have prepared this Op well in advance. It was beyond impressive.

Boyd tried to unlock the car's doors and windows but couldn't get them to respond, and the manual override refused to return control of the car to him as it was designed to do.

Kelly Connolly whitened as the reality of what was happening finally sank in. They were trapped inside a streaking vehicle that was delivering them to a destination of someone else's choosing. "Can you get us out of this?" she asked anxiously.

"Absolutely," he said with confidence, but this was false bravado for Kelly's benefit. The truth was that they were up against the very best, a team who wouldn't leave anything to chance.

The truth was that Justin Boyd had no idea what might come next, or the odds that they'd survive it.

9

The black ops major paused in thought as the car streaked down the highway. "It's only been a few minutes since Sage alerted us that all signals are down," he said, thinking out loud. "Whoever is behind this wouldn't expect us to catch on so quickly, but they'd know we would eventually. Well before we arrived at . . . *wherever*. We'd check our phone. Or the car would miss a turn it was supposed to take. Something. And once I learned that we were trapped inside a flying steel prison, I'd be sure to destroy the dark energy generator so they couldn't get their hands on it."

His jaw clenched tight. "And they can't let me do that," he added. "So how would they stop me?"

Boyd's eyes widened as he seized upon the answer to his own question.

"Sage!" he blurted out in a controlled panic. "Scan for the scent of all known knock-out gases. Hurry!"

"Detecting Zanamine 4 at two parts per billion," said Sage, who had access to an olfactory sensor embedded in Boyd's shirt that was sensitive enough to put a bloodhound to shame. "But this level is many orders of magnitude below what would be required to incapacitate a human being," she pointed out helpfully.

Of course it was, thought Boyd. Because the AI was detecting just the tip of the iceberg. The rest of the iceberg was no doubt about to make an appearance in violent fashion.

"What does this mean?" said Kelly.

Boyd had begun rooting through his duffel and now removed a small mask, just large enough to fit over a mouth and nose.

"It means we're about to be gassed," he said as calmly as he could, reaching toward her. "Stay still," he added, quickly fitting the mask over her face and ratcheting it tight. "This mask has a substance inside that can mop up toxins, purify air. A substance like activated charcoal, but much more effective. It won't let any Zanamine reach your lungs."

"What about you?" she said, her words now muffled through the mask.

"Don't worry about me. I can—"

A playing-card-sized section on the back of Boyd's headrest exploded with a loud crack, right on cue, followed by the loud hiss of gas leaving a tiny canister that had been embedded there. A thick haze quickly enveloped the car's two inhabitants.

"Stay calm," said Boyd. "Breathe normally. You can speak, but keep the movements of your mouth small, like you're working a ventriloquist's dummy."

"How can *you* speak?" said Kelly, her words tinny and hard to make out. "And how are you still conscious?"

"I only had the one mask," he replied. "But my blood stream is enhanced with mechanical red blood cells."

So much for keeping EHO secrets, he thought. But if this didn't constitute a *need-to-know* situation, nothing ever would.

"They're called respirocytes," he continued, "perfected just last year. Essentially, they're spherical nanobots the size of blood cells. They function as tiny pressure tanks that can be stuffed with oxygen and carbon dioxide. Each can store, transport, and release over a hundred times more oxygen than a natural blood cell. I can go almost twenty minutes without taking a breath. None of us breathe while we're speaking, but I've trained myself not to take a breath afterward, either, in this type of emergency circumstance."

"Wow!" said Kelly in awe as the gas continued to collect around them. "Then why do you even carry a mask?" she added, her words continuing to be muffled and hard to decipher. "In case you're next to a damsel when a gas attack happens?"

He shook his head. "Some gases can outlast even my ability to hold my breath," he explained.

"Was this gas supposed to kill us?"

"No. They appear to want us alive. They couldn't risk blowing up the car or crashing us into a building, since this might damage the generator. But they also could have used lethal gas, and didn't."

"But who? And why?"

"Don't know, but they're extremely sophisticated and competent. Almost certainly backed by a major country," he added, still not having taken a single breath.

"Sage," he continued, "access the self-driving system and tell me where these hostiles are taking us. Also, wrestle back control of the car."

"Working," responded his personal AI. "They are taking us to a location twenty-seven miles northwest of our intended destination, on the Pennsylvania side of the Delaware. I estimate we'll arrive there in forty-one minutes. As for retaking control of the autopilot, I'm doing everything I can, but after they broke in, they used an encryption to block anyone from following. One that I've never seen before. I'm trying to crack it now, but have no idea if, or when, this might be possible."

"Keep trying," said Boyd. "In the meantime, if I shot out the engine from here, would we survive?"

"Impossible to know, but we are now traveling at seventy miles per hour, so this is certainly a risk. You're wearing advanced body armor and have been genetically altered to heal quickly, so your chances of survival are much better than your companion's."

"Speaking of my companion," said the major, "call her Kelly. And until further notice, interact with her as you would me, including taking orders and sharing classified information. Understood?"

"Understood," repeated Sage.

Boyd reached into a small outer compartment of his gray duffel and removed a case with a ball-bearing-sized plastic ball inside. "Put this in your ear," he said, handing it to Kelly.

She studied it warily, making no move to do as he asked.

"It's harmless, I promise. Once inserted, you can use it to communicate with me and Sage over great distances. Or about a mile if no Wi-Fi or cell signals are available, since both Sage and the comms have a limited radio transmission capability. I can speak to you subvocally, soundlessly. And while you won't be able to do the same, the comm is sensitive enough to pick up a whisper. It's activated when anyone sends a transmission to it. Or you can initiate a call by tapping a finger twice just outside your ear canal. Sensors will pick up the vibrations and turn it on. You turn it off the same way."

"If I put it in my ear," she said, "it'll just roll out again."

"No, it won't," replied Boyd, after pausing briefly to reconstruct her words. She would have made a horrible ventriloquist. "It's *very* sophisticated. It will travel to your cochlea, open up, and insert itself with sub-millimeter precision. You won't feel a thing."

Kelly winced, but to her credit, she did as he asked without complaint, despite still wearing a snug mask, and despite gas continuing to swirl around her.

"Sage, is it safe to breathe yet?" Boyd asked his AI.

"Negative. But I estimate it will be very soon. I will alert you when it is."

"Thank you," said Boyd as he removed the dark energy generator from his duffel bag and placed it on the floor. He then proceeded to crush it to tiny pieces with the heel of his shoe, destroying it beyond repair, while Kelly looked on in fascination and horror.

"It is now safe for you to breathe," reported Sage.

Boyd nodded and finally took a breath, unhurriedly, even after all this time, instead of having to gasp it in like a desperate swimmer exploding to the surface to fill aching lungs.

Kelly removed her mask and handed it back to him. "Thanks," she said gratefully.

He nodded and returned it to his gray duffel.

"You know," she said, "back in Spokane, I thought you were a little anal to keep your combat gear so close while in friendly territory." She winced in an exaggerated fashion. "But there's a *teensy-weensy* chance that this assessment may have been a bit . . . *hasty*."

Boyd laughed, but only for a moment. They were far from out of the woods. "Sage," he said, "were you receiving data from traffic cams before our signals were blocked?"

"I was."

"Still have this footage stored in temporary memory?"

"I do."

"Search it for any activity that looks suspicious, especially in the vicinity of where we'll be ending up. Also, tell us what you can about the nature of the destination."

"Working," said the AI, and then a moment later added, "request completed. Traffic cams show a pattern of activity suggestive of an ambush. I can give you details of the full analysis, but the bottom line is that several hours ago, four vehicles, each with four men inside, were picked up on cameras entering the general vicinity of this car's destination. There could well be other vehicles doing the same who took routes not covered by a traffic cam. Yet up until a short while ago, when I lost my connections with the cams, there was still no sign that any of these four vehicles had left."

Kelly caught Boyd's eye. "They probably just stopped off at a religious retreat, right?"

"No doubt," he replied wryly. "Or else they're camped out around our arrival point with enough firepower to stop an army." He shrugged. "You know, either way."

The corners of Kelly's mouth turned up into just the hint of a smile.

"My maps show that our destination is within a deep woods," continued the AI, "about fourteen by eighteen miles thick. The car is taking you to a clearing near the center."

"So a place so secluded," said Boyd, "that a war could break out and no one would hear it. Just what I'd expect from this group. They think we're unconscious, but still plan for a possible battle."

Kelly blinked in confusion. "How does Sage know the dimensions of the woods?" she asked. "She can't connect with online mapping programs."

"She has a huge memory and onboard database. Enormous. Think a Wikipedia-sized information base times a thousand, complete with maps. If she is cut off from the internet, EHO made sure she could still serve operatives as a massive storehouse of knowledge."

"Remarkable," said Kelly. "The government must have spent tens of billions of dollars on R&D to perfect this stuff. How much does it cost to even outfit a single EHO agent?"

"You don't want to know," said Boyd with a smile. "Well, you clearly *do* want to know. But I *definitely* don't want to tell you."

Kelly returned his smile, but only for a moment. They were both trying to inject levity into the conversation, but neither was much in the mood for laughter.

"Sage, any progress taking back control of the car?" asked Boyd.

"I haven't cracked their firewalls yet, but I'm devoting all of my capabilities to the task."

"Any chance she'll take it back in time?" asked Kelly.

"We can only hope. They expected us to be safely unconscious for the entire trip. I'm pretty sure they know I'm with EHO, and what this might entail. But even if I managed to stay conscious, they can't possibly have imagined that I'd have access to a supercomputer that doesn't require Wi-Fi."

He shook his head gravely. "But even so, they went to the trouble of sealing the autopilot back up so tightly that even Sage is having trouble regaining control. This shows an extraordinary level of competence, caution, and contingency planning."

"They really have you worried, don't they?"

"They're very, very good," said Boyd miserably.

The major stared intently into the green eyes of his companion. "You heard what I asked Sage earlier. I could try to shoot out the engine. Try to stop the car before it plants us on the center of a bull's-eye. But there's a chance that this could also lead to . . . bad things."

"Like me dying?" she said, swallowing hard.

He nodded solemnly.

"But you think that we should risk it?"

"Yes."

"But why? You said they want us alive."

"They do. For now. But that won't last long. We're looking at capture, followed by torture, followed by death. There's a small chance they'll let *you* live, for the right inducement. But once they get what they can from me, my fate is sealed. I'm too powerful, and I've witnessed too much. I have a lot of tricks up my sleeve, so there's a good chance we can escape. Even so, I think it's worth the risk of a few slugs in the engine to see if we can't stop this runaway train."

Kelly gritted her teeth and held the straps of her seat belt. "Do it," she said bravely.

Boyd removed a handgun from the bag and screwed a silencer onto its barrel, so he wouldn't make them temporarily deaf.

"You're sure?" he said.

"Not even a little," whispered Kelly, "but do it anyway."

Boyd took aim at a point below the dash that he guessed would hit the engine and fired.

The instant he depressed the trigger a loud metallic clang sounded, and the bullet ricocheted backwards, nearly taking off his head as it embedded itself into the back seat.

"These assholes are really getting on my nerves," he said through clenched teeth, seething. "They must have installed a hardened steel barrier to prevent anyone from shooting the engine from inside the car."

He pointed the gun at his window, but then lowered it again as he thought to examine the glass more closely. "Transparent aluminum," he said after a careful inspection. "Something else I missed," he added in disgust. "I can't even shoot out any of the windows. The preparation behind this Op is extraordinary," he concluded, almost in admiration.

Kelly looked ill. "Does this mean we're forced to go with the 'capture, then torture, then death' option?"

"No it doesn't," insisted Boyd. "I'll find a way to get us out of this. Might as well prove that my enhancements are worth the money."

"You know," said Kelly wearily, "it occurs to me that self-driving rental cars aren't as fun as I initially thought."

Despite everything, Boyd couldn't help but laugh. Nothing impressed him more than a woman who could embrace gallows humor as disaster loomed.

"Sage, I know you're still shut out," he said, "but have you come across any software or hacking signatures that might tell you who's behind this?"

"Affirmative," said the AI. "The telltales are unmistakable. The work bears the signature of the People's Republic of China."

Boyd let out a curse. "It's possible this is a false flag operation," he said to Kelly, "but unlikely. I was already becoming convinced that China was behind this. I was just hoping I was wrong."

"Why were you hoping you were wrong?"

"Because given what I know of their capabilities, this is very much a worst-case scenario."

"Thanks," said Kelly grimly. "I was *hoping* for more bad news."

10

From the journal of Otto Richter

Where do I begin to describe my meeting with Heinrich Himmler? Even though it happened many years ago, in some ways it seems like it took place yesterday. In others, like I wasn't even involved, like it happened to someone else.

My memory is excellent, but time, emotion, and maturity tend to distort all things. I only wish I had been allowed to keep a journal of my experiences just after they had happened, to compare my recollections now to my observations then, but alas, this was not to be.

After Gruppenfuhrer Becker and his SS thugs pulled me from my home, Becker made sure he washed his hands of me, relegating me to underlings. Himmler must have ordered him to retrieve me, but judging from his manner, he found this duty demeaning, and adhered only to the letter of his boss's order. He fulfilled his duty by retrieving me and he was gone, off to ply his cruelty and sadism elsewhere.

I was held for several hours before a long drive to Wewelsburg, three hundred miles away. Not that I knew where I was being taken at the time. After I made an inquiry, I was told to shut up and stop asking questions by my charming escorts, who viewed me with contempt. I was a scrawny adolescent who somehow warranted a meeting with Reichsfuhrer Himmler, and I had a feeling they sensed I found them abhorrent, as much as I tried to hide it.

I was torn up inside, and I spent the long drive pulling myself together. My parents were wonderful people, whom I loved and respected, and I had a sick feeling that I would never see them again. Still, this storm had been coming since before I could remember, and I had fared better than many. And I had always known that it was only a matter of time before the Reich would come for me, to press my intellect into furthering their twisted purposes.

We finally arrived at our destination, Wewelsburg Castle, and I was pushed across the moat bridge forcefully, even though I showed no sign that this was necessary. My SS escorts felt the need to show dominance, to make sure I knew who was boss, like primitive apes beating their chests.

The castle was as magnificent as it was horrifying. Large, stark, and looming. A vast, elongated triangle in shape, with three round towers connected by imposing walls. Hitler and Himmler were nothing if not masters of imagery, symbolism, and propaganda, and Himmler's acquisition of the renaissance castle in 1934 was inspired in the Nazi Party's sick and twisted way.

Whatever the case, it was well known that Himmler adored the castle, intending for it to serve as the central site for the cult of the SS. Rumor had it that he dreamed it would one day become "The Center of the World" in the Nazi SS religion.

The head of the SS was also obsessed with archaeological excavations, a critical part of his never-ending quest to distort history to support the racism and delusions of the Nazi party. He soon made Wewelsburg Castle the home base of archaeology in the region. The Ahnenerbe, also known as the Ancestral Heritage Research and Teaching Society, was the SS's propaganda arm, dedicated to spreading mythology to give historical credence to the Nazi's claim of Aryan ancestry and superiority, and this group ensured the castle was well stocked in ancient relics.

Himmler had seen to it that the moat was lowered to make the castle seem more like the one in the mythological legends of King Arthur, who had magically become an Aryan in Himmler's mind. The Reichsfuhrer was obsessed with Arthur and the Holy Grail legend, even to the point of naming one room in the castle the "Grail" room, and another the "King Arthur" room.

Mysticism, occultism, and belief in witchcraft reigned in the Reich, spearheaded by the psychotic men at the top—*especially* Himmler—whose distorted point of view was so diseased as to be unrecognizable as human. And Wewelsburg Castle was the perfect embodiment of this warped, twisted madness.

How had so many of my fellow citizens been gripped by mysticism and the supernatural? By mass delusion? How had reality become so distorted?

I knew that part of the answer, of course, was that after my country's crushing defeat in the First World War, the collective souls of many of my fellow Germans had been scarred, disfigured beyond recognition, and open to believing almost anything, no matter how insane. It terrified me to realize just how easy it was for mass delusion to overtake large swaths of humanity. That just below the surface of human kindness was a seething pool of unfathomable ruthlessness and cruelty, unequaled in the animal kingdom.

My escorts and I waited outside a room until we were summoned by the man inside. The moment we were, I was shoved through the door into a massive, medieval room and pushed down into an ornate chair that sat in front of an imposing wooden desk.

The floor was a shiny, rose-colored marble, and it was truly beautiful, although I had no time to appreciate my surroundings as I tried to size up the man across from me. He was seated at the desk, and after he and my escorts traded a perfunctory *Heil Hitler*, he dismissed them with a flourish of his hand.

As they left, I felt my own right arm shoot out and heard myself saying *Heil Hitler* also, a greeting that had been mandatory for civilians for over a decade. Hitler's efforts to indoctrinate all Germans into becoming obedient drones was insidious and horrific—but also chillingly effective.

In the early years, those who refused to use this greeting were often beaten by the zealous, and by the end of 1934, special courts had been established to punish those who refused to salute. The brainwashing began in kindergarten, where children were already being taught to thrust out their right arms to routinely express their fealty to a ruthless psychopath. Students and teachers would salute each other at the beginning and end of the school day, and between classes.

The combination of punishment for those who didn't comply, and brainwashing of an entire generation of children, was extremely potent, and the salute had soon become part of everyday German life. Postmen used it when delivering letters, and department store clerks did so while greeting customers with a hearty, "Heil Hitler, how may I help you?"

I had railed against this despicable greeting from a very young age, but my father had softened the blow, reminding me that "heil" had more than one meaning, being the imperative of the verb "heilen"—to heal. Like many others, whenever I uttered this nauseating phrase, I was imploring the gods to *"heal Hitler!"* despite my certainty that the malignancy that filled this tyrant's soul was well beyond the possibility of repair.

But now, more than ever, I knew I had to sublimate my abhorrence of all things Nazi. I had to park every ounce of my contempt and hostility, and of course, intelligence and rationality, at the door. If I ever hoped to strike out against this ignorance and malevolence, it would pay to be on good terms with the man who was arguably the second most powerful in all of Germany, and almost as great a psychopath as his boss.

The man across from me appeared meek and unimposing. Thin, weak-looking, and slightly below average in height, he had the oval face and round glasses of an accountant, with the obligatory Hitler mustache under his nose. He wore his uniform in a prim and officious manner, and at first glance appeared to be completely harmless. At first glance.

But I quickly began to sense the malevolence just under the surface, and I'm convinced that this wasn't simply because of what I already knew about him. Somehow the rage, hatred, and psychosis that was churning and erupting like lava inside his soul couldn't be fully contained. Almost, but not fully.

Himmler was like a pastoral field littered with hidden mines. If one came upon it unaware, one would admire the calm serenity of the pasture and feel perfectly safe, having no idea that a single misstep could turn it into a bloody killing field.

But I knew. I was never so nervous as I was during this meeting. I was dealing with a madman who was completely unpredictable. Docile until he wasn't docile.

And what might trigger the beast? I had no idea, but I had a bad feeling that it would be random, and I'd never see it coming. A compliment could set off a hidden landmine just as surely as an insult.

The general who had visited my home was cruel and malevolent, wearing these attributes on his sleeve. But Himmler could fake normalcy, which I found to be far more chilling than if he were a snarling barbarian.

"It is a great honor to meet you, Reichsfuhrer Himmler," I heard myself say, as bile literally rose in my throat. Perhaps this is why my memories are so clear this many years later, but yet so faint. Because the entire meeting was like an out-of-body experience as I pretended to be the opposite of who I really was.

Himmler stared at me for what felt like forever, as if I were nothing more than an insect pinned under a microscope. "Do you know why I brought you here?" he said finally.

I shook my head. "No, sir."

"Come now," he said, sounding irritated. Had I triggered a mine already? "Surely you must have some idea."

"Only what General Becker told me, Herr Reichsfuhrer. That since I've excelled in certain academic pursuits, you and the Reich have a project that you would like me to focus my energy on."

"I couldn't have said it better myself," said Himmler disarmingly. Not that I was fooled. I wasn't about to lose my focus, or my fear, for an instant. I was locked in a cage with a lion, and my every sense would be heightened until I was out once again.

I was young, slight, and physically unimposing, but I had always compensated for feelings of physical intimidation by counterbalancing feelings of mental maturity and superiority. But I had never felt younger, or smaller, or more helpless than I did then.

"Rather than keeping you in suspense," said Himmler, "I'll give you a brief summary of what you'll be working on now. Then, after further discussion, I can provide more details."

The SS chief paused. "I have a fascination with the supernatural, as you know," he continued. "In fact, I'm in possession of many thousands of books, journals, parchments, and so on, purchased or taken from numerous collections. Many of these are well over a thousand years old, and all pertain to the occult and supernatural. I'm convinced that within these books are important clues to the glorious past of the Aryan race. I have sent archaeological teams around the world in search of artifacts and relics, and to track down yet additional relevant texts. I have followed up on hundreds of leads. Admittedly, most of these have been dead ends."

He paused for effect, and then raised his eyebrows. "Until now."

I found myself both fascinated and confused. Was this yet another of his delusions? Or had he finally uncovered something worthwhile?

Even if he had, I couldn't imagine what it might have to do with me. At sixteen, I was perhaps the leading physicist in the world, even though the Nazis had gone to great lengths to keep my existence a secret. But what I was most certainly *not* was an archaeologist.

"Recently," continued the head of the SS, "we found an obscure reference that led us to something truly astonishing, thousands of miles from Germany. A find beyond our wildest hopes. An object that proves, conclusively, that ancient, pure-blooded Aryans possessed the power of the gods."

"Ah . . . that is truly remarkable," I said, sensing that he wanted a response.

"The object is shaped like a cube, about the size of a crystal ball," he continued. "With other shapes inside, either spinning or stationary. It's an object that produces impossibly strong beams of light that streak forth from each vertex, one that throbs with energy. A truly hypnotic object that can harness nearly unlimited power."

"Can you tell me the highest level of power that's been measured so far?" I said, having become convinced that this was nothing more than a test of my thought process—or my gullibility.

He smiled. "None has been measured. The power is somehow constrained within the cube. But the truth of its immensity requires no measurement. When you see the object, you will know in your very being that it represents the ultimate dynamo. You will know that it is an object that only the true Aryans of Atlantis could have possibly produced."

"May I see it now?" I asked.

He frowned. "It isn't here," he replied. "You'll have to travel to where it was found. It's behind enemy lines," he added, "although in a remote location. Far from any human activity."

I nodded. For some reason, I had guessed it had been found in America, but if it was behind enemy lines, this could not be true. The Americans hadn't joined the war until the very end of 1941, so at the time of the meeting there was no certainty that they would join the fray.

But in truth, I didn't believe this bizarre cube he described was *anywhere*. How convenient for Himmler that the object was so far away that his propaganda could not be confirmed. Just another Nazi fantasy tale.

"Forgive my ignorance, Herr Reichsfuhrer," I said as timidly as I could, "but if the object is a small cube, wouldn't it be easier to bring it to Germany to study?"

"I'm afraid that this has proven to be impossible. In fact, we haven't been able to move it as much as a millimeter, no matter what we've tried. The head scientists on the team estimate that it weighs many millions of pounds."

It took all of my focus not to laugh in Himmler's face, but I knew this would be a fatal error. I had thought this a test. I had thought it propaganda. But now I saw the horrifying truth.

These were nothing but the ravings of a madman. Not mad with power, but literally, *clinically* mad. The second most powerful man in all of Germany had lost his mind entirely.

And this was the most terrifying realization I had ever had.

11

The black Lexus sedan, a car now possessed by a demon AI, pulled off the highway and was soon taking more and more obscure roads, leading ever deeper into an endless woods, reducing its speed to a bumpy thirty-five.

Kelly Connolly found the beauty of the lush, multicolored leaves that now surrounded them breathtaking, and cursed the fact that she didn't have the luxury of basking in this splendor.

"Sage, what's our ETA?" asked Boyd.

"Thirty-one minutes."

Kelly was a whirlpool of conflicting emotions. She was terrified, fearing for her life, but yet in a strange way, exhilarated. She couldn't help but be enthralled to be around a man so competent and decisive. And so confident, even as he was admitting to uncertainty. Women might claim to want a Clark Kent, but nature had evolved their genes to fall for his more powerful, tights-wearing alter ego instead.

Boyd fell silent for several minutes, alone with his thoughts, and as much as Kelly knew he needed time to think and plan, she couldn't handle the quiet. She needed to distract herself from the coming showdown, when the Lexus finally reached its destination. When the music finally stopped and a deadly round of musical chairs began.

"Tell me more about this supercomputer of yours," she said to her military companion, interrupting his reverie. "And your AI, of course. She seems like a handy tool to have around."

Boyd told her the basics, subvocal communication, the advanced architecture of the computer, and how it was affixed to his thigh.

"So Sage was with you in Spokane," said Kelly. "Which explains why you seemed so knowledgeable, so impressive." She raised her eyebrows. "Because you *cheated*."

"It's nice to know that you found me so impressive," he said with the hint of a smile.

"Did you miss the part about cheating?"

His smile broadened. "No, I just liked the other part better. And the truth is that I *didn't* cheat. Not really. Almost all of what I claimed to know, I really did know. Being able to secretly communicate with a supercomputer AI is great if you're in a trivia contest. But it's less and less helpful the more complicated the subject matter. And we were talking about some very complicated things."

The major paused. "In this case," he continued, "having Sage with me was like taking an open-book test back in college. You remember those. Whenever you had a test that was open book, you knew it was going to be brutal. You knew the professor expected you to have mastery of the subject matter and to use your brain, not just find the answer in the book."

Kelly nodded. She had to admit he made a good point.

"My biggest cheat," continued Boyd, "was searching for your dark energy credentials when the subject came up, to learn just how expert you were. I had read a short bio on you before arriving in Spokane, but your background in dark energy research was barely touched upon. So I called up a number of papers you had written on the subject on my smart contact lenses."

"Smart contact lenses?" she repeated. "How *smart* are we talking?"

"Pretty smart," he said. "Not that they need to be, since they're tied into Sage. But they contain a nearly microscopic onboard computer and an invisible antenna. Sage can see what I see, and can record it all. She can also send 3D images and video to my lenses, which seem to float in front of my face.

"I can view anything you can view on a computer without anyone knowing," continued Boyd. "Videos, schematics, tactical displays." He paused and gestured at his fellow passenger. "Journal articles written by Kelly Connolly," he added pointedly. "Anything."

"How do you control it all?"

"I can order Sage to do it, but it's faster using blink patterns and subtle contractions of ocular muscles. I practiced for over a year, so I can do this without anyone knowing."

"I certainly didn't."

"The lenses also annotate any object or person I see. If I look at a tree and blink in a certain way, Sage will identify the type of tree and display information about it, which will seem to hover beside it. Same goes for a person—assuming Sage is able to get his or her identity. If I'm reading something and I focus on a word or phrase in a certain way, additional information relevant to this word or phrase will appear."

"Like clicking on a hyperlink," said Kelly.

"Exactly."

"Impressive. Anything else?"

"Yes. I can zoom in on distant objects, like having an internal pair of binoculars, and switch to night vision with a blinked command."

"Night vision?" said Kelly incredulously. "In contact lenses?"

"I was just as skeptical," said Boyd. "But our scientists figured out a way to use a single layer of carbon atoms to pick up the full spectrum of light, including infrared and ultraviolet. So they can provide thermal imaging that outdoes bulky night-vision goggles."

"Wow. These lenses of yours seem quite . . . handy."

"You have no idea. If you think a smartphone is addictive, wait until you've gotten used to the combination of Sage and smart lenses. They become indispensable."

"I don't doubt it," said Kelly. "So how about telling me the rest," she added, locking her gaze onto his. "And if you say that I still don't need to know, I'm going to kill you myself."

"That's tough, but fair," said Boyd in amusement.

The major went on to rapidly describe a litany of enhancements. His undergarments provided greater protection from bullets than a Kevlar vest. Made from flexible sheets of graphene, which were honeycombed arrays of carbon one atom thick, they were a supple material that would instantly stiffen to diamond-like hardness when hit with a bullet or a thrown knife.

His second layer of clothing, which looked like casual civilian wear, was a soft endoskeleton of fabric and carbon fiber, with an electroactive coating. Human muscles exerted their force through controlled expansion and contraction, and this flexible woven material could do the same, expanding and contracting in response to the application of a low voltage, giving it the ability to actuate the same way as muscle fibers. Sage could precisely control where and when current was applied to the material, amplifying Boyd's muscle power whenever the AI sensed that this was required. All in all, with Sage's help, Boyd could almost triple his strength for brief periods.

This didn't make him a Marvel superhero, Kelly knew, but it sure would make rearranging the furniture a lot easier.

The comm embedded in Boyd's ear was superior to the one he had given her, able to pick up and amplify sound well beyond the range of normal human hearing, allowing him to eavesdrop on whispered conversations thirty yards away.

Boyd also disclosed that several implants were embedded in his brain. When electrically stimulated, these implants could amp up his mental and physical acuity to great heights for short periods, leading to superhuman reaction speeds—even without his electroactive body suit. Military experiments had demonstrated the cognitive enhancement potential of transcranial electrical brain stimulation for some time, and the technology had been field tested on Navy SEALS as far back as 2016.

Kelly was absolutely fascinated. The major was a repository of revolutionary techniques and technology. And while the scientific rationale and underpinnings of these enhancements could be found in the scientific literature, few could ever guess that they had actually been perfected.

These technologies were bolstered by genetically engineered modifications that provided EHO operatives with a host of additional advantages, using the immensely powerful CRISPR gene editing system. Enhancement of NMDA glutamate receptors was long known to improve memory formation and long-term potentiation, such that Boyd was able to learn faster and retain more information. Modifications to Boyd's LPR5 gene strengthened his bones. Modifications to his myostatin gene—which had first been shown to result in super-muscular pigs and dogs—resulted in muscles that were stronger and leaner than a non-enhanced human could ever achieve.

Other genetic manipulations conferred superhuman reflexes, and provided a form of super-adrenaline that could heighten the major's performance even more, not just in short bursts, but giving him increased strength, speed, and stamina for extended periods.

Kelly's eyes were wide when he finished the list. Along with Sage, his smart contacts, and his respirocytes, the technology was truly next level. It was now clearer than ever why the military had gone to such great lengths to ensure that only the most ethical of soldiers become EHO agents, since their enhancements made them all but unstoppable.

Boyd had raced through his enhancements very rapidly, providing little detail. But this had served brilliantly to distract her from what they were about to face.

"Anything else?" she said hopefully when he had stopped.

"Probably," he replied as the car took a dirt road that branched off from the narrow paved one it was on. "But we only have nine minutes before we . . . land. And I need to mentally prepare for what we might face."

He sighed. "Before I do, I want to tell you how sorry I am that you've become involved in this. I signed up for dangerous duty—you didn't. And I need to be honest. I expect to have to use lethal force. We'll be greatly outnumbered, so I can't just knock them down. I have to be sure they can't get up again. I'm a living, breathing treasure trove of game-changing technology, so lethal that our own government only trusts it with a select few. So it's critical that it not fall into anyone else's hands, no matter what it takes."

Kelly already felt queasy, and her stomach suddenly took a turn for the worse. She was fearing for her own life. But she hadn't considered that she might soon be witness to the violent deaths of others, which was something she had never expected to experience. She had seen men slaughtered in movies, but could only imagine how truly horrifying something like this would be in real life. Apparently, she was about to find out.

"I understand," she whispered finally.

"Good," said Boyd. "I need you to expect surprises. Be prepared for *anything*, at any time. And follow my orders, my lead, without question. Got it?"

She swallowed hard. "Got it," she confirmed.

"Sorry to interfere with your pending preparations, Justin," said Sage's voice over the speaker, "but the signal suppression field around the car has been disengaged. Wi-Fi and communications are now enabled, but only within a five-mile radius, centered on our destination. We still can't reach anything beyond this bubble, nor can any signal reach us."

Kelly shot the major a quizzical glance. "I don't get it," she said. "Why this change?"

"Because they have numerous soldiers within the bubble," said Boyd. "Probably a lot more than the sixteen Sage already identified. And they're taking nothing for granted. If I give them a fight, they want to be able to communicate with each other through their comms. Since we have no allies here, they figure the limited range won't help us."

Boyd shook his head. "But they've made a significant miscalculation."

"How so?"

"I can have Sage control certain drones, which they'll never expect."

"Because they'll never guess you're wearing your own supercomputer."

"Right."

Kelly's eyes narrowed. "What about—"

"I really need a few minutes of thought," interrupted Boyd. "We'll be stopping very soon. When we do, leave your phone in the car, since they can trace it. I'm sure it's been backed up fairly recently, but I'll have Sage place a copy in her memory just in case."

"Uh . . . thanks," said Kelly. "I guess."

The inside of the Lexus fell silent for five minutes as the car continued its journey over the narrow dirt road. Finally, it arrived at a clearing, about the size of a basketball court, completely devoid of trees. As the rental rolled to a stop in the center, Boyd carefully unzipped his duffel bag.

The major blew out a long breath. "I'm going to protect you, Kelly," he said solemnly, holding her gaze. "I promise."

She nodded, temporarily speechless, as her heart began pumping so powerfully she thought it might explode through her chest.

The locks on all four doors popped open with a sound that seemed deafening, and Kelly almost jumped out of her skin.

Ten men emerged from the woods on all sides and approached the Lexus, each dressed in autumn camouflage, and each pointing a submachine gun at the vehicle.

"Get out of the car with your hands up," shouted a beefy giant of a man, apparently their designated spokesman. "You have three seconds."

12

Boyd scanned his surroundings with practiced efficiency as a calm settled over him. The calm before the storm.

He was now so proficient at operating his lenses they had become like his own eyes, doing his bidding without any conscious thought. His contacts zoomed in on several of the hostiles' weapons belts to find tranquilizer guns in each case, as expected. The submachine guns were just for show, for intimidation. He already knew they wanted to take him alive and wouldn't use them. But when the shit really did hit the fan, now they'd have to take an extra few seconds to drop the lethal weapons they were holding and grab their non-lethal counterparts instead.

Idiots.

Sage was able to identify six of the men, all known mercenaries. Since all ten were either Caucasian, black, or Hispanic, Boyd had already guessed that they were soldiers of fortune, hired by the Chinese to make sure their American victims didn't know who was really pulling the strings.

The major triggered all of his enhancements to sharpen his thinking and pump up his reaction times, making the wait for Kelly to exit the car seem far longer than it was. Finally, she stepped out of the car, and he moved across the seat and followed behind her, leaving the door ajar. He quickly ushered her away from the open door, stopping just a few feet beyond the hood of the car.

"Sage," he said subvocally, *"fly all eight dragonfly drones about an inch above the ground until they reach the nearest tree line. Then spread them out to all compass points and identify any additional hostiles within fifty yards. When this is done, give me a count of protected versus unprotected comms."*

"*Understood*," replied the AI, as dragonfly surveillance drones lifted silently from his unzipped duffel still inside the car and flew unobserved through the lowest part of the open door.

The hostiles continued to converge, pulling the circle in so that now all ten were facing the two new arrivals to their north, knowing that the car was blocking any escape to the south. The soldiers fanned out and stopped about twenty feet away, their submachine guns still pointed squarely at the two newcomers.

The man who had already spoken stared at them in disbelief. He locked his eyes on Justin Boyd. "How are you even conscious?" he asked.

Sage displayed the leader's bio in Boyd's field of vision, just next to the man's face. Boyd smiled arrogantly. "Oh, I'm full of surprises, Master Sergeant Knudson," he said. Then, raising his eyebrows, he added, "Oh, sorry. I know you prefer to be called *Dredd*. Like the judge, I guess."

"How do you know that?" said the man in dismay.

"I know *everything*," replied Boyd haughtily, trying to rattle them as much as possible. He waited a moment for this to sink in and then continued. "Look, you guys are in a fight that you didn't choose. I do realize that this is what mercs *do*," he added, "but this time you're in over your heads."

"Yeah, we've heard all about you," replied the mountain of a man who served as the mercs' leader. "Why do you think there are *ten* of us? The boss told us to expect you to be the most badass commando we've ever seen. And that if you didn't arrive unconscious, to knock your ass out right away."

Boyd laughed in an overly loud, mocking manner. "You poor shithead," he said in disgust, casting a quick glance at Kelly beside him to gauge her alertness. "You have *no idea* what you're up against here. So I'm prepared to show you mercy. Walk away with your men right now, and I'll pretend this never happened."

Dredd shook his head in disbelief. "Who are you?" he whispered.

Boyd glared at him with unbridled arrogance but didn't respond.

"*The dragonflies have identified ten additional mercenaries in the woods surrounding you,*" blurted out Sage at three times her normal speaking rate. *"Comm signatures indicate the twenty mercenaries identified are from two distinct groups brought together for the occasion. All ten in the woods, and five of those in the clearing, are from one group. All fifteen members of this group use the same make of comms, which are all protected. An additional five mercenaries in the clearing are from a second group, and they are all using unprotected comms."*

"Send three of the drones farther afield to look for additional hostiles," ordered Boyd subvocally, *"and keep five near the clearing."*

While he and Sage communicated at a dizzying speed, Dredd was surveying his immediate surroundings, as if to reassure himself that he was sane, and that he and his force still outnumbered the man holding his hands in the air ten to one.

"We aren't walking away," he said to Boyd. "That's for damn sure. But I do have a counteroffer."

Dredd removed a small bottle from his camouflaged vest. "Catch," he said, chucking the bottle toward the major, who snatched it from the air. "Either take one of these tranquilizer pills voluntarily," he added, trying to sound as menacing as he could, "or we'll paint the Lexus behind you red with your blood."

"Wow, did you rehearse that?" said Boyd mockingly. "Paint the Lexus red with my blood? Really?" He shook his head. "The good news for you is that, despite your cringe-worthy threat, I'm prepared to give you one last chance to live."

He gestured to Kelly beside him, who looked justifiably horrified to be facing so many men and guns, but seemed to be holding up as well as could be expected. "Let my friend drive out of here unmolested," said the major, "and I'll take your pill. And I'll fully cooperate once I awaken."

He paused. "She doesn't know anything," he added. "She's an innocent egghead, totally harmless. So let her go, and I'm yours. Otherwise, I'll have to kill all of you in front of her, which I'm hoping to avoid."

Dredd shook his head. "I'd love to take you up on the offer," he said. "But—funny thing—we were told just this morning that *she* is our main priority. You're important, but secondary. Likely more dangerous, so we need you to go to sleep first. But, actually, if we had to choose just one of you to capture, it'd be *her*."

Boyd wavered for the first time, glancing at the woman beside him in disbelief. *"Sage, is this true?"* he asked silently.

"Master Sergeant Knudson is too far away to get biometric readings, but his micro-expressions indicate that he's speaking the truth. With a greater than seventy percent confidence level."

Boyd's eyes narrowed. What in the world? His mind was cranked up to its maximum level of focus and enhancement, but this didn't begin to make any sense to him. Being outnumbered twenty to one didn't trouble him nearly as much as *this* revelation.

He tilted his neck so he was looking above the heads of all ten submachine-gun-toting soldiers. "Whoever is really running this show," he bellowed to the sky, "why don't you come out from behind the curtain. I know you're there. I get you're too afraid to show yourself, but are you really too afraid to even communicate with me? I have a deal to make, but only with you. This is your chance to keep ten of your hired hands alive."

A hologram materialized about twelve feet ahead of Boyd, hovering at head height. The 3D figure looked like nothing more than a shiny silver soccer ball, enlarged by a factor of three. "All right, Major," said a booming voice coming from the ball. "You want to chat before we knock you out. You have two minutes."

"Impressive English," said Boyd, staring at the ball. "And I like how you're using a geometric hologram rather than showing yourself. I get it. You don't want these men to see your nationality. You don't want them to know that Chinese intelligence is pulling their strings. But I'm afraid I have to let the cat out of the bag."

"That is an unfortunate disclosure, Major," said the voice. "I'll make sure you're tortured in a way that reflects our displeasure."

Boyd turned away from the silver soccer ball and faced the mercenary leader. "What he means by *unfortunate disclosure*, Dredd and company," he said, "is that since you now know China is in control, he can't let you live. So even if you survive me, which you won't, he'll have to kill you. Not a great spot to be in, is it? So now would be a *really* good time to walk away."

"Nice try, Major Boyd," said the voice coming from the hologram. "I considered various weapons you might deploy, but I never thought that your *mouth* might be one of them. Unfortunately for you, these men are exceedingly well paid, and know that you're lying. They aren't going *anywhere*."

Boyd surveyed the mercs and confirmed that this was true. None of them had moved, nor had they lowered their useless submachine guns an inch. They were too stupid for words.

The voice emanated from the hologram once again. "So how did you and Dr. Connolly manage to stay conscious when the gas canister went off in the car?"

"Gas canister?" said Boyd, feigning confusion. "I'm not sure what you're talking about. Maybe your people put it in the wrong car," he added helpfully.

"I'm beginning to really like you, Major. You're quite entertaining. With any luck you'll cooperate so I can keep you alive."

Boyd glared at the hovering hologram. "Why don't you come out and show yourself?" he said. "I'm guessing you're fairly close by. Although not too close, right? I know you're afraid of being caught up in the carnage."

"Let's just say I'm waiting in the wings. Well situated to observe the proceedings. I have no doubt that as soon as I give the word, you'll be knocked unconscious, just like any other man. But if you are able to put up a fight, however briefly, watching you operate will be quite . . . instructive."

The voice of the hovering silver ball paused. "But I really don't want any trouble. So you should know that if you were to somehow get past these men, there are ten more mercenaries in the woods. More importantly, if you somehow get by all twenty, I have yet another team waiting even farther back in the wings. A team I brought in from home. One comprised of individuals who are much more your match."

"Your version of EHO?" said Boyd.

"Very good, Major."

"Not very brave, are they?" said Boyd in disgust. "I guess they're trained to let other men do their fighting for them. Do you also teach them to hide behind women and children?"

A laugh issued from the floating hologram. "Not cowardly, Major. Smart. For the prize that you two represent, we can't afford to take any chances. I had planned for this enhanced force to engage you in Spokane, if you made it that far. I didn't want to use them first and show our hand if I could help it. And I didn't expect you to be making the guesses you have as to our origin."

"What do you know about Spokane?" demanded Boyd.

"We've had your Uru facility under surveillance for some time."

Boyd's amped mind jumped to the proper conclusion instantly. "Using the same remote transmission tech you used to take control of my car when all signals were down."

"Correct again. You're as astute as I thought you'd be."

"So why the change of plans?" said Boyd. "What caused you to race your people here, to lurk in the woods of Pennsylvania like cowards?"

"Kelly Connolly caused it," the silver hologram said simply. "We've known who she was, of course, for some time. We know all Uru personnel. A few days ago, the plan was to kill her and capture you. But last night she became the most important person on the entire planet. Someone we're willing to risk being discovered for. Someone whose capture is worth risking a possible *war* to achieve."

Boyd's eyes narrowed. There was something he was missing. Something enormous. He tossed the bottle of pills toward the wall of soldiers facing him, unceremoniously. "Before the fireworks begin," he said, "I don't suppose you'd be willing to tell me under what delusional rationale this woman has become so important to you."

"Why not? After all, I listened in to your conversation with Harry Salazar earlier. I find it ironic that we maintain extensive surveillance inside your Uru facility—but you *don't*. It's very sad. We have cameras pointing at your Enigma Room and in a dozen other locations. Those pointing at the cube are blinded, of course, but they can see your people and experiments, and pick up what is being said.

"So imagine our surprise last night," continued the voice, "when we captured Dr. Connolly on video. Captured her walking out of your facility—with the Enigma Cube *in her hand*. She did this just an hour or so before she left her home to take a flight to Philadelphia. The cube looked solid, and showed up on video, so we weren't sure if it really was your Enigma Cube. But we confirmed it readily enough, when it became clear the cube was missing."

There was a short pause. "And your companion was carrying it *effortlessly*," added the disembodied voice. "As if it were as light as aluminum. Just before she concealed it inside a purse. Unfortunately, we didn't review this footage, which we had expected to be routine, until after she was in the air. But you can see why we'd *very much* like to talk to her. Learn how she managed to do this. And why. And where she hid the cube."

"You're out of your mind," spat Boyd.

"Am I?" said the hologram. "Why don't you ask Dr. Connolly if what I'm saying is true."

Boyd glanced at Kelly for the first time in minutes and his breath caught in his throat. She was white as a ghost, and several tears were streaming down her face.

She *had* taken the cube. Her reaction left no doubt.

Despite himself, Boyd's head was spinning, just when he needed to be at his most focused to escape.

What in the hell was going on?

"When we get out of this," he said out loud to the woman beside him, "you and I need to have a very long talk."

PART 3

Russia's and China's "Enhanced Human Operations" Terrify the Pentagon
Popular Mechanics, Dec 16, 2015

U.S. adversaries are already working on something America is reluctant to: Enhanced Human Operations (EHO). EHOs entail modifying the body and the brain itself, creating what some have called "super soldiers." At a press conference laying out the Defense Department's future research and development strategy on Monday, Deputy Defense Secretary Bob Work warned that America would soon lose its military competitive advantage if it does not pursue such technologies. "Now our adversaries, quite frankly, are pursuing enhanced human operations, and it scares the crap out of us," Work said.

Superpowers aren't just for superheroes anymore. Want some?
San Diego Union Tribune, September 14, 2017

. . . the revolutionary CRISPR gene-editing tool can be used, not just to repair biological flaws, but in god-like fashion to engineer improved biological performance.

But there is also a chance that human enhancement will devolve into a Wild West free-for-all. Because the geopolitical stakes are too high. This explains why in 2015 the Pentagon announced it had begun its Enhanced Human Operations program, which is expected to use all the tools described above and probably quite a few that we don't know about. With archrival China undertaking a heavily funded similar program, as well as engaging in unprecedented human genetic engineering, the US government has a primal reason (survival) to shift to anything-goes mode.

Be terrified, be fascinated, be appalled, or be skeptical—but most of all, be ready. If sophisticated human enhancement is crucial to dominating the twenty-first century—as the world's greatest powers have concluded—it's coming.

13

My mind raced as I considered what the head of the SS had just told me. A small, all-powerful cube that weighed millions of pounds?

It was preposterous, the wild ravings of a lunatic. Still, what choice did I have but to take it seriously? If an armed escapee from an insane asylum asks you to talk to his imaginary friend, you talk to his imaginary friend. The *last* thing you do is tell him you can't see anyone, and question his sanity.

"So you have a team in place studying this object, this cube," I said to Himmler, pretending to see his invisible friend. "Is that correct?"

"Yes," said the head of the SS. "But before we continue with the cube, I want to have a brief discussion. Get to know you better. I've been told that you're the most brilliant of all of us. I wanted to see this for myself before I finish your briefing and send you off."

"Of course, Herr Reichsfuhrer," I said, more wary than ever.

"Can I assume that you're familiar with World Ice Theory?" he asked me.

"I am," I replied immediately.

"And what is your scientific assessment?"

I struggled to find an acceptable answer. The truth was that World Ice Theory was ludicrous. Nonsensical. A travesty of reality. It made a mockery of science, and it was pure propaganda.

Einstein and other German Jews had revolutionized mankind's understanding of the universe. But in a demonstration of cosmic irony at the Nazis' expense, the very men at the vanguard of the greatest revolution in human thinking ever, men lionized the world over for their genius, were Jewish. Germany could have become the very center of the scientific world, in historic, breathtaking fashion, but its malicious leaders chose instead for it to become a historic center of *barbarism.*

Meanwhile, Europe and America would reap the fruits of exiled minds like those of Einstein, Leo Szilard, John von Neumann, Edward Teller, and so many others for decades to come.

Even more ironically, Germany had a significant head start in the race to build the atomic bomb, kicking off their secret program, which they dubbed "uranium club," in 1939. The US government only became aware of the German program when Einstein wrote a letter to President Roosevelt, issuing a warning and describing the possible destructive power that could be unleashed by the bomb. If not for the contributions of German Jews to America's *Manhattan Project*, the Americans never would have succeeded.

But during my meeting with Himmler, America's success was still many years in the future. The salient point was that the Nazis had exiled their greatest minds, believing all Jews to be vermin, including so many physicists who would go on to win the Nobel Prize.

But this created a logical conundrum. If these men were vermin, how could their revolutionary theories be correct?

The answer was that they couldn't be. The Nazis needed a theory of their own, one that discounted Jewish theories and elevated Aryans at the same time. Facts, reality, truth, had nothing to do with it.

Which is where World Ice Theory came in. If I were a fantasy writer, I'd be embarrassed to spread a theory with so little logic behind it, and yet Hitler and Himmler had convinced themselves that it was real, and were intent on convincing the world.

This was suddenly not so surprising to me, given that Himmler had also convinced himself that he had found an all-powerful cube that weighed more than the castle we were now in.

"World Ice Theory is brilliant, Herr Reichsfuhrer," I once again heard myself say.

Never before, and never after, have I been so sickened by my own words. But again, if you find yourself in an insane asylum, feigning insanity isn't such a bad idea. "Absolutely groundbreaking," I added.

"How so?" he asked, studying me intently.

I swallowed hard. "The truth of the theory is intuitively obvious," I replied. "Which is how any great cosmological theory should be judged," I added, testing the limits of my own inventiveness. "Any theory can be made to seem impressive mathematically. I'm good enough at math to know that this is a tool that can be misused to show anything a talented charlatan wants to show. I can write out a mathematical proof that shows one equals two, but that doesn't make it so."

"And Jewish physics?" said Himmler.

"Ridiculous," I said, hating myself. "I've studied the math and logic of it, which are purposely misleading. Not to mention preposterous. World Ice Theory is elegant and intuitive. Jewish physics is exactly the opposite. Are we truly to believe that time itself slows to a crawl at a high enough speed? Or that energy can somehow magically be turned into matter?"

"Why do you believe World Ice Theory makes such intuitive sense?" he asked, challenging me.

My mind had never raced so fast, or scrambled for footing so desperately. Could I find a rational defense for the indefensible in seconds? Or would it become clear that my earlier statement had been nothing more than saying what Himmler wanted to hear, which could well incur his wrath.

"It has a beauty to it," I said, as a rationale that I knew would seem compelling appeared in my head, fully formed, almost magically. "Water is the perfect molecule, upon which all life is based. We are largely made of it, and totally dependent on it. All liquids contract when they freeze—except water. It does the opposite."

I paused. "Because this miracle substance expands when it freezes," I continued, "ice is less dense than water. So it floats instead of sinking. If this wasn't the case, entire rivers and lakes would ultimately become blocks of ice, killing all life within. Instead, ice forms a ceiling, a layer of insulation, to protect life in these bodies of water."

I was riffing now, like a talented fantasy writer or musician might, and I could tell from Himmler's reaction that he was impressed. More than impressed, that he had never heard this line of reasoning before, even from his so-called *experts*.

"Not only is the idea that the Earth has repeatedly been hit by falling ice-moons a beautiful one," I continued, "but it explains so much. Why there is so much water and ice on our planet. And only an event as cataclysmic as an ice-moon strike could disrupt the almost god-like Nordic race, the pure Aryans of Atlantis, whom you already mentioned. Only an ice-moon strike could destroy their impossibly advanced civilization, and disperse them to all corners of the globe."

Himmler scowled. "Where they've become contaminated by the lesser races," he spat.

I nodded. "Exactly."

"This contamination explains why civilization has never again reached its former heights," he added. "But it will. *We* will. As soon as we purify the species once again. We will produce many more like you, Otto. True scientists who will return the world to the former glory of Atlantis."

The accountant-shaped madman leaned toward me intently. "Can I assume that you're prepared to give every last ounce of your energy and passion to help this come to pass?"

"Of course, Reichsfuhrer Himmler."

Himmler's demeanor changed in the blink of an eye, from serene to absolutely *demonic*, as the violent rage he was keeping suppressed burst through every pore of his body. "Lie to me again, boy," he said chillingly, "and you'll never walk again."

I found the psychotic intensity of his whispered words far more terrifying than if he had shouted them at me and drenched me in spittle.

Even though I had known he could turn suddenly, I felt like a mouse who had been hypnotized by a snake, not even realizing the reptile had moved until I felt the searing pain of fangs sinking into my neck. And I had foolishly been congratulating myself on my skill at picking my way around landmines.

"I'm sorry if I offended you, Herr Reichsfuhrer," I stammered, my throat suddenly dry. "But I don't—"

"Pretend that you have no idea why I accused you of lying and your mother will lose both of her hands."

My eyes widened in horror, and my tongue froze in my mouth. Himmler had just begun to spearhead the machine-gunning and gassing of millions of helpless innocents in a systematic, horrifically efficient slaughter the likes of which the world had never seen. But I didn't need this information to know that he would happily carry out his threat on my mother without a second thought.

"What's the matter, young Otto?" he said icily. "No more clever responses? Did you really think you could tell lie after lie about your true beliefs and I wouldn't know? Do you think me a fool?"

There was no acceptable answer to this, so I remained silent, fighting back the vomit that suddenly threatened to erupt from my throat. My heart was beating out of my chest, and I knew that he would mutilate my mother without a second thought if I didn't find a way to up my game.

"Do you think me unaware that your parents aren't fully loyal to the Third Reich?" he demanded in contempt. "That they had close friendships with a sickening number of Jewish professors? That they were attracted to these Jewish swine like flies to shit? Do you think we wouldn't be keeping tabs on you, a boy who is arguably the most brilliant German to have ever lived? Do you think it was lost on me that you *refused* to join the Hitler Youth, even after membership became mandatory?"

For just an instant I thought to correct him, but clamped my lips shut. My father had arranged for me to get a special exemption from this brainwashing organization, arguing that the Reich would be better served if I spent all of my time on scientific scholarship. But I was sure that Himmler was well aware of these facts. And also that facts didn't matter to him in the least. In his mind, I should have *fought* to join the Hitler Youth. I should have walked barefoot across broken glass if this were required. To him, my unwillingness to do so was a terrible transgression.

"Do you think I don't know you've done only minimal reading on World Ice Theory?" continued the madman, still seething. "That, conversely, you've found ways to get a hold of forbidden scientific journals filled with *Jewish Physics*. Do you think we don't know everything you've read in the past five years?"

I just stared at him, speechless, praying to a god I wasn't sure I believed in to spare my parents any harm due to my miscalculation.

"Just because you're more intelligent than me," he continued slowly, as if he were stabbing me with every word, "doesn't make me an *imbecile*. I know *exactly* where you stand. I have an unequal knack for reading people, no matter how duplicitous. And I despise those like you. Aryan, *superior*—yet stubborn. Soft. Unwilling to face the truth that's staring them in the face. Refusing to believe in a Master Race, even though you could be the finest example of it. Believing that sparing lesser races is compassionate, when it is, in fact, the opposite.

"To truly forge a great civilization," he continued, "one rivaling even Atlantis, requires a purging of the lesser races. You do no favors to the future with false compassion, which will eventually sow the destruction of the world. Yet you have the audacity to feel morally superior to those of us dedicated to preventing this disaster. Those of us willing to do what is needed to elevate civilization to god-like heights, no matter how unpleasant."

There was a long silence in the room, which seemed now to be spinning rapidly around my head. I may have been able to master calculus at the age of six, but I had absolutely no ability to predict where things might go from here.

"So let me tell you what will happen," continued the Reichsfuhrer. "You will be smuggled in to where our team is studying the cube, along with other new personnel. And, as the most brilliant among us, you *will* learn what makes it tick. Other scientists have so far failed. But *you* will not. You will find a way to harness its power. To rediscover science lost to the ages. You will find a way to use this knowledge to create a superweapon that will end the war in one fell swoop."

I still didn't trust myself to speak, but my head bobbed up and down, nodding my acquiescence—anything to pacify this madman and get out of the room.

"And you *will* impress me," continued Himmler. "If reports don't consistently sing your praises, I will mutilate your parents, little by little."

He paused to let this sink in. His general had made a similar threat when he had come to collect me, but Himmler's threat hit home in a far more visceral manner.

"Despite the difficult logistics," he continued, now seemingly calmer, "we have the most advanced scientific equipment in existence on site. We will make sure you have any additional equipment that you find is currently lacking. Whatever you need.

"But rest assured that SS soldiers are there as well, and will be told of your attitude, your lack of loyalty. I handpicked these men, and all are expert at reading deception, like me. You will not be allowed to write down any account of your experiences. No journals or letters home. Scientific writings only. And while my soldiers won't recognize legitimate scientific writings, there are other scientists on the team who will, scientists who are almost your equal.

"In short, we will own you. Your every breath will be at our forbearance. You will do nothing but eat, sleep, work on solving the cube, and read and discuss Nazi ideology."

Saying this, the last of Himmler's demon rage faded away and his face became the serene mask he had worn at first. "My hope is that you will find your way, young Otto," he said pleasantly. "That you will embrace your heritage.

"Despite pretending otherwise, I know that you scoff at World Ice Theory. At the concept of our Atlantean ancestors. But this cube will convince you otherwise. For there is no other explanation for its existence. It had to have been created by Aryan supermen from Atlantis. And when you do come around to realizing this truth, to changing your attitude, I'll be the first to welcome you to your rightful place as chief scientist of the Third Reich."

I nodded, still afraid to speak, and still afraid to tell him I didn't believe a word he had said about his imaginary cube. And even if everything he said *were* true, of course it didn't prove the existence of Atlantean superscientists. If the cube had been found among a vast field of Atlantean ruins, this would be one thing. But it had not been, or he would have told me so. Which meant that if the Atlanteans had made it, they would have had to *move* it to its current location.

But how?

The answer was obvious. The only way the small object he had described could weigh so much was if it were made of neutron star matter, which had only recently been hypothesized to exist. The only problem was that absolutely none of this material could be found on Earth, even in the mythical land of Atlantis. The cube had to have been brought here by sentient life that had been born around another star.

So I had bad news for the madman across from me. Even if his preposterous fantasy turned out to be true, the superscientists responsible had *not* been Aryan. They hadn't even been *human*.

But I said nothing of this, of course. I simply nodded, counted my blessings that I was still alive and Himmler seemed to be settling down, and continued to pray, despite having always fancied myself an atheist.

14

Justin Boyd stood in a clearing surrounded by endless trees and a rainbow of leaves, well aware that he had no time to consider the implications of what he had just learned. Or at least what he *thought* he had learned. The idea that Kelly Connolly had removed the Enigma Cube from the Uru facility was *preposterous*, even if it weren't impossible.

But why hadn't she objected when accused? And why was she reacting like someone who was guilty as charged?

"As fun as this has been, Major Boyd," said the voice coming from the soccer ball hologram, "the nap I had planned for you to take in the car is long overdue."

Boyd knew that the voice was seconds away from ordering the mercs to shoot him with multiple tranquilizer darts. He needed to find a stall *immediately*.

"Okay," he said slowly, outwardly calm and unhurried while inwardly churning. "You win. Let me pick up the bottle of pills I threw on the ground, and I'll take one. I won't resist. And I'll even cooperate afterwards. All you have to do is promise to tell me what you learn from your interrogation of Dr. Connolly."

There was a long pause, during which Boyd issued quick instructions to Sage to reposition the five dragonfly drones nearby.

"Agreed," said the voice finally, but Boyd was only vaguely aware of it, as he had already begun having his AI send a communication to Kelly's comm, using his voice. *"Sprint for the nearest tree line on my mark,"* he told her, *"but stop five feet short of entering the woods and wait for me. I guarantee that you'll be fine. They need you alive, and I'll be creating a diversion."*

He really couldn't make such a guarantee, but worst case, she'd be hit with a tranquilizer dart and knocked unconscious, and he wanted to calm her fears as much as possible. Despite the recent bombshell revelation about her, he had to assume that they were still allies, at least until he learned otherwise,.

"Scratch your leg to confirm you understand," he finished.

Boyd glanced sideways to see Kelly scratching her leg as he walked slowly to the bottle of pills fifteen feet away. Fifteen feet closer to the array of soldiers facing him, which is where he wanted to be.

"Sage," he said subvocally as he walked, *"are the dragonfly drones in place and ready to go?"*

"Affirmative."

"Three seconds after Kelly begins sprinting for the trees, send a debilitating audio frequency to the five men wearing unprotected comms."

"Understood," said the AI.

Boyd bent over to pick up the bottle of pills. *"Kelly go!"* he ordered through her comm. *"Now, now, now, now!"*

To her credit she followed his order without hesitation, abruptly racing toward the tree line with greater speed than he had expected.

All ten mercs dropped their useless submachine guns to the ground and reached for their tranquilizer guns, almost in unison, as he knew they would.

Before any of them could get off a shot, Sage carried out her orders, and five of the mercs screamed in agony as a shrill, penetrating screech issued from their comms, driving into their brains like ice picks and causing blood to leak slowly from their ears. All five fell to the ground, writhing. They clutched at their ears as the devastating, *piercing* frequency continued unabated, as did their bloodcurdling screams, straight out of a horror film.

The instant Sage's sonic attack hit, Boyd sprinted toward the nearest dropped submachine gun with superhuman speed, and all five remaining mercs trained their tranq guns on him instead of Kelly and began firing. She was the higher priority, but if they didn't stop *him*, they'd be dead in seconds.

Given Boyd's speed, and the chaos surrounding the men who were firing at him as their comrades continued screeching on the ground, it was unlikely any of them could hit an exposed part of his body with a dart before he reached the gun, but the stakes were too high to take chances.

"*Dragonflies now!*" he ordered his AI as he ran.

The five remaining mercs dropped to the ground in a panic as the unmistakable sound of machine-gun fire issued from speakers in Boyd's tiny dragonfly drones, which were hovering just a few feet behind them.

As these men whirled around to face the phantom threat, Boyd retrieved a fallen submachine gun and sprayed them with enough rounds to turn them into bloody Swiss cheese. He then immediately pivoted and put the five men hit by Sage's sonic attack out of their misery, becoming a blur of motion. In seconds the clearing had become reddened with gallons of blood, and littered with viscera and brain matter from ten shredded bodies.

Even so, Boyd sprayed the fallen mercenaries one more time, just to be certain, and raced to join Kelly, stopping at the car along the way to retrieve his duffel bag.

"*There are ten more mercs in the woods,*" he told her through her comm as he ran, "*like the voice said. So stay put until I join you.*"

"*Hurry!*" she whispered, unnecessarily.

Boyd pulled up beside her seconds later. He removed a gun from the duffel, zipped it closed, and handed the bag to Kelly. "*Carry this so I can use both hands,*" he said through his comm. "*And stay behind me.*"

She nodded anxiously and took the bag.

"*Sage,*" he said, temporarily remaining in the clearing, "*project a tactical display just to my left, showing my position and the positions of all remaining hostiles in the woods.*"

A three-dimensional map of the area appeared instantly, showing one green ball, representing him, and ten red ones, representing mercenaries.

"*I should caution you,*" said Sage, "*that this display has been out of date for minutes, since you had me reposition all eight dragonfly drones, and the mercs are sure to be on the move.*"

"Deploy the five drones nearby to reacquire the locations of the mercs, and notify me immediately if any are found within thirty yards of us."

"Understood," said the AI.

Boyd frowned. They couldn't stay unprotected in the clearing any longer, even if this meant venturing into the woods without accurate reconnaissance data.

"Follow me," he whispered to Kelly. He crossed the tree line into the thick woods and began moving at a fast jog. When they were eight yards in and picking up speed, Boyd saw movement to his right out of the corner of one eye. He quickly spun Kelly to the ground, rolled in the opposite direction, and came up firing, his superhuman reaction speed allowing him to do so in the blink of an eye, and he planted a bullet through the forehead of a merc, killing him instantly.

It had all happened so quickly that the merc was dead before Kelly even realized she was now lying on dirt, leaves, and vegetation that had been beneath her feet a moment earlier. She began to lift her head to see what was happening when Boyd's amplified comm caught the sound of a twig breaking to her left, and he wheeled around once more.

"Down!" he shouted at her as he sent several bullets flying over her head, which connected cleanly with their target, putting him down.

Just over a minute had now passed since Kelly had begun her initial sprint, and after being in the woods for a mere eight seconds, two more mercenaries were dead, and additional human blood was pooling on the ground, soon to become fertilizer.

Boyd pulled his female companion up from the ground and made sure she had the large duffel before he continued running through the woods, maintaining a pace that he knew Kelly would just be able to manage. Her heart began to race, and in less than a minute she was gasping for air, while Boyd's oxygen-hoarding respirocytes ensured that his vitals were as relaxed as if he were sound asleep.

"Two soldiers at your seven o'clock!" said Sage, as the dragonflies finally proved useful once again. *"They're about thirty yards distant and moving in your direction."*

Boyd stopped abruptly and pulled Kelly in position behind a thick tree trunk before venturing forward. He blinked his contacts to ten times magnification and spotted the two mercs before they could see him. Both were dressed in autumn camouflage, as their brethren had been, and Boyd took steady aim with his handgun. He waited until they closed the distance, so fewer trees would be in his way, and his enhanced focus, smart-contact-aided vision, and enhanced musculature allowed him to squeeze off two perfect shots, which somehow threaded between multiple tree trunks before exploding through the heads of his two targets, who were dead before they even had eyes on the black ops major.

Four down, six to go, thought Boyd, as he rejoined Kelly where he had parked her, still hidden by a thick tree trunk.

"Have the drones discovered any additional forces?" he asked Sage silently. *"The voice bragged that there were Chinese EHO commandos hanging farther back from the clearing."*

"Not yet," said the AI. *"I'll alert you the moment this changes. But the drones do have a bead on the six remaining mercenaries, so your tactical map is now accurate."*

"Well done," he said to Sage, fully aware that the AI needed no praise, but unable to help himself.

Kelly was shuddering beside him, and her eyes were vacant, shell-shocked.

"These men had lives," she whispered softly, words that Boyd only heard because Sage amplified them. "Families. I know you warned me . . . but they were *shredded*. Cut to pieces. So much blood. So *horrible*."

"I know," Boyd whispered back.

How could she not be near an emotional meltdown, despite his warning? She was a scientist who had never experienced violence, suddenly finding herself in a war zone. In minutes, she had witnessed more horrible deaths than had the majority of seasoned soldiers.

"But you have to get a grip, Kelly," he added as gently as he could. "No one deserves to die like this, but they aren't choirboys. They'd kill you without a second thought. You don't have the luxury of sinking into this quicksand right now."

The light slowly returned to her eyes, and he could see her ratchet up her resolve on the spot. She had realized he was right, and had the strength of will to harden herself to the massacre, at least temporarily.

She turned to him, stared deeply into his eyes, and nodded, knowing enough not to distract him further. She was pacifistic and empathetic by nature, but she was also a survivor, and her spirit and sense of fight were climbing back off the mat, with a vengeance, right before his eyes. She had been to the brink, but he had managed to pull her back, without even resorting to the cliché move of slapping her in the face.

Boyd nodded back firmly and turned his attention once again to the battlefield. *"Sage, are you able to transmit a message through the comms of the six remaining mercs?"*

"Affirmative."

"Great. Impersonate the voice that came from the hologram in the clearing. Using this voice, I want you to say the following."

The major paused in thought. *"To all remaining mercenary forces,"* he began slowly, *"disengage immediately and leave the area. My personal team will handle things from here. You will receive payment for this mission, as promised."*

Boyd thought about what he needed to accomplish for a few seconds longer and then continued. *"Disable comms immediately after receiving this message. We've learned that Major Boyd can use them to deliver a devastating sonic attack if he gets within a quarter mile of you. He can do so even if your comms are protected, and thus designed to prevent this. I repeat, disengage, leave the area, and disable comms immediately."*

"Sending message now," said Sage after Boyd conveyed that he was done. About fifteen seconds later, the AI reported that the message had been delivered.

Boyd waited an additional ten seconds. *"Did any of the mercs question the order?"* he asked.

"Negative," the AI responded. *"And all six have now disabled their comms."*

Boyd breathed a sigh of relief. Not only did this indicate compliance with his order, it ensured their real commander could no longer reach them to set them straight, which was the only way his false order to disengage could possibly work.

"Based on footage from the drones," continued Sage, *"they all appear to be standing down and leaving the area as instructed."*

"Outstanding," said Boyd happily. What he had told Kelly was true. These men would have happily killed *them* if this had been the order. Still, he had no interest in taking any more lives than were absolutely necessary.

"One of the dragonflies just identified the additional force you were looking for," said Sage. *About a mile and a half away. Eight men, all Chinese, and all dressed in brown camouflage. The drone that identified them was detected and shot down seconds after coming upon the group."*

Boyd's stomach tightened. Detecting and killing a drone this small and silent was an impressive feat. He had taken out the junior varsity team, but the force that remained was at another level entirely. These men were sure to have some serious enhancements, and some serious skills.

But even so, they had stationed themselves too far away. What could they have been thinking? They couldn't possibly make up a mile and a half on him. He could outdistance them until he got beyond their no-communications bubble, and could then call in reinforcements, even with Kelly slowing him down. He could carry her while he ran if this proved necessary.

"I should also tell you that the entire group is moving quickly in this direction," continued the AI, *"riding XJ-27 dirt bikes with advanced noise-canceling technology."*

Boyd sighed. So much for outdistancing them.

"Well that really, really sucks," said Kelly out loud, having listened to his exchanges with Sage through her comm, and knowing there were no mercs left in the area to hear her.

"Yeah, it's not . . . *ideal*," said Boyd.

"Nice use of understatement," she said, rolling her eyes, which demonstrated more than anything she could have done that she had found a way to distance herself from the carnage and regain her equilibrium.

Kelly blew out a long breath. "But you *are* going to get us out of this, right?" she continued. "I mean, I abhor violence and all, but you're fricking *amazing* at what you do. A one-man army." She shook her head. "And I thought you were impressive for knowing about neutron stars," she added wryly.

Boyd sighed. He had shown a side of him that he'd hoped to never have to reveal to *anyone*, let alone Kelly Connolly.

"So what's an XJ-27 dirt bike?" she asked.

"Perfect for use in the woods. Lightweight, so it won't sink into the ground. Ideal for riding over rough and uneven terrain. A stiff suspension that's great for jumps, and for minimizing otherwise jarring impacts on a rider's spine and bones."

"Perfect," said Kelly sarcastically. "Any way we can make it to safety before they catch up to us?"

Boyd shook his head. "Not a chance in hell," he said gravely.

15

From the journal of Otto Richter

When I first saw what the SS were calling the *Atlantis Cube*, I thought I must have already gone insane, and was surely in a fantasy construct produced by my own tortured mind. A mind fleeing the reality of Nazi Germany.

And if I were truly schizophrenic, I was most likely experiencing these fantasies from within a Nazi camp, awaiting death. The Reich, *brimming* with compassion as they were, couldn't tolerate anyone who didn't live up to their Master Race standards, and by the end of the war, had exterminated two hundred thousand physically or mentally disabled innocents, to add to their list of atrocities.

In the end, as I gazed upon the Atlantis Cube in awe, I decided I had to believe it was real. What other choice did I have?

The cube was everything the psychopathic head of the SS had said it was.

And more.

The small object throbbed with the infinite, like an entire star shrunk down to cubic form. Like an omnipotent deity, utterly glorious and terrifying. The human psyche wasn't built to behold something this magnificent, this unstoppable. It was akin to staring into a bottomless abyss or an active volcano. Or standing before an approaching tidal wave, or a four-story wall of fire. Human breath couldn't help but stop in the face of such ultimate power. Human knees couldn't help but turn to jelly in the face of a threat too awesome to truly comprehend.

But while having the chance to view the cube was a priceless experience, my day-to-day life was a *nightmare*. Week after week, month after month, I experienced hardships, cruelty, and loneliness without end, a suffering that went beyond anything that physical torture might deliver. It was a cold, sparse life, controlled to the inch by paranoid sadists, without a single woman among our contingent to soften the fanatical intensity.

For much of two years I was lost and alone. I was in the wilderness, both figuratively and literally—the wilderness of Canada.

Himmler hadn't lied about the cube being behind enemy lines, as the Canadians had joined the war in 1939, more than two years before the Americans.

I had memorized an atlas when I was four, and I knew that Canada had the second largest land mass of any nation, just ahead of the United States and China, and the number of square miles of wilderness within its boundaries was immense.

I had little idea precisely where I was within this vast nation, but it hardly mattered. All I knew was that I had been deposited into the heart of a Canadian forest, which soon became my entire universe.

Apparently, there was a tale in some ancient mystical text that Himmler had acquired about a man, an explorer, who had stumbled upon a magical cube in the forest, located in this general region of Canada, which emitted powerful beams of light from its corners. But try as he might, the man was unable to carry it away, or even budge it a millimeter. He was forced to return home, and was never able to find the object again. Even so, the man spread the legend of the cube far and wide. A legend that no one ever took seriously.

No one but the head of the SS, that is, obsessed with proving a warped thesis of Aryan ancestry. Himmler had gone to the trouble and expense of sending a large team to comb the Canadian wilderness region cited in this fable, just before Germany declared war on the world.

It had been a horrible misuse of resources and effort. Of course the fabled cube wasn't real. And even if it was, the odds of finding it were exceedingly small. Which just goes to show, sometimes the Universe decides to reward the foolish over the wise.

By the time I arrived on site, the encampment was quite extensive. It consisted of five sizable buildings, constructed from thin, prefabricated sheets of metal, each separated from the others by large swaths of trees to make the structures less conspicuous. Each roof was entirely covered by a canvas painting affixed to a canopy of chicken wire. A painting of the surrounding woods, which conferred surprisingly effective camouflage when seen from above.

A runway had been carved into the forest a little more than a quarter mile from the encampment as well, painted a mottled green and brown, although this was only used to transport personnel to or from Germany. Food and supplies were parachuted down to us by low-flying planes, under cover of darkness, about twice a month, although members of the SS took to hunting as well, to obtain food that was decidedly fresher.

The distance between Germany and Canada represented the operation's biggest challenge. But this had been overcome by transforming a tiny desert island in the Hudson Bay, the second largest bay in the world, encompassing almost half a million square miles, into a refueling center, with fuel transported there by seagoing ships in the strictest secrecy and by cover of night. In this way, long-range transport planes could land on the island and get a full tank, more than enough for them to land on our makeshift runway and return to the island for additional fuel to get them back to Berlin.

The secret encampment housed thirty-seven scientists from a number of disciplines, including chemistry, physics, and geology, and twenty-five *Waffen SS* thugs, who watched over the scientists and patrolled the forest for miles around.

With Hitler's approval, Himmler had grown the once tiny SS—by far the most racist of any part of the Nazi war machine—into a behemoth that consisted of divisions with a variety of responsibilities. One group served as Hitler's personal bodyguards. Another, the *Totenkopfverbande*, or *Death's Head Unit*, ran the Nazi's extermination camps. And yet another, the military branch of the SS, the *Waffen, or Armed SS*—basically Hitler's private army—was comprised of hundreds of thousands of combat troops.

Having to live at the mercy of twenty-five soldiers serving in Germany's regular army, the *Wehrmacht*, would have been bad, but possibly tolerable. But living at the mercy of twenty-five members of the *Waffen SS* was most certainly not. These men had been intensely indoctrinated into Nazi ideology, were fanatically loyal to Adolf Hitler, and seemed to thrive on bullying and cruelty.

If only the Canadian government had discovered what was going on under their noses, our contingent wouldn't have stood a chance, as isolated from German forces as we were. But, alas, this was not to be.

All in all, I spent two years in this forest. Two years that seemed like decades, and that aged me even more. The two most arduous, horrible, and tortured years of my life.

But also my most productive.

Shut off from love, comfort, and any distractions of civilization, forced to endure constant venom and sadism from seemingly all quarters, my mind fled to higher planes, tried to lose itself in prolonged bursts of theory and intuitive scientific thinking.

Also, trying to solve the impossible had a way of freeing my mind, getting me to think of hidden forces and dimensions. Given the Atlantis Cube's existence, what idea could possibly be too wild for me to consider?

I have no doubt that the last three months of this two-year period were my most productive of all. With all due modesty, I'm convinced that during this time I achieved breakthroughs that not even Einstein and Faraday, standing on the shoulders of another Einstein and Faraday, could even begin to imagine.

But I'll never know the full extent of the scientific insights I achieved, as my memory of these months is gone entirely. Wiped clean, no doubt, by some voodoo energy of the cube I inadvertently unleashed.

But I'm getting ahead of myself.

I was miserable, but so were we all. The forest was magnificent. Camping here for two weeks, surrounded by the glory of nature, could have made for a great vacation. But being *banished* here for years without end, not once returning to civilization, was a *nightmare*. Especially since a camper would choose his two-week stay during the spring or summer months, not during the rainy season or the middle of a frigid, snowy winter. And no vacationer had ever imagined that bringing along dozens of SS psychopaths might be fun.

We had electric generators that enabled us to power certain experiments, but electricity was in short supply for other luxuries. Running water and indoor plumbing soon began to seem like distant memories. We were filthy for much of the time, mostly bathing only after collecting rainwater or melting snow.

We were all aware that this was wartime, and men around the world were facing much worse duty than we were, in bigger hellholes, with tanks and bombers and machine guns trying to cut them down. But during the cruel, endless winters, this was little consolation. Knowing that others were suffering worse than we were was helpful, but it didn't lessen the actual suffering.

And we all blamed the despised cube for our plight. We had been exiled to the bowels of hell, and solving the cube was the only way out.

And it was *not* cooperating. Nothing we did could affect it one iota. It *mocked* us.

And the longer we went without making progress the more irate Himmler and the Fuhrer became. They made their fury known to the commander of our secret encampment, Colonel Bruno Zimmerman, and he made sure that this venom was passed on to us—with interest.

So we took abuse from the SS, tinkered with the most advanced equipment of the day, and worked on esoteric scientific theories, trying anything and everything, while the cube just sat there *laughing* at us.

Still, during this time I made breakthroughs that surprised even me. For instance, I proved the existence of *nullpunktsenergie*—zero-point energy—something my countryman Max Planck had theorized to exist in 1911. My experimental proof was more complete and profound even than the work of Dutch physicist Hendrik Casimir a few years later, which ultimately gained him considerable notoriety.

In any case, I believe that this discovery is what led me down the path that enabled me to *finally* unlock the cube.

But, again, I'm getting ahead of myself.

For the most part, every day blended into every other, but there was one day, about fourteen months in, that changed *everything*.

I was working out complex fifth-dimensional mathematics, in furtherance of an idea I had to unify relativity and quantum mechanics, when Colonel Zimmerman and his second-in-command, Major Kurt Hahn, rushed around the compound, flushing out all but five members of the SS as if they were quail in the brush.

Apparently, a Canadian family of four, lost for days on a hike, had made it within sight of our encampment, a clear sign that the SS soldiers manning various outposts and patrols had been asleep at the wheel. Sadly, the family had seen one of our buildings and had made the mistake of thinking it would be their salvation, when just the opposite was true.

Zimmerman and Hahn were furious, and sent all their men, save five, out to search for additional Canadians until the wee hours of the night. This was done more as a way to punish those who had dared to miss this wandering family than with the expectation that the SS troops would find any others.

At dawn the next morning, all of the scientists gathered outside at Zimmerman's insistence, so he could demonstrate his utter ruthlessness, in case we had a doubt. We didn't. Neither he, nor his second-in-command, Major Hahn, needed to worry that we might ever think them human.

The family members had been tied securely to four tall, thin poplar trees growing almost in a line, and had been left ungagged. Zimmerman and Hahn *wanted* us to hear their pleas for mercy.

The family members were terrified, and rightly so. Nothing like being in Canada, thousands of miles from any front, and coming across dozens of SS soldiers in your *backyard*.

The mother and father looked kind, compassionate. I could see it in their teary eyes. Even in their panic, their love for each other was readily apparent. They had two little girls, one who looked to be about eight, and another who looked about six. And even at this young age, both knew that they had walked out of the frying pan—and into a nuclear furnace.

Although a nuclear furnace was bound to be more merciful.

Tears streamed down the faces of all four, and the parents pleaded for mercy in English, a language I had spoken like a native since I was four. Not mercy for themselves, because they understood that this wouldn't happen, but mercy for their innocent, helpless daughters.

The father knew the German word *bitte*, for please, and little else, and was beseeching us for mercy, repeating the word over and over again, in between begging for us to spare his children.

Most of the scientists looked properly horrified, but the two SS commandants of our encampment remained stone-faced, unaffected, and even seemed to be enjoying the intense suffering of their prey—animals toying with their food.

Utterly sickened, I walked silently back inside the main building, the largest one, which housed the cube in a separate room in the back. Just because this poor family was as good as dead, and I knew I couldn't save them, didn't mean I had to watch it happen.

Major Hahn tore after me like a cheetah chasing a gazelle. "*Where do you think you're going?*" he bellowed from behind me as he entered the building. Himmler had made certain the SS here were far rougher on me than on any other scientist. My attempt to win the Reichsfuhrer over had backfired, hard, and I paid the price every day.

Himmler needed me, which is why I was still alive, but he despised me for being an Aryan of undeniable genius who he knew mocked everything he believed in. And he believed that the only chance to make a diamond of me was to have his men here apply soul-crushing pressure, which took the form of contempt and continual mistreatment.

"I have some work to do," I answered tiredly. "I've come up with a possible new way to get at the cube."

"That can wait!" yelled Hahn, clutching my arm in a painful grip and dragging me back outside. He pulled me through the thick throng of scientists and to the front, closest to the four victims.

"Herr Richter here thinks he's better than us!" he announced to the entire crowd, which consisted of Colonel Zimmerman, a collection of scientists, and five SS soldiers. "He thinks he's too good to witness any suffering! We all know that you refused to join the Hitler Youth," he added, now addressing me directly. "That you demanded special treatment. That you believe yourself to be our moral and intellectual superior.

"Well, you're about to turn eighteen," Hahn continued, "and this is the perfect occasion for you to get down off your high horse. To get your hands dirty!"

The major handed me a gun. "Shoot them all in the head, Herr Richter."

My mouth dropped open, and I looked back at him in horror.

"*Now!*" he shouted. "Do it! Shoot them in the head this instant!"

I just stood there, frozen.

Hahn's lip curled up into a malevolent sneer. "If you don't shoot *them*," he hissed, "then I'll do the same to *you!*"

16

"How long until the Chinese commandos arrive on their dirt bikes?" asked Major Justin Boyd out loud.

"*If they maintain their current average speed,*" replied Sage through his and Kelly Connolly's comms, "*I estimate in three minutes, thirty-eight seconds. But they are not moving close to maximum speed. Apparently, they are exercising a degree of caution.*"

"Who can blame them?" said Kelly. "You just tore through their force of twenty soldiers without breaking a sweat—*literally.*"

"*I just lost the feed from the one drone surveilling them,*" reported Sage. "*I assume it was spotted and brought down. Would you like me to send the other dragonflies on an intercept course to get eyes on the approaching commandos?*"

"Yes," replied Boyd. "Immediately."

"*Carrying out this order now. I can also report that just before the drone went down, it identified another Chinese soldier hanging even farther back.*"

"Display this soldier," said Boyd, and an instant later the man's face seemed to hover in front of the American major, fully annotated, indicating his facial recognition data was in Sage's database. He was Commander Shen Ning, and US intelligence had identified him as a real up-and-comer in the Chinese military. Best guess was that he wasn't enhanced like his eight comrades on the bikes, but he was known to be both clever and ruthless.

Boyd had no doubt that this was the man in charge, the man who had masterminded this brilliant, self-driving-car-assisted ambush, and the man whose voice had emanated from a silver soccer-ball-shaped hologram. This was a warrior not to be taken lightly, even without enhancements.

Boyd called a halt and unzipped his duffel bag once again, this time pulling out a device that looked like nothing more than a black, plastic TV remote, with a tight coil of thick, insulated green wire emerging from one end, and a single button in its middle.

"Sage, tell me when all eight dirt-bikes are within half a mile of us."

"*Will do*," acknowledged the AI. "*I estimate they will reach this point in two minutes, ten seconds.*"

"How many dragonfly drones are close enough to return here in that time period?" he asked, continuing to speak aloud since no one but Kelly could hear.

"*Three*," replied Sage.

"Fly them into my duffel bag at best possible speed," he ordered.

After Sage confirmed the order, Kelly eyed the device Boyd now held. "So what do you have in mind?" she asked.

"Have you ever heard of an EMP?"

"Of course," said Kelly. "Stands for *electromagnetic pulse*. Nukes produce them. They wipe out all electronics in their path. So you don't have to hit a country with a nuke to do damage. Just explode one above a city and watch as their power grid goes down, airplanes and cars crash, every phone and computer gets fried, and civilization returns to the Dark Ages."

"I like a woman who knows her EMP," said Boyd wryly. "You're correct. And this device," he continued, nodding at the object in his right hand, "can generate a mini-EMP. Most people don't realize that EMPs come in all sizes and power levels. You don't need a nuke. If you go online, you can even find recipes for do-it-yourself EMP guns."

"Definitely something I wouldn't have guessed," said Kelly. "But I assume that your device only has a half-mile range, right?"

"Exactly," replied Boyd with a smile. "Once they're in range, which should be in less than a minute, I'll point and shoot in their direction. Since we'll be behind the origin of the pulse, our electronics will stay safe and snug, while theirs will be fried. The pulse won't kill the soldiers, but it will cripple some of their equipment, and stop their dirt bikes cold."

Kelly brightened upon hearing this last.

"Given that they're enhanced," continued Boyd, "and I have . . ." He paused. He was going to say, *I have you to slow me down*, but thought better of it. "Given that they're enhanced," he began again, "a half mile will put them too close for us to outrun. But this will buy some time for Plan B."

"What's Plan B?"

Boyd grimaced. "No time to tell you," he said, which was a lie. The truth was that he had no *interest* in telling her. That he was ashamed and horrified to tell her. Plan B was a means of killing that he found detestable. Unconscionable. But in this case, unavoidable.

"The three drones just returned to your duffel bag," said Sage.

Kelly's eyes narrowed. "I'm standing a few feet away from the duffel," she said, "and I didn't see or hear a thing."

"They're built to be soundless and nearly invisible."

"All eight bikes are now within half a mile of your position," said the AI.

"I'll be creating the pulse in just a few seconds," he told Kelly, knowing that she had heard Sage's report. "I want them to get a little bit closer. Just to be sure."

Boyd was moving to depress the button on his EMP gun when his comm detected a sound much too faint to hear with the naked ear, but Sage recognized it for what it was immediately. *"Two hostile drones at twelve o'clock!"* she blurted out urgently at four times normal speed.

Boyd dived to the ground and spun Kelly down with him, hitting the button on his EMP gun as he did so.

He rolled and came up searching for the drones, but realized immediately that the electromagnetic pulse would have surely knocked them out. He blew out a sigh of relief.

"Don't worry about the drones," he said, turning back to Kelly. "I fried them in time."

But Kelly Connolly didn't reply. Instead, she remained flat on the ground, still and unbreathing, showing no signs of life.

The EMP *hadn't* taken out the drones in time after all. One of them had gotten off a shot before going down.

A shot that had connected squarely with his companion.

Boyd lifted her gently in his arms, and his eyes welled up with tears. "Nooo!" he screamed in anguish, overwhelmed by emotions more potent than he had ever experienced. This woman had somehow come to mean more to him than he had even known.

But this realization had only come now, when it was already too late.

17

From the journal of Otto Richter

I stared at the gun that the SS major, Kurt Hahn, had shoved into my hand, and at the poor family I had just been ordered to execute, each tied to a tree like a human scarecrow.

I was nearly paralyzed, but couldn't help but notice that Colonel Zimmerman was looking on approvingly, surprised by this spectacle brought on by his second-in-command, but wholly supportive. No doubt Zimmerman saw this as a great way to beat me down further, and as a sort of cruel, demented entertainment.

I evaluated the situation in an instant. Rationally, intellectually, this poor family was going to die. There was no way out for them. And morally, I knew I wouldn't be in any way responsible for these deaths. I was as much a tool in someone else's hands as was the gun.

The father and mother, still firmly tied to trees, and still facing us, teared up even more, the last bit of moisture in their bodies serving the purpose of signaling severe distress to fellow humans, begging for compassion.

Unfortunately for them, compassion was an emotion the SS monsters in charge were incapable of feeling.

Tears began to roll down my own face as I gazed upon the heartbreaking sight of the two small, helpless girls. These innocent children should be basking in the warmth of their family and playing with dolls, not facing an execution simply for being in the wrong place at the wrong time.

I looked at the gun in my hand and then back at the family, and the solution to the equation was clear. I *had* to do this. I had absolutely no choice.

And yet, here was a moment beyond math, beyond rationality.

I realized that I couldn't do it. I *wouldn't* do it.

I doubted Zimmerman would allow his second-in-command to kill me. But I would surely be beaten severely for my refusal, and then treated even worse from now on than I was already being treated, which was difficult to even conceive.

My refusal would turn my life into an even greater nightmare, while not changing the fate of these helpless innocents in the least. Still, I couldn't stare into the large, teary eyes of a six-year-old girl and calmly snuff out her life. And this applied equally to each of them.

The fact that I would be an unwilling weapon, forced by others to kill, would be of little consolation. I might be a weapon, but I was a *sentient* weapon, with the power to refuse.

I shook my head wearily. "I won't do it," I whispered softly.

"What did you say?" demanded Major Hahn in disbelief.

"I said I *won't* do it!" I repeated, this time so forcefully I surprised even myself.

Hahn slapped me in the face so hard that I thought my head would be ripped from my shoulders, and pain erupted from my cheek. An open-handed slap, yes, but much harder than I had become accustomed to.

"You have one minute to shoot them all!" he barked. "Or I won't just shoot you. I'll break every bone in your body before I let you die."

I glared at him with a searing hatred, refusing to be a sheep any longer. "You won't kill me," I said defiantly. "But I can promise you this. Break one bone in my body and I'll kill *myself*. I swear to it! And then you and Colonel Zimmerman can explain to the Reichsfuhrer how you let his prize genius die here."

Hahn hit me again, this time with a closed fist, and tore a gash in my cheek, which began to slowly bleed.

"The Reichsfuhrer is well aware of your insolence," he said through clenched teeth. "You now have thirty seconds to end their lives," he added cruelly.

I let the gun fall from my hand and to the ground, shaking despite myself. If I had miscalculated, and they were really ready to kill me now, so be it. At this point, death would be a blessing.

Major Hahn looked at me with utter contempt and picked up the gun I had dropped. He took several steps toward the nearby row of captives and shot each between the eyes at point-blank range, including the two little girls, ignoring their terror as they cried and screamed hysterically, having just seen their parents murdered before their eyes, and knowing they were next.

I fell to my knees and vomited on the forest floor.

"*Get up!*" demanded Hahn.

I wiped the vomit from my lips and chin with several fallen leaves nearby and rose.

"Kill me now," I said in resignation, glassy-eyed. "Please."

Hahn glared at me in contempt once again. "Not a chance!" he bellowed so everyone in the clearing could hear. "Death would be too easy a punishment for you."

Zimmerman ordered the gathering of scientists back inside to return to their work.

Hahn waited for them to disperse before turning to his commander. "Request permission to discipline this pathetic excuse for a human, Colonel," he said.

"Permission granted," said Zimmerman. "But don't break any bones, Major. Don't even injure him," he added, clearly disappointed to have to add this restriction. "The Fuhrer and Reichsfuhrer both expect him to solve this cube and bring them the superweapon they crave."

The colonel frowned. "I just got an update last night," he added. "Apparently, one of the other superweapons the Reich is pursuing, something called an *Atom Bomb*—which the Reich has had high hopes for, but which I've always thought to be fantastical nonsense—isn't going well. Which makes our success here even more critical."

"Understood, sir," said the major.

He carefully undid the rope that still pinned an adult male corpse to a tree. "I'll take young Otto away from here, so his screams don't disturb the other scientists. I'll hang him by his arms and ankles from a tree for extended periods. He'll live, and I'll make sure he isn't injured, but the pain will become excruciating."

"Excellent choice, Major Hahn," said Zimmerman.

The major shoved me forward to begin our trek away from the encampment, baring his teeth like fangs and relishing what was to come. "Don't wait up," he said to Zimmerman, who returned his cruel smile.

We walked for almost twenty long minutes through dense forest before finally stopping.

"Sit down," said Hahn in low tones when we came to a halt, gesturing to a large rock outcropping that could serve as a natural seat. But as he said these words, his face transformed from raging barbarian to something else. Softer. Thoughtful. Human, even.

Surely, I was reading him wrong.

"Let's talk," he said quietly when I sat, making no move to do the same.

He carefully surveyed our surroundings. Even though we were at least a mile from our encampment, it was possible that one or more of his men might venture near us on a perimeter patrol. The fact that he was worried that we might be overheard was either a good sign—or a very, very bad one.

"First off," he began, "I'm not going to hang you by your arms and legs. Just say that I did when we return."

"What *are* you going to do to me?"

"Nothing. I just want to talk."

I stared at him suspiciously as a pair of squirrels scurried up a nearby tree. "Why?" I asked. "What do you want?"

"I want to help you."

I couldn't help but laugh. "Sure you do," I said. "After more than a year of treating me like something you scraped off your boot. After trying to force me to kill little girls, and then doing so yourself. After almost breaking my cheekbone."

Hahn took a deep breath. "Look . . . Otto," he began. "I'm truly sorry about that. But we're of like mind, you and I. I've sworn to devote the rest of my life to undoing some of the evil that Hitler has unleashed upon the world. There are more good men than you know in the Nazi ranks. Fewer than there should be, but more than you know. The problem is that Hitler has seen to it that no one can trust anyone else. It's never clear who is a spy. Or who has become brainwashed but is pretending otherwise. I never thought I'd see the day when young children would be turning their loving *parents* into the secret police. But even this has been happening—for many years now."

"Are you saying you thought that *I* was a spy?"

"I thought you might be, yes. Himmler painted you as having deep-seated anti-Reich sentiment." He raised his eyebrows. "Which might be true. Or which might make you the perfect lure to draw out traitors to the Reich, whom you could then expose."

My eyes widened. As twisted as his logic was, it was accurate. And it was logic that I, myself, had used. I had initially hoped to make friends among the scientists, but this was not to be. Himmler had made sure to poison the well, to isolate me, even from them. He had fostered jealousy and competition among the scientists, thinking that this would somehow improve the chances we would succeed, when it was sure to do just the opposite.

But worse, even if he had tried to foster friendship and camaraderie, I knew I could never be sure whom to trust, even among the scientists. Nazi Germany was built upon a foundation of mistrust and fear, of justifiable paranoia.

George Orwell captured this culture of distrust and oppression brilliantly four years after the end of the war in his book *1984*. He wrote of the *Thought Police*, Gestapo wannabes who monitored and punished any citizen committing "thoughtcrimes" against the state, in many cases luring them to do so by pretending to be in solidarity with their goals. The book was presented as a tale of the distant future, but it was really a chronicle of the recent past, with Hitler, the SS, and the Gestapo the clear antecedent for Big Brother.

"To trust someone in these times," continued Hahn, "is to put your life in their hands."

He sighed. "But I'm doing that now, Otto. I'm trusting you with my life. Because I was finally able to give you the ultimate test. One that enabled me to confirm where you really stand, once and for all. And you passed with flying colors, as I hoped you would."

"Are you seriously saying that trying to force me to kill innocent children was nothing more than a test?" I spat in disgust.

"That's exactly what I'm saying. And your refusal, even upon threat of death, told me everything I needed to know. I'm very proud of you, Otto. And very impressed."

I shrank bank in horror. "But *you* killed them without a thought. And it looked like you *enjoyed* it."

The major's face fell, and he looked as pained as if I had knifed him in the stomach. "It made me sick," he said in disgust. "Absolutely sick. A blight on my soul—one of many—that I can never erase. But it served a greater purpose. This poor family was going to die today, one way or another. They were dead the moment they saw us. You know it too."

He paused to let this sink in. "But for me to do lasting damage to the Reich, I have to do it from within. I have to earn the trust of my superiors. And the best way to do this, the best way to advance, is to pretend to be even *more* ruthless than they are. Even *more* psycho-pathic. I've been brutal to you since the beginning. But think about what this has gained us. Do you imagine Zimmerman suspects that I'm having this conversation with you now? That I'm being *nice* to you? That I want to be your ally? Do you imagine that when we re-turn, and I tell him I tortured you, he'll doubt my word?"

His logic was unassailable. "So you've gone out of your way to make my life miserable—because you're really on *my* side?"

"I *hoped* we were on the same side," replied Hahn. "I was sure about *me*. But I couldn't risk everything until I was sure about *you*. So I've been biding my time, staying above suspicion, and monitor-ing your progress in solving the cube. And you've made more than the others realize, haven't you? I know a little science. You've proven the existence of zero-point energy. The other scientists pretend not to be impressed, but I know better. It's a mysterious, invisible force that no one has demonstrated before. If anything can unlock the cube, it's advances like this one."

I continued to be struck by the stark dichotomy of the past hour. I had gone from being pressured into committing a despicable act, to believing I was seconds away from being tortured, to now learning that the man I hated the most in all the world might be my only ally. It was dizzying.

I watched a stick bug walk along the ground and for the first time in hours allowed myself to hear the chirping and singing of the myriad birds all around me.

"It became clear to me early on," continued Hahn, "that you were obsessed with solving the cube—before anyone else. I reasoned that if you aren't a spy, a lure, and truly despise Hitler and everything he stands for, like I do, you're obsessed for the right reasons. Not to gain personal glory, and not to ensure a victorious Reich. But because if any other scientist beats you to the punch, they might deliver Hitler his superweapon. I grew to believe that if you solved it first, you planned to destroy it." He paused. "Even if this cost you your life."

I studied him in astonishment. He was right in every respect.

"You couldn't be more wrong," I said firmly. "My goal is to repair my image by demonstrating my loyalty to the Nazi Party. I plan to solve the cube and help our Fuhrer win a glorious victory. So that I might eventually become the chief scientist of the Third Reich. What you just suggested would be *treason*."

Hahn sighed. "Yeah, I know. I don't expect you to admit it. You'd be crazy to. I've abused you, and now I say I'm your friend. This could easily be a plan to gain your confidence, so I can hang you with it later."

I remained silent.

"I can't blame you for not trusting me," he continued. "After all, I only began to trust you completely an hour ago, after putting you through an obscene test that no one should ever have to face. But even if you never come around, I plan to help you to the best of my ability. My hope is that one day, through my actions, I'll be able to *earn* your trust."

I considered. "Help me, how?"

"First, I should tell you that I *have* been helping you. I'm responsible for delivering personnel reports back to headquarters. And I've been giving you glowing reviews. Telling headquarters that you remain our best hope, and that I believe you are giving maximum effort. All this is true, they just don't know that your efforts are at cross-purposes to theirs. I'm also giving you high marks for coming around to Nazi ideology, telling them that I believe our indoctrination discussions have been effective."

"Why would you do that?" I asked.

"Two reasons. One, glowing reviews ensure your parents remain safe. And two, if this quest to understand the cube ends in failure, which seems likely, and you're recalled, I want you to be trusted. I've been implying that you're closer to a breakthrough than you really are, just to be sure they don't pull up stakes prematurely. If this project is canceled, I believe they'll want your genius on the atom bomb program, which Zimmerman just mentioned. It's apparently not going well, but we can't be sure this won't change. So if you are assigned to this program, I need you to be more trusted than you were at the start here, so you can make sure it's sabotaged."

I studied Major Kurt Hahn with newfound respect. I had thought him nothing more than a cruel buffoon, one sure to lose to a *rooster* in a game of checkers. Instead, he had been playing high-level chess all along.

"But this is how I *have been* helping you," he added. "You wanted to know how I can help you going forward. So I'll tell you. I can see to it that you sleep with the cube."

My eyes widened. I had requested this very thing so often that Zimmerman had finally threatened to cut out my tongue the next time I did.

I had told him that I found the cube soothing and that it would help me sleep. That I was often struck by eureka ideas while I tossed and turned at night, but ideas that were quickly forgotten. I had insisted that sleeping in the same room with the cube would allow me to test my ideas the moment I awoke, before they vanished.

This was all nonsense, of course. Like everyone else, I found the cube extremely disquieting. No one in their right mind would want to sleep anywhere near it, even if it was covered by a metal box that blocked its blinding rays.

But I needed to overcome my aversion and sleep in the same room with it anyway. After a month or two, the SS would take this strange behavior for granted, and not give it a second thought. It would be just another example of the inexplicable peculiarities of genius.

Once this happened—assuming I continued to make break-throughs—I could awaken in the wee hours of the night and carry out experiments, very quietly, without anyone being the wiser. In this way, if I did solve the cube, I could do so without anyone knowing. And I could *destroy* it without anyone knowing.

My guess was that I couldn't destroy it without also destroying myself, and maybe even hundreds of miles of forest, but it would be well worth it. Giving Hitler the kind of power the Atlantis Cube could unlock would lead to the deaths of uncountable millions. Not to mention ensuring that humanity would be enslaved for decades, or even centuries, by a self-perpetuating ruling class of psychopaths, making the world depicted in Orwell's book seem like a *paradise* by comparison.

Hahn waited patiently for my response.

"Why would you bring up sleeping with the cube?" I asked him. "I haven't mentioned that in a long time."

"Because it's vital to your goal—*our* goal—and we both know it. We both want you to be in position to conduct secret experiments on the cube, so you can discover a way to destroy it."

I wanted to nod my agreement, but shook my head in feigned disgust, instead. "Once again, you have me all wrong," I protested. "The cube soothes me. And sometimes I awaken at night with fleeting ideas that I want to try. These are the *only* reasons I want to sleep in the same room with it."

"Whatever you say, Otto. Again, I don't blame you for not trusting me."

"So how would you manage this, anyway?" I asked. "The colonel is dead set against it."

"I've given it a lot of thought," he replied. "I'll tell Zimmerman that while you were hanging upside down from a tree, I got you to admit that the cube evokes a primal fear within you. It evokes a primal fear within *everyone*, as Zimmerman well knows. So I'll tell him that you only requested to sleep with it to appear willing to go the extra mile, so your parents wouldn't be harmed, knowing that your requests would be denied."

I nodded as I guessed where he was going.

"Then I'll suggest to the colonel that we should *force* you to sleep near this object," he continued, "*because* it spooks you so bad. As punishment for your disobedience. And as a way to make a man of you, and to get you even more receptive to accepting Nazi ideology."

A smile slowly crept across my face, despite myself. It was an inspired strategy. Zimmerman would never agree to such a thing if he thought it's what I wanted. But if he thought it was a *punishment*, that was a different story.

Hahn sighed. "I do a good job of pretending to be a psychopath," he said in disgust. "*Too* good of a job. But the colonel *is* one. Trust me, if I convince him this will be your worst nightmare, he'll go for it."

I turned away in thought, but didn't reply.

"I assure you, Otto, that we believe the same things. Hitler is as insane as he is evil. I've had to become evil myself to fit in, to solidify my cover, and to excel. But this just makes me even more determined to stop this bastard and make amends. I'd give my life twenty times over to do this."

He paused. "All I ask is that if you do figure out the cube, you promise to destroy it. Unless you can use it to destroy *them*. Either way, you can't hesitate."

"I won't," I said under my breath.

"Sorry. I didn't quite catch that."

I nodded. He wasn't meant to. "Look, Major, you've said a lot of traitorous things. But I'm not going to turn you in. Because I know that you've simply been testing me. Of course I don't want to destroy the cube. All I want to do is solve it, as commanded, and provide it to the beloved Reich. You can have total faith in me."

I paused. "*Heil Hitler!*" I added for good measure, thrusting out my arm.

Hahn frowned, not returning my salute. "We both know that Hitler *can't* be healed," he said. "My dream is to one day return to

Germany, more trusted than ever, and be in a position to kill that monster. Destroy the evil little prick, once and for all. In the meantime, it's great to finally be convinced that you aren't part of a clever trap set by the Reichsfuhrer to ensnare me.

"So when others are watching," he added, "I'll continue treating you with contempt. But behind the scenes, I'll be helping you achieve our goals. If you create revolutionary technology, I'll help you hide it. If you need equipment you don't want other scientists to know about, I'll acquire it for you. I hope that eventually you'll come to trust me, and know that there is at least one other person in this with you."

He paused. "But even if you can never trust me, I'll be doing my absolute best to help you defy the Reich."

As I gazed into the eyes of the man I had come to despise above all others, who had made my life a living hell, I decided that I believed him. Not that he still didn't need to earn my trust. This could still be a double-cross. He said he would help me solve the cube so I could destroy it. But he could be *pretending* to help me, only to swoop in and hand the spoils to Hitler himself. Or maybe his goal was to use the power of the cube, not to *end* Hitler, but to replace him.

I couldn't help but flash on the numerous cruelties I had witnessed Hahn commit, including the recent execution of two children. Could a decent human being bring himself to be so utterly cruel and callous to maintain his cover?

Maybe so. But maybe not.

Despite these misgivings, something in my gut told me he was being sincere.

And I began to feel a glimmer of hope for the first time since I could remember.

18

Justin Boyd sat on the leaf-strewn ground and cradled the lifeless figure of Kelly Connolly, wondering how she had come to mean so much to him in such a short time.

And now he had lost her. Despite possessing superhuman reflexes, he had been a moment too slow.

His eyes widened as he detected the slightest rise and fall of her chest, and the obvious finally hit him. *Of course* she wasn't dead. He had been on too many missions where the prospect of either side using non-lethal force was laughable.

But not this time. This time the Chinese wanted him alive. And even *more* so, they wanted his scientist companion alive. And Boyd hadn't seen any blood, just an unconscious figure he assumed was dead.

He searched over Kelly's fallen form and quickly found a tranquilizer dart in her leg, which he promptly pulled out, while his AI confirmed the presence of a slow but steady pulse.

Boyd closed his eyes and basked in pure, unadulterated relief—but only for a moment.

Disabling the dirt bikes had slowed the Chinese commandos down, but the clock was still ticking.

He lowered Kelly gently to the ground and reached into his duffel bag once more, this time unzipping a small inner compartment.

"Sage, activate the HK drones," he ordered subvocally.

There were nine remaining hostiles and he only had eight HKs, but he could easily handle the un-enhanced Commander Shen, no matter how brilliant a tactician and strategist he was.

"I assume you have enough visual history on the eight commandos who were on the bikes to differentiate between them all," he added.

"Affirmative," replied the AI.

"Assign each HK drone to one of the eight and let them fly. Have them target a centimeter above the bridge of the nose."

"Launching HKs now," confirmed Sage.

"Tile the feeds from all eight drones and display them on my lenses," said the major, and an instant later a display appeared a foot in front of his face, showing eight video images of a tree that was just beyond where the HK drones were now emerging from his duffel bag. All eight tiles displayed the same tree, just at slightly different angles, but their views would diverge considerably as the mission proceeded.

Boyd watched the eight tiny quad-copter drones hover above his bag, just for a moment, before streaking off through the trees toward their targets. Each was just slightly larger than his thumb.

And each was an *abomination.*

But they were abominations that contained breathtaking technologies. Night vision, noise cancellation, and advanced facial recognition, along with decision-making capabilities that enabled them to actively conceal themselves at all times. And one other item. A potent explosive packed into their minuscule nose cones.

These tiny drones were basically autonomous bullets. Bullets capable of hunting a victim down, of stalking him or her for hours on end. Tiny self-guided missiles that never missed, and that were treacherously difficult to bring down, moving as they did at over a hundred miles an hour and capable of evasive action. Smart bullets able to navigate around corners and obstacles on the way to a target, striking with perfect accuracy every time to blow a hole in a helpless victim's forehead.

While US black ops had dubbed these drones HKs, for *Hunter-Killers*, they were more commonly known around the world as *slaughterbots*, after a short film of the same name made years earlier. The seven-minute film was fictional but showed simulated graphic scenes of attacks by these lethal, autonomous microdrones, and it had gone viral, shocking the conscience of the world.

As well it should have. These weapons, whether called HKs or slaughterbots, were utterly *despicable.* Inhuman. And recently deemed by international treaty—signed by numerous countries, including China and America—as being too barbaric even for war, along with bioweapons, chemical weapons, and nerve gases.

And the HKs would only get more abhorrent from here. At some point soon, the technology would advance so that each bullet could take out more than one victim. Like the whistle-powered arrow from the movie *Guardians of the Galaxy* that had unerringly pierced through dozens of hostiles in seconds, zigzagging to hit each one in turn, this development would represent the ultimate horror show.

Still, Boyd carried these eight illegal HKs to use as a weapon of last resort, and only when much more than his own life was at stake. In the current case, his capture would yield EHO secrets that he had vowed to do everything in his power to protect. And the information they could get from Kelly Connolly could be even more of a game changer than what they could get from him.

Who was this woman? Was she an alien?

If she really had moved the Enigma Cube, this would make the most sense. But Boyd refused to believe it. Her every expression and reaction, down to her tears, were as human as he had ever seen.

Yet there was far more to her than met the eye, this much was obvious.

He sighed, knowing that this was a riddle he wouldn't be solving for a while.

Boyd monitored the progress of the tiny drones, which were now in position. A small red dot appeared at the top of each of the eight tiles, indicating that each drone had located its target, and was now hovering out of sight, awaiting Boyd's order to finish its task.

"Sage, have all HKs strike in ten seconds," he commanded. *"I want a freeze-frame image from each of them a hundredth of a second before impact with their target,"* he added.

This was the only way to ensure that the targets were down without having a dragonfly drone available to confirm the kills. An image taken a hundredth of a second before impact would show the target just before death. A hundredth of a second *after* would show nothing, as the charge would not only kill the target, but the drone and its video equipment, as well.

"*Striking now,*" reported Sage, and over a quarter-mile distant, each of the eight drones accelerated to over a hundred miles an hour and unerringly zeroed in on the foreheads of their respective targets. In his mind's eye, Boyd imagined each drone striking above the bridge of each target's nose and blowing their charges, obliterating eight heads, and splattering the grisly contents for many yards around them, like a watermelon dropped from a skyscraper.

Five of the tiles showed Boyd what he expected to see. Images of Chinese faces, likely having no idea that death was streaking toward them, one hundredth of a second away.

But three of the tiles were totally blank.

What?

He opened his mouth to query Sage, but she answered his question before he could ask. "*It appears that five of the drones completed their mission,*" said the AI, "*while three of the drones were taken out.*"

"Taken out *how*?" demanded Boyd. The Chinese commandos had downed dragonfly drones, sure, but these were slow and unable to take evasive action. Taking out a slaughterbot was like hitting a bullet with another bullet.

"*Unknown,*" replied Sage.

Boyd cursed to himself. If he was going to sell his soul and use a despicable, illegal weapon, he should at least put an end to the conflict. But he had not. Three enhanced Chinese soldiers still lived, along with their commander.

Boyd knew he needed a new plan, and he needed it now. The four remaining hostiles would *not be happy*, and three of them would be running through thick trees and underbrush at speeds an Olympic sprinter would envy.

The major lifted Kelly effortlessly, with Sage boosting his strength by sending controlled currents through sections of his soft fabric endoskeleton. He draped her over his shoulders in a fireman's carry and began sprinting off through the woods, giving the men behind him more distance to close before they reached him.

As he ran, he considered multiple plans, but quickly discounted them all.

All except one.

It was simple, but his gut told him it would work. It would *have to*.

Because he was all out of options.

19

Kelly Connolly's consciousness swam slowly to the surface, and she felt as relaxed and content as she ever had.

Where was she?

Part of her didn't care. Part of her wanted to luxuriate in the comfort of being mostly asleep, numb, and of continuing to rest a mind and body that seemed more spent than she could remember.

A sharp bolt of electricity coursed through her system as her memory of recent events came flooding back. She had been with Justin Boyd, and they had been in trouble. Boyd had defeated twenty seasoned mercs with effortless efficiency, and had then been desperately trying to slow down a much more formidable force using an electromagnetic pulse.

But why didn't she remember anything from there? And where was she now?

Her eyes fluttered open, and for a moment she wasn't sure of what she was seeing above her, or the nature of the surface below her.

And then it all became clear.

She was lying on her back across the back seat of the Lexus rental car that had driven them here, to the ninth circle of hell, against their will. In this case, a hell disguised as a magnificent autumn woods. She glanced up at the headrest and confirmed that she was right—it still had a chunk missing from where the gas canister had revealed its presence.

She gasped at the incongruity of it all and began to rise.

"Don't get up," cautioned Justin Boyd, his voice coming from the front of the car, where he was also lying across the seats. "We can't risk being seen."

"What . . . um, what . . . happened?" she said. She felt dazed, groggy. Maybe even a little high.

"You were drugged," he replied. "Hit by a tranquilizer dart fired from a drone. After you were out, I triggered the EMP, and I also managed to take out five of the Chinese commandos."

She blinked as her addled brain tried to do the math. "Which means that there are . . . three left, right?"

"Actually, four. Their commander is out there also. The voice from the hologram. In this case an actual commander, although not enhanced, by the name of Shen Ning."

Kelly could feel her mental acuity returning, but she still felt sluggish and slower than usual. "Why are we here?" she whispered slowly. "How . . . long?"

"We're safe," he assured her. "The drug will be completely out of your system any second, and you'll be back to normal. You've been out for about four hours, and we've both been right where we are now for all but a few minutes of that time. Sage and I tried to start the car, but no luck."

He paused. "Once you were knocked unconscious, my options became limited. I'm not sure I could have beaten these three enhanced commandos under the best of circumstances, but with you out cold, I wouldn't have had a chance."

"Unless you abandoned me."

"Which was never going to happen," replied Boyd emphatically. "So I ran off with you in one direction, and had Sage use a dragonfly drone to lead them in the opposite direction."

"How?"

"We had the drone fly ahead of them and broadcast faint sounds of me running through the woods with you draped across my shoulders. Snapping twigs, bent branches whipping back into position after I passed, that sort of thing. The actual sounds I was making, just closer to them, and coming from the wrong direction."

"Smart," said Kelly.

"Maybe," he allowed, "but only a temporary solution. They figured out they were being misled soon enough. I thought about running beyond the signal dead zone to call for reinforcements, but decided I'd never make it. Besides, I'm the highest value target China has ever had in their sights." He raised his eyebrows. "Well, other than *you*, apparently."

Boyd sighed. "So you can bet Commander Shen contacted his people to have them extend the signal dead zone," he continued. "And that every Chinese satellite in existence is monitoring motion within these woods and all exits, making sure we don't escape. With this vast expanse of woods to look for us in, they have a big needle-in-a-haystack problem. But you'd better believe they've at least made certain the needle is forced to stay within the haystack."

"Wait a minute," said Kelly, realizing that her normal mental acuity had fully returned. "Slow down, Justin. How would this Chinese commander . . . Shen . . . contact associates to make this happen? I get he has some special new frequency that we don't. But I thought you fried their electronics?"

"Very true," replied Boyd with a sigh. "But an outfit this good will make sure that at least one phone or comm is protected from electromagnetic radiation by a Faraday Cage, or some other means. And also other select equipment. My duffel bag, for example, is lined with a layer of aluminum, which can fend off an EMP attack, as long as the bag is zipped closed."

"So tin-foil hat people aren't so crazy after all?"

Boyd laughed. "No, they're still mostly crazy. But they are right about aluminum fending off electromagnetic radiation."

"So you figured you couldn't get reinforcements," said Kelly, "and you couldn't outrun them. So lying low was your best bet."

"Our *only* bet. It probably took them a while to get their satellites redeployed and programmed for us, but after that happened, we'd have been screwed. Their satellites won't miss us moving through the woods, even one this dense. They'll have algorithms that will be able to distinguish us from woodland creatures. They might not detect us the first hundred yards or so—*might* not—but the longer we're moving, the more sure it becomes.

"After Shen failed to detect us for a while, I'm sure he guessed that I'm hiding to make sure this doesn't happen. Hunkered down like a spider, setting up booby traps around me, waiting for them to venture close enough to strike."

"Why here?"

"There are endless places in the woods for me to hide us. So I'm counting on them not guessing I'd return to where this whole thing began. To the one spot for miles that has *no* cover."

"Other than the car we're in," said Kelly.

"Other than the car we're in," he repeated. "I have the two remaining dragonfly drones monitoring our immediate vicinity, just in case they think to look here. Nothing so far."

"Should we be talking like this?" she asked in low tones, suddenly apprehensive. "Won't they have comms that can amplify sound like yours can?"

"They can amplify away," said Boyd. "Lexus does a good job of soundproofing their cars. And transparent aluminum is even better at shielding noise than glass."

"Is there anything aluminum *can't* do?" asked Kelly wryly.

Boyd laughed. "Sage tells me that as long as we don't raise our voices, we can talk in here without danger of attracting any attention. It'll be pitch-dark outside in just about three hours," he added, "and then I'll have the advantage. I can go on offense, if necessary. Bottom line is that I should be able to get us out of here by morning, one way or another."

Kelly considered. "*Why* will you have the advantage?" she asked. Then, after a moment's thought, she answered her own question. "Because you have night vision and you think they don't?"

"That's right. Our intel suggests that their smart lenses don't have night-vision capabilities. If they brought goggles, these are likely fried. But I doubt they brought them. They expected us to arrive here unconscious and to mop us up before noon. Intel suggests they're engineered to be able to see better at night than the average human. But still not nearly as well as I'll be able to see."

"You are a lot more impressive than I'd ever have guessed," said Kelly earnestly. "You aren't just a badass because of your tech and enhancements. You're sharp as a razor. And you seem to have great judgment. Exceptional instincts. Not to mention being lightning quick on your feet, decisive."

"Thanks," said Boyd, almost shyly. He blew out a long breath. "I just hope your praise isn't premature. Once it's dark, we *should* be able to work our way free of this trap. Their satellite motion sensors should detect us, even at night, so at some point I'll need to engage the enemy. But I should have enough of an advantage to prevail. As soon as I can get a signal, I'll contact Colonel Osborne to send in reinforcements."

"How many?"

"I'm pretty sure *all of them*," said Boyd wryly.

Kelly smiled.

"Thirty to fifty men, to be on the safe side," said Boyd, serious once more. "We'll need exfiltration, and a team has to move in and mop up any remaining enhanced hostiles. And I wouldn't be surprised if they bring in a large number of their own reinforcements by morning."

Kelly was about to ask another question when the comm in her ear suddenly sprang to life. *"Hello to my two American adversaries,"* said the same voice that had come from the hologram in the clearing, which Boyd had identified as belonging to Commander Shen Ning. *"If I've timed this right, Dr. Connolly,"* continued the voice, *"you should now have recovered from the tranquilizer dart we hit you with. I wanted to wait until you were awake so I could greet you both together."*

"He's just trying to bait us to respond," said Boyd. "Fishing. He can't track us if we're just passively receiving."

"Don't all rush to respond at once," said Shen after waiting just over twenty seconds. *"I'd prefer to have a two-way conversation, but at the risk of seeming rude, I'll just continue with a monologue. The EMP was a nice touch, Major, but much of our equipment is protected. As you've no doubt guessed by my ability to broadcast this message.*

"I'm asking you to save all of us a lot of trouble and surrender now. You're clearly aware that you're pinned. That our satellites are scanning the area for motion. So you have no options, and time is running out. It'll get pretty cold out here soon, and the noose is tightening. I have massive reinforcements set to arrive before morning."

Kelly nodded to herself. Boyd's guess on the reinforcements had been spot on. When she had told him how much he had impressed her, she had meant it. And he was *continuing* to impress.

"In short," continued Shen, *"you have no chance. You know I want to keep you both alive. But I promise to go much easier on you if you surrender voluntarily. And this promise is a very big deal,"* he added, his tone darkening considerably, *"given how badly I want to cut you into little pieces for killing five of my comrades."*

Shen paused again, as if wanting to give them a few seconds more to come to their senses and surrender.

"You're basically defenseless at this point," he continued finally. *"As you Americans say, you failed to keep any powder dry. If you had any more HKs, you'd be using them,"* he added, *"since it's clear you missed class the day they reviewed the slaughterbot treaty. Not that I'm in any position to file a complaint, since I'm here on American soil trying to capture American citizens. But let's just say that I'm not the only party here breaking international law, am I?"*

"What is he talking about?" said Kelly.

Boyd ignored her as Shen continued trying to goad them to respond, surrender, or make a mistake for another five minutes. Finally, the Chinese commander gave up, with a promise that he would find them, wherever they were hiding, and that their capture was inevitable.

"So what did he mean by saying we were breaking international law?" asked Kelly yet again, once it was clear the Chinese commander had finished.

Boyd shook his head. "Look, Kelly, I made sure I filled you in on how we got here, and my plans for escape. But I haven't forgotten why Shen now seems to want you even more than me. So now that his little interruption is over, don't you think it's about time you answered *my* questions?"

Kelly cringed but remained silent.

"I'll take that as a *yes*," said Boyd. "So first question: did you—or did you not—take the Enigma Cube from the Uru facility?"

Kelly's breath caught in her throat. "I did," she said softly. "And I can't tell you how sorry I am."

Boyd shook his head in disbelief. "Incredible," he whispered. "I mean, when Shen made his accusation and I looked over at you, my gut told me he was right. But I can't tell you how hard I've been trying not to believe it."

"I'm *sorry*," said Kelly again. "But I had my reasons. At least I *thought* I did. I had a tough call to make, and I made it. And I'm willing to walk you through my thinking."

"Wait," said Boyd after he had digested what she had said. "Let's back up. Before we get to *why* you took the cube, why don't you begin with *how*. As someone once said, the cube is a *fricking immovable object*." He shook his head. "Are you even *human*?"

"All too human, I'm afraid," said Kelly with a sigh. "Look, I've come to like and respect you, Justin. *A lot*. And my instincts tell me you feel the same way about me. There seems to be strong chemistry between us, for reasons I can't explain. Is this just a normal consequence of two people being thrown into the trenches together?"

"Sometimes," said Boyd. "But I've sensed the same chemistry between us that you have. And I'm pretty sure we both felt it even *before* we were in the trenches." He frowned. "But that was also before I learned about your activities last night. Now all bets are off."

"I understand," said Kelly miserably. "But despite how it looks, we're on the same side. At least I hope we are. I'd never do anything to hurt you or my country. To hurt *anyone*. I don't even kill spiders. I know that not everyone will agree with my reasons for what I did. That *you* might not. But you should know that my intentions were good."

"The road to hell is paved with good intentions," said Boyd.

"So is the road to *heaven*," she countered. "Which road we might be on is in the eye of the beholder."

Kelly paused, and a wry smile came across her face. "I just hope that a little thing like me stealing a priceless alien artifact from the most secret, high-profile black ops facility in the world, which you'll soon be in charge of, doesn't, you know . . . *hamper* our relationship."

Boyd couldn't help but laugh at the playful audacity of her statement. "Well, yeah," he replied, "when you put it *that* way . . ."

The major paused and became deadly serious once again. "Look, Kelly, I can't tell you how much I'd rather be your friend than your adversary. But that all depends on how you were able to move an immovable object. And why you took it. And what in the hell is going on!" he finished emphatically.

"It's a bit of a long story," said Kelly.

"Good," he replied. "Turns out that I don't really have anywhere to be just now."

PART 4

"Any sufficiently advanced technology is indistinguishable from magic."

—Arthur C. Clarke

20

When Justin Boyd had first situated them in the car, he had felt ridiculous being sprawled out across the front seats of an unmoving car, while a woman he was surprisingly drawn to was sprawled out across the back seat. And the hours he had waited for her to regain consciousness hadn't helped.

Now that she was awake, he *still* felt ridiculous. But in addition, he also found it surreal to be having a calm discussion under these bizarre circumstances, especially since the discussion topic itself was considerably *more* surreal, *more* bizarre than the venue itself. And that was really saying something. Not only were they both on their backs in a car, like patients on a psychiatrist's couch, but the clearing they were in was still littered with the fresh remains of the ten men Boyd had slaughtered, which he had purposely failed to remind his companion of.

When he had picked up Dr. Kelly Connolly at the Philadelphia International Airport that morning, he couldn't have possibly imagined any scenario in which he would be where he was now, in the fight of his life, waiting for nightfall, in a dead car in the middle of a Pennsylvania woods.

And yet, even this would have been more believable than the idea that the woman he'd be with in the car had casually walked off with an object that all the resources available to the US military couldn't move.

"As eager as I am for you to begin," said Boyd, "there's a house-keeping item that we should take care of first."

"Housekeeping?"

"Yes. I've decided to trust you. I'm not sure why. But I'm going to let myself believe that you mean well. That we're still friends and allies. And who knows, maybe someday more than that."

Boyd sighed. "I do think we're going to get out of this," he continued. "But what you know is likely too important to chance it falling
into Chinese hands. They may not think to check this car for days, or
they may be seconds away. We can't risk keeping your secrets unprotected any longer."

"I'm not following you."

"I have a truth-serum blocking agent in my duffel bag. It's experimental, but it works. I propose using it on you right now, just in case
we get caught before you finish your, ah . . . long story. It will protect
your secrets from both truth serums and torture."

"*Torture?*" said Kelly in alarm.

"Again, I don't think we'll get captured. This is just a precaution."

"How would that work, anyway?" she said. "How can a chemical
protect me from *torture?*"

He winced. "It can't. But it *can* prevent you from spilling your
guts."

"I see. So while *they're* spilling my guts, *literally*, it prevents *me*
from spilling my guts, *figuratively*."

Boyd cringed. "A graphic way to put it," he said. "But I suppose
so. I have a small vial of the stuff. It's extremely potent, so I only
need to use what fits into the very tip of a small syringe. Here's how
it works. First, I'll inject you. After that, I need you to concentrate
for all you're worth, for about ten minutes. I need you to think hard
about all the secrets you wouldn't want the Chinese to have. In as
much detail as possible, and really dwell on them."

"And that will protect this information from coming out?" she
said skeptically.

"Exactly. If you're drugged or tortured, you'll be unable to dis-
close it."

"How could that *possibly* work?"

"I'm not entirely sure. It's very complicated. One component of
the drug blocks truth serum. That's the easy part. The other component preferentially migrates to the memory traces that you re-trigger
during your ten-minute walk down memory lane. It sets up a matrix
that locks them up, but only if you're under duress. The gist is that
your brain chemistry is different when you're being tortured, a loved

one is being threatened—that sort of thing. So under duress, it isn't that you won't be *willing* to give up the information. It's more like you won't even *remember* it. It won't be there for you to access."

"Hard to imagine that this could really work."

"It does, believe me. Very well. It acts like a chemical version of a Chinese finger trap. The harder you try to pull out of it, the harder it grips you."

"So the more I try to remember, the less likely I'll be able to."

"Right. But if you aren't under duress, you'll be able to access all of your memories freely."

"That's quite the trick," said Kelly.

"It is. And it's pretty foolproof."

"And more than a little . . . *disturbing*."

"This is true," said Boyd. "But you should know that by doing this now, I'm taking a big chance with you."

Kelly pondered this statement for a moment and nodded. "Because if I lied about wanting to confide in you of my own free will," she said, "then *you* won't be able to get at this information, either."

"It is nice to be around someone I don't need to spell things out for."

"It's nice being around someone willing to trust me," said Kelly. "Especially when I've given you every reason *not to*." She paused. "Thanks, Justin. I won't betray your trust."

The major drew up a tiny amount of the drug into a small syringe and placed the vial back into a separate compartment in his duffel. Kelly thrust her arm through the narrow middle gap between rows and Boyd injected her. Ten minutes later, she reported that she had dredged up every last memory that should best be kept secret.

"What about you?" she said when this was done. "Are you going to inject yourself?"

"Already covered," replied Boyd. "Unfortunately, my technology and genes will tell quite a tale, even if I don't." He paused. "But now that we have that out of the way," he continued, "the moment of truth has finally arrived. You have the, ah . . . floor."

"Or at least the back row of the car, at any rate," said Kelly with a smile.

She took a deep breath, gathering her thoughts. "Give me just a few more seconds," she said. "I'm trying to decide where to begin."

"How about at the beginning?" said Boyd wryly. "Or is that too cliché?"

"Okay, beginning it is. Any guesses as to when that might be?"

Boyd considered. "When you first joined Uru?"

"Good guess," she said. "But you had no chance of getting it right. Turns out the beginning is just a little bit earlier than that. In 1939, in fact."

Kelly blew out a long breath. "And in the center of Nazi Germany."

21

Boyd's eyes widened. Once again, he had thought he was prepared for *anything*. But he had been wrong.

"Nazi Germany?" he repeated stupidly. "Your story begins in Nazi Germany? Are you *kidding* me?"

"Yeah, because who doesn't kid about Nazi Germany?" she said wryly. "It was such a whimsical place."

Boyd sighed. "Okay," he said. "Go ahead. I'm listening. *Intently*."

"Were you aware that the Nazis were into mysticism and the occult?"

"I wasn't, no."

"Well, they were. In a *big way*. Have you ever seen the old Indiana Jones movies? You know, beginning with *Raiders of the Lost Ark*?"

"I have."

"If you remember, in the first one, the Nazis were pretty eager to get their hands on the Ark of the Covenant. And in the third one, on the Holy Grail. Well, this sort of interest wasn't just fictional. The Nazis were obsessed with stuff like that. And Christian-inspired supernatural objects were only the tip of the iceberg.

"In 2016, a collection of thirteen thousand occult and witchcraft books were rediscovered in the National Library of the Czech Republic. They had originally been just one part of a vast collection of occult books that belonged to Heinrich Himmler, the head of the Nazi SS. The Nazis plundered hundreds of libraries and archives across the world for material like this."

"Why?" said Boyd simply.

"A long story. One for another time. But they were also obsessed with what they called *Wunderwaffen*—German for *Miracle Weapons*. Usually referred to as *superweapons* in English. Several of these weapons programs were somewhat mainstream, simply ahead of their time. Like super battleships, super-tanks, and jet-powered aircraft. And all manner of advanced rockets."

"I'm aware of the Nazis' advanced rocketry programs, at least," said Boyd. "They were far ahead of the rest of the world. After the war ended, the United States secretly employed sixteen hundred German scientists and engineers, including Wernher von Braun and his V-2 rocket team, under a program that was code-named *Operation Paperclip*."

"I've heard about that," said Kelly. "Weren't a number of these scientists part of the Nazi Party, or even Party leaders?"

"They were. But our government looked the other way. To be honest, they felt they had no other choice. Operation Paperclip was in direct response to a similar operation conducted by Russia. The Soviets pressed even *more* German scientists into service than we did. So Germans ended up playing key scientific roles on both sides of the Cold War. And the Space Race. In fact, Von Braun was responsible for our Saturn V rocket. Without him, America would have never made it to the moon."

Boyd paused. "But getting back to Nazi Germany," he said, "you began listing a few superweapon programs that were on the mainstream side. I assume they had others that were . . . less so."

"A *lot* less so. Really, really far out. Hard to believe, even. They were working on the bomb, of course, but this was just the beginning. They had a program to develop something called a Sun Gun. A huge reflector in space, three and a half square miles in area, that they believed could focus the sun like a giant magnifying glass, boiling the ocean or burning a city."

"But they had no means of getting anything into space," pointed out Boyd.

"You can't say they didn't think big," replied Kelly. "Let me give you a few more examples. They worked on massive sonic emitters, to do what you had Sage do to those mercs in the clearing. They tried to build vast cannons on railroad tracks, four or five stories high, which would weigh over three million pounds, and which would fire twenty-thousand-pound shells the size of cars.

"But I saved the best for last," she added. "Toward the end of the war, the Nazis had a major effort underway to crack *anti-gravity*. Something I suspect our friends at Haycock Township are aware of."

"This had to be the earliest effort ever."

"It was," replied Kelly.

"But more about that later," she added with a sly smile. "First, let me circle back to the Nazis' occult obsession. In one of the thousands of books Himmler acquired, there was a tale about a magical cube. It was fabled to be in a certain area of Canada, deep in a forest, and its description couldn't have matched the Enigma Cube any closer."

"Fascinating," said Boyd.

"Oh no. The fascinating part is coming. Himmler sent a team to scour this area for the cube, and in a huge stroke of luck, his people actually found it. He called it the Atlantis Cube."

"Atlantis Cube?"

"Long story. But the name makes sense if you're familiar with crackpot Nazi theories. Anyway, Canada joined the war effort while the SS team was there. But even so, Himmler was so excited, he ventured behind enemy lines to see this find for himself. And after he left, he maintained a large team in the forest to study it. A team consisting of dozens of scientists, and dozens of SS soldiers."

"That's actually the first thing he did that makes sense," noted Boyd. "If you find an Enigma Cube, you do whatever you have to do to unlock its secrets, *wherever* it is. Well, at least to *try* to unlock its secrets. I'm sure they didn't get anywhere."

"I get why you say that. But much of today's fundamental quantum physics and general relativity was known at the time."

"Maybe so, but it wasn't nearly as developed as it is now. And neither was any other scientific discipline. *Our* people spent years without getting anywhere, and they had advanced technology the Nazis couldn't even dream of."

"Very true," said Kelly. "But the Canadian encampment had something *we* don't." She paused for effect. "They had Otto Richter."

Boyd tilted his head in confusion. "What's an Otto Richter?" he asked.

"The greatest mind humanity has ever produced. A mind the Nazis kept hidden from the world. An Aryan who soared above even the brilliant Jewish physicists of the time.

"In 1941, Richter was sixteen," continued Kelly, "and already producing work that was arguably more impressive than anyone else in the world. So Himmler pressed him into service to solve the cube, about eighteen months after the project had begun. If anyone could solve it, then or now, it would be Otto Richter."

"You make him sound like a *god*," said Boyd. "The Nazis must have done a phenomenal job of keeping him secret for no one to have ever heard of him."

"They did," she confirmed. "But to continue, Hitler and Himmler were aware that young Otto didn't subscribe to Nazi ideology. But they had no idea just *how much* he despised them. They had no idea of the sacrifices he was willing to make to hurt the Third Reich. Even so, they made sure the SS soldiers in Canada kept a sharp eye on him."

Boyd continued to hang on her every word.

"Fortunately," she continued, "young Otto knew he couldn't trust anyone, so he watched his steps very carefully. And luckily for him, after a little more than a year in the forest of Canada, he found an ally. The second-in-command of the SS contingent there. A major named Kurt Hahn."

Boyd's eyes narrowed. "How is it that I didn't know any of this?" he said suspiciously. "After I first met you and Harry last week, I reviewed the origins and history of the Uru group. It turns out that Colonel Osborne conducted a thorough records search when your facility was being constructed. He looked for any reference to anything that might vaguely resemble the Enigma Cube. And found nothing. It's understandable that he missed the obscure reference in Himmler's private occult collection. But if the Nazi program in Canada was known to history, his search would have found it."

"I don't doubt it. He didn't find it because it *isn't* known to history. I tried to find it, too, and struck out just as completely."

"Then how can you possibly know so much about it?"

Kelly sighed. "Because Otto Richter was my grandfather."

22

There was a long silence inside the car as Kelly let her companion digest what she had just said. Boyd was reeling yet again, something that had begun to happen with increasing frequency since he had first set eyes on the cube.

This took surreal to another level.

The car was quiet as a tomb. Outside in the clearing, an ever-growing number of insects and birds were feasting on the fresh bits of human flesh that Boyd had so kindly provided. Sage had positioned a display to his virtual right, one showing the feeds from the two remaining dragonfly drones, but he had chosen not to share this grisly scene with his companion.

"Until about sixteen months ago," said Kelly, picking up the narrative yet again, "I had no idea that an Otto Richter from Berlin even existed—let alone that he was my grandfather. All I knew was that my dad's dad had died before I was born. And I had been told that he had been a man named Jim Connolly, from Clear Lake, Iowa."

"So your family was lying to you?" said Boyd.

"No. Otto was lying to *them*. They still have no idea. In fact, not even my grandmother—his wife—had any idea who he really was. Or his history. No one in my family does even now, because I haven't told them."

"So what happened sixteen months ago?"

"My father passed away," said Kelly softly, and the pain in her voice was unmistakable.

"I'm so sorry."

"Thank you. He meant a lot to me. But after mourning for longer than I should have, I've moved on. Still hurts when I think about it, but he'd want me to get over it and be as happy as possible. He had a big influence on my life."

"I don't doubt it," said Boyd. "I should have guessed that he'd be a world-class physicist also."

"Are you cheating again, Justin?" she said. "You do know it's rude to use your personal AI and smart contacts to learn about someone you're talking to."

"Sorry," he said sheepishly. "Force of habit."

"I know Sage is cut off from the internet, so I'm impressed that her onboard database is comprehensive enough to have my father in it."

"She does come fully loaded," said Boyd with a smile. "As I said earlier, the entirety of Wikipedia is just a tiny fraction of the whole." He paused. "But please continue. And I'll try to control my database searching."

Kelly nodded. "My father was seventy when he passed away from a heart attack," she said. "Information I suspect Sage has already displayed for you. Anyway, this was tragic, but not entirely surprising. My dad had undergone open heart surgery twelve years earlier, and we knew this was an issue for him.

"Anyway, after the funeral my sister and I stayed with our mom, who is ten years younger than my dad, for several weeks. We were there to console her, and to help her sort out what to do with the house, financial issues, that sort of thing. Our family has always been well off, so she was in good shape, but she still needed company and guidance.

"My grandfather, Jim Connolly," she continued, "really Otto Richter, had been an inventor of some acclaim. No one in the family knew, including me at the time, that he was capable of so much more. That he was arguably the most brilliant man who ever lived. His inventions had been fairly small-time. Nothing too showy. But they had netted him about fifteen million dollars. A sizable amount, but again, not so sizable that he stood out. Which was true of everything he did. He had a gift for languages, spoke English like a native, so he chose to pass himself off as farm boy from Iowa. After living and working in Hitler's malignant Nazi regime, and so soon after the end of the war, it isn't hard to understand why he didn't want to share his past. Or even admit to being German."

"Is that why he chose to go by the name of Connolly?" asked Boyd.

"Absolutely. Nothing says *German* like the name Otto Richter. He purposely chose a name that everyone would recognize as being of Irish origin. *Connolly* comes from an Old Gaelic name meaning 'fierce as a hound.'"

"Seems to fit *you* fairly well," said Boyd in amusement. "I mean the *fierce* part, of course," he added quickly. "Not the *hound* part."

Kelly smiled. "Thanks for the clarification," she said. "In any event, my grandfather's earnings from his inventions allowed all of us 'Connollys' to live fairly comfortably down through the generations. He was quite a generous man."

"So when, and how, did you find out about him?"

"While I was staying with my mom in the weeks after my dad's funeral. She had used her entire attic as a storehouse. So I was going through it all, trying to help her organize, and I came across dozens of boxes of old books, which had belonged to my grandfather Jim. I decided to look through them, to determine if any were valuable, should be kept as heirlooms, or should be finally tossed away.

"I was astonished by their titles," she continued. "Heavy duty physics and mathematics texts that even world-class physicists would struggle with. I knew my grandfather was smart, and an inventor, but had no idea he was interested in physics. Not just interested, but obviously quite accomplished. My father must not have ever opened these boxes after his mother passed away, because he would have told me about this."

"Right," said Boyd, "because you and your dad were both physicists. And it would have meant a lot to both of you to discover how much this interest had run in the family."

"Exactly. I opened up a number of the boxes, fascinated. Finally, I came upon an entire volume devoted to zero-point energy, which has always been an interest of mine. I knew that it had first been theorized more than a century earlier, and that Casimir had demonstrated the effect in the forties or fifties. But this field had been largely ignored, until recently. So I was surprised to find an entire book on the subject that was so *old*."

She paused. "So I opened it. And I found that it *wasn't* an entire volume on the subject after all."

"I don't understand," said Boyd.

"The book was *hollow*. Inside was an old, leather-bound journal. My grandfather's journal. More to the point, *Otto Richter's* journal. A journal he had kept up with until just before his death."

"I see," said Boyd slowly. "So that's how you learned about the Nazi program in Canada."

"And a whole lot more. He wasn't able to begin keeping a journal until he was finally out of the Nazis' clutches, but he had a very good memory. And he wrote it in English. I made a digital scan of it so I could keep electronic versions on my phone and in the cloud. Which means that Sage now has a copy too, since you had her suck in the contents of my phone."

Boyd nodded slowly. This was another unexpected turn. "I won't read a word of it unless I have your permission," he said.

"I appreciate that. But given where things stand, I'll probably end up *encouraging* you to read it. But for now, let me just tell you the basics. My grandfather wrote of his upbringing in Berlin, and the astonishing things he was able to accomplish, even before he was ten. He was a prodigy's prodigy. He wrote about being pressed into service to solve the cube when he was sixteen, and of meeting Heinrich Himmler himself."

Boyd let out a soft whistle. "Now *that* must have been an interesting passage," he said.

"I certainly thought so," she replied. "He then wrote about his time in Canada and his work on the project. How miserable he was. Living and working in harsh, primitive conditions, with even harsher, *more primitive* human beings. Still, he was able to do extraordinary work. Revolutionary. His journal had much more to say about this time in his life, but skipping ahead, his work culminated in the creation of a dark energy generator."

"A dark energy generator?" said Boyd skeptically. "Are you sure about that?"

"Positive."

"That would be absolutely incredible," said the black ops major. "Our people have only now pulled this off. More than eighty years later."

"Not to rub it in," said Kelly, "but his was more powerful. Still weak, but more powerful than the one the Haycock group developed."

"But I thought dark energy and dark matter were only hypothesized very recently."

"They were. My grandfather—Otto—didn't call it dark energy, of course. And he didn't have the cosmological evidence that caused physicists to posit it in the first place. But, like Leonardo Da Vinci, he was *generations* ahead of his time. His generator was about the size and shape of your EMP gun. Very rudimentary, but absolutely amazing. It incorporated breathtaking ideas that not even modern science has rediscovered.

"When I found his journal, there was a key taped to the back of it. The key was to a safe deposit box in one of the oldest banks in Manhattan. He had paid for the box in advance for a hundred years. Inside the box, I found his generator, safe and sound. I was able to improve it using modern technology, and I built a more powerful, more reliable version of my own."

"So why haven't you introduced it to the world?" asked Boyd.

"I'll get to that soon. But let me get back to Canada and back up a little. Before my grandfather perfected the dark energy generator, he obtained permission to sleep, alone, in the same room as the cube, so he could perform secret experiments at night. His SS ally, Major Kurt Hahn, helped him with this by sleeping just outside the room. Whenever Otto was conducting experiments, Hahn would only pretend to be asleep, and would make sure my grandfather wasn't discovered.

"As I'm sure you can appreciate from Uru's track record," she continued, "none of his experiments had any effect on the cube at all. But this changed dramatically when Otto hit the cube with his newly developed dark energy generator. It was the key that finally unlocked the thing.

"The moment he trained the generator on the cube, the blinding beams of light streaking from the cube's corners, which had seemed eternal, vanished." She snapped her fingers. "Just like that. And whereas it had been a cage before, with ever-changing spinning and not-spinning geometric figures inside, all six faces of the cube suddenly filled in, turning the cube solid. With a glossy finish that looked like white marble."

"How in the world did it do that?"

"How does it do *anything* it does?"

"Good point."

"After Otto got over his absolute shock," continued Kelly, "he began to experiment—*frantically*. He still couldn't move the cube, and if he couldn't get it back to its original configuration by morning, the Nazis would discover he had found a way to affect it.

"Whether due to genius-level intuition or just plain luck, he discovered a second required key. If he pressed his fingers on all four vertices at the top of the cube, and held them there for several seconds, the cube transformed again. This time, it maintained its solid form, but fifteen hieroglyphs suddenly materialized on all six of its faces, glowing red, as if they were on fire. But despite their appearance, they were cool to the touch.

"Three of the cube's faces contained a single hieroglyph, and the other three faces had four, evenly spaced. The glyphs that had cube faces all to themselves were the most prominent and stood out the most, of course. Later, Otto found that if he didn't touch any control for exactly three minutes and twenty-three seconds, or if he pressed and held all four top corners again, all the glyphs would disappear, leaving a solid, barren cube."

She paused for an extended period to let Boyd digest this revelation and get a picture of what she was describing in his mind's eye.

"The glyph on the top face," she continued, "was clearly a depiction of the Enigma Cube itself, and showed forces acting *on* it. It had one notch above it, and one below, that could well have been the alien version of arrows. Otto learned that if he pressed on the notch below this glyph, the cube would suddenly shed its enormous weight and become light as a feather.

"If he then pressed the one above it, the cube would gain weight, at an ever-accelerating rate. If he pressed this notch and held his finger down for a few seconds, the cube would jump immediately to its original weight and form. It would once again be an immovable cubic cage, with blinding lights streaming from each vertex."

"So probably not a good idea to be holding it when you make *that* happen," noted Boyd, as he imagined clutching an object that jumped instantly from feather weight to the weight of a skyscraper in one fell swoop.

"Not a good idea at all," agreed Kelly with a smile. "A good way to lose a hand. Fortunately, Otto had thought of that, and always left it where it was originally sitting."

"But the bottom line is that he solved it," said Boyd in wonder. "He discovered that the cube, *itself*, is an anti-gravity device."

Kelly shook her head. "It isn't just an anti-gravity device," she said. "It's *much* more impressive than that. It doesn't just *reduce* gravity. It *controls* it. Absolutely. Increases as well as decreases. Which means that its weight doesn't come from neutron star matter after all. It comes from an ability to mold spacetime like so much clay. The implications go far beyond simple anti-gravity, but I'll save these for later."

"Understood," said Boyd. "Go on."

"The other two stand-alone glyphs were on side faces. One showed a depiction of the cube, just like the glyph on top. But this time, instead of showing what seemed to be forces acting *on* the cube, it showed forces emanating from the cube and acting on *another* object. This one had *eight* distinct notches arrayed around it, which served as control notches."

Kelly paused. "He didn't explore this glyph the first night," she continued. "But he did extensively over the next month with Hahn acting as guard. As Otto had guessed, this one could control the gravity being experienced by *other* objects. He experimented on rocks that he could sneak in and out of the room so as not to leave evidence of his experimentation.

"The implications soon became abundantly clear. If he were to point the vertex of the cube nearest this glyph at a tank, for example, he could make its gravity increase so much that it would implode like a crushed aluminum can. He could point the cube at advancing soldiers and crush them into *paste*. And so on."

Boyd's eyes widened. "Which would make the cube every bit the superweapon Hitler hoped for," he said.

"That's right. But Otto was smart, and cautious. He only experimented with these two glyphs, which had seemed to have more obvious functions, not any of the other thirteen. But because of these numerous others, it seemed clear to him that he was only tapping the tip of the iceberg of what the cube could do."

She paused. "And I can tell you, based on theoretical work that has been developed since the 1940s, the possibilities are even more staggering than Otto Richter imagined."

"What about the third glyph that was all by itself?" asked Boyd. "Seems like an obvious one for him to try."

Kelly frowned. "It was a large red dot in the center of its cube face. The dot was surrounded by what looked to Otto to be the glyph equivalent of a cloud. And there were no control notches of any kind. He didn't think this cloud was suggestive of explosive debris—*necessarily*—but he definitely didn't want to take that chance."

Boyd nodded, totally engrossed. "Go on," he said again.

"His goal was to destroy the cube. But he couldn't find a way. It was just as invulnerable in its active, solid-cube state, as it was in its original state. He thought maybe one of the other controls might have done the job, but he refused to access any of them. The longer he experimented, the more determined he was not to press his luck. He had stuck with the most prominent, obvious controls and had survived. But if he tripped the wrong one, he was convinced the cube could melt down the entire area. Maybe even the entire *planet*."

"Yeah, I get why he might think that," said Boyd, glad that he had seen the cube for himself. If he hadn't, he would have thought the idea that it might be capable of destroying the Earth ridiculous. But after seeing it for only a few minutes, it was easy for him to believe the cube's destructive power was limitless.

"Since he couldn't destroy it," continued Kelly, "he decided he had no choice but to steal it out from under the Nazis' noses. He discussed this with Hahn, whom he had grown to trust. He couldn't let

Hitler have it. So he would activate it, use it to wipe out everyone in the camp, except for his ally, and take it where the Nazis would never find it. He would create a crater, an earthquake, that Himmler would think had killed everyone not on patrol at the time. Himmler would believe the cube had blown up, and that would be the end of it. Hitler would be denied his alien superweapon."

Boyd was mesmerized. "So this Otto," he said, "your *grandfather*, must have succeeded. If not, he wouldn't have lived to write his journal."

"He did succeed. He just wasn't quite sure *how*. Because one day he found himself in the woods of Spokane, Washington, holding the cube—and he had no idea how he had gotten there."

Boyd's mouth dropped open. "Spokane, Washington," he repeated in dismay. "I'll be damned," he whispered. "How did I not see this coming? So the Nazi cube you were talking about isn't just *like* the cube we've been studying. It *is* the cube we've been studying."

"Yes it is," said Kelly simply. "And no worse for wear," she added with a smile.

23

Boyd couldn't believe his ears. Did the cube *ever* run out of surprises?

"As I was saying," continued Kelly, "Otto Richter found himself in Spokane, with the cube, without knowing how he had gotten there. Months had passed since he had prepared to put his plan into effect, but somehow his memory of carrying it out was gone. Along with everything that happened since."

She paused. "Given that he was in Washington State, which bordered Canada, and which would be an obvious place for him to journey to after taking the cube, it was clear to him he *had* carried out his plan. He chalked his loss of memory up to some strange effect caused by prolonged contact with the cube."

"Incredible," said Boyd to his companion in the back seat. "So your grandfather stole the immovable cube from the *Nazis*. And you decided to follow suit by stealing the very same cube from *us*."

Kelly sighed. "And I'm getting to my reasons for that," she said. "But do you want to hear the rest, or not?"

"By all means. Please continue."

Kelly took a moment to gather her thoughts. "Otto was eighteen years old when he found himself in Spokane. In his pocket, he found a diagram of the cube and the results of extensive experiments he had done with it, in tiny print. In *his* handwriting.

"The experiments he had performed in the Nazi camp had been necessarily limited, so he must have done these on his way to Spokane. Experiments such as using the cube to crush a boulder the size of a car. Or using it to levitate a thirty-foot tree. Or having the cube increase gravity in a circle around him, while leaving his own gravity untouched. He had apparently learned to use the eight controls surrounding the glyph I told you about with exquisite accuracy, sensitivity, and versatility. He had been able to wield the cube to carry out his will like a veritable magic wand."

Boyd nodded, spellbound.

"Even so," continued Kelly, "he dug a hole in the woods where he was, returned the cube to its original immovable setting, and covered it with dirt.

"One quick digression," she added. "Uru has been confused by how the cube's downward weight isn't nearly enough to account for its enormous resistance to lateral movement. But the thing can manipulate gravity as effortlessly as you can change the channel on your television, and with the precision and flexibility of a gymnast. So my guess is that the aliens gave it a tricky default setting—which Otto called its *lockdown mode*—in case it fell into the hands of primitives like us."

"With its lockdown mode being the way it was when I first saw it, right?"

"Right. In this mode, the cube's gravity in the downward direction is set lower than its gravity in the lateral direction. In this way, it can sit on the ground, or a surface—provided it's a very, very sturdy one—without crashing through it. But at the same time, it still can't be moved."

"So the aliens made sure it could sit there, stably, and mock us for eternity," noted Boyd wryly.

"Exactly," said Kelly. "Bastards!" she added with a smile.

"In any case," she continued, "the cube you saw in our facility was, indeed, in lockdown mode. Inert and inactive. With blazing light pouring from each of its eight vertices, and its twelve edges forming a cage rather than a solid. And as you know, in this mode, it isn't going anywhere, nothing on Earth is going to affect it, and there are no glowing red glyphs to control it."

"And the only power on Earth that can activate it, take it *out* of lockdown mode, is a small dose of dark energy."

"As far as anyone knows."

"But why dark energy?" asked Boyd. "What's your guess?"

"Otto conjectured, and I agree, that it's an alien test of maturity. The cube itself makes use of dark energy, so only a civilization advanced enough to wield this energy for itself is qualified to activate the cube. Nothing less. And we weren't even close to being qualified in the 1940s. Otto Richter was just *way* ahead of his time."

"Interesting theory," said Boyd. "I also find it interesting that dark energy is the key to unlocking the cube, because it clears up a mystery I was trying to solve."

"What mystery is that?" said Kelly.

"The mystery of your uncharacteristic behavior. Which occurred twice, both times involving the Haycock group's prototype dark energy generator. When I first proposed testing it on the cube, you disparaged their work. You argued *fiercely* against even making the attempt."

"*Fiercely*?" repeated Kelly. "Really? Is that another reference to *Connolly* meaning *fierce as a hound*?"

"Absolutely," replied Boyd with a smile. "But you can see where I'm heading with this. Now I know why you acted the way you did. You weren't worried that trying the generator would be a waste of time. You were worried that it *wouldn't be*.

"You did everything you could to talk me out of it. And when you failed, when we were a day away from our breakthrough, you just removed the cube on your own. Which is why you were so surprisingly amiable this morning with the Haycock team, and didn't argue against their generator at all. Because you knew it didn't matter any longer."

"You're right," said Kelly softly. "And I felt like a real ass disparaging their work. But I thought it was for the best. I didn't count on you being so stubborn in the face of my objections."

Boyd nodded. He hated when things didn't make sense, and was glad that order had now been restored to this part of his universe. "Before you finish your story," he said, changing gears yet again, "I need to ask about something I've been avoiding."

"Go ahead."

"Can I assume that you didn't bring the cube with you on this trip?"

"Of course not."

"Shen wanted you to tell him where you hid it. Which implies his people haven't found it yet. Given the resources he's no doubt plowing into this task, I'm surprised."

"I don't want to tell you where it is quite yet, Justin," she said. "I need to see if we're on the same page. And I have a lot more thinking to do in any case."

"I understand," said the major. "I *think*."

"But I did hide it well. And I hid the dark energy generator separately, not that anyone could possibly be looking for that. When I took the cube, I was *extremely* paranoid. I've never so much as stolen a candy bar before. I was convinced that somehow Uru would be on to me, even though it was after hours. I never expected *China* to have seen me, that's for sure. Still, I tried to be very clever about how I hid it, and where."

"I'm sure you were," said Boyd. "Did you leave it in lockdown mode?"

"No. It's in a temporary hiding place. I planned to find a better one when I returned from this trip. But I hid it inside something that couldn't contain its light in lockdown mode, so would advertise its presence. Besides, in its active form, after making the glyphs disappear, it looks like a harmless marble paperweight. Even Uru personnel wouldn't guess what it was. And a thief wouldn't bother stealing it."

"Yeah, but given what we know now . . ."

"Given what we know now," said Kelly, "I'd feel *a lot* better if it was locked down. But at the time, I thought the worst case was that Uru would get it back. In what world does a foreign power catch me stealing it when our own government doesn't?"

"Yeah, tell me about it," said Boyd miserably.

"Fortunately," said Kelly, "without the glyphs being activated, the cube is useless."

There was a long silence. "You should get back to your story," said Boyd finally. "I interrupted. You were saying that Otto Richter had buried the cube in the woods."

"Right," said Kelly after taking a moment to gather her thoughts. "And after he hid it away, he had a tough decision to make. His first thought was to give it to the Americans. To the Allies. Who could probably use it to win the war."

She paused. "But in his short life, he had witnessed more human evil, delusion, cruelty, and barbarism than most of us can even comprehend."

"I don't doubt it," said Boyd.

"The list of Nazi atrocities goes on and on," she continued. "Burning books, enforcing ghettos, and starving millions into *skeletons*. Rounding innocents up in train cars and sending them to work camps, where they would be exterminated by the millions in the most callous, systematized means imaginable. Absolute control of speech, of thought. Doctors conducting gruesome experiments on non-anesthetized human beings. An entire culture fostering sadism and cruelty."

She shook her head. "If you think you're familiar with all of the horrors of Nazi Germany, do an hour of research, and you'll find even more. What happened there makes your worst nightmares seem like rainbows and unicorns."

"So Otto hadn't exactly seen humanity at its best."

"Which is why he finally decided not to give the cube to the Americans after all. He had witnessed untold human evil, human cruelty, his entire life. And even the most compassionate of the species could be corrupted by absolute power. Even angels in heaven could be corrupted, as Satan himself proved only too well."

She sighed. "So there was no way he was letting any human being gain control of the cube, and especially not a government or military. He couldn't trust anyone with this kind of power. And not just this single cube's power to implode tanks and wreak havoc. But the even greater power to be gained from the study of the unlocked cube, assuming its scientific secrets could be learned. Besides, he hadn't forgotten that he had only activated *two* of the glyphs. There were still thirteen left to try."

Boyd frowned. It was hard to argue with Otto Richter's reasoning.

"So he decided to build a cabin around the cube, and set it in eternal lockdown mode. To buy the land around it under an assumed name, cover his tracks, and keep careful watch of it. Even in the unlikely event that someone stumbled upon it, it wouldn't matter. They couldn't budge it, and when he discovered the trespass, he would simply move it somewhere else."

"Why not just leave it buried?"

"He wanted it to be easily accessible to him—just in case. He didn't want anyone to have it, but he did recognize it as the ultimate fail-safe. If Hitler was on the verge of winning the war, he would give it to the Americans then. Or if the Earth was ever about to be struck by an asteroid the size of Texas, he would use the cube to deflect it and save the planet. He slept easier knowing it was within easy reach."

Kelly paused to collect her thoughts. "He described all of this in his journal in great detail. Including a diagram of the activated cube, with glyphs, and a detailed instruction manual.

"After he built the cabin, he became an upstanding citizen of Spokane, keeping a very low profile. He was afraid to even attract the attention of the scientific community. He had heard rumors that any number of German scientists were in America, and he didn't want anyone who knew about the cube program to know he was alive. Any one of them could have been shown his photo while still in Germany, and briefed on Otto Richter the prodigy.

"He also made inquiries and learned his parents had died in the war, never learning exactly how. He was heartbroken, but when Himmler separated him from his parents, he had the feeling he would never see them again. And although he tried, he never did learn the fate of his sole ally, Kurt Hahn.

"Finally," continued Kelly, "one last point of interest before I move on. I'm convinced that when the Nazis discovered their Atlantis Cube was gone, knowing how much it weighed, they must have figured some sort of anti-gravity tech had to have played a role. How else could it have been moved? I think this explains their anti-gravity program during the war. We can never be sure, but I think the timing of this program is too much of a coincidence."

"I suspect you're right," said Boyd.

"You're up to speed on much of the rest," she continued. "The Allies won the war, and time marched on. Otto Richter became Jim

Connolly, and made a great living as a small-time inventor, studying physics in secret. All in all, he felt good about his life, about what he had accomplished. He went on to achieve any number of breakthrough physics results, but only for his own edification. He disclosed none of these, and while their nature was touched upon in his journal, none were elucidated.

"Ultimately, he decided he would pass knowledge of the cube down to his descendants, so it wouldn't be lost to humanity. He didn't know whom he could trust, but he hoped his offspring would share his values. He hoped they would watch over the cube in the cabin when he was gone. Be there to wield it in emergencies. He saw himself, and his family, becoming humanity's caretakers."

She paused. "So he wrote of his experiences in a journal and hid it in a book about zero-point energy. The discovery of this energy was his first big breakthrough in Canada, and had ultimately led to his dark energy generator. He hoped the journal would be handed down by his descendants, generation after generation, for centuries. Until mankind had matured enough to be ready to handle the kind of knowledge the cube represented. And he wrote dozens of pages in the journal pleading with his eventual offspring to resist the temptation of giving the cube to the world. His arguments were brilliant and eloquent, as might be expected of the greatest genius mankind has ever produced."

"Were his arguments all centered on humanity's *inhumanity*?" asked Boyd. "And our tendency to let power corrupt us?"

"Much of them, yes. But he also knew that his descendants would see the immense good the cube could do. And he knew how painful it would be for them to turn their backs on the extraordinary knowledge the cube represented. So he asked for their forbearance, and argued that there would come a time to reveal the cube to the world. But that whoever was the caretaker at this point had to be *certain*. Once the lamp was rubbed, there would be no way to put the genie back in.

"He recounted the story of Adam and Eve, who were banished from paradise because of their curiosity. Their inability to resist the temptation of the forbidden fruit. Which itself was a metaphorical stand-in for knowledge and power. He urged us to find the restraint needed to resist the temptation of the cube—the biblical apple in modern garb. He urged us to remain in Eden until we were able to work out the knowledge the apple offered, all by ourselves."

Kelly fell silent, allowing her companion to ponder all he had heard.

"I need you to back up a bit," said Boyd after nearly a minute had passed. "Your grandfather wanted his journal to be handed down through the generations. So how is it that no one in your family knows anything about it—or the cube—to this day? And how is it that *you* only know about it through chance alone?"

"Good question," said Kelly. "My grandfather wrote the journal—and continued to make entries—with the plan of sharing it, and his history, with his firstborn when he or she turned eighteen. Introducing his firstborn to the lifelong responsibility of watching over the cube, and of using it if the fate of humanity hung in the balance."

"So what went wrong?

"My grandfather died suddenly one day from a heart attack. Before my father, his firstborn, reached eighteen."

"You did say that heart problems ran in the family, didn't you," said Boyd solemnly. "Along with the dazzling brilliance that you've clearly inherited."

"Nice of you to say, but no one can hold a candle to my grandfather. Genetic dilution, I guess. My father and I became world-class physicists. But Otto Richter was in a league no one else has ever achieved."

"How old was your father when Otto died?"

"Fifteen. Otto Richter/Jim Connolly married my grandmother when he was twenty-eight, and she was twenty-three. They had my dad in 1956, when Otto was thirty-one. And Otto died fifteen years later, at forty-six, without any warning."

"What a loss to the world."

"No doubt," said Kelly sadly. "My understanding is that he seemed healthy as a horse at the time. But the heart attack killed him in minutes. My grandparents were in separate rooms when it hit. My father told me that my grandfather had gone to heroic efforts to pull himself across the floor as he was dying to see his wife one last time. But the last words he managed to gasp out before he died weren't 'I love you' or any other such sentimentality. They were 'open zeer.'"

She paused. "This became lore in my family. All of us took a crack at trying to discern what he might have meant by *zeer*. But we failed, of course. We decided that my grandfather had been too far gone to think clearly, and these words were little more than gibberish. Or that my grandmother had heard him wrong."

"But she had heard him perfectly, hadn't she?" said Boyd. "He was trying to say *zero*, but he died before he could utter the second syllable, so it came out *zeer*."

"That's almost certainly right," said Kelly. "Knowing what I do now, it's clear that he was trying to say 'open zero-point energy book.' He was desperately trying to hand down knowledge of the cube in the seconds he had left to live." She frowned and shook her head. "But he came up just short."

"So your father grew up knowing nothing about it."

"That's right. For all intents and purposes, the information, and the cube, were lost to the world. When my dad was thirty-seven and my mother was twenty-seven, they had my older sister. Four years later—thirty years ago—they had me."

"And then, just sixteen months ago, your father died, and you rediscovered Otto and the cube. So you salvaged his legacy after all. It just skipped a generation."

"Except it wasn't that simple," said Kelly. "Because, as you know, the cube was found in the meantime, during a time when no Connolly was keeping watch. When no Connolly was around to whisk the cube to a new location before the Uru facility could be completed."

"Good point."

"My grandfather's journal had the exact coordinates to the cabin. After I read it through, you can imagine how eager I was to see the cube for myself. But when I ventured out there, I found that the government had bought up hundreds of acres of woods around the cabin. Which shouldn't have been possible, because there wasn't a seller. My grandfather had bought the land under an assumed name.

"The area was covered by surveillance cameras. It took me a while, but I learned how to beat them, and eventually managed to get inside the cabin. And you know what I found. It was empty. But even though the hole around where the cube had been was filled with concrete and covered up, I found evidence that it had been lowered underground. Which is why the cabin wasn't all that well guarded by then, since the cube was a half mile of granite and concrete away."

"So how did you manage to join the team?" asked Boyd, fascinated.

"I knew whatever team was studying the cube must be traveling through a tunnel to reach it. It took me a few months of reconnaissance, but I eventually identified the fake factory that served as the entrance. Then I kept careful track of who was coming and going."

Boyd whistled. "You might be in the wrong line of work. You'd make a hell of an enhanced commando."

"Wow, you really know how to flatter a girl," said Kelly in amusement. "But there's no way in hell I'd have ever found it if my grandfather hadn't given me the precise coordinates of the cabin. He gave me a great head start. It occurs to me the Chinese could never have found it, either, unless they knew where to look."

Boyd frowned. She made a good point. "But how could they possibly know where to look? Are you suggesting we have a mole?"

"No. I'm suggesting they are somehow able to detect the energy of the cube when it's in lockdown mode."

"Interesting theory," said Boyd. "One I'd like to explore further when we get out of this. But go on. What did you do after you identified Uru personnel?"

"I contacted one of them, Claude Pascal. Academic to academic, not letting on that I knew anything about the cube. I'm an accomplished enough physicist that Pascal didn't find this strange. I proposed collaborating on several experiments that I knew would get his attention. I got to know him, built a working relationship. I thought if I skirted around the edges, brought up provocative topics and ideas that he might find useful in his Uru work, he'd eventually realize I'd be a good addition to this secret project."

"Sure enough," said Boyd, "when I reviewed your file a few days ago, it did indicate that it was Dr. Pascal who recommended you for the team. Truly outstanding," he added. "Even though you learned of your legacy too late to stop the world from discovering the cube, you found a way to position yourself to guard its secrets after all."

"Exactly. Although I never expected to have to . . . relocate it. Until you came to visit. You and your inspired idea. Another reason I'm so impressed with your instincts. I mean, who comes to see the cube for the first time and suggests the one experiment that will actually *work*?"

"So you knew the gig was up?"

"Yes," said Kelly. "After I failed to talk you out of trying the generator."

She sighed. "So then I had a decision to make. I could do nothing, and pretend to be astonished when Haycock's dark energy beam kicked the cube out of lockdown mode. Or I could take and hide the cube. I could honor my grandfather's wishes that it not be activated unless the Connolly acting as caretaker was certain that humanity was ready. Or to fend off an asteroid or some other potential crisis. But you know, make sure it was kept out of human hands."

"And especially kept out of government or military hands, if my memory serves."

"Yes."

Boyd considered. Perhaps they were on the same side after all. She had done what she had done for what she considered the right reasons. And who could say she was wrong? Given everything he had heard, could he really blame her for her actions? Hell, he might have made the exact same choice. He had also seen the underbelly of humankind, and it wasn't pretty.

"If I'm going to be honest," he said finally, "I can't really fault your choice. I mean, the dangers of this thing couldn't be any greater."

Kelly sighed. "Thanks, Justin. But if *I'm* going to be honest, so is its potential. To lift humanity to greater heights. And while humanity is still barbaric in many ways, we've come a long way since Nazi Germany. This time we didn't get to the dark energy key because of a genius that only comes along once every thousand years. Our civilization got to the level of scientific maturity required to *earn* this breakthrough.

"Ironically," she added, "you were the one who kicked this all off, without knowing it. But before I met you, my decision would have been simple. I was convinced that letting the unlocked cube fall into military hands would turn my grandfather's dire prophecies into reality.

"But after meeting you, I wasn't so sure. Maybe our military *has* become mature enough to handle it. After all, look how mature they've been when it comes to the EHO program. I never thought I'd find a soldier I could trust it with. But I was wrong. I'd trust it with *you*."

Boyd stared deeply into her arresting green eyes and knew that she was being sincere. "That means a lot to me," he said. "But I still think you did the right thing," he added, finding it hard to believe that these words were actually coming from his mouth.

"Maybe. But maybe not. It was a very tough call, balanced on the edge of a razor. I suspect you only think I did the right thing because we've been focusing on mankind's barbarism, and on the destructive, negative things the cube can do. But it's likely to be able to do a host of positive, *miraculous* things also. And after I've described these, you may feel differently."

"Well, we have more than an hour in this car before it gets dark enough to leave," replied Boyd. "So describe away."

24

"Before I give you a crash course on the cube's potential," said Dr. Kelly Connolly, "would it be too much of a risk for us to sit up?"

"Yeah, I've been wishing for that too. The risk is small, but we've come this far, so it isn't worth taking."

"I thought you might say that," said Kelly in disappointment. "Second question. You don't happen to have a blanket in that miracle duffel bag of yours, do you? Shen was right. It's getting a little nippy as the day goes on."

"Sorry, I don't. I've been genetically modified to be able to maintain body temperature better than average. All I can offer is sharing body heat if it gets too uncomfortable for you. I could join you in the back and hold you, but it'd be pretty tight quarters."

"Body heat?" said Kelly with a smile. "Really? My mother warned me about boys like you when I was in high school. Boys who might pretend their car had died when we were in the middle of nowhere. And then try to grope me under the guise of conserving body heat."

"I didn't say anything about *groping*," said Boyd with a smile. "But I do like how you think."

She laughed. "It's nice to know that you aren't letting a little felony like Grand Theft Enigma get in the way of our budding chemistry."

"I don't know. You could make the argument that the cube is a family heirloom, and that you're the owner. This won't stop the government from taking it, but they might forget about the felony charge. And, you know, the whole *treason* thing, if they tend to see the theft that way."

"Now I'm liking how *you* think," said Kelly. "I'll tell you what, let me describe the wonders of gravity control, and if it isn't dark when I'm done, maybe I'll take you up on your offer to keep me warm."

"Great," said Boyd with a playful smile. "Then you'd better hurry up and get through it."

"I'll do it so fast, you'll hardly notice," she replied. "Here goes. I know you're well versed in science, for a layman. So you may be aware of some, or all, of what I'll be saying. But I'll just say it anyway, rather than ask you if you already know it. That'll make it faster."

"I won't be offended if you tell me something I already know."

"Good. So let me start by giving you a quick overview of gravity. First, it's extraordinarily weak. The weakest of the known forces, by far. For example, the electromagnetic force is thirty-six orders of magnitude stronger. That's a trillion, trillion, trillion times stronger."

"I don't doubt you," said Boyd, "but I have to say, gravity seems pretty strong to me."

"That's because it's produced by mass, and there's so damn much of it. The entire weight of Earth is trying to pull you in, yet you can lift your leg off the ground with ease. A magnet the size of your thumbnail can pull a paperclip from the ground, easily winning a battle of forces against a planet weighing thirteen trillion billion tons."

"Okay then. Good examples. Weak it is."

"But the *most* important thing to know about gravity is that it's a warp in spacetime itself. In the very fabric of our universe. If spacetime were a trampoline, our planet would be a bowling ball in its center, indenting it. This indentation, this warp in the trampoline, is gravity, and would cause any matter nearby to roll toward the bowling ball. Are you with me?"

"Yes."

"Another important thing to know is that spacetime isn't just about space. It's about time also. The stronger the gravity, the bigger the dent in spacetime, and the slower time will run. GPS satellites in orbit experience less gravity than we do on Earth, so their time moves faster than ours. Their onboard atomic clocks have to be corrected for this, using Einstein's equations. If not for these corrections, they'd be off by more than six miles after a single day."

Boyd raised his eyebrows. "I can see how that would make them less useful for navigation."

Kelly ignored him and continued. "So gravity attracts all objects, all mass. Anti-gravity and dark energy—which could well be one and the same—*repel* mass. But the Enigma Cube can do both at will. And modulate levels of both at will. So what it really gives you is absolute control of nothing less than the fabric of spacetime itself," she added emphatically. "As I said before, the cube allows you to mold spacetime like clay. Which opens up a staggering array of possibilities, as you can imagine."

"Well, yeah," said Boyd. "The possibilities *couldn't* be more obvious." A wry smile came over his face. "But just for fun," he added, "why don't you pretend that I don't know *any* of them."

Kelly laughed. "Will do," she said. "The first is the production of traversable wormholes. And by traversable, I'm not talking about the better-known Einstein-Rosen Bridges or Schwarzschild wormholes formed by black holes. I'm talking about hyperspace tunnels through spacetime that can connect remote regions of our universe. If you can manipulate spacetime in any way you want, you can create these shortcuts and stabilize them. This would allow you to pop through a wormhole and reach a planet a thousand light years away in seconds. If you want instant access to a certain region of space, just be sure to build a bridge to it. The cube makes this possible."

"And you're *sure* about that?"

"Yes. You and I already talked about how our government finally admitted to taking UFO sightings very seriously. I'm sure you're also aware that the government has been studying wormholes and other advanced physics concepts, trying to figure out how aliens could possibly traverse interstellar space."

"I am."

"As you know, much of this work, done under the auspices of the Defense Intelligence Agency, was declassified and published in 2019."

Kelly paused for a moment in thought. "Sage," she continued, "search your database for a Defense Intelligence Agency report entitled, 'Traversable Wormholes, Stargates, and Negative Energy.'"

"*Report found,*" said Sage immediately.

"Good. Can you read the first sentence of the paper's conclusion for us."

"Affirmative," said the AI. *"Reading now. 'Implementation of interstellar travel via traversable wormholes generally requires the engineering of spacetime into very specialized local geometries. Analysis of these via the general relativistic field equation, plus the resultant source matter equations of state, demonstrates that such geometries require the use of "exotic" matter, which includes anti-gravity, in order to produce the requisite FTL spacetime modification.' "*

"Thanks, Sage," said Kelly. "You can read the entire report later, Justin, but I think you'll find it offers ample support for what I'm saying."

"I'm sure it does."

"The second huge, huge possibility the cube opens up," continued Kelly, "is a working warp drive. Wormholes are like galactic superhighways. But if you want to get around between exits, you need a faster-than-light drive."

"Nothing can go faster than light," said Boyd. "I know that for certain. Wormholes may be able to get around this by cheating, by creating shortcuts through spacetime, but no ship traveling through space can exceed light speed."

"Very good," said Kelly. "But the universe offers another cheat. It's true that nothing *in space* can go faster than the speed of light." She raised her eyebrows. "But space, *itself*, can. So if you could speed up space and stick to it like glue, you'd come along for the ride. Like a stationary passenger on a moving walkway. Or maybe a better analogy would be a surfer, with space being the wave. You and your surfboard don't move much, but if you ride the right wave you can get to shore in a hurry."

"But how would you turn space itself into a moving walkway? Or a wave?"

"Good question," said Kelly. "Let me point to one last DIA report. Sage, pull up the report entitled, 'Warp Drive, Dark Energy, and the Manipulation of Extra Dimensions.' Got it?"

"I have it, yes," said the AI.

"Read the first paragraph about warp drives."

"The warp drive," began Sage immediately, *"involves local manipulation of the fabric of space in the immediate vicinity of a*

spacecraft. The basic idea is to create an asymmetric bubble of space that is contracting in front of the spacecraft while expanding behind it. Using this form of locomotion, the spacecraft remains stationary inside this 'warp bubble,' and the movement of space itself facilitates the relative motion of the spacecraft. The theory of relativity places no restrictions on the speed of motion of space itself, thus allowing for a convenient circumvention of the speed-of-light barrier."

"Thank you, Sage," said Kelly. "We know that space is already expanding at great speed. Which is the very observation that led cosmologists to realize that dark energy exists, and that it's a repulsive force like anti-gravity."

"So the cube, by manipulating spacetime, can give us both wormholes and warp drives."

"A more impressive piece of technology than you thought, isn't it? If you can manipulate the fabric of spacetime itself, the universe is your playground. The same paper talks about the possibility of manipulating higher dimensions. I want to get to the part of our program where you and I exchange body heat, so I won't go into this in much detail, but imagine what it would mean to be able to tap higher dimensions."

"Again, assume I'm not expert."

"Imagine you lived in a two-dimensional world, on the surface of a vast sheet of paper. If I, a three-dimensional being, drew a circle in front of you, would you know that it was a circle?"

Boyd thought about this. "No, because my eyes would be smashed down on the 2D surface. So I'd only see a convex line, or maybe a straight one."

"Good. You wouldn't be able to see the back of the circle at all, unless you traveled around to that side. And you couldn't see the circle shape in its entirety no matter what you did. Because you're a 2D being and can't lift yourself off the page. And if I placed a dime inside the circle, you could never see this, either."

"Right. I'm following you so far."

"But a 3D being like me, looking from above, can easily see the entire circle, and what's inside.

"If I drew a line down the middle of the entire page, I'd split your 2D world in half. I'd have created an impenetrable wall, blocking you from ever crossing to the other half. But I, the 3D god that I am, could just step over the line. Easy as pie.

"If you put 3D me in a 2D prison, only my footprints would be visible. And when I lifted up my feet to step over the prison walls, you'd see my footprint disappear, and then reappear outside the prison. Or perhaps a considerable distance away.

"To a 2D being, there is no up and down, just side to side. No matter how hard they try, they can't pry their eyes or bodies from the page. They can't see the world above and below it. Nor can they view their own world from above or below. They can't possibly imagine such a 3D world, such a 3D viewpoint, even existing."

Boyd nodded. "I think I see what you're getting at," he said. "In the same way, we can't see or imagine a fourth spatial dimension. One could be right above us, so to speak, but we can't look up."

"Exactly," said Kelly. "And just as we 3D beings can easily perform feats that 2D people would find impossible, miraculous, imagine what we could do from the vantage point of a higher dimension than *ours*. A 2D being who wanted to extract the dime from inside the circle would have to drill a hole in the circle's perimeter. But I could just reach down from above, straight into the circle's *stomach*, without penetrating its skin, and pluck it out.

"So someone in a higher dimension could do the same to us," she continued. "Could remove a tumor without breaking our skin, coming in through an avenue that we're incapable of perceiving. Or could enter one of our closed bank vaults at will, and could then appear to teleport out again. These and many more miracles not only suddenly become possible, they become *easy*. Unspectacular."

"You said in Spokane that the cube was a showoff," noted Boyd. "But I didn't know the tenth of it, did I?"

Kelly shook her head. "You *still* don't know the tenth of it. Even if the cube couldn't create wormholes, warp drives, or higher dimensional miracles, it could still bring a paradise to Earth. The ability to mold spacetime gives us more power to transform civilization than all other major advances in history, combined. Free energy is a given.

A revolution in transportation a given. We would have free and absolute mobility. Not just flying cars. Flying *everything*. From trains to ocean cruise ships. Highways and train tracks become useless. Cargo ships largely useless. Mining and construction revolutionized as the heaviest loads, the heaviest girders, can be manipulated effortlessly."

She paused to catch her breath. "And then there's space travel. Local space travel, since we're stipulating uses for the cube that don't involve wormholes or warp drives. No more strapping ourselves to the tops of rockets. Space travel becomes dirt cheap, and absolutely safe. Settling the solar system becomes a breeze, as does mining any metal or precious material from the asteroid belt."

"Does seem to be an attractive future," said Boyd, in what had to be the greatest understatement ever.

Kelly sighed. "Still think I did the right thing by preventing Uru from unlocking the Enigma Cube?"

"A little less than I did before, I have to admit."

"Then let me go the other way for a moment. I presented much of the cube's promise, so let me revisit its peril for a while. I studied my grandfather's instructions for operating the cube, the capabilities he discovered, until I memorized every last one. And the variety of settings is breathtaking. It can be used to make an object heavier by increasing the force of gravity below it. Or it can be set to what I think of as *implosion mode*, instantly increasing gravity in the center of an object to a level that will draw the object in on itself, explosively. In short, it's a more versatile weapon even than it seems."

"Of course it is," mused Boyd, no longer surprised by anything.

"Imploding tanks and the ability to crush troops like grapes are only the beginning," continued Kelly. "You think you could sink a battleship if you could make it weigh a billion tons? Bring down a jet? What about a skyscraper?

"And while you could flatten an entire army into liquid, you could use the opposite setting to send them rocketing into the sky, only to reverse it when they got to a hundred yards up."

Boyd swallowed hard. "Not the sort of technology you'd want a terrorist to control," he said.

"Or any army," said Kelly. "And even what I just listed are fairly benign possibilities. There could well be a setting that allows you to create and destroy black holes at will. Create one, let it swallow an entire city, and then kill it.

"Or just lift a skyscraper ten miles up and let it slam back to Earth at free-fall speeds. The faster an object goes when it hits something, the more power it unleashes. A bullet hitting you at one mile per hour doesn't hurt a bit. One traveling *five hundred* miles per hour blows through you like you're made of cotton candy. So imagine the enormous crater something as heavy as a plummeting skyscraper would make. It would release as much energy as a nuclear bomb."

She paused, and there was an extended silence once again inside the Lexus.

Boyd finally spoke. "Clearly, your decision as to whether or not to move the cube was even more difficult than I knew. *Insanely* difficult."

"Good thing there was nothing important riding on it."

Boyd laughed.

"I agonized over what to do," said Kelly. "It was as close to fifty-fifty as it could be." She sighed. "But no use revisiting my decision just now. I say we call a halt to our discussion—at least for the moment."

"Agreed," said Boyd.

"Good. Because I really am starting to freeze my butt off. I think it's time you honored your offer and paid a visit back here."

Boyd checked the drone feeds to make sure the coast was clear. "I'll be right over," he said. "You know," he added with a grin, "I haven't shared the back seat of a car with a woman since I was a kid."

"Well, I've *never* been hunted by enhanced Chinese commandos," replied Kelly. "So I guess new experiences are the order of the day."

25

All things considered, thought Kelly Connolly, things were going well. At least, a lot better than she had any right to expect after being attacked, knocked unconscious, hunted, having her theft discovered, and being trapped inside a car.

Not that exceeding expectations when the bar was set this low was saying all that much, but a lot of positives were coming out of this. She was falling for a major, a *commando* no less, in a big way. She would never have believed it. And she knew that he was falling for her, too.

She was relieved to have come clean about the cube. The burden of knowing about its origins, about her grandfather, about her responsibilities, and not being able to share this with anyone had been crushing. And Boyd had at least understood why she had done what she had done, and was sympathetic, if not outright supportive. She felt like the weight of the world had been lifted from her shoulders— or the weight of the cube in lockdown mode at any rate.

But now she was focused on nothing more than the man lying beneath her, and the passionate kiss they were sharing. Their mouths had found each other, almost of their own accord, and seemed locked together as if by an irresistible force. It was *electric*. Gentle, yet ravenous, as the bottled-up feelings they had for each other revealed themselves in a way that was primal, undeniable. On paper, there was no way they should have clicked, but, inexplicably, something about them seemed to fit together like a puzzle.

She felt Boyd finally pull away and turn his head, making it clear that he wanted to stop the proceedings. "Sorry," he whispered. "I'm a little embarrassed, but I feel like a teenager. I seem to be having trouble keeping my engine in, ah . . . *idle.*"

Kelly grinned. "Yeah, I could tell that something had come *up*. Something *big*."

Boyd laughed. "I knew there was a reason I liked you."

"But I agree we should stop," said Kelly. "Why torture ourselves? Don't want to heat up your engine with no place to go, since there's nothing we can do about it now. And nothing we *should* do about it. I mean, we could continue to get lost in each other's eyes, or we could try to stay alive."

"Tough call," said Boyd with a smile.

She rested her head on his chest and he put his arms around her. She really had been getting chilly, and she welcomed both the warmth and intimacy.

"I get that we need to restrain ourselves," said Boyd, "but I am going to insist on a raincheck."

"Keep me from being captured, and I'll give you two rain checks."

"Deal," said Boyd immediately.

They laid together in silence for several minutes, basking in the temporary comfort their entwined bodies were providing.

"So do you do this often, Justin?" she said softly. "I don't want to think that you take all of your dates here."

"When you find the ideal spot for a first date," he replied in amusement, "you don't change things up." He paused for several long seconds. "But you have nothing to worry about," he added. "I haven't even had a date for more than six months now."

"That's surprising. Even when you don't show your superman side, you have a lot to offer."

Kelly knew this was an understatement. He was handsome and smart. And she could tell he was quite compassionate, which wasn't easy for a man to show while he was leaving dead bodies in his wake like a runaway weed-wacker. Finally, he had a great sense of humor, which seemed to blend perfectly with hers. There was nothing about him *not* to like.

Boyd sighed heavily, and she could feel his chest move as he expelled air from his lungs. "Women seem to like me well enough," he said in a way that didn't seem boastful, "but it turns out I'm a little too picky. Plus, having to keep so much of my life secret doesn't help."

Kelly's ears perked up at this. Sounded exactly like her, although having to keep secrets was a fairly recent development in her case.

"Plus," he continued, "I've been on a lot of missions, which makes a long-term commitment difficult. I've had some shorter relationships during the past few years, but nothing more substantial. I was hoping that now that I'm transitioning out of a pure commando role, this might change."

"Oh yeah," said Kelly wryly, "you've left the commando part of you *way* behind. You've been acting like a paper-pushing accountant all day. You must be bored out of your mind."

Boyd smiled. "Just to get back to the part about me being picky," he said. "A woman needs to have a number of qualities for me to really fall for her. She has to be bright. Being brilliant, like you, is a bonus. She has to have a great sense of humor—like yours. And finally—even though I sound like I'm reading from a Kelly Connolly resume—she has to be independent. *Fiercely* independent."

"You mean as independent as an Irish hound?"

"Couldn't have said it better myself."

"You do know that I'm not actually Irish, right? I'm really a Richter. Which is German for *Judge*. Not quite as interesting as *fierce as a hound*. Worse, I grew up being misled that I *was* part Irish. Should have taken one of those DNA tests."

"Well, the Irish thing wasn't a bad cover," said Boyd. "You do have green eyes and a light complexion."

He paused. "So what about you?" he continued. "Any other guys you've been hiding in the woods with lately?"

"None. Or doing anything romantic with. Not in almost a year. I'm a lot like you. I'm picky. I like men who are smart, and even though I'm around a lot of them, I haven't seemed to find the right one. Besides, while you seem to go for women you consider brilliant, funny, and fiercely independent, I think most men become intimidated by this type of woman." She raised her eyebrows. "So maybe today is my lucky day."

Boyd sighed once again. "If we can get out if this, it just might be," he said. "Mine too."

Kelly put her head back down on his chest, as content as possible under the circumstances.

"Given everything the cube can do," said Boyd softly after almost a minute had passed, "why do you suppose the aliens would just leave it here?"

She shrugged. "It could be the drive from one of their starships, jettisoned just before a crash. But I think it was left by super beings wanting to help shape our future. To provide a ticket to the universe when we become advanced enough to unlock it."

"So if we're worthy we gain a ticket to the infinite. If we're unworthy, we destroy ourselves."

Kelly was about to reply when her comm became active, startling her yet again. "*Hello again to my two American adversaries,*" said the voice of Commander Shen Ning. "*Congratulations on eluding us for this long. Whatever hole you're hiding in has served you well.*

"*Make no mistake, we still intend to capture both of you. And we will, especially after my reinforcements flood these woods. But this has become less critical than it was an hour ago. Why? Well, you'll be pleased to know that my team in Spokane was finally able to find your cube, Dr. Connolly, weighing so little that a child could lift it. And it will soon be on its way back to China.*"

Kelly lifted her head off Boyd's chest and stared into his eyes in horror. "He's bluffing," she said. "I was too careful."

"*But nice hiding place,*" added Shen. "*inside the furry abdomen of a giant spider being used as a Halloween decoration—one hanging inside a home. The fact that the home it was in wasn't yours is what made this so impressive and hard to find.*"

The blood drained from Kelly's cheeks, and she looked like she might be sick.

"Maybe not so much of a bluff after all," she said grimly.

26

"*You have really impressed me, Dr. Connolly,*" continued the voice of Commander Shen Ning straight into the ears of the two Americans lying together in the backseat of a Lexus. "*You've previously been a model citizen. Yet you managed to steal a priceless, immovable object and keep it hidden for a very long time from the vast manpower I put on this case. Truly remarkable.*

"*You led us on what you Americans call a wild goose chase. Street cameras we hacked showed you stopping at two wooded locations, a store, and your home, before heading to the airport. So at three this morning, my men were tearing your house apart like a piñata, and digging up every inch of your yard. But they found nothing. Everything inside your house is now in shreds. Your walls, drawers, cupboards, toilet tanks, furniture, and everything else. We gave your car this same rectal exam, and hunted for footprints in the wooded locations you visited, digging up more than I'd care to admit.*

"*We were about to give up when my comrades back in China provided us with your hacked phone and text records. We learned that your neighbors ten houses down the street, Ryan and Charity Lee, are out of the country for two weeks, and you've volunteered to bring mail and packages inside.*"

Shen paused. "*And Enigma Cubes, apparently,*" he added smugly. "*When the Lees return from vacation, they may find their home a little . . . torn up. But at least it was for a good cause.*"

Kelly issued a bloodcurdling primal scream, unable to keep her rage bottled up any longer, but Boyd used superhuman reflexes to slap a hand over her mouth after the first few seconds and stifle the earsplitting shriek.

"*Anyway, I just wanted you to know. I'll leave you to your hiding and cowering. I'm sure we'll be with you in no time.*"

With that, Shen discontinued his unilateral broadcast.

Tears welled up in Kelly's eyes. "This is all my fault," she said. "I should have put the cube in lockdown mode. How could I have been so careless?"

Boyd was roiling inside but fought to maintain his calm. "You're being too hard on yourself, Kelly. You had no idea the Chinese were in the picture. And even so, they were lucky to find it. Despite pulling out all the stops, and using massive manpower and intelligence resources."

"I took it because I didn't want the *American* military to have it," said Kelly. "So how bad is *this*?"

Boyd frowned. "*Devastatingly* bad," he said. "Worst-case-scenario bad. China is one of only two superpowers on Earth, and they haven't made their interest in global domination a secret. They're a ruthless, totalitarian regime. One that has done a brilliant job of showing a friendly, benign face to the world, and managing public relations. Partly because with almost a billion and a half people, more than four times our population, they wield considerable financial resources and punish anyone in the West who tells the truth about them."

Kelly winced. "I do know this. I was just hoping you'd tell me they were beginning to trend more democratic."

"Just the opposite. The Chinese are a wonderful people. But the president and politburo have become Big Brother. They've turned China into a surveillance state, with hundreds of millions of cameras that use algorithms to make sure citizens are toeing every line. China's human rights record, rarely mentioned, is atrocious. They have the lowest level of internet and media freedom anywhere in the world, no religious freedom, and absolute ideological control of education. They discriminate against women, convict dissenters without trial, and have over a million Muslims in detention camps."

Boyd shook his head miserably. "Short of Iran or North Korea gaining control of the cube, this is as bad as it gets."

"Then we have to get it back," she said adamantly. "This is *my* fault. I have to rectify it."

If Boyd wasn't already smitten with Kelly Connolly, he would be now. His chivalrous instincts balked at the idea of letting her take this kind of risk with her life. But he knew she had to. They *both* had to. He was bracing himself to persuade her of this, but *she* had come to this conclusion on her own. She was truly remarkable.

"I have to contact Shen," insisted Kelly. "Right away. I have to be sure his people don't activate the glyphs, either accidentally or on purpose. Make them properly terrified. And then I have to surrender. So I can go where the cube goes. Which is what they want anyway. And I have some ideas as to how to get it back."

Boyd stared at her in wonder. Her thinking was as clear as anyone could want, and the courage she was showing was off the charts. But he had to be sure she understood just what it was she was suggesting.

"It's almost nightfall," he said. "We're *very* close to being able to escape. If you surrender, I'll surrender with you. But you have to know it's a suicide mission."

"We have to do this, Justin. *We have to.* I was willing to commit treason to prevent my own government from wielding the cube's power. But we *cannot* let the Chinese have it, under any circumstances. You know that better than I do. If we die trying to stop it, so be it."

She paused. "How can a man—or a woman—die better?" she added. "Right?"

Boyd shook his head in disbelief. Had she really quoted a line from *Horatius at the Bridge*? From a stanza that he, himself, had recited in his mind when facing impossible odds for a worthy cause.

He barely knew this woman, yet he could easily see himself falling in love with her. Instead of having to convince *her* to volunteer for a suicide mission, she was attempting to convince *him*. It was extraordinary. It didn't seem fair to have finally found a woman this perfect for him, only to learn that both their lifespans were now measured in days.

"If we're going to do this," he said, "we have to do it together. If we want any hope of getting the cube back, we'll likely have to spill blood. Probably *lots* of it. And not just me. *Both* of us will have to." He paused for this to sink in. "Are you really prepared for that?"

Several tears rolled down Kelly's face. "No!" she said emphatically. "Not at *all*. I consider myself a fricking *pacifist*." Her hands balled into fists and she blew out a long breath. "But even though I'm not prepared for it, I will do what I have to do. I give you my solemn vow. The cube is just too dangerous for them to have."

"Okay," he said softly. "Then let's do this thing."

Kelly wiped the tears from her cheeks, and they both rose to a seated position. After a few minutes of discussing strategy, her expression hardened, and her eyes gleamed with absolute resolve.

"Commander Shen!" she bellowed out once Sage had established a link to the man's comm. "We need to talk. Now! Respond!"

A few long seconds passed. *"Dr. Connolly,"* said Shen in delight, *"what a nice surprise. Are you and the major finally ready to surrender?"*

"If you honor our conditions, yes."

"Is the major with you?"

"I'm here, Shen!" snapped Boyd.

"Curious that an esteemed major like you would let a civilian scientist negotiate your surrender for you."

"You were the one who said she's the more important of the two of us."

"This is true," replied the Chinese commander. *"Okay, then, Dr. Connolly, go ahead. Tell me your conditions."*

"I have four of them," said Kelly. "First, you have to promise not to hurt us. That's obvious. Second, you have to promise to keep us together at all times when we're in your custody. Third, and most important by a long shot, you have to make sure your people don't touch the cube any more than they already have. Not in Spokane, and not while they're transporting it to China. Put it in a box and don't touch it again. You have *no idea* what you're dealing with, and when you might handle it in just the wrong way."

She paused. "Which is why you want me in the first place, right? Because I know what makes it tick. Mess with it randomly and risk losing more than just your people. More than China itself. This thing has the power to accidentally destroy *ten* Earths and not even feel it. You're not a child playing with dynamite. You're a child playing with a *hydrogen bomb*. Please tell me you understand what I'm telling you."

"I do," said Shen. *"So what is your last condition?"*

"You bring us both to where the cube is. So we can make sure you don't do anything . . . *apocalyptic*. You know I'm the only one who knows anything about it. Which is why you're so eager to capture me in the first place. So I'll surrender, and all you have to do are the things you want to do in the first place. Make sure the cube doesn't accidentally blow up in your face. And let me tell you how to operate it properly."

"You drive a hard bargain," said Shen wryly. *"Of course I agree. But what about you, Major? Are you on board? Do you agree not to resist when we come to round you up?"*

"I do," said Boyd. "But you had better take what Dr. Connolly said very seriously. Touch that thing wrong, and not even Earth's cockroaches will survive."

"You've made your point," said Shen. *"I'm perfectly willing to wait until Dr. Connolly can guide me through its operation."*

Boyd nodded somberly. "In that case, Commander, we're in the car we were in when we first arrived here."

He glanced at Kelly and nodded as reassuringly as he could. "Come and get us."

PART 5

Then out spake brave Horatius, the captain of the gate:
"To every man upon this Earth, death cometh soon or late.
And how can man die better, than facing fearful odds.
For the ashes of his fathers, and the temples of his gods."

—Thomas Babington Macaulay, *Horatius at the Bridge*

27

Kelly Connolly awoke inside a small, empty room, numb, with her eyes and mind still not in focus. She sensed that she had been out for at least twenty-four hours, maybe longer—ever since they had surrendered in Pennsylvania. Boyd had tried to hide his duffel bag, hoping Shen would overlook it, but this was not to be, as the duffel had also become of great interest to the Chinese commander. Once the bag had been retrieved, the commander had handed them each a pill to swallow, and that was the last thing she remembered.

The room she was in contained a single cot and nothing else. It was white, antiseptic, and its only decorations were two small cameras attached near the ceiling, watching her as if she were a specimen in a zoo.

She gasped as her mental numbness finally wore off, and it hit her with a start that she was alone. Where was Justin Boyd? Her heart began pounding wildly and a chill swept up her spine.

When he had been by her side, no odds had seemed too daunting. But now that he was absent, she felt just the opposite. She felt out of her depth, foolish—*helpless*.

What had they done with him? Was he okay?

As panicked as she was to be alone in what were surely desperate circumstances, she was *more* panicked at the prospect that he was hurt. Or worse. Or that she might never see him again.

If any of these possibilities came to pass, she would never forgive herself. This was all her fault. *She* had taken the cube out of a secure black ops facility. *She* had failed to lock it down. And *she* had persuaded Boyd to surrender.

Kelly knew she was in a downward spiral and needed to get a grip on herself. Right now. This was no place or time for weakness. No place or time to be squeamish.

She realized that while unconscious, she had been bathed, and all of her clothes changed, down to her panties. This was uncomfortable to think about, but also something she appreciated after a red-eye and then a very long day of sweating and crawling in dirt. She was now wearing soft, faded jeans and a thin black sweatshirt.

She tried the steel door that trapped her in the room, but it didn't budge, as expected. Then, feeling silly, she proceeded to clap out twenty jumping jacks to get the blood flowing into her extremities, and especially into her brain.

Kelly paced for what was probably thirty minutes, although it felt like much longer, and reviewed the cube's various control operations in her mind, over and over, to keep from becoming hysterical or losing her mind.

Was she in solitary confinement? Was Shen leaving her here to soften her up?

He must know that after waking up this way, alone, with no idea where she was, the longer she had to think, to worry, to imagine one horrific scenario after another, the weaker her psyche would become. She was meat, and this treatment was tenderizer.

She was barely able to stop herself from screaming, from staring into one of the cameras and demanding that Shen acknowledge her existence. But she knew that this would give him exactly what he wanted, so she somehow found the strength to fight off an impulse that was quickly becoming overwhelming. She *refused* to let him know just how easily she could be broken.

Finally, after an agonizingly long time, a bald Chinese official in an unrecognizable military uniform opened the door. He was escorted by two guards, who both held their guns extended toward her, although their listless demeanor made it clear they were as worried about a possible attack from Kelly Connolly as a lion was worried about a possible attack from a newborn beagle puppy.

She was relieved to have a visitor and get out of her own head for a while, but refused to show it. "Where is Major Boyd?" she snapped. "I was promised we'd be kept together."

"You'll be seeing him very soon," said the man in perfect English.

"Then I demand to see Commander Shen Ning!"

The man smiled. "I can't tell you how much your demands mean to me," he said dryly. "But I'm afraid he isn't here. I'm Colonel Wu Fen, and you're now in my humble hands."

"So Shen's promises to us mean *nothing?*"

"*Less* than nothing," replied Wu. "But it's cute that you think they might."

Kelly knew she shouldn't have been surprised. All was fair in love and war. And the truth was, she had no intention of honoring the bargain she had made with Shen, either.

"Where am I?" she said, suspecting he would tell her, since he was sure to believe that she would never leave captivity again.

"You are on a man-made island in the South China Sea," said the colonel. "A combination advanced research station and military base."

"Lucky me," replied Kelly unhappily.

They had been smart. The cube was a mysterious dynamo that she had already warned could be volatile and unleash untold destruction. So better to study it on an island than in mainland China. And the combination of military base and top-secret research facility was ideal.

"You must be hungry and thirsty," said the colonel.

Kelly considered her response. Was he genuinely wanting her to be comfortable? Or was he making it clear that he had the power to starve her at his whim?

"I want to see Justin Boyd!" she demanded, ignoring his question.

Wu nodded. "I admire your persistence. Follow me."

He began walking away from the room and down a hallway, while the two guards waited for Kelly to follow, taking up positions behind her as she passed.

Wu led her through a maze of rooms and laboratories until he arrived at the biggest room of all, half the size of a football field. The immense room was filled with high-tech equipment of all kinds, dozens of lab benches and other lab stations, twenty or more scientists, and maybe fifteen soldiers ringing the perimeter, each carrying a machine gun that was extended in her direction.

Kelly had flashbacks to the clearing in the Pennsylvania woods. She had never even seen a gun in person before her trip to Haycock, and now having multiple soldiers pointing machine guns at her was becoming commonplace.

She caught Wu's eye as he continued leading her into the room. "Do you think you have enough men?" she asked in disgust.

The flicker of a smile crossed the colonel's face. "The majority of the people here speak English," he pointed out. "Those who don't are receiving a translation through comms."

Kelly barely heard him as she spotted the activated Enigma Cube sitting on a stainless steel table in the center of the vast room. Her eyes widened, and she was relieved to note the absence of any glyphs. Wu halted and gestured to her right, directing her to look about fifteen yards in the distance.

She gasped as she realized what he wanted her to see. Justin Boyd. He was hurt. *Badly.*

The EHO major was pinned on his back to a stainless steel gurney by a series of restraints that looked formidable enough to keep Steve Rogers down. His advanced clothing—the thin graphene body armor and electroactive weaved shirt—had been replaced by jeans and a thin black sweatshirt to match hers.

The sleeves of the sweatshirt had been pulled up, and his bare forearms were now covered in blood, as was much of his shirt. He was unable to move any part of his body even an inch, including his head, which was locked vertically into place by a silver vise-like device. Opaque goggles had been placed over his eyes to blind him, and his mouth was duct-taped shut.

And he didn't appear to be breathing.

Kelly charged across the room toward the American major, closing the distance between them like an Olympic racewalker. She ignored Wu, his two guards, and every other soldier or scientist in the room as if they didn't exist. She was frantic to reach Boyd's side. To confirm that he was alive. To hold and comfort him.

As she rushed ahead, she surveyed the area around the American major in a few quick glances. His ever-present duffel bag was open on a table nearby, with its contents strewn about. The bag had been depleted by overuse in Pennsylvania, so the contents now consisted simply of several first-aid vials, truth serum, truth serum blocker, three chocolate-flavored energy bars, a spray can of wound-sealing foam, four flashbang grenades, a Glock 22 semi-automatic pistol, a few diminutive electronic devices, and what looked to be plastic explosives.

His smart contact lenses had been removed from his eyes and were being examined under a scanning tunneling microscope, which was recording every circuit on a monitor above it.

Several Chinese scientists in lab coats were studying small vials of his blood, running them through genetic sequencers or other tests. If the respirocyte technology was secret, that wouldn't be the case for much longer.

"Justin?" she whispered in a panic as she reached him, barely fending off hysteria. "Justin?" she repeated as tears once again welled up in her eyes. She gently lowered her head to his chest, the only area of his torso not soaked with blood, and listened for a pulse, felt for the rise and fall of his rib cage.

She finally detected both, but they were exceedingly faint. He likely only had minutes to live. "Hang on, Justin," she pleaded, as tears now dripped from her face. "I'm going to get you medical help if it's the last thing I ever do."

Wu's two guards had long since caught up to her and now forcibly pulled her away from the supine major. Colonel Wu followed, pressing a nearby button that retracted the vise holding Boyd's head in place. He removed the opaque goggles from Boyd's eyes and then violently ripped the duct tape from his mouth.

Boyd turned his head to gaze upon his American compatriot. "I should never have let you surrender," he said, regret etched in every line on his face. "No one should have to go through this. *Especially* not you."

"How are you even able to speak?" said Kelly in dismay.

Boyd sighed. "Because I'm fine. Really. The cuts are superficial."

"But what about your heart rate? Your respiration?"

"My enhancements suppress both," said Boyd. He shook his head miserably. "I'm afraid this was nothing more than a setup."

"A setup?" she repeated in confusion.

"Tell her, Wu," said the American.

"Oh no. Why don't *you* tell her, Major."

Boyd blew out a long breath. "They made sure my eyes were covered and I couldn't move or talk. And they made sure to make me as bloody as they could. The blood soaked into my shirt isn't even mine. They wanted me to look like I was nearly dead. Then they brought you in. Wanted to see how you'd react. Get a sense of how much you cared for me, on a scale of cold and clinical on the one hand, to absolutely devastated over the possibility of losing me on the other. The more deeply you seem to care, the more leverage they have over you."

Kelly felt the room begin to spin around her. Of course that's what had just happened. She had fallen for their trap. She had let them see just how vulnerable Justin Boyd made her. Five minutes earlier the Chinese had no idea how much he had come to mean to her.

But now they did.

What a fool she had been. She had played right into their hands.

"Justin, I am so sorry," she said to him. "I should have known."

"Don't be sorry," he replied. "How can I be upset with you for caring about me?"

Wu caught Kelly's eye. "I'm pleased that you two have become so obviously . . . close," he said. "But things are going to get very rough for your friend here." He shook his head. "You brought this on yourselves."

"Sure we did," said Kelly in disgust.

"In fact, you did," said Wu. "We found a truth serum blocker in the major's bag. And then faint traces of it in your bloodstream. I know enough about this blocker to know that drugging or torturing you will prevent you from talking." He raised his eyebrows. "But if we torture Major Boyd here, I have a feeling you'll want to tell us what you know to get it to stop."

"That's still duress," said Boyd. "The drug will react to it the same way it reacts to torture. She might *want* to tell you, but she still won't be able to."

The colonel shook his head. "We both know that *being* tortured is different than *reacting* to the torture of another. You just better hope that she can stay calm. That she can fool the drug into thinking she *wants* to cooperate. Because if she doesn't tutor us on the cube's operation, you are going to have a very bad day."

He turned to Kelly. "We wanted the major to *look* bad, to test your reaction, but made sure that he's actually largely undamaged. Because we want you to be able to witness his transition from good health to a hacked-up shell of a man. We'll begin by stabbing out his right eye. Then we'll chop off his fingers, one at a time. Then, if you still haven't told us what we want to know, we'll get even more creative."

Wu paused to let this sink in. "Major Boyd is enhanced, so he'll have a very high pain threshold. But even so, he'll be screaming so loud he'll wake the dead."

"You are one demented bastard," whispered Kelly in disgust. "I already told Shen I'd teach you how to control the cube."

The colonel smiled. "We didn't believe you for a second." He motioned to a man in a lab coat, standing over Boyd's immobilized form. "Stab him in the right eye," he ordered.

"Wait!" screamed Kelly, as the man Wu had spoken to lifted a scalpel from a tray nearby. "I'll help you. You haven't given me a chance! Let me do it *now*. The more you torture him, the less likely the drug will *let* me help you."

Wu faced the man with a scalpel and shook his head, rescinding the order. "Okay, Dr. Connolly," he said. "You've bought the major a temporary reprieve."

"Kelly, no!" shouted Boyd. "You can't do this! Let my death have *meaning*. You said you would do whatever was necessary! You vowed it!"

The orderly standing over the major elbowed him hard in the mouth, drawing blood. Wu issued an order in Chinese, and the man held down Boyd's head while an associate sealed his mouth shut with tape once again.

Kelly looked as if she had been punched in the gut. "I'm so sorry, Justin," she said, shaking her head sadly. "I thought I could do what it took. But I was wrong. I'm not strong enough to watch you get *mutilated*. I'm not."

"Major Boyd is very brave," said Wu, as if trying to console her. "But you're doing the right thing. I'll make sure he stays healthy. And if you tell us how to operate the cube, we can avoid any more . . . discomfort."

The colonel paused. "So go right ahead, Dr. Connolly," he said. "You have the floor."

28

There were from thirty-five to fifty people in the sprawling laboratory, mostly men, and the entire room was utterly silent, as if breathing, and even heartbeats, were no longer allowed.

All eyes, near and far, along with those watching remotely, were firmly glued to Kelly Connolly's face, ready to hang on her every word.

"I can't just *tell you* how to operate the cube," she began. "It's not as simple as that. You have to *learn* the controls. *Feel* them. It's like playing the violin. I can give you the sheet music for Beethoven's *Violin Concerto* and tell you how to play the instrument, but without showing you how it's done, you have no chance of getting it right."

Wu shook his head in disgust. "As you Americans like to say, that's a load of crap. The next time I order Major Boyd's eye taken out, I won't be rescinding the order."

"It isn't crap," insisted Kelly. "It's the truth. Control of the cube isn't just about what hieroglyphs you hit. Or what order you hit them in. It's also about the amount of pressure you apply. The controls are exquisitely sensitive."

"What controls?" snapped Wu. "What hieroglyphs?"

"I'll show you. But I want your assurances that you won't hurt either one of us. If I live up to my end, you have to treat us well from here on out. I get that you won't let us go, but let us live together in peace. Find a prison that gives us privacy and feels like house arrest. Remember, you never know when I can be useful going forward."

Wu considered. "Agreed."

"Good," she replied. "Then I need you to get pressure sensors that can stick to the tips of my fingers. Sensitive ones. You'll want to measure the exact pressure I apply, along with the order of controls I touch, because not even *I* know how much pressure I use. I've just developed a feel for it. And I was very lucky. Knowing what I do now, I came very close to disaster on several occasions. I was a fool for doing random experiments, which is why I can't let you do the same."

Wu issued orders and two male scientists rushed out of the room to locate the specialized sensors Kelly had demanded.

With this in motion, the Chinese colonel and his two guards ushered their American prisoner over to the cube where it rested on a stainless steel table, halting five feet away.

A full forty-five minutes passed, and time seemed to stop. Everyone in the room remained silent, alone with their thoughts, with their attention still on Kelly, although the fifteen machine-gun-wielding soldiers were allowed to lower their weapons and rest their arms until the scientists returned.

Finally, the two men returned with what were clearly jerry-rigged sensors. It appeared they had located tiny round labels, colored a bright fluorescent orange, used to mark boxes or other inventory, and had stuck minuscule, threadlike pressure sensors to the adhesive, possibly taken from cell phones or other electronics.

Kelly held out her hands while electric-orange labels were affixed to the tips of each of her fingers.

She was then instructed to press down on a table with all ten fingers while the scientists consulted a computer monitor to make sure the sensors were working and the wireless signals were being received. Finally, Wu indicated they were ready to proceed.

The Chinese colonel issued an order in Mandarin, and three of the fifteen soldiers in the room, who were once again pointing their weapons at Kelly's chest, peeled off from the phalanx and double-timed it to the gurney on which Boyd was restrained. In seconds they were standing over him with machine guns pointed at his head at point-blank range.

Wu gestured toward the cube. "It's all yours," he said to Kelly. "But if you even _blink_ funny your friend will be dead before you can blink again. If you do anything that seems more threatening than a blink, my men will cut you down where you stand, regardless of your potential importance. Do you understand?"

Kelly swallowed hard. "You have nothing to worry about, Colonel," she said, approaching the cube. Wu and his guards stayed ten feet back and off to the side, not wanting to be collateral damage if his men had to open fire.

Several video cameras surrounded the cube on all sides, and these now zoomed in on the alien object, displaying its white-marble-like splendor in exquisite clarity on dozens of television and computer monitors arrayed around the room.

"First," said Kelly when she reached the object, "I'm going to place my thumb and index finger on two of the cube's vertices on top, and my other thumb and index finger on the other two. Then I'll press down on all four corners at once for several seconds. I'll leave it to you to measure the precise length of time I do this, and the pressure I'll be using."

Kelly proceeded exactly as she had specified, and a collective gasp broke out among dozens of observers as fifteen blazing red glyphs burst onto the surfaces of the cube, looking as if they were on fire.

"You'd think these glyphs would be as hot as the sun," she said, "but they're the same temperature as the rest of the cube."

If her audience was captivated before, they were now *spellbound*. The Chinese observers could have been thrown in vats of acid and wouldn't have taken their eyes from her or the monitors.

Kelly lifted the cube and turned to face Wu. "Now, I'm going to unlock additional controls," she said, "which will float above the cube as holograms."

She gestured to a face that showed a glyph of what appeared to be the cube itself, acting on another object, with eight distinct control notches arrayed around it. "The holographic controls are unlocked by touching this glyph, then three notches around it in succession, and then touching the glyph again while sliding my fingers outward—like I'm trying to enlarge a photo on my phone. All right?"

Wu was clearly mesmerized by the glyphs. "Understood," he said. "Please proceed."

Kelly manipulated the controls as she had promised. "Now," she said when this was complete, "if I touch the glyph in the center one final time, the holographic controls will appear."

She hesitated.

"What are you waiting for?" demanded Wu. "Don't make me have to torture Major Boyd after all."

Kelly shook her head sadly. "I won't," she said, pressing down on the glyph one last time.

The cube immediately carried out her preset instructions, leaving the gravity in a three-foot circle around her untouched, while sending out a wave at the speed of light that, for just an instant, increased the force of gravity ten thousand fold inside every object for almost thirty yards, in a band that began at about chest height and ended approximately four feet higher.

The upper torsos and heads of all soldiers and scientists in the room burst inward into vapor, leaving legs, waists, and stomachs untouched, as though a scythe made of light-saber energy, four-feet thick, had neatly erased the upper halves of their bodies.

Blood poured from the gaping openings that remained, as if severed veins and arteries were momentarily unaware that the hearts that controlled the circulation of the bodies they were in had been crushed into liquid.

To Kelly, it all seemed to happen instantly—and simultaneously. The sickening popping sounds of dozens of human implosions. The wrenching groan of steel as the parts of equipment rising higher than four feet were compressed into a dense amalgamation the size of a flea, like a car crushed all the way down to a metal sugar cube. And the loud boom from broad sections of two walls that splintered in on themselves and were ground into dust.

The room was rectangular, and the two nearest walls now had gaping three-foot-wide bands missing, from four to seven feet off the floor. The enormous laboratory was only standing because the farthest two walls were unaffected, and provided just enough structure to prevent the room from collapsing.

Kelly heard a hysterical shriek that seemed to go on forever, and realized only after it had ended that the scream had come from her own throat.

She had known exactly what to expect, but this was still too much. Too much death. Too much blood. The reality was far more gruesome, far more horrible, than her mind had been capable of imagining beforehand.

She didn't even like killing *insects* if she could help it. And now *this*. When she had told Boyd she was willing to do what it took, she was telling the truth. But how could she ever recover from what she had just wrought?

Kelly fell to the floor and vomited—but nothing came out. She hadn't eaten in days, leaving her stomach completely empty, which resulted in a series of dry heaves. She had read her grandfather's journal dozens of times and recalled that he had vomited also after witnessing two little girls being shot to death by his soon-to-be ally, Kurt Hahn. Perhaps this reaction ran in the family.

She was numb, paralyzed, and found herself wishing that she were dead too. Anything not to have to face her role in the gruesome, senseless executions of dozens of men and women.

She forced herself to fight through the shock to her system, through the debilitating horror of it all. The only way she could possibly handle this psychologically was to convince herself it wasn't real. That she was inside a particularly graphic haunted house on Halloween and nothing more.

She finally managed to stumble to her feet, dazed, and make her way over to Justin Boyd. The floor around his gurney was now littered by the severed lower bodies of the three soldiers who had been standing over him. He had been lying below the implosion zone, so was unaffected, but even after all he had seen in his career as a commando, he was stunned speechless from the grisly, barbaric scene he had just witnessed.

Kelly vaguely realized that an alarm was now blaring at ear-crushing decibel levels, no doubt triggered by a human or AI who had been watching the video feed remotely, as most of the video cameras were above the implosion zone and remained operational.

Boyd shouted out instructions to her on how to undo his restraints, and when she had finally freed him, he rose and held her for almost ten long seconds, keenly aware of how psychologically devastating her actions had been. The plan they had devised just prior to their surrender had called for her to pretend to cooperate with the

Chinese—to get her hands on the cube—so when Boyd had insisted she let him be tortured to death, it was only for show.

"We have time before reinforcements arrive," he bellowed, words that she barely heard over the blaring alarm. "No one's rushing into this room after seeing what happened on the feed."

He walked ten feet away to where his smart contact lenses were being scanned by a powerful digital microscope, which had been just below implosion height, and inserted them carefully back into his eyes, while Kelly peeled the makeshift pressure sensors from her fingertips.

"They didn't find Sage or remove my comm," said Boyd's voice in Kelly's ear. *"I assume they haven't removed your comm yet, either. Nod if you can hear me?"*

Kelly nodded vigorously while the major retrieved the can of wound-sealing foam that had been in his duffel bag, sprayed both of his forearms, and then covered them with his sweatshirt once again, not even bothering to wipe away the blood first.

Boyd handed her two of the three chocolate-flavored energy bars on the table and insisted that she eat them to maintain her strength, taking the third for himself.

While she bit off a portion of the high-calorie bar and began chewing, the major shoveled the rest of the items arrayed around the duffel bag back inside it, save for the Glock 22 semi-auto, which he kept in his right hand, appraising it like it was a long-lost friend.

This finished, he turned to Kelly. *"We're getting out of here,"* he said through Sage. *"I need you to put this place out of your mind forever,"* he added. *"You did what you had to do. You know they were going to kill us both once they got what they wanted. And this carnage took only an infinitesimal fraction of the cube's power. If that doesn't underscore why we can't let the Chinese military have it, nothing ever will. The freedoms of hundreds of millions, if not billions, of people around the world are at stake."*

Kelly nodded, but tears once again began sliding from the corners of her eyes and streaming down her face. She hadn't cried in many months, yet had recently let this become as common as breathing. She fought to regain her composure, knowing she had to toughen up.

Justin Boyd looked heartbroken to see her in such pain, but there was nothing he could do to help.

"Stay behind me," he said, this time carrying the duffel bag for himself. *"You and the cube have done enough."*

He nodded at the gun in his right hand. *"I'll take over from here."*

29

Boyd found himself marveling at Kelly Connolly's resilience as he waited for her to finish the second protein bar. Yes, she was in immense pain, and her psyche was in an alarmingly fragile state. Even so, there were hardened veterans who would still be shell-shocked after the massacre she had unleashed. He hadn't been at all sure that she'd be able to bring herself to do it, no matter what the stakes.

And few could have pulled it off so effectively. It wasn't just her mastery of the cube, but the way she had played her role to perfection. She had been so *in control*. Even though he had known that a second set of holographic controls didn't exist, she had been so convincing he half expected to see them materialize anyway.

She was clearly torn up inside. How could she *not* be. This massacre would have shaken a *serial killer*. Kelly now had deep emotional scars that might never heal. Seeing her suffering so acutely was more painful to him than he could have imagined. But the faster he could get her out of the room, get her focused on other things, the better.

"Sage," he said subvocally, "*extend your sensors to maximum range. Also, increase reception on my comm to maximum range. But instead of funneling amplified sound into my ear, monitor it yourself. I want an immediate warning if you detect any possible hostiles, or any autonomous weaponry.*"

"*Understood,*" replied the AI.

With this completed, Boyd led Kelly from the laboratory and up two flights of stairs. They came to the ground floor, as evidenced by several windows, and entered what appeared to be office space. Office space that showed clear signs of having been abandoned in a hurry.

The alarms that had been screeching into their brains abruptly stopped, and Boyd let out a heavy sigh of relief. "Did Wu give you any idea of where we are?" he asked Kelly, relieved that he no longer needed to shout, or communicate through an impersonal comm.

"He said we were on a man-made island in the South China Sea."

Boyd's eyes widened. "Of course we are," he mumbled to himself.

It was a perfect location. China had been expanding their presence in the South China Sea for decades, muscling into international waters despite considerable pushback from the world community, along with the strident objections of Vietnam, the Philippines, Malaysia, Indonesia, Brunei, and Taiwan. One early island that had become a Chinese military base, Fiery Cross Reef, was almost eight hundred miles from mainland China, but less than two hundred miles off the coast of Vietnam.

All in all, China had created seventeen such islands by depositing millions of tons of concrete and sand on top of coral reefs. And while China's Xi Jinping had promised not to create any further islands after the first handful, he had broken this promise as early as 2015.

Boyd rushed through the first floor of the building, with Kelly in tow, and soon found what he was looking for, a large corner office, hastily abandoned like all the rest. He entered, checked for cameras, and deposited his duffel bag on the floor behind him.

"Perfect," he announced.

"Perfect how?" said Kelly.

Boyd gestured to two walls of windows that met at the far corner of the room. "This gives us the broadest view outside. Gives us a chance to see what we might be dealing with."

Beyond the north window was perhaps twenty feet of sand that dropped off into a stunningly blue expanse of endless ocean. The adjacent window, facing east, showed any number of buildings, some with radar and satellite equipment on top, extensive storage facilities, and five basketball courts arranged side by side, a favorite recreation of the Chinese military.

No one was in sight outside, as if the two Americans had materialized in the island equivalent of a ghost town.

"Sage," said the major, "can you get internet access?"

"Negative. I've found a network, but the encryption protecting it is keeping me out, at least for now."

"Keep trying. Meanwhile, based on the layout I'm seeing, what island are we on?"

"Sun Island," replied the AI. *"The second smallest of the man-made Chinese islands, three hundred miles southwest of mainland China."*

"Where are the runways?"

"On the opposite side of the island," replied Sage, *"just over two hundred yards distant."*

"Figures they'd be the maximum distance away," he said to Kelly with a frown. "We wouldn't want this to be too easy."

"So we're going to steal a military jet?"

He nodded.

"And you can *pilot* one of those?"

Boyd swallowed hard. "Sure," he said unconvincingly. "I've had some training. Sage can walk me through the rest."

Boyd waited for an ironic reply, like 'that's comforting,' but none came. This was the starkest indication of all that Kelly was in a very bad way. Her sense of humor had survived every hardship. But it was finally nowhere to be found. She was a shell of her former self, listless and emotionally drained.

"Let's go," he said, lifting his duffel. "They're bound to regroup any moment."

"Okay, but *I'm* leading," said Kelly, seeming to come back to life as she made this proclamation. "And I'm going to make sure that no one else dies. I could've gotten us out of there without using lethal force. I *should* have. I'll never forgive myself for that mistake. But no more innocents are being sacrificed on my watch."

Boyd knew that she was right. No one in that room had deserved death. He felt the tragic, horrific loss of life almost as deeply as she did, he just had more experience suppressing it. Most of the men and women killed had been pressed into service and were just trying to get by. Provide for their families. Many were victims themselves, appalled by their leaders but powerless to do anything to stop them.

He had hoped that Kelly would focus on Wu and his sadistic threats of mutilation, and not on the fate of so many others who were little more than collateral damage.

"So you think you can clear a path to the runways without killing anyone?" he asked her.

"I do."

"Good," said the major. "Then I'm all for it."

Boyd paused and shook his head. "But you need to know that you *had* to use the force you did," he added. "And you have to find a way to forgive yourself. The colonel had guns pointed at both of us, held by scores of men with itchy trigger fingers, watching you like hawks. He threatened to kill us if you *blinked* funny.

"Yes, non-lethal force might have worked. *Might* have. But you only had one chance at this. If you miscalculated, we were dead. And the Chinese would control the cube until the end of time. You used the force you did because you had to be sure."

Boyd waited several seconds for this to sink in. "So I'm all for using non-lethal force going forward," he continued. "But I won't let you rewrite history. I won't let you second-guess yourself and succumb to self-loathing. Sometimes very good people have to make very hard choices."

Kelly didn't reply, but he sensed that his words had helped.

They exited the building and headed across the island. They crossed about twenty yards of sand and were nearing the first outdoor basketball court when Sage came to life. *"Incoming military drones at eleven o'clock,"* the AI blasted into their ears.

Kelly's fingers raced across the cube like a concert pianist as four unmanned aircraft came into view in the distance, streaking over the horizon. They looked more like small, windowless fighters than standard issue octo-copter drones, and far more deadly.

Kelly struck the last glyph, aiming another implosion beam outward, just as each drone fired two missiles, which leaped toward them eagerly. An instant later, all four drones and eight missiles imploded in spectacular fashion, close enough to have pulverized the two Americans had the gravity field not kept the destruction self-contained.

"Alert," said Sage once again, but Boyd had already launched himself at Kelly, dropping his duffel and driving her onto the sand, as a barrage of bullets pierced the air where their heads had been a

moment before. In one smooth motion Boyd landed on the ground, rose to a crouch, and dragged his companion behind a concrete bathroom facility near the first basketball court, all at a speed that no unenhanced human could hope to achieve.

Kelly rolled to her elbows, still holding the alien object in one hand, as dozens of men with machine guns, grenades, and missile launchers advanced from the north. Her hands flew over the cube once again, and she thrust one corner toward the incoming platoon, lifting them all into the air at once. Several dropped their weapons in panic, and several others wet themselves.

Not yet done, Kelly worked the cube further, demonstrating what exquisite control of the fabric of spacetime could do, and the men careened toward the ocean in an upright position. She stopped their surreal flight fifty yards past the edge of the island and dropped them, screaming, into the tranquil blue sea. They would live, but they wouldn't be troubling the two Americans for some time.

"I'm hearing approximately twenty-five more hostiles approaching from the east," said Sage.

Boyd hastily escorted Kelly to the west side of the concrete outhouse as a second small army, much like the one that was now swimming, made itself known.

This time Kelly took a different approach, increasing the gravity *under* the group. She pointed a vertex of the cube at the approaching platoon, and all of them crashed to the ground, as if they were covered in steel and walking on a powerful electromagnet. All were instantly pinned there, every inch of their bodies and cheeks pressed against the ground, unable to move a millimeter.

Kelly realized that this was effective, but she couldn't hold the cube on them all day. "Sage," she called out. "How many Gs does it take to knock a man out without killing him?"

"Air Force officer John Stapp survived over forty-six Gs for almost two seconds. But without a special compression suit, nine G's for twelve seconds should do it."

Kelly nodded, fiddled with the cube's settings, and held it on the men. During the seconds she did, they looked like fighter pilots undergoing full acceleration, their skin and hair stretched toward the ground as if pushed there by hurricane force winds. Finally, after counting to twelve, she discontinued her effort, and there was no doubt that they had all blacked out as expected.

She and Boyd both continued to frantically scan the area, looking for additional threats, while Kelly tried to catch her breath.

"Enough!" shouted a voice in the Americans' ears. The all-too-familiar voice of Commander Shen Ning. *"I've called off all further attacks. I have what I want. More than I could have hoped for. So it's time to end this, once and for all."*

30

Shen paused for several seconds. *"Why am I not hearing a reply?"* he continued. *"You're really starting to hurt my feelings. I already know exactly where you are. You understand that, right? Just use the same broadcast frequency you did in the woods, and I'll pick it up."*

Boyd made sure Sage was continuing to monitor for hostiles, not trusting that Shen had really called off the dogs, and then turned to Kelly. "He's right. We have no reason not to reply. Let's find out what we're up against."

She nodded.

Boyd ordered Sage to broadcast his voice. "Where are you calling from, Commander Shen?"

"So glad to hear from you, Major," replied Shen. *"I really do treasure our discussions. I'm many, many miles away from your island. But rest assured that I've been monitoring you and the esteemed Dr. Connolly this entire time. Colonel Wu only thought he was running the show. In reality, I'm in charge, put there by our president himself."*

"I wouldn't boast about that," said Boyd. "Your president isn't going to be happy with you."

"On the contrary, Major Boyd. My job was to find out as much as I could about the operation of the cube. And I've done that. I set up a scenario in which I couldn't lose.

"If you cooperated with the colonel, then I would get what I wanted. If you failed to cooperate, the only way you could escape would be to use the cube as a weapon—while I was watching—and I'd also get what I wanted."

"So you considered Colonel Wu and his people expendable?" said Kelly in disgust.

"*Regrettably, yes. But they could not have died more honorably, sacrificing themselves for their country.*"

"So this was just another setup?" said Kelly.

"*Let's just say that your actions were a contingency I was prepared for. Did you really think we were so sloppy that we wouldn't find the supercomputer affixed to the major's leg? Or fail to remove the comms embedded in your inner ears? We left them in place so that if you weren't planning to cooperate, you'd feel more comfortable using the cube to escape.*"

He paused. "*I thought there was a good chance you would find a way to use the cube against us, Dr. Connolly, while pretending to show us how it worked. I'm sorry that I was right. But I did warn the colonel of this possibility. Apparently, he didn't take me as seriously as he should have.*

"*But the result of this is that we have more than just a precise record of how you controlled the cube inside our main lab. We also now have a record of how you controlled it to fend off our three attacks on the surface. There are dozens of drones hovering out of your sight, with telescopic cameras trained on your hands, and they picked up your every movement.*

"*Despite this success,*" continued Shen, "*I've decided no further attacks are necessary. We now know enough to figure out the rest for ourselves. So why risk losing additional men?*"

"Your compassion is truly inspiring," said Kelly.

"And once again," added Boyd, "you've made sure you aren't anywhere near where the bullets are flying. So your bravery continues to amaze, as well."

"*Bravery used unwisely isn't a virtue.*"

"Spare us your lame rationalizations," said Boyd.

"Your plan may *sound* good," said Kelly, "but it gets you nowhere. So you know how to call up the glyphs," she added, "and perform some rudimentary operations. So what? How does that help you?"

"Exactly," seconded Boyd. "You've been too clever by half. You may have learned how to control the cube, but only by letting *us* have it. Which is a *huge* mistake. We'll take out this entire island if that's what it takes to escape. You'll never see the cube again."

"This is where you're wrong," said Shen. *"Why would you think taking out our entire island would trouble me? In fact, that's exactly my plan to get the cube back."*

"What are you talking about?" snapped Boyd.

"I'm talking about overwhelming firepower. And you should also know that when we do remove the cube from the vapor-stains that used to be your bodies, it will be our second one. *We've been studying a cube of our own for many months now."*

Boyd shook his head in alarm. "You're bluffing," he said. "It's not like the aliens dole them out to every superpower."

Shen laughed. *"Very true,"* he said. *"We started with none, in fact. But we recently developed a sensor that just happened to be able to pick up these cubes while they're in a state of immobility. That's how we found the one in Spokane. And it turns out that there are two on this planet. The other one wasn't in China, unfortunately, but at least it wasn't in North America either. It's in a desolate location, in fact. So we bought up the land and established what is purported to be a climate station around it."*

"I still don't believe you," said Boyd, but his expression indicated otherwise.

"Believe what you want," said Shen. *"I'm sure you've wondered how we found your operation in Spokane. This is how. And while we were conducting our own experiments on our own cube, we were looking over your shoulder in case you unlocked yours first."*

"Which we did," said Kelly.

"Which you did. And we're still unsure how, since we couldn't get any images of you when you were in your cube room and about to steal it."

"Sorry to hear that, Shen," said Kelly. "So at the end of this, we'll have an active cube, and you'll have one that does nothing but mock you. If you can't unlock it, you can't move it, and you can't get at the glyphs."

"I wasn't finished," said Shen. *"We aren't sure how you did it, but we kept searching all the places you visited after you stole the cube. And yesterday, we found a strange device that no one recognizes. One*

that doesn't seem to do anything. So we plan to train it on our cube tomorrow and see if this is the magic key."

Kelly closed her eyes and cringed. They had found her dark energy generator. Things kept going from bad to worse.

"And you still aren't getting this," continued Shen. *"We're prepared to do anything to get the cube you're holding now. Anything. I'm prepared to unleash what you Americans call an Armageddon of biblical proportions.*

"I had hoped my comrades on the island would be able to get the cube back after your initial escape. But it's become clear that this isn't going to happen. Fortunately, I have a backup plan. It turns out that China has a number of nuclear bombs stored on the island you're on. I'll give you a few seconds to have your supercomputer confirm this, Major."

Sage quickly confirmed this intel, and Boyd's face contorted as if he were eating a particularly sour lemon. "Okay, Commander," he said. "So you have nukes on site. Are you telling me that you'd nuke your own base?"

"That's exactly what I'm telling you. Ten minutes after I sign off, I will detonate one. I'm betting the Enigma Cube weathers the nuke just fine. Probably won't even get a scratch. What about you, Major? Do you have a DNA upgrade that lets you withstand a thermonuclear blast?"

Boyd's jaw tightened but he didn't reply.

"I didn't think so," continued Shen. *"So once the island finally cools down, we'll simply locate the cube and decontaminate it. Nullify the pesky radiation. Then we'll have two of them, and the rest of the world will have none."*

"You'll be killing thousands of your own people," said Boyd.

"Unfortunate, but acceptable. Now there is a chance that the cube, in Dr. Connolly's expert hands, can protect you somehow. Throw up a gravity shield that not even a nuke can penetrate. If it can do this, then we want it even more. We'll then bombard the island with a blizzard of lethal weapons. Missiles, additional nukes, poison gas, you name it. From fighter jets and battleships and subs. A simultaneous

bombardment the likes of which the world has never seen. And we'll keep at it until we finally overwhelm your ability to counter us."

"Do you have any idea of the international backlash you'd be facing from just the detonation of a single nuclear bomb?" said the major.

"Every idea," said Shen calmly. *"Our president is prepared to handle it. To apologize for such a tragic accident, which, after all, will have only killed his own citizens. He believes the breathtaking advances the cube makes possible justify any means used to acquire it."*

Shen paused. *"Naturally,"* he added, *"we're hoping that you just surrender before the ten minutes are up. We'd save a perfectly good base, and some good people. Not to mention your lives. And the end result will be the same. If you think this is a bluff and don't surrender, so be it. That will be the last poor decision you ever make. But I'm going to sign off now. You have exactly ten minutes."*

He paused for effect. *"And the clock starts . . . now!"*

31

"Sage, hover a small digital timer just above my right lens," ordered Boyd, "counting down from ten minutes, starting the instant Shen signed off."

Kelly stared deeply into the major's eyes. "I don't suppose you have any idea how to get out of this?"

"None. But my gut tells me he isn't bluffing. Any chance the cube can help us withstand everything he's prepared to throw at us?"

Kelly frowned. "Let's say for the sake of argument that it could form a protective gravity bubble. One that could block us from temperatures of millions of degrees, winds of six hundred miles per hour, and shock waves that could split a mountain. Even so, it would have to block air from reaching us also, as this would be hot enough to melt our lungs. Not to mention radioactive. So we'd die of suffocation."

Boyd shook his head. That was a worse alternative than being instantly vaporized.

"Then we have no choice," he said. "We have to surrender. If they're going to get the cube regardless, we have to live to fight another day."

Kelly blew out a long breath. "There is one other option. A long shot. A *dangerous* long shot."

Boyd looked confused. "Then it's one that I'm missing."

"I can activate one of the other controls on the cube. See what happens. We discussed the possibility of teleportation. Of higher dimensions. Maybe this thing can get us out of this after all."

"Or destroy the solar system with a wrong touch."

"I've given this a lot of thought in the past sixteen months," said Kelly. "A doomsday button is possible, yes. But if we're in a universe with aliens who would put a button like that on such a nifty cube," she added wryly, "then I don't want to live in that universe."

Boyd smiled. *Welcome back, Kelly*, he thought. Her gallows humor had returned.

As devastated as she had been after being the instrument of a massacre, this blow had been lessened by the realization of just how ruthless China's president was prepared to be. Just how many thousands he was prepared to kill without a second thought. A sobering reminder of what was at stake if she let this man have his prize.

"If you were going to try a new glyph," asked Boyd, "which one would it be?"

"The third one that's all by its lonesome. The cloud around the dot might be blast debris, but it could be *anything*. And this glyph is bound to be important, since it warrants its own cube face."

The major glanced at the digital clock hovering in front of him. They had just over seven minutes before they surrendered or died. "Let's do it," he said decisively.

Kelly nodded, but before she could touch the glyph, Boyd swept her up in his arms and kissed her with unbridled passion, as if he didn't want to ever stop.

"What was that for?" she said when they had finally separated.

"For luck," he replied with a smile. "And if we're *out* of luck, and this kills us, I can't think of a higher note to end things on than kissing you."

"Wow. Men facing imminent nuclear attacks say the sweetest things."

With that said, Kelly Connolly turned the cube so the glyph in question was facing her, nodded at Boyd, closed her eyes, and pressed down on the center—waiting for oblivion.

32

Nothing happened for several seconds after Kelly pressed the glyph, and she opened her eyes once again.

Hello, Kelly, she said to herself.

Why had she done that?

"You aren't talking to yourself," said the same voice in her head. *"What you call the Enigma Cube has a telepathic AI on board, which you've just activated."*

Kelly gasped.

"Why did you just gasp?" said Boyd, blinking in confusion. "Nothing happened, right?"

"Not exactly," she said hastily. "But give me a few seconds."

"Enigma Cube AI," she thought at the object in her hand, *"are you picking up my thoughts now?"*

"I am."

"Can you communicate with my companion also?"

"I can, but I won't. I'm programmed in very specific ways."

"Please elaborate. And hurry, we don't have much time."

"I carry out orders given by the first being who activates me," responded the AI, its directed thoughts now coming at her more quickly, displaying the urgency she had called for. *"Provided I deem the being worthy, well-intentioned. A being who ultimately wants to use the power of the cube for constructive, rather than destructive, purposes. I can answer certain questions, but I'm precluded from answering others. I can help you wield what you call the Enigma Cube, but I can't answer questions involving the science behind its operation. You have to figure that out on your own."*

Kelly turned to her human companion, her eyes wide. "This is *incredible*," she said. "Justin, the glyph activated a telepathic AI inside the cube. I swear to God. I'm conversing with it now, but I can't conference you in."

Boyd's mouth dropped open. If he had been given a thousand guesses as to what might result from Kelly trying the new glyph, this wouldn't be on the list. Even so, he didn't doubt her for a moment. "Okay," he said, "an unexpected development, for sure. But it beats the hell out of a doomsday button."

"I'm going to see if it can save us. How much time is left?"

"Just over five minutes."

"Thanks," said Kelly. "I'll be conversing telepathically, but I'll get back to you as soon as I can."

"*So, Enigma AI,*" thought Kelly, not wasting a moment, "*how much do you know about our current situation? Have you been monitoring it?*"

"*I hear everything that is said for miles around me. This was also the case inside your Uru facility. In addition, I routinely access the entire contents of your internet, which enables me to understand the context of what I hear.*"

"*Do you believe Shen will do as he says?*" asked Kelly. "*And can you protect all life on this island?*"

"*The commander will do as he threatened. And the fact that you asked me to protect all life, instead of just your own, confirms my assessment of your good intentions. But I can't save your lives. Not from this. Your analysis in that regard is accurate.*"

"*Can you teleport us out of here?*"

"*I can only teleport objects, or beings, between two cubes, provided that both cubes are active. There is only one other cube on Earth, and it's currently in what you call lockdown mode. So this won't work. I could also teleport you to locations at which wormhole gates have been established, but you would arrive in the vacuum of space and die horribly.*"

Kelly cursed to herself. "Time?" she said out loud to Boyd.

"Just under four minutes."

Kelly's eyes widened once again. She had just shouted the word *time*, which had been like waving a neon flag in front of herself. As she had told Boyd, the cube didn't just impact the *space* part of spacetime. It impacted the *time* part as well. She hadn't gotten into all of the time possibilities with Boyd in the car because they were even more speculative than wormholes and warp drives, and she had been eager for him to join her in the backseat.

"*Enigma AI*," she thought urgently, "*what about time travel? Can you send us into a different time to escape this threat?*"

"*I can.*"

"*Outstanding!*" thought Kelly excitedly.

"*But to be clear, I won't send you into the future, meaning to a point in the timeline beyond that which any possible version of you has already reached. So your travel can be to the past only.*"

"*I'll take it!*" thought Kelly. "*Send us back to five days ago. Immediately.*"

"*This particular time is also off limits. There are certain rules. First, I can only send you back to a time, and place, where this exact cube existed previously. Period. It has to create a tunnel through time, and be there to anchor the tunnel on both ends. And it has to be in active form in both time periods.*"

"*Second,*" continued the cube's AI, "*I'm also not authorized to send you to a time when you already exist. You can only travel to a time before you were born. And even then, you will not be permitted to communicate with yourselves in the future.*"

"*When was this cube last active prior to my birth?*"

"*In 1943.*"

Kelly rolled her eyes. *Of course* in 1943.

"*And when before that?*" she thought at the AI.

"*Prior to various brief periods of being active in 1943, it was in lockdown mode in what is now Canada for over four thousand years.*"

Kelly swallowed hard. That didn't seem ideal. The year 1943 wasn't ideal either, but at least electricity and cars had been invented.

"*If we change things in the past, will this change the future?*"

"*Yes. And I would only let you go because I've read your mind and I believe you will make every effort to blend in and not alter history. Please confirm this is accurate.*"

"It is," thought Kelly. *"I promise to try to minimize changes and make sure Justin does the same. But even if we inadvertently change things, it won't affect our future, right? Our timeline is set in stone. Change something in the past and a new timeline branches off, but the original timeline remains."*

"You've been watching too many movies. That isn't how it works. One universe, one timeline. The timeline doesn't branch off, it gets re-made. And the universe will not allow paradox. Whatever is changed is changed, without regard to causality. So changes to history do affect the one true future. But history has an inertia, and if it played out a certain way in the initial timeline, it will not easily be pushed into a new course."

"Less than two minutes left, Kelly," called out Boyd anxiously. "If you and the cube are still looking for a way out of this, now would be a good time to find one."

"We have," she replied hurriedly. "One only. We'd have to travel back in time. To 1943. Long story about why that's our only good option, but it is. Are you in?"

Boyd was momentarily stunned, which Kelly found unsurprising. Nuclear threats, alien cubes, telepathy, and now time travel. It would blow the mind of the most stable man, test the credulity of the most believing.

"Is this really what you want to do?" asked Boyd feebly, still trying to digest the idea that time travel might actually be possible.

"Yes!" she said emphatically. "It's what we *have* to do. If we surrender, we're dead, like you said. And they get the cube. Time travel is insane. *Insane.* And being stranded in 1943 is a nightmare. But it's our only chance."

"Then I'm in."

"Good. I need you to leave the gun and duffel bag behind. We don't want to risk bringing items from our day that might alter the course of history. Sage is okay, because they'd have no idea what to make of her, and no way to reverse engineer her nanocircuitry. Same goes for your contacts."

Kelly could tell Boyd had a thousand questions—as did she—but time was running out, so without another word, he tossed the bag aside. He didn't look happy to have to abandon it after managing to hold on to it through all the bedlam, but he knew better than to argue.

"*What else can you tell me about time travel rules?*" Kelly asked the Enigma AI telepathically.

"*There are too many complexities for you to grasp in the time remaining. But if you'd like, I can implant a brief overview of the implications of time travel into your brain, instantly, as you're leaving.*"

"Yes, do that."

"Thirty seconds, Kelly," said Boyd hurriedly, a note of panic in his voice. "Why aren't we in 1943? If we're doing this, we need to do it *now.*"

"*Send us back,*" Kelly thought at the AI. "*Immediately!*"

"*This cube was activated and then deactivated more than once in 1943. Which of these activation intervals do you want to travel to?*"

"Ten seconds!" shouted Boyd.

"*I don't know,*" she thought frantically to the telepathic AI. "*Just pick one. Now!*"

Seconds after Kelly issued this order a blinding white fireball more than three miles across erupted eleven miles into the air, exactly as Shen had threatened, topped with a distinctive mushroom cloud.

For a brief instant the temperature given off by the detonated thermonuclear device rivaled that at the center of the Sun, exceeding a hundred million degrees. Everything on the surface of the island was instantly vaporized, including any number of substantial concrete structures, trees, runways, and thousands of people. Millions of tons of sand were blasted into glass, and the ocean boiled for miles around, killing millions of fish and other sea creatures.

This inferno, this maelstrom of energy and death that made the bowels of hell look like Disneyland, would later be called a tragic accident by China's president. And almost no one in the international community would believe him.

But that didn't matter. Because only a few people on Earth, all of them in China, would ever have any idea of what actually happened here—or why.

PART 6

"I myself believe that there will one day be time travel because when we find that something isn't forbidden by the over-arching laws of physics, we usually eventually find a technological way of doing it."

—David Deutsch (Oxford physicist who laid the foundations for quantum computing)

33

Kelly Connolly's brain was on fire as it was barraged by input it had no way to interpret, which she could only guess was higher dimensional reality her 3D mind was ill-equipped to digest. The colors, tastes, sounds, and smells that assaulted her senses were almost too much to take in, like she was on an acid trip that was taking an acid trip, and her mind began to melt down.

The world suddenly, mercifully, collapsed into the one she was used to, but her mind and eyes were foggy, and she had a sense that her brain would be shutting down within minutes, if not sooner, desperate for the reboot that sleep would provide.

Kelly heard a gasp in front of her in the small, dark room, lighted only by a single lantern, and through blurry eyes made out the figure of a gangly young man, holding an enigma cube in his hand, its burning glyphs blazing in the dimness. He jerked back explosively, reflexively, upon seeing her materialize in front of him, and immediately tripped over a shoe, one belonging to Justin Boyd, who had arrived behind him.

The boy, who Kelly realized had to be the young Otto Richter, crashed to the hard floor, the back of his skull hitting first, and was still, either temporarily stunned, knocked out, or dead.

Justin Boyd shot her a pained, confused look and then collapsed to the ground as well, unconscious.

Kelly almost joined him, but used every last ounce of her will to fight off the darkness that was enveloping her mind, just for a few seconds longer. She was stunned and confused, but she knew that she had to be at the Nazi compound in Canada. And from the commotion she was now hearing in the outer room, their arrival must have made enough noise to rouse the SS soldiers sleeping there. They would be entering the room to check on things any moment. Kurt

Hahn would stall them, but not for long without raising too much suspicion. And if the SS came in and found the cube active, it would be the ultimate disaster.

Kelly fell to the floor, her wobbly legs no longer able to support her weight, and crawled the short distance to the cube, which had dropped from Otto's hand to the hard floor. She reached out and pressed the glyph that called up the telepathic AI.

"Welcome to 1943, Kelly," the cube thought at her immediately.

"Return the cube to its original position in the room," she ordered telepathically, *"and return it to lockdown mode. Immediately!"* she finished.

Kelly battled ferociously to remain conscious, to ensure her instructions were carried out, but this was not to be. Instead, clinging to reality by her fingertips, her grip finally slipped, and she plummeted into the cold, dark oblivion that had beckoned since her arrival.

34

Justin Boyd awoke with a start to find himself sitting on the floor of a small room in total darkness, his back against a corrugated steel wall. He blinked on the night vision feature of his contacts and took stock of his situation and surroundings. His wrists and ankles were bound by steel cuffs, anchored by a chain to a bolt embedded in the concrete floor.

Kelly Connolly was sitting beside him, restrained in the same way he was, and he could see her stirring from her sleep, opening her eyes to absolute darkness. Against the opposite wall, maybe twelve feet away, was an unconscious teen, of average height but thinner than he should have been, also propped into a seated position against the wall, and also restrained.

Boyd decided it wasn't necessary to use Sage to broadcast his voice directly into his companion's ear, as they were almost touching each other. "Kelly," he whispered softly.

She jumped, surprised to hear a disembodied voice so close to her in the cave-like darkness.

"Justin?" she whispered back in relief, still groggy, staring at his face just inches away but still unable to detect it. "Where are we? How long have I been out?"

"We're in a small room," he answered in low tones. "I've put my contacts in night-vision mode. I awoke just a few seconds ago myself. But for some reason, I don't think we've been out for long."

"Yeah, now that I'm more fully awake, I get that sense too. Maybe an hour or two at most."

"How are you feeling?" he asked her.

"Still a little rattled. But I'll be okay."

Boyd pulled against his restraints with all of his might, but his enhanced strength was still no match for them, especially without his electroactive clothing. "Are we really in the past?" he asked. "Or am I in the psych ward of a hospital?"

"I wouldn't rule out anything," said Kelly, "but I'm pretty sure we really did travel in time."

She tilted her head in thought. "I remember the Enigma AI flashing information about time travel into my memory the instant we left. Then my mind was flooded by a barrage of—well, by a barrage of *something*. Sensory input I can't possibly describe. Even so, it was almost as if part of me was witnessing the island being destroyed, wiped clean by an incomprehensible fire. It was devastatingly real, and devastatingly terrifying."

Boyd nodded slowly. "Now that you mention it, I remember the same. The cube must have wanted us to get a taste of the nuclear cataclysm we narrowly missed. And then I remember suddenly finding myself standing in a room."

He thought hard but finally shook his head. "I don't remember a thing after that."

"We arrived at the Canadian encampment where the Nazis were studying the cube. The encampment Otto Richter described in his journal. And things went south in a hurry. Otto was there, holding the activated cube. But we startled the hell out of him by appearing out of thin air, and he tripped over your foot and hit his head."

"That would explain the unconscious kid cuffed to the wall across from us. I'm pretty sure that's Otto."

"There's been someone else in the room with us, and you didn't tell me until *now*?"

"I was getting to it," said Boyd, realizing just how lame that sounded.

"Any others I should know about?"

"No, just the three of us."

"That's good to know," replied Kelly, irritated.

She blew out a long breath. "But on the bright side, at least we know Otto is still alive."

"So what happened next?" asked the major.

Kelly told him, about how he had fallen unconscious just after Otto, and how she had activated the telepathic AI and ordered it to cover Otto's tracks before the SS soldiers rushed in.

Boyd shook his head. "Since we left Haycock," he said, continuing to speak in a whisper, "the impossible has become *routine*. I've imagined myself in all kinds of hostile settings and disaster scenarios. But I have to admit, I never imagined being a prisoner of the *Nazis*."

"Brace yourself, then," she whispered back. "Because this is the *least* of our worries. If the Enigma AI didn't return the cube to its original position and lock it down, then Hitler has his superweapon."

Boyd shrank back in horror. "Yeah, that's *much* worse."

"Oh, but there's more," said Kelly in disgust. "I'm pretty sure the cube from our time didn't make the trip with us. I think it's still in the future, on the island. It makes sense now that I think about it. The Enigma AI did say there had to be one on both sides of the time tunnel to anchor it. But it would have been nice to make this more explicit. I don't do my best thinking while sitting on top of a thermonuclear warhead."

Boyd looked ill. "So Shen will get the cube after all, once it's been decontaminated. And assuming it survives the explosion."

"I'd be amazed if it didn't."

"Perfect," he said bitterly. "If we had known we'd be leaving it with China, we'd have surrendered. At least then we'd have a *chance* of getting it back. So now, impossibly, we've handed unlocked cubes to both Hitler *and* the totalitarian regime in China."

"We aren't sure about the situation here. I'm still hoping the AI carried out my order and put the cube back in place before the SS entered. If not," added Kelly, shaking her head, "we won't have to worry about China. Because we'll have changed history so that Germany dominates the world, and China never becomes a world power."

"But won't the future we lived in still happen?" said Boyd. "Won't the changes we make here just branch into a second timeline? In this second timeline, history will play out differently, but the first will remain. Right?"

Kelly couldn't help but smile. "Incredible," she said. "We seem to be on the same page. I thought that's how time travel would work, also. But the Enigma AI says it doesn't."

"Did your telepathic friend bother to tell you that time travel would cause us to black out?" asked Boyd.

"No. Another small item it neglected to mention. Although, to be fair, I wouldn't be surprised if we were the first humans it ever sent back. And at least it sent us back fully *clothed*. We can be thankful for that small mercy."

"Not having the chance to see you naked is a *mercy*?" said Boyd, faking dismay. "Then why do I think of it as a *crime*?"

Kelly grinned. "It's pretty scary that you can joke under these circumstances," she said. "And even scarier that I find you amusing."

She paused. "But in all seriousness, we couldn't have screwed things up any worse."

"So do we tell Otto who we really are?"

Kelly considered. "I think we have to," she said. "If all he knows is that we're strangers from North America who popped up out of nowhere, even he won't be on our side. And we desperately need to win him over if we want to have any chance of surviving this. And even more importantly, Kurt Hahn, who's the number two ranked SS officer here."

"Are you certain that you can trust this Hahn?"

"Not at all. But Otto ended up trusting him. Hahn may have double-crossed Otto at the end, and he wasn't aware of it. So trusting Hahn is still a gamble. But one we have to take."

"What about changing history?" said Boyd. "This will do it for sure. If Otto knows his future, he'll surely change it. Which means you'll probably never be born. Do you really want to take that chance?"

"The telepathic AI implanted knowledge of time travel logic in my mind just before we traveled back. Yes, if we change Otto's history, I probably won't be born. But this still won't erase me from existence. The rules dictate that the universe rolls with the punches. Just because I'll never have been born doesn't stop me from existing now.

If I'm already here, I stay here. We can discuss time travel logic at another time. The bottom line is that we need to tell Otto the truth."

"Why do you think he's chained here also?"

"Because of us," replied Kelly with a frown. "The Nazis here trusted him alone in their cube room, just like his journal said. But our arrival must have really thrown them. So now they don't trust him anymore." She shook her head. "We do seem to make everything we touch a lot worse."

"You're being too hard on yourself. I can't gloss over just how bad things look right now. We failed in the future, and we might be failing in the past. To be fair, we've been up against incredible odds, and we've had some very bad luck. But the past few days has shown me that we make an extraordinary team. So don't let yourself get down. We've found a way out of impossible situations before. So if there's a way to get out of this one and set things right, I guarantee we're going to find it."

She nodded but didn't reply.

"And speaking of getting out of this," he continued, "I need time to think. We don't know who will come through the door first. If it's Kurt Hahn, then we'll tell him the truth. But if it's anyone else, I need to have a backstory planned. A way to justify what happened here, at least with enough plausibility to keep us alive through the first five minutes of any encounter."

"I doubt that's possible," said Kelly. "I mean, we appeared from thin air into their Enigma Cube room—what they call their Atlantis Cube room. A room in the center of a top-secret facility in the middle of a forest. One that only a few people in the world, all in Germany, even know about. And then we promptly passed out. If you can explain that away, you're a magician. I don't even speak German. Do you?"

Boyd shook his head. "Sage can translate if need be. I learned some Chinese, Arabic, and Farsi on the job. But America hasn't had any conflict with Germany for a long, long time," he pointed out. "You know, other than *now*."

"Well, if we screw this up," said Kelly grimly, "the entire *world* will be speaking German."

"Then it's time for me to have some solitude and think of a back-story for us. This will be the biggest bullshitting challenge I've ever had," he admitted. "But since joining EHO, I've had to BS my way out of dicey situations any number of times. I've told whoppers that you wouldn't believe. It's a matter of knowing the audience inside and out, being quick on your feet, and letting your imagination fly. And, most importantly, not being afraid to be bold or outrageous."

"This last technique was formalized by Hitler himself," said Kelly. "Although you're using it for good, not evil," she hastened to add. "In his book, *Mein Kampf*, he coined the term *große Lüge*, which means Big Lie."

"I thought you didn't speak German."

"I don't. But since finding my grandfather's journal, I've done a little research on the period. Anyway, Hitler believed that the bigger the lie, the more audacious, the more likely it was to be believed. Because who'd imagine someone would have the nerve to spread such a colossal lie? And the more such a lie was repeated, the more likely it would be accepted as truth."

Kelly paused. "But I need to stop talking now and let you think."

"Thanks. If someone comes in, close your eyes and pretend to be unconscious."

"Sure. My eyes are useless anyway. I can't even see my hand."

"Keep pretending to be out cold until we know who entered, and we can get a sense of what they're up to. We'll go from there, depending on who it is. If it's Kurt Hahn, you take the lead. If it's anyone else, I will. And we *are* going to get out of this," he added emphatically.

Kelly nodded, feeling much more hopeful than their situation seemed to warrant. But she was buoyed by Boyd's calm, his decisiveness. He had a can-do, never-say-die attitude that was inspiring.

Once again, when she was by his side, no odds seemed too daunting to overcome. She found herself believing that anything was possible, and that they could extricate themselves from any trap, no matter how foolproof.

But while this belief had been tested before, she had no doubt that the ultimate test was yet to come.

35

SS Colonel Bruno Zimmerman stood outside on the starless spring night holding a lantern in one hand and a flashlight in the other, and both revealed that he was *seething*.

"Report!" he shouted at his second-in-command, Kurt Hahn.

"Nothing new," said the SS major as a never-ending chorus of crickets chirped in the background. "The patrolmen on duty at the time saw nothing. And the larger group we sent out afterward hasn't seen or found anything either. Every tripwire is still in place, and no other telltales have been found. No footprints, broken branches, or anything else."

After the Canadian family had stumbled onto their encampment, Zimmerman had made sure a series of nearly invisible tripwires, tied to small explosive charges, were laid at key points of possible ingress to make it all but impossible to sneak up on them again. And an alternating group of six SS soldiers patrolled the perimeter each night.

Hahn was vaguely aware of light in the distance, no doubt generated by more than a dozen SS soldiers with flashlights. They had now fanned out through the forest, slowly crisscrossing the perimeter of the encampment, searching ever so carefully for any clue that might explain what had happened.

"In addition," continued the major, "none of the men assigned to sky watch this week have reported seeing a single aircraft in the area." He frowned. "In short, we still have no idea how this man and woman could have possibly gotten inside the Atlantis Cube room."

"This is unacceptable!" screamed Zimmerman as several bats winged by overhead, passing briefly from the dark shadows into the limited illumination thrown off by the lantern. "This has to be the boy's doing. When he comes to, we'll finally find out how he pulled it off."

Hahn cursed inwardly. How had this happened? Who were these trespassers? They could ruin *everything*. Otto had been completing careful experimentation on the cube, and they were just days away from using it to wipe out the encampment, ensuring it was removed from Nazi hands once and for all.

Worse, the timing had become more critical than ever. They had been forced to move up their schedule recently when another top scientist in the group, Alex Wentz, had discovered one of Otto's notebooks that the boy had thought was properly hidden. It had been a disaster. Wentz was brilliant, but loyal to the Third Reich, the worst possible combination. And the notebook he had found was the one containing Otto's equations and diagrams for the generator he had created.

Otto told him he had found flaws and was embarrassed by the work, which is why he never shared it. But Wentz thought it was worth trying, and took it upon himself to bring Otto's invention to life. It might only be a matter of days before he succeeded. If the cube wasn't gone before this time, Hitler would get his prize.

"Respectfully, Colonel," began Hahn, aware of just how carefully he needed to tread, "the boy had nothing to do with this. No one despises him more than me. You know that. Which is why I volunteered to sleep outside the cube room so he can never leave at night. So he never gets a reprieve from the thing that terrifies him the most. I don't like sleeping anywhere near that thing, even in the room beyond. No one does."

Hahn paused to let this marinate. He wasn't telling Zimmerman anything he didn't know, but it was worth a reminder. The cube was walled off in its own space at the back of a large room, and the colonel had insisted that five soldiers sleep in the outer room. But the cube evoked such primal fear and superstition in the men that they objected even to this arrangement, and Zimmerman was forced to rotate different groups through the assignment, just as he did with the night patrols. Only Hahn slept there every night, ostensibly out of hatred, so this was worth reemphasizing to the colonel.

"So I would love nothing more than to pin this on Otto Richter," continued Hahn, "and then break his scrawny, arrogant neck." He shook his head. "But the boy couldn't possibly have been responsible for this."

"No, Major, *only* he could have been responsible. We've been told his genius is unparalleled. So when the impossible happens, who else could be behind it? And it can't be a coincidence that these two intruders were found in what amount to his private sleeping quarters."

Zimmerman's already grim expression darkened further. "So he stays chained in there," he continued, gesturing toward the small structure out of sight through the trees, which was normally used as his private conference room, but which was now doubling as a prison—and soon an interrogation site.

Hahn thought about where he should go from here, as an owl hooted in the high branches of a massive tree behind him. He had committed unconscionable acts to ingratiate himself with the SS, to ensure that he rose well above any possible suspicion. But all of this effort might quickly unravel if he let this situation get away from him.

"You make some good points, Colonel," he said finally. "Although I don't think the boy is nearly the genius we've been led to believe. But as I told you, I was wide awake the entire night. Couldn't sleep to save my life. And my cot is closest to the cube room. I assure you, sir, I saw no one pass. And I saw no one inside the room when I deposited Otto for the night. And it isn't as if there is anywhere to hide in there."

"We're going in circles, Major," said Zimmerman. "All reason says this couldn't have happened. Yet it did. We just haven't figured out how yet. But it smells very fishy to me. All we know is that they passed our defenses, the soldiers in the outer room, and you, without being detected. But isn't it interesting that they ended up with Otto Richter."

"And also knocked him out," noted Hahn. "He now has a knot on the back of his head. Surely not the act of an ally. Which is why I'm confident we'll find an explanation that doesn't involve the boy. Every magician appears to do the impossible, until his trick is revealed, and the solution becomes obvious."

Light and shadow flickered across the colonel's face, causing his eyes to gleam. "Let me go over this one more time to be sure I have it right," he said. "You were awake, but the men with you were not. No one heard or saw anything, until two loud noises coming from the cube room startled all of you. And, apparently, the noises sounded like two nearly simultaneous cracks of a giant's whip."

"That's what happened," confirmed Hahn.

"Did you find any whips inside the room? Or anything that might account for that particular noise?"

"No. Nothing."

Zimmerman paused in thought. "Well, we're not going to solve this mystery based on what we know now," he said. "So break the men into two groups. I want one group to continue patrolling and trying to find clues as to what happened here, while the other sleeps. With a shift change in four hours. The two of us will alternate shifts also. Is that clear?"

"Yes, sir," said Hahn. "Why don't you get some sleep. I'll take the first shift."

"Not necessary, Major."

"I'm having trouble sleeping, anyway, sir, and in four hours perhaps we'll find something that's worthy of your attention. I'll check in with the prisoners every twenty minutes, and try to rouse them."

The colonel considered. "Okay. But if any one of them regains consciousness, I want you to wake me *immediately*. Don't talk to them, don't interrogate them, just come and get me. Are we clear?"

"Yes, sir."

"And before I return to my quarters," said Zimmerman, "I'll be assigning four of the men to stand guard inside the cube room. Not the outer room, but the Atlantis Room itself. From now on, I want them there, and awake, every night. Otto Richter will no longer sleep there. He'll sleep in the outer room, with you, and won't be allowed near the cube unless supervised by at least three of our men."

He raised his eyebrows. "And this is assuming we clear him of involvement with . . . well, whatever this was tonight."

Hahn stared straight ahead, woodenly, and somehow clamped down on the primal scream that was desperate to erupt. These intruders were ruining *everything*. He wanted to shout his protest of this new edict, but he could hardly argue against it on the grounds that it would ruin his plans to commit treason against the Reich. "I think this is a wise step," he said instead, biting off the words as if they were bitter.

"As soon as both intruders are awake," said the colonel, "we'll begin the interrogation. We'll torture the girl first, in front of her partner. One of them will talk if we have to skin her alive."

Hahn nodded. He was just as eager to learn what the intruders had been up to as the colonel, and he would do whatever it took to clear Otto's name.

"But no matter what," continued Zimmerman, "I want both of them dead by tomorrow night."

"What if they're able to hold out and we don't learn anything?"

The colonel shrugged. "Hard to imagine that will happen," he said. "But if it does, so be it. I don't know how they ended up where they did, but I find them troubling. I want them dead, even if this has to remain a mystery."

"And Otto?"

"We'll see what he has to say for himself. And how it meshes with what *they* say. I'm not a fool, Major. The boy is Reichsfuhrer Himmler's chosen one, as you know. So he dies only if we have incontrovertible evidence of his involvement. And then only if we get the go-ahead from the Reichsfuhrer himself. But if we do have the proper evidence, I won't be shy about recommending the boy's execution."

"And I'll happily add my voice to yours," said Hahn. "This little weasel might pay lip service to Nazi ideals, but we both know he's mocking everything we stand for on the inside. So if you do get permission, I hope that you'll let *me* carry out the execution."

"Perhaps I will, Major. But for now, I'm going to see to it that the cube room is manned at all times, day and night, and then try to get some sleep. Again, let me know the moment you're able to rouse the intruders."

"I will, sir," said Hahn dutifully. He thrust out his right arm. "Heil Hitler."

The colonel thrust out his own right arm, maintaining his grip on the flashlight. "Heil Hitler," he replied.

36

"Otto, wake up!" said a familiar voice coming from light years away, or perhaps from inside Otto's own mind—he couldn't decide. "Wake up," the voice repeated, and Otto felt himself being shaken gently, and then felt cold water being flicked onto his face.

His eyes fluttered open to see Kurt Hahn standing in front of him with a flashlight and canteen of water. A large lantern was on the floor nearby, providing dim illumination to the entire room. Otto felt a throbbing pain at the base of his skull, but when he reached back to explore what it might be, his hand was yanked to a stop.

His mind swam into focus, and he realized he was chained to the floor, causing adrenaline to course through him. "Where am I?" he whispered. "Why am I chained?"

"We had intruders in the cube room," said Hahn. He gestured at the two unconscious prisoners across from Otto. "Here, have a drink," he added, putting the canteen to the boy's lips and pouring gently while moving his own lips inches from Otto's right ear. *"Their loyalties are uncertain,"* he whispered so faintly that he was nearly inaudible. *"Be careful."*

The major finished streaming water slowly into Otto's mouth and screwed the cap back on his canteen. "So tell me what happened," he said, still speaking in low tones, but no longer in a whisper.

"I don't know," replied Otto. "I was working out a physics equation in my head," he lied, taking Hahn's warning seriously. He had actually been experimenting with the active cube, but he wasn't about to admit to that when he might be overheard. "Then, from out of nowhere, the woman over there," he continued, gesturing to the female prisoner across from him, "materialized in front of me. And I mean from out of nowhere. One instant she wasn't there. The next she was. That's it. Then I woke up here."

Hahn studied the adolescent for several long seconds. "We found both of the prisoners in the room with you, and all three of you were out cold. The blow to your head must have caused you to hallucinate."

"It was no hallucination," insisted Otto. "The woman appeared out of nowhere."

"You do know that's impossible?"

"I do," replied the young scientist. "But so is the cube." His jaw tightened. "Believe me, Major, I know what I saw."

Hahn thought about this for a moment and decided to change gears. "Look, Otto, however it happened, Colonel Zimmerman suspects you were working *with* them. Is that true? You need to tell me if it is."

"That's preposterous. Of course I wasn't. No one was more surprised than me."

There was a long silence, until the woman they had thought was unconscious cleared her throat to draw attention to herself. Hahn wheeled around to face her as if he had been struck by a cattle prod.

"We're prepared to talk," she said quickly in English. "Prepared to tell you what this is all about."

"How long have you been awake?" demanded Hahn with a heavy German accent.

"You speak English," said the woman excitedly. "Great! I wasn't sure."

"How long have you been awake?" repeated Hahn.

"Since before you entered."

Hahn turned to face Otto. "I have to go," he said in German. "The colonel insisted he be notified the moment they were conscious. We'll interrogate them and get to the bottom of this. And make sure your name is cleared."

"Wait!" said the male prisoner. "We're ready to talk, but only to the two of you. If you hear us out for five minutes, we promise to tell you everything. Fetch your colonel right now, on the other hand, and we promise the opposite."

"No deal," said Hahn, rising to leave.

"We know a lot about you," said the woman. "You're Major Kurt Hahn, and the young man near you is Otto Richter. Trust me, you're going to want to hear what we have to say."

"How do you know our names!" demanded the SS major.

"We're happy to tell you," said the woman. "But again, *only* you."

"You have five minutes," snapped Hahn.

"Thank you," said the woman in evident relief. "My name is Kelly. Kelly Connolly. And my friend here is Justin Boyd. We're Americans."

"Why are you here?" demanded Hahn. "And how did you get here? And how do you know who we are?"

"I wish we could have a preliminary conversation," said the woman named Kelly. "So we could convince you that we're normal, rational people. But there's no time for that, and no easy way to explain what's going on. So I need you to be as open-minded as you've ever been."

"Go on," said Hahn.

"We know all about your Atlantis Cube," she continued. "We know that it's immovable, unless it's hit with a beam of specific energy. Energy we know that young Otto here managed to generate. Blending principles of relativity, quantum mechanics, and the zero point field."

She paused. "Before I continue, Major Hahn, you sleep closest to the door, so can I assume that you entered the room first?"

Hahn's eyes narrowed. "Just how much do you know about me?" he asked warily.

"Did you enter first?" pressed Kelly.

"Yes."

"Was the cube in its usual place when you did?" she asked. "With light streaming from its corners?"

"It was," confirmed the SS major.

Both American prisoners blew out sighs of relief. "Thank God!" said Kelly for the both of them. "And the generator Otto used to activate it. Were you able to keep it from being discovered, and hide it, as usual? In the hollowed-out section of a fallen tree?"

Hahn gazed at her in disbelief. "Yes," he replied again. "But how can you possibly know all this?"

She nodded at the young man chained to the floor near the SS major. "I learned it from him," she replied simply.

37

Otto Richter noted absently that Kurt Hahn had jerked his head around to stare at him, not knowing what to think, but this didn't impact the delighted grin Otto now wore on his face in the slightest. "So you must be time travelers," he said matter-of-factly. "When you first materialized in the cube room, I had it narrowed down to two possibilities, teleportation or time travel. I have to admit, I was betting on teleportation."

Boyd shook his head in disbelief. "You had these two hypotheses in mind in the fraction of a second between when Kelly startled you and you lost consciousness?"

He shrugged. "They both just jumped into my head. That happens a lot."

"Time travel?" repeated Hahn, his thick German accent offering a stark contrast to the boy's perfect English. "That's ridiculous."

"Maybe," replied Otto, "but it's also obvious. The cube manipulates the fabric of spacetime. So both teleportation and time travel become possible. And maybe even access to higher spatial dimensions."

"Wow," said Boyd simply. "You're every bit the genius Kelly said you were."

"How far in the future are you from?" asked Otto, ignoring the compliment. "And why are you here? Did you invent the cube?"

"They haven't even confirmed they really are from the future," said Hahn, struggling to take it all in, and failing miserably.

Otto couldn't blame him. Unless he had read H.G. Wells's *The Time Machine*, which was highly unlikely, his SS ally hadn't even *imagined* time travel as a possibility.

"There's no other explanation," said Otto. "It accounts for their Houdini entrance, their knowledge of the science behind my generator, their knowledge of us—*everything*."

"You're correct in every regard," said Kelly. "And thanks for catching on so quickly. Saved me a lot of explaining and convincing. Knowing how bright you are, I should have realized that you'd be way ahead of me, but I guess I hadn't thought it through. We're from the year 2027."

"My God," said Hahn, "that's, that's . . ."

"Eighty-four years," said Otto effortlessly. "Eighty-four years in the future. And what a relief to learn that Hitler ultimately fails."

"What makes you think that?" said Hahn.

"They can't even speak German," explained Otto. "Besides, they don't seem to be ruthless psychopaths."

"Thanks," said Kelly with a smile. "That may be the strangest compliment I've ever been given, but I'll take it. But to give you one back, it's beyond extraordinary that you were able to solve the cube. Even in 2027, we were just beginning to get there. That's how far ahead of your time you are."

Otto considered. "You said you learned what you know of us and the cube from me. Given that you look to be between twenty-five and thirty-five, we must not have met until I was quite old. Unless you're much older than I think, and humanity has found a way to stop the aging process?"

"No such luck, I'm afraid."

"Then how do I know you?"

"Good question," said Kelly. "And I have a wild answer for you." She paused for effect. "It turns out that you're my grandfather."

Otto's eyes widened. His first reaction was disbelief, but only for an instant. Why would she lie now?

His initial skepticism was followed immediately by a feeling of exhilaration. He had an actual granddaughter. And one who was arrestingly beautiful.

Knowing that he would have a granddaughter was extraordinarily gratifying, in and of itself, but her presence suggested he had likely married a bright, attractive woman. More importantly, it made it clear that his biggest fear would not come to pass.

He would not die a virgin.

Growing up in Nazi Germany, Otto expected to have a relatively short lifespan. Especially since he was prepared to die to stop the Third Reich. But death wasn't his biggest concern. For several years now, ever since puberty, his biggest fear was to die without ever knowing the touch of a woman, the softness of her skin, the warmth of her embrace.

Despite his unparalleled genius, he was not exempt from normal human needs and desires. He knew full well what was behind them—evolution's inexorable will to drive every animal into reproductive acts to ensure the survival of the species—but this intellectual analysis didn't prevent him from being a slave to his drives just the same. Didn't stop him from longing to experience something that billions of humans had experienced before him.

"So you're a *Connolly*," he said finally, careful not to sound as elated as he felt. "Might be your mother's married name, but it sounds like a name I'd take on as an alias."

"You do catch on fast," she said appreciatively. "Yes, you changed your name to Connolly."

"And you're American," he said. "We're in Canada now. So I must have crossed the border with the cube, as planned, and settled there. Makes sense I'd change my name to something less German under the circumstances."

Otto's elation was short-lived as his mind continued to race ahead. "But you must be aware of the danger of telling me any of this," he said with a frown. "You could change the future in dramatic ways. Much more so than might be readily apparent," he added. "I've come up with a series of equations that suggest even a minor change to the initial conditions of certain complex, dynamic systems can lead to unexpectedly large changes in outcomes."

Kelly nodded in awe. "This is true," she said. "And you've just precisely described what we call *the butterfly effect* from a branch of mathematics called Chaos Theory. You've come up with equations that the rest of humankind won't formalize and refine for decades to come."

She blew out a long breath. "I need to discuss time travel theory and the possible effects on the future our visit might have. But before

I do, I should tell you how we ended up here. I'll make this as quick as possible. To begin with, Otto, we never meet. You steal the cube from the Nazis and hide it in Spokane, Washington. You decide it's too powerful for anyone to have, and employ your descendants as caretakers, in the event that the need to use it becomes unavoidable somewhere down the line. So you write a journal detailing your history. You write of how the SS barged into your home to take you away. You write of your meeting with Himmler. And you write of your time here, including how you discovered that Major Hahn was an ally. Just after he executed a Canadian family who had wandered into your camp."

Hahn grimaced. "That was the most horrific thing I've ever felt forced to do," he whispered. "And that's saying a lot."

"It was despicable," agreed Kelly. "But as you said at the time, there was no way to save them." She lowered her eyes. "And I've felt forced to do some horrific things recently, too. So I'm not sure I'm qualified to judge."

"Do you still doubt that these two are time travelers?" Otto asked his German ally.

"No," said Hahn. "Not at this point."

Kelly continued her brief overview. She told them of how she had unlocked the cube and taken it from a secure government facility, intent on honoring Otto's wishes that no military ever have a chance to use it. Of China, a major superpower in the future, coming after them and the cube. And, finally, of being trapped on an island and threatened with a hydrogen bomb—which she explained was a thousand times more powerful than the atomic bomb Hitler was after—and that time travel had been their only escape.

She only hit the highlights, and her entire story, from start to finish, took less than fifteen minutes.

"Fascinating," said Otto when she was done. "Truly fascinating. But we really do need to turn back to time travel. Your actions here are bound to change history. Have already."

"He's right," said Hahn. "Colonel Zimmerman intends to increase security in the cube room going forward. He's implemented the changes already. Otto will now have to sleep just outside the cube room, where I've been sleeping, and soldiers will now be stationed inside the cube room day and night. Otto will no longer be allowed to even go near the cube unless accompanied by three soldiers. It's become much more unlikely that we'll be able to steal it now. Which means that Otto will never make it to America, never leave the cube there, and never write his journal. Especially in the limited time now available."

"What do you mean, *limited time?*" asked Kelly. "You should have all the time you need—within reason."

"*Should* have," said Otto, who then went on to explain how Alex Wentz was in the process of recreating his work with the generator, putting a loaded gun to their heads with respect to timing.

"Well, isn't this great," said Kelly sarcastically. "Because, you know, things weren't sucking enough."

"Sucking?" said Otto. "Like a vacuum?"

"Never mind," she replied.

"Let's get back to the changes in history that you're causing," said Otto. "They go much deeper than Zimmerman's increased security." He nodded at Kelly. "There is now little chance that you'll be born. But since you haven't vanished, and you know a lot more about this than I do, I must be missing something."

He paused, as if double-checking his analysis. "In my mind, the butterfly effect you spoke of makes it clear that the slightest change in my thinking, the slightest change in even a single minor decision, will lead to dramatically different outcomes. Such as missing a chance encounter with my future wife, perhaps. Or, if I do still meet and marry the same woman, an infinitesimally small change in the time or place of conception will lead to a different sperm winning the race to my wife's egg, resulting in a different child."

He tilted his head in thought. "Unless we're in a closed loop," he said, as if thinking out loud. "One that's played out infinite times. And your presence here is what *causes me* to live out a future that leads to your birth."

"I think we probably are in a closed loop," said Kelly. "But maybe not. History also has an inertia that counteracts the butterfly effect," she said, relying on the information the telepathic AI had planted in her mind as they left Sun Island. "It wants to stick to the path it took before. You can push on the timeline a lot more than you'd think, and history will find a way to repeat itself. You have to do something fairly big, really kick it in the teeth, to get it to change paths."

"Which is counterintuitive," said Otto.

"Very, but that's how it seems to work. With the butterfly effect, small changes get amplified in a big way. You'd think this would be truer than ever with history, but it's the opposite. In many cases, small changes are shrugged off as history fights and claws its way to return to its original path."

Hahn frowned. "I feel like I stepped into an advanced course on this subject," he said, "without taking the introductory one first."

"Sorry," said Kelly. "I can try to simplify things and start from basic principles. Since this will be very relevant to our future decision-making, I think it's worthwhile."

Hahn glanced at his watch, squinting to read it in the dim light. "We have just under three hours before the colonel's shift begins."

"I should only need about ten minutes," said Kelly. "Not that you'll really understand time travel when I'm done. I'm not sure it *can be* fully understood." She gestured toward Otto. "But I do know this, if *anyone* can understand it, it will be my, ah . . . *grandfather*."

38

Kelly was delighted by the young Otto Richter, although it was difficult to get her mind around their relationship. She hadn't compared notes, but she was pretty sure that none of her thirty-year-old peers had an eighteen-year-old grandfather.

Regardless of Otto's appearance and youth, his mental age was staggering. His mind was even more dazzling than she would have thought. There were so many topics she wanted to explore with him, but she was acutely aware that the clock was ticking.

She considered telling him about the telepathic AI that had implanted knowledge of time travel reality into her mind. But explaining the nature of a telepathic artificial intelligence would take too long in an age when the computer had yet to be invented.

In fact, Alan Turing had created the progenitor of the modern computer just a year earlier at Bletchley Park, England, a feat that would lead in no small part to the eventual defeat of the Nazis. This primitive, room-sized computing device had enabled the decryption of the Nazis' secret code, which was also called *Enigma*, but had nothing to do with an alien cube.

Kelly waited for the SS major to reposition his lantern in the center of the small room and then began, drawing on the information the AI had given her, but describing it in her own way. "Ironically enough," she said, "the most famous time travel thought experiment of all is called the *grandfather paradox*. I'm not sure when it first arose, but it's been debated for generations. And the crazy part is that we're more or less recreating it in real life right now."

"Lucky us," mumbled Boyd.

"This is the gist," continued Kelly. "Say you go back in time and kill your grandfather when he's a boy, before he has any children. What then? Well, if you do that, then you never come into existence."

Kelly paused. "I have to admit, I'm not sure why they used a *grand-father* in the thought experiment. Why not just imagine killing your *mother* before she has children? Same result, and a simpler example."

She shrugged. "But anyway, if you kill your grandfather before he has kids, you're never born. But if you're never born, then you can't kill him. But if you can't kill him, you *do* get born, and then you *can* kill him. But if you *do* kill him, you're never born, and you can't again."

"And so on," said Otto.

"And so on," repeated Kelly. "This is just one example of how changing the past can lead to unresolvable paradoxes. And it's easy to come up with endless others. Which has led many scientists to conclude that time travel is impossible. But not all of them. Because there might be ways around the paradoxes.

"One way is to introduce the possibility of multiple timelines, multiple universes. In this scenario, once the grandfather is murdered, the timeline branches into a new universe from that point on. The original universe, the trunk of the tree if you will, remains unchanged. In the new, separate universe, the grandchild never comes into being. But so what? The grandfather can still be murdered by the grandchild from the *original* universe, who can come back just before the branch point to kill him."

Kelly paused. "So if you have two universes," she continued, "you get zero paradoxes. In this scenario, all of the consequences of the murder are shunted off to a new universe."

"But you're about to say it doesn't work like that," said Otto.

"That's right. There is only a single timeline, and a single universe. No branches. But still no paradoxes. Because it turns out the universe stubbornly refuses to allow them, no matter what rules of logic it has to break."

"I see," said Otto thoughtfully.

"I don't," said Justin Boyd.

"It works like this," said Kelly. "Go back in time and kill your young grandfather. He never has a son, so you're never born. But it doesn't matter. The sole timeline, the sole universe, is rewritten going forward because of your actions. Even so, you remain as a fully formed adult. Just because you were never conceived in the rewritten timeline doesn't matter. You don't vanish from reality."

She raised her eyebrows. "You could even say that you're . . . *grandfathered* in. Whatever exists in the universe exists, even if it violates cause and effect. Even if it violates all logic."

"So even though you were never born," said Boyd, "the universe just ignores this inconvenient truth. It refuses to react as if it's a paradox."

Kelly nodded.

"Given only one timeline," said Otto, "one universe, this raises the stakes substantially. Because if you change history, the consequences don't just branch off into a new timeline. The one true universe is stuck with them."

"That's right," said Kelly. "Unless you create a recursive loop, which keeps the changes confined. As you said, Otto, unless the changes in the past actually create a future that leads back to the changes in the past."

"What?" said Hahn in utter confusion.

"Say I'm sitting in a room in the year 2000," said Kelly, "when a 2003 version of me, wearing a blue shirt, barges in and hands me instructions for how to build a time machine. I spend the next three years building it. When it's done, in 2003, *I* put on a blue shirt and visit the me in 2000, handing her the instructions to build the thing."

Kelly raised her eyebrows. "So who invented it in the first place?"

She waited for Hahn and Boyd to consider this, knowing that Otto had been way ahead of her from her first sentence. "The answer is that *no one* did," she said finally. "At least within this loop. But it *was* invented. It had to be. Only it must have been invented in a *different* version of the timeline.

"Maybe originally, after decades of toil, I invented a time machine in the year 2040, and then came back to 2000 to give myself the instructions. This would then change history. Now that young me has the instructions, she can make the time machine come into being by 2003, instead of 2040—which kicks off the infinite recursive loop. The version of me who toiled to invent it never comes into existence.

Still, she is grandfathered in and still exists, but leaves an infinite recursive loop in her wake."

"And you think we might be in one of these loops?" said Boyd.

"Maybe," replied Kelly. "Otto, you write in your journal that you have no memory of several months' time leading up to Spokane. Which is why I had no idea that another scientist had found your notes on the generator and is racing to complete it.

"You write that you find yourself in Spokane, with no awareness of how you got there. So maybe you were just covering for our visit. Maybe you were aware of what happened tonight when you wrote the journal. And you purposely left out that you met me, along with everything else you now know about our future, so history repeats itself in an endless loop."

"But we can't be sure of that," said Boyd. "This could be the first and only time any of this has happened. Otto suspected in his journal that being exposed to the active cube for a long while is what led to his memory loss. This could also be true."

"Agreed," said Otto. "So let's analyze both possibilities, using Kelly as the subject of the thought experiment. If we are in a loop, and history repeats itself exactly, Kelly will be born again in our future. She'll grow up. She'll travel from 2027 to 1943. And once in this time, she'll kick off the very events that will lead to the cycle repeating. Which, presumably, she's doing now. In this case, despite being born in the nineties, she'll live out the rest of her life in this time period.

"If we *aren't* in a loop," continued Otto, "your presence here will change the future. Assuming the changes are big enough to overcome the inertia of history, then I'll likely marry someone different this time. Or the wrong sperm will hit the wrong egg. Either way, this time Kelly is never born. But as she said, the universe doesn't care. She's here now, so will remain here. She doesn't vanish."

"So both outcomes are the same," said Boyd in astonishment. "Either way, she lives out her life in this time period."

"Actually, it's stranger than that," said Kelly. "Because there are a few relevant points I haven't shared with Otto. The cube will allow you to travel into the future. But only as far ahead in time as any version of you has ever been. And it won't allow two versions of the same person to exist at the same time."

"You're saying that the *cube* won't allow it," noted Otto. "Meaning the builders of the cube won't. That isn't the same as saying the laws of physics won't allow it."

"I think that's right," said Kelly. "But until we can invent time travel on our own, we're reliant on the cube. And its rules mean, ironically enough, that if our presence here changes the future, such that I never get born again in 1997, the cube *will* send me back to 2027. Because I'd be the only version of me there.

"On the other hand," she continued, "if I *am* born as before, then, ironically, my presence in the future blocks me from traveling there. So I end up trapped here for the rest of my life."

"Wow," said Otto in fascination. "Didn't see that coming."

"And the same would apply to me," said Boyd. "If Kelly isn't born, the me in the future doesn't meet her. So I never end up here. But if she is born, I do—and I'm just as stranded."

Kelly winced. "Sorry about that."

Boyd appeared lost in thought. "If this happens," he said, "I'll let you make it up to me."

"How?"

"If we're stranded here together," he replied, "you have to promise to marry me."

Kelly looked stunned. "I know we, ah . . . *necked* in the car," she said, purposely using the most innocent, old-fashioned word she could find. "But aren't you pushing this relationship a little fast?"

"No doubt about it. I'm aware that we don't love each other. Well—yet. But if we're banished here forever, we'd have to stay out of the limelight so as not to change the future. And who else is going to understand us, other than *us*? Talk about people not getting our pop culture or tech references. Believe me, we're both going to want to be able to share our lives with the only other person in the world who knows our secret, who knows our *era*. If not, we'll lose our minds."

"I'll be damned," said Kelly. "You make a strong case." She paused in thought. "Okay, if we do get stranded in this time period forever, marriage it is."

"Are you two *finished*?" said Hahn irritably, shaking his head. "You're in a top-secret Nazi base in chains, not on a date. You do know that other things are going on here, right?"

"Right," said Boyd. "Sorry. How much time until the shift change?"

Hahn consulted his watch. "Just over two hours."

Boyd pursed his lips in thought. "I say we make our move right now. There's a lot of chaos out there. Your men are reacting to the surprise of our arrival. We should strike while they're still preoccupied. If we can get an active cube into Kelly's hands, we can destroy this encampment like you planned. And then get Otto's ass to Spokane, Washington."

The SS major stared at his American counterpart in thought.

"If it helps," added Boyd, "I'm pretty handy in a fight."

"You have *no* idea," Kelly said to the two Germans. When she had described how she and Boyd had ended up in the past, she had purposely failed to mention her companion's enhancements. "Training techniques and physical conditioning have come a long way in eighty years."

"I do like the idea of striking now," said Hahn. "The problem is that I don't have the key to any of the cuffs. Zimmerman does. And trust me, not even Harry Houdini could pick the locks on these."

"So sneak into Zimmerman's quarters and strangle him," said Boyd, as casually as if he were ordering from a takeout menu. "Then bring the keys and a backpack full of guns and grenades back here. We'll fight our way into the cube room. Then we just have to keep your people at bay for a few minutes while Kelly does her thing."

"Does her thing?" said Hahn in confusion.

"Uses the cube to end the conflict," said Boyd.

Hahn paused in thought for several seconds. "Otto?" he said. "What do you think?"

"It's a tough call," replied the eighteen-year-old. "There are extra soldiers awake tonight, and they're agitated. It might be best to wait until tomorrow night, when things have settled back down."

Hahn frowned. "*Scheisse*!" he said miserably. "I just remembered. We can't wait until tomorrow night. The colonel plans on killing these two by then, no matter what. So it really is now or never."

Before this sentence was even finished, the door burst open, and a tall, imposing man in a colonel's uniform entered with a lower-ranked soldier on either side, all three holding guns pointed at Kurt Hahn.

"*What* is now or never, Major Hahn?" demanded Zimmerman in English.

He then switched to German and continued. "And think very hard before you reply," he said, "because your life is riding on the answer."

39

"Stand against the wall, Major!" ordered the colonel as he placed a second lantern beside the first, increasing the illumination inside the room considerably. He motioned for Hahn to stand just to the left of where Otto Richter was seated on the floor.

Sage transmitted the translation of these words into the comms of the two Americans, as she had done previously when Hahn and Otto had been speaking to each other in German.

Boyd desperately wanted to intervene but couldn't until he learned more about what the German colonel knew.

Kurt Hahn was frozen, but only for a moment. His fearful expression turned into one of irritation, even anger, as he pressed his back against the wall. "Colonel, what is going on here?" he said. "Is this how you repay my loyal service? With suspicions, threats, and guns in my face?"

"Save your indignation, Major, and answer my question. Yes, you've been loyal. A model officer. But odd things are happening tonight, with their arrival," he said, gesturing to the two American prisoners. "So all bets are off."

Hahn stared deeply into his commanding officer's eyes, not backing down. "I was just about to get you, Colonel," he said. "I was telling the prisoners that I'd try to persuade you to show mercy if they cooperated. But that they would only have one chance to avoid torture. It was now or never."

"Why don't I believe you?" said Zimmerman. "Oh, right, because I gave you explicit orders to alert me the *moment* either of them regained consciousness. And I know you understood the order."

"Sir, I—"

"Not another word!" barked Zimmerman. "I couldn't sleep, so I checked on the men. And I ran into Sergeant Vogel. He told me he heard you speaking with the prisoners twenty minutes ago, and that you were keeping your voices low. Twenty minutes ago! It could have begun sooner than that for all I know. Vogel could tell you were conversing in English, even though he doesn't speak it. And he said it sounded more like a *tea party* than an interrogation."

The SS colonel paused, fuming. "So how do you explain it?" he demanded. "Are you working with the prisoners?" He gestured to Otto. "Are all *four* of you working together?"

Hahn's eyes were wild, and Boyd could tell his mind was racing.

"This is my fault, Colonel Zimmerman," said the American major from out of the blue.

Zimmerman rushed across the six feet of floor separating him from Justin Boyd and drove his boot into the prisoner's gut. Boyd gasped, fell to his side, and clutched at his stomach, dragging his chains along as he did. If not for his genetically modified muscles, increased pain tolerance, and oxygen-rich respirocytes, he would have been gasping for breath and moaning in agony.

"Did I say you could speak?" hissed the colonel in English, his accent as thick as Kurt Hahn's. "Right now, I'm trying to find out why the major disobeyed a direct order. And why you and he seem so . . . chummy."

Boyd knew he had to risk the boot again, or worse. He had been putting the finishing touches on a backstory just before Hahn had entered, and he was the only one who could get them out of this.

"He failed to follow orders because of me," said Boyd as quickly as possible. "I had him mesmerized. Not his fault."

Boyd waited for another kick, but it didn't come, either because his words were sinking in, or Zimmerman was impressed that his prisoner had the balls to speak again after being savagely attacked. "He wanted to get you," continued the American, "but I controlled his mind so he didn't."

The colonel's restraint was short lived as he suddenly kicked Boyd a second time, just as ferociously. But this time Boyd was prepared. He coughed weakly and pretended to be more hurt than he was. "Not a great way to treat the man who will win this war for Germany," he croaked. "Kick me again and I won't tell you how. Instead of being rewarded by your Fuhrer, you'll earn an execution."

Zimmerman's eyes narrowed, and he studied Boyd like he was a particularly venomous snake. "You must have a death wish," he growled.

"I have a wish for *glory*. And there's enough of that for both of us to share."

"You're insane," said the SS colonel, but Boyd could tell he was now intrigued.

"Am I? If I'm so insane, how did my wife and I make it past your guards?"

"Only to promptly pass out," said Zimmerman. "All in all, an unimpressive effort."

"I know you don't mean that," said Boyd. "Assist me, and I'll see to it that you become part of the Fuhrer's inner circle."

When Zimmerman didn't respond, he hurriedly continued. "My name is Justin Boyd, and this is my wife, Kelly Boyd," he said. "We're Canadians."

"Get lost on a hike?" said Zimmerman, crouching down and leaning close to the prisoners. His lip curled up in disgust. "And why are you both dressed in black sweatshirts and blue jeans? And unusual ones at that. Is this some kind of uniform?"

Boyd sighed. "Not a uniform. Just very comfortable. And my wife likes it when we wear matching clothing."

Zimmerman shook his head. "You really expect me to believe that *you're* the man who can turn the tide of the war?"

"Even the strongest man indulges the whims of his woman, Herr Colonel. Even at the expense of looking like a fool."

Zimmerman smiled. "You have balls, Justin Boyd, whoever you are."

"I also have skills. And so does my wife. That's how we met. In a group of Canadian clairvoyants."

"Clairvoyants? Like *seeing the future* clairvoyants?"

"Yes. And I can see the future with greater clarity than anyone who ever lived," said Boyd boldly.

"I am so disappointed, Herr Boyd," said the SS colonel in disgust. "I really hoped you had something real to tell me. But this is *Scheisse*! I don't believe in the supernatural. So tell me what you're really doing here, or your wife will be dead in *minutes*."

Saying this, his arm shot out in the blink of an eye, savagely back-handing Kelly across the face, drawing blood.

Boyd hurled himself against his restraints so forcefully it seemed like the building itself might come down, but he was stopped just short of contact with the colonel, like a rabid lion charging a zoo visitor just beyond his range.

"You have very strong feelings for this woman, don't you?" said Zimmerman. "Are you sure she's your wife and not your mistress?" he added, grinning at his own joke.

His smile vanished, to be replaced by a scowl. "But it occurs to me, Herr Boyd, that I'm making the wrong threat. How about this one? Stop trying my patience or I'll do *worse* than kill her. I'll give her to my men to pass around like a cheap cigar. Am I clear?"

"If you or any of your men ever touch her again," hissed Boyd, his eyes burning with enough intensity to melt lead, "I'll see to it that the Fuhrer douses you with gasoline and sets you on fire."

"Are you actually *threatening* me?"

"You may not believe in clairvoyance, but Himmler and your Fuhrer both do. *Strongly*. And when I prove my abilities, I'll become your Fuhrer's right-hand man. We both know that if not for Erik Jan Hanussen, Adolph Hitler's reign would never have even begun. Well, I make Hanussen look like a two-bit tarot card reader."

Boyd had at first considered telling the truth to explain their presence, at least a doctored version, but had discarded this idea for numerous reasons. Most importantly, convincing the Nazis that he had traveled through time was more likely to rewrite the future, as Sage had found no records of any such claim. She had found endless records of claims of clairvoyance, on the other hand.

Erik Jan Hanussen had been a famous con man and performer in the 1920s, who had billed himself as a clairvoyant. In March of 1932, when Hitler's political future was teetering on the edge of a cliff,

Hanussen claimed to foresee the resurgence of the Nazi Party, bailing Hitler out and becoming his confidant.

Then, in 1933, Hanussen correctly predicted an arson attack on the German parliament, which came to be known as the *Reichstag fire*. Hitler blamed the attack on communist agitators and clamped down on civil rights, which allowed him to seize absolute power.

Historians later suspected that the fire was a false flag operation spearheaded by Hitler himself, and that Hanussen's prediction was based on insider information. Hanussen was assassinated days later, either because of his knowledge of who had really ordered the fire, or because Göring and Goebbels were threatened by his growing closeness with Chancellor Hitler.

"I'm sure you're well aware of the influence Hanussen had on your Fuhrer," continued Boyd. "Well, *my* influence will be ten times as great. Believe me, you want me as your friend, not your enemy."

Zimmerman paused in thought for several long seconds, and Boyd couldn't guess how he might respond. The smart play for him would be to hear Boyd out, on the remote chance he could back up his claims. The colonel had nothing to lose. If Boyd failed, the SS colonel could always have him tortured and killed.

"Okay, Herr Boyd," said the colonel. "I'll listen. But you'd better get to your proof quickly."

Boyd could detect a subtle release of tension in his three fellow captives, one that he fully shared. He knew this had been a close call, and he had made it worse by not being able to control his rage when Kelly Connolly had been brought into the line of fire.

"My wife and I together are even more clairvoyant than we are apart," said Boyd. "It amplifies itself. My clairvoyance kept pushing me to come here. I had no idea where *here* was, and still don't. But I knew the general area, and my gifts guided me to this location."

He paused. "And now I know why. For two reasons. First, I've long been eager to join the Nazi war effort. My own people have no appreciation for the occult. But yours do. Your Fuhrer will take me as seriously as I deserve, and will offer the rewards that I deserve. When Germany controls the entire world, Kelly and I will be supported, will be encouraged to hone our abilities. Which is something we've long wanted. I didn't know I was walking into a Nazi camp, but my intuition knew. It was following a higher occult power."

Boyd paused to let this sink in. "But the second reason I had a calling to come here is even more shocking to me. When we got closer and closer to this site, our psychic powers increased dramatically. When we were about a hundred yards away, we were thrown into a trance. This higher power took over, directing us when to move, when to pause, and where to step. We were able to slip past your people undetected because we were guided by supernatural forces."

Zimmerman rolled his eyes but didn't interrupt.

"Then, when we entered the final room," continued Boyd, "the indescribable happened. We were bombarded by light, and we both had the same vision. It was a vision of a small cube, but one that pulsed, *throbbed*, with extraordinary energies. It was dazzling. And it charged up our powers to impossible heights. I was clairvoyant before, but now I'm a seer beyond all seers. I'm able to see every future battle, every surprise attack, every pivotal moment in the days and years ahead. Thanks to the incomprehensible psychic energy in that room, with me at Hitler's side, Germany can't lose."

"As long as you don't keep passing out," said Zimmerman dryly.

"Absorbing this energy was like drinking from Niagara Falls," explained Boyd. "Our minds almost exploded. As I was losing consciousness, I tripped a young man who was already in the room and knocked him out. This was accidental, I assure you."

The colonel considered. "And that's your entire story?"

"Almost," said Boyd. "When Major Hahn entered this room, I mesmerized him. So he would tell us about you, yes, but mostly so he would regale us with what he knows about the mystical beliefs of the members of your High Command. He wanted to alert you that we had awakened, but I was too eager to satisfy my curiosity. I had no idea this would get him in hot water. But he had no free will. He was completely under my control."

"You really must think I'm a fool," said Zimmerman. "If you were able to do something like this, you'd have seized control of me already."

"No need," said Boyd. "I saw the future and knew you would come around. And controlling him weakened me considerably. Besides," he added, "it's a lot harder to influence a mind as strong as yours."

"Flattery now?" said the colonel. "Or just more stalling? It's time for you to convince me of your clairvoyance. I won't ask again."

"What's today's date?" asked Boyd.

"You don't know?"

"We hiked for many days. I just want to be sure."

Zimmerman told him.

"Give me a moment to find the most important vision to share," said Boyd, closing his eyes.

"Sage," he said subvocally, *"I need a short list of World War II battles and engagements that will happen within the next twelve hours. Immediately!"*

"Understood," replied Sage. *"I'm displaying them on your lenses now."*

Boyd swayed back and forth, as though in a trance, while choosing an entry and expanding upon it. Seconds later he stopped his swaying and opened his eyes, facing Zimmerman.

"Okay, Colonel," he said. "I've seen the future, clear as a bell. The allies will be raiding one of your most important submarine bases tomorrow—in Naples, Italy. A surprise attack initiated by hundreds of American B-17 bombers." He squinted as if trying to see something far away. "The Church of *Santa Chiara* and the *Santa Maria di Loreto* hospital will be destroyed in the raid, as well."

Boyd sighed and tried to look woozy. "That's all I see for now. But you need to transmit this information to your people in Naples immediately. If they act now, they'll be able to thwart the attack."

Zimmerman shook his head. "I don't know what game you're playing," he said derisively, "but there's no way I'm telling my superiors about this supposed attack on your word alone. When the attack doesn't happen, I'll be the gullible fool who raised a false alarm and caused unnecessary redeployments."

He pulled a handgun from his holster and shoved the barrel against Boyd's forehead. "Much simpler just to kill you now!" he said icily. "Bet you didn't see *that* coming?"

Boyd forced a relaxed smile. "Actually, I did," he said calmly. "And you won't pull that trigger. The Naples raid is going to happen tomorrow. *Guaranteed.* And you know that if it does, if I prove I can foresee every attack before it happens, this war is as good as over.

"If I'm right," he continued boldly, ignoring the presence of the gun digging into his skin, "all I ask is that you bring me to your superiors' attention. In exchange, I'll bring you into the High Command."

Boyd paused. "If I'm wrong, on the other hand, kill me and my wife in the most horrible way you can think of." He shrugged. "Or let your men pass her around like a cheap cigar. *That's* how sure I am."

Zimmerman's eyes narrowed in thought.

A fearful intensity came over the American major. "But it goes without saying," he hissed, "that if anyone lays a hand on me in the meanwhile, or even *thinks* about laying a hand on my wife, the deal is off."

The colonel studied him for several long seconds and then reholstered his gun. "Agreed," he said simply.

Zimmerman turned to the two SS soldiers. "Get them water," he ordered in German. "Chain Major Hahn along with them, and make sure they're all gagged. They stay here until I get word on the goings-on in Naples. Post a three-man guard outside."

"I don't understand, Colonel," said Hahn. "I'm your most loyal man. You know that."

"I've always thought so, Major. And if Herr Boyd is right, and the Naples attack happens, I'll believe you behaved the way you did because you were under a spell. But until then, you aren't going anywhere."

"And if I have to pee?" asked Hahn.

"Pee on yourself," said Zimmerman callously. "It'll help keep you warm."

40

The prisoners slept fitfully, their shackles and gags not lending themselves to slumber.

The emergence of dawn came as a relief, and even though several soldiers came for them before noon, the wait seemed endless. Boyd used Sage to communicate subvocally with Kelly just enough to keep her spirits up, and to share the time, since without this knowledge he knew its passage would seem interminable to her. If only she hadn't been gagged, they could have had a two-way conversation, but this was not to be.

Boyd watched several World War II documentaries on his lenses as time marched on, and he read a number of detailed summaries and analyses of the war, knowing that much more than their lives might ride on this knowledge. Projections onto his contacts required only a trickle of power, but he hated to use any.

At long last four SS soldiers unchained them and pulled them from the room, removing their gags and the shackles around their ankles, but leaving their hands cuffed. They led the prisoners away from the encampment, past scientists who were conversing and preparing additional useless experiments to try on the cube.

"Wait here, Herr Boyd," said one of the men in German when they had reached a nearby clearing, devoid of human activity. "I'm taking the other prisoners to use the outhouse and for food. You'll be next. And then Colonel Zimmerman will join you."

Kurt Hahn translated for the two Americans, not knowing that Boyd had a magical device affixed to his thigh that could translate German and communicate with Kelly, in addition to numerous other capabilities he would find nearly impossible to believe.

The guard led the other prisoners away, leaving Boyd with three SS soldiers alone in the small clearing. They each eyed him with what looked like utter contempt.

"Do any of you speak English?" asked the American prisoner after several long seconds of tense silence. There was no response, or even any indication that he had been heard.

"You guys don't happen to know *edelweiss* from the *Sound of Music* do you?" continued Boyd to amuse himself. "It's a movie—a period piece," he added helpfully, making sure not to mention that the Nazis were the villains. "We could do a singalong."

The soldiers' scowls intensified. "By making into Atlantis Room," said one of the three in broken English. "We look like *fools. Du wirst zahlen!*" he finished, which Sage translated as *you will pay.*

Before Boyd could digest these words, the soldier delivered a savage, viper-like strike at his skull with the butt of his automatic rifle—but Boyd's skull had moved in the fraction of a second it took for the blow to arrive, and the German hit nothing but air.

Astonished, as if he had witnessed an optical illusion, the soldier instantly followed up with two additional lightning-fast thrusts of his rifle, which Boyd also dodged with superhuman agility. The American's enhanced musculature and reaction time made the athletic soldier appear to be moving in slow motion, and Boyd deftly sidestepped a fourth jab while sweeping the soldier's feet out from under him.

The two other soldiers charged at the prisoner, and even though Boyd's hands were locked together, he easily blocked an incoming fist and spun around to dodge a knife coming toward his leg, elbowing one of the men in the face, blocking a second blow, and sweeping one of the two men to the ground. The only German left standing tried to dive on Boyd and turn it into a wrestling match, but the American sidestepped the dive and used the man's momentum against him, driving him into the ground.

The first soldier sprang to his feet to reengage when the voice of Bruno Zimmerman bellowed through the woods. "*Enough!*" he shouted in German. "Disengage!"

The SS colonel entered the small clearing with a gun shoved into Kelly Connolly's back. "Nicely done, Herr Boyd," he said. "Now raise your hands while my men retrieve their weapons and retreat."

Boyd smiled. "Of course, Colonel. We were just getting some exercise."

Zimmerman allowed himself an icy smile as his men hastily retreated to a safe distance. Two more soldiers entered the clearing and escorted Major Hahn and Kelly Connolly to Boyd's side, but Otto was not in sight.

"What is this all about, Colonel?" asked Boyd.

"Your prediction has been confirmed," said Zimmerman. "The submarine base in Naples was attacked exactly as you described."

"I never had a doubt," said Boyd. "So why did your men attack me? I've proven to be what I say I am, the greatest weapon your Fuhrer could ever want. Surely you can trust me now."

Zimmerman shook his head. "Less now than ever before, Herr Boyd."

"I don't understand."

"Of course you do," said the colonel. "You made a prediction that turned out to be uncannily accurate. So there are two possible explanations. One, that you're clairvoyant, as you say. Or two, that you're a talented spy, a key piece in a game of chess being played by the Allies. They simply had to feed you detailed intel on their Naples operation so you could *prove* your supernatural abilities. Taking special care to obliterate a church and a hospital to make your details come to life."

"You'll believe anything rather than admit clairvoyance is real, won't you?" said Boyd sadly.

"A brilliant plan, really," continued the colonel as if Boyd hadn't spoken. "The Allies are well aware of the superstitions of many of our leaders. And they risk very little by letting you spill the Naples operation, since only a fool would believe you. So you get to establish your credentials without paying any military cost. Sell your wild story. Ingratiate yourself. Burrow your way into our High Command. The perfect double agent."

Boyd looked disgusted. "If you think this is the case, I can provide another demonstration. And another. Eventually, even you'll have to admit the truth."

"I don't have time to play games," said Zimmerman. "So I've seen to it that you're now the Reichsfuhrer's problem. Because you made a mistake, Herr Boyd. You were far too bold last night. No Canadian civilian throws himself at me when he's chained, outmanned, and outgunned. Not even battle-tested soldiers would have this kind of arrogance."

He paused to let this to sink in. "So I set up a little experiment of my own just now. Had my three best hand-to-hand fighters attack you, with orders not to kill, but at least put you down. I predicted you'd prevail, even cuffed. But I didn't predict just how effortlessly you would do it.

"I've never seen any man move with such speed, grace, and decisiveness. I'm pretty sure you could have bested *ten* of my soldiers. Which makes sense. My guess is that you're really an American officer, spy, and commando. For an operation designed to place you into the heart of the Fuhrer's inner circle, I would expect the Americans to send their very best man."

Boyd frowned deeply, furious with himself. Maybe it was the aftereffects of time travel, but he had been uncharacteristically sloppy. First, he had exactly mirrored the mistake Kelly had made on Sun Island, when she had let their Chinese captors know how much Boyd meant to her.

But she had made this mistake as an inexperienced civilian. His lapse was unforgivable.

And now this. He should have realized he was being tested. He would have if he had been up against a colonel from his own time. But he had let down his guard here. Just because a man lived in primitive times and was part of a barbaric movement didn't make him *stupid*.

"I see why you're so misguided," said Boyd calmly, trying to salvage the situation. "First, I have to admit to being a hothead. Even so, I normally would have been cowering in fear last night. But the power I absorbed in that room was exhilarating. I was a little bit drunk with it. I felt *invincible*."

He paused. "Second, I'm a true seer. When your soldiers attacked me, I knew what moves they were going to make before *they* did. Do you really think the most gifted clairvoyant on Earth could be beaten by a few men? Foresight is the ultimate advantage in hand-to-hand combat."

"You didn't foresee my boot," said Zimmerman.

"Of course I did," said Boyd. "But I was chained to the floor. How was I going to dodge it?"

The colonel paused for almost a minute in thought. Boyd knew he hadn't been expected to put on a defense, especially one that made sense.

"This may be true," said Zimmerman finally. "You may be exactly what you say. But it's now out of my hands. I've transmitted details on everything that happened here to Reichsfuhrer Himmler. I told him of my concerns, and he is eager to sort things out. I'm either sending him a brilliant clairvoyant," he added, "or a master spy. Either way, he's sure to find you useful.

"As it happens," continued the colonel, "a long-range transport plane was scheduled to arrive here tonight to drop off supplies. But rather than head back empty, as had been the plan, it will now carry three passengers. You and Major Hahn will be flying to Berlin in the cargo compartment, and your wife in the cockpit. If you try to resist us at any time, your wife will pay the price. If you *are* a spy, she probably *isn't* your wife. But I know that whoever she is, she means a lot to you."

"Colonel?" said Hahn, his tone almost pleading. "Request permission to stay here."

"Sorry, Major, your request is denied. Until we're certain his story checks out, you continue to be under suspicion, and will continue to be a prisoner. If his story checks out, I will personally see to it that you get a well-deserved promotion."

Justin Boyd gritted his teeth, disgusted with how this was turning out. His backstory had backfired in a big way. Scientist and Nazi loyalist Alex Wentz was maybe days away from solving the cube. Otto

Richter was under intense scrutiny. And he and Kelly were being banished to Germany, taking Otto's only ally along with them.

Still, he knew that there hadn't been another choice. Zimmerman had been intent on killing them while they were helpless, and this had been their only way out. Theirs and Kurt Hahn's both, since he had been sinking fast before Boyd had interjected. Still, they were now heading thousands of miles in the wrong direction, and would need to return in a hurry.

"What of the boy who was chained in the room with us?" asked Kelly. "Why is a sixteen-year-old even at this encampment? And why are you punishing him? He did nothing but get knocked unconscious."

"He is *eighteen*," said Zimmerman. "And he will be restored to his former duties. We'll just be keeping a more careful eye on him from here on out. And this is your fault for exposing the vulnerabilities in our security. Normally, I'd be worried that you know our location. But since neither of you will ever be out of sight of the SS unless you've proven yourselves beyond all doubt, I will continue to sleep soundly."

"You should, Herr Colonel," said Boyd. "Because soon I'll be guiding your Fuhrer and High Command, and this war will be over quite quickly."

PART 7

"Fairy tales do not tell children that monsters exist.
Children already know that monsters exist.
Fairy tales tell children that monsters can be *killed*."

—G.K. Chesterton, (English writer and philosopher)

41

Major Justin Boyd awoke on a hard cot and took in his surroundings. He was shackled to a concrete floor once again, but this time inside a dim, dreary prison cell that looked ancient, exactly the way he imagined a medieval dungeon might appear, except it wasn't underground.

The cell was tiny, illuminated by a single low-watt bulb out of reach in the ceiling above, with bars extending deep into concrete walls, and a tiny, barred window to the outside that was too small to wriggle through, even if the bars were absent.

Even so, given his shackles, the Nazis had decided the prison cell alone wasn't enough to contain him. Zimmerman must have made sure that news of Boyd's extraordinary combat skills, and his likely identity as an enemy spy, had arrived long before he had.

Boyd had no memory of his recent trip, just of ten hours of solitude in Canada before the long-range transport plane had arrived. He had read for most of this time, having Sage display the parts of Otto's journal having to do with the Nazis on his lenses, along with as much information on the war and key players as he could possibly suck in.

After being chained inside the plane, an injection had been administered to knock him out, and he made the trip unconscious, the same way he had traveled to Sun Island. In all his years as an enhanced commando, he had never been drugged into unconsciousness a single time, and now it seemed as though it was becoming a daily occurrence. This time, however, he was grateful. He had no interest in staying awake for twenty-five to thirty hours of cramped, chained travel.

The major rose and walked to the tight bars in front of him, his chain providing plenty of slack, and was able to make out almost a dozen additional prison cells, all of them empty.

He looked through the tiny window to a dark, starless sky, although the grounds were surprisingly well lighted. He could make out two medieval guard towers and at least three nested layers of unclimbable walls, the last two of which were topped with electric wire and barbed wire, respectively. But just like the inside, the grounds appeared to be deserted.

"*Can you identify this place?*" he said subvocally to Sage.

"*Yes. Based on your visual input, there is a greater than ninety percent likelihood that you are in Spandau Prison in western Berlin, which was built in 1876.*"

"*Why does it seem deserted?*"

"*It was last fully occupied in 1933,*" reported the AI. "*Adolf Hitler used the Reichstag fire that year as a pretext to round up journalists and other opponents and put them here in what he called protective custody. The Gestapo also used this prison to torture enemies. But in 1933, the first Nazi concentration camps were completed at Dachau and other locations, and all Spandau prisoners were transferred to these sites.*"

As Sage was finishing her reply, an SS captain marched into Boyd's view wearing a neatly pressed uniform. "Welcome to Berlin, Herr Boyd," the man said with a heavy accent. "My name is Eckhart Pelzer."

"How did you know I was awake?"

"I've been checking every fifteen minutes," replied Pelzer. "I'll have some food and water brought in right away."

Boyd considered him carefully. "I'm surprised you know English."

"One of the reasons I was assigned to this duty. I'm told you've attracted very rarefied attention, Herr Boyd, but that no one is sure what to make of you. You could be a hated enemy, or a highly valued guest. So I've been told to treat you as well as possible under the circumstances."

"Does that include reopening Spandau Prison just for me?"

Pelzer smiled. "Very temporarily, I assure you. And if you prove yourself, I'm told you'll be treated like a king. For the time being, I can make sure you get high-quality food, and have your shackles removed long enough for you to shower. When you're finished, I can give you fresh underclothes and have your outfit washed and pressed. Looks like you've, ah . . . lived in those clothes for quite a while."

An image of a woman sitting at a soapy washboard and bucket flashed into Boyd's mind. *"When were electric washing machines invented?"* he asked Sage subvocally.

"1908," replied the AI immediately.

I'll be damned, thought Boyd. "That would be appreciated, Captain," he said out loud.

"I've seen jeans and sweatshirts before," said Pelzer, "but never any like yours."

"Well, you know what they say," replied the American prisoner, barely managing to keep a straight face. "Canada is the undisputed fashion capital of the world."

Boyd's eyes narrowed, and his expression became gravely serious. "There was a woman who was flown to Berlin on the same plane I was," he added. "My, ah . . . wife. Where is she?"

"She's been taken to Rolling Hills Mansion, a more comfortable, secluded estate about thirty miles from Berlin. She'll be well treated while we . . . evaluate your situation. As long as you cooperate, of course."

"Of course," repeated Boyd.

"An SS general is on his way here and will arrive before dawn. I'm told that if you prove yourself to him, you'll be joining your wife within just a few days."

"I'll look forward to that," replied Boyd. "And what of Major Hahn? He was also on the plane with us."

"He's at Rolling Hills Mansion, as well. In a different wing than your wife. He's had a distinguished career, and is only under suspicion, so he's entitled to civilized treatment. Not that the mansion isn't extremely well guarded. You'd be there, too, except that Colonel Zimmerman thinks you could take out an entire platoon single-handedly, and he warned us to be very, very careful with you."

Boyd had known the Germans would still be wary of him, thinking he was much more likely a spy than a seer. The quicker he could reverse this perception and get them to lower their guard, even slightly, the sooner he could reunite with Kelly and escape back to Canada.

To do this, he had to find ways to accurately predict the future without harming the Allies or changing history, a difficult task. During his long wait for the transport plane, he had searched for just the right piece of intel to offer up on his arrival in Germany, based on a rough estimate of how long the travel would take.

He had hoped to find an Allied attack that had failed, so that tipping the Germans off wouldn't change things. Instead, he had stumbled upon something that would serve even better, occurring in the German occupied territory of Norway. As long as he wasn't speaking to a member of the German High Command. And assuming he arrived before it happened—which still remained to be seen.

"What time is it?" he asked the captain.

"Just before eleven p.m."

Perfect! thought Boyd. He had made it here with four hours to spare. "Then we're in luck," he said aloud. "There's still time."

"Time for what?"

"I realize I'm supposed to prove myself to the general who is on his way. But I've seen a future that I can't wait until dawn to report."

The captain considered. "Go on," he said.

"I'm going to need you to call your Fuhrer immediately. I have some critical intelligence for him that is very time sensitive."

Pelzer looked amused. "I'm afraid I can't do that," he said.

"Do you know who I am?" said Boyd, striving for the right degree of haughtiness. "What I can do?"

"Yes. I've been told you're either the world's most brilliant clairvoyant. Or the world's most brilliant spy."

"I'm a seer, not a spy. And you must also be aware that I'm on the radar of both Heinrich Himmler and Adolf Hitler, correct?"

"I've never heard that expression before, *on the radar*," said Pelzer. "But I think I understand your meaning. Yes, I'm aware that you've attracted their attention."

"A clear measure of the potential they see in me, Captain. And in just four hours the Allies will succeed in delivering a major blow to your war efforts." He raised his eyebrows. "Unless I alert your Fuhrer in time."

"Then you first need to tell *me* what's going on."

Boyd sighed. "If that's what it takes," he said, "I will. I had a very powerful and specific vision just before I awoke. I saw a team of maybe ten Allied commandos scaling a cliff and crossing a gorge. Their target is something called the Vemork power station in Norway. I don't have the exact location, but your Fuhrer will know where it is. Unless I alert him, the Allies will succeed in sabotaging a section of the station that's dedicated to processing water. As I said, in about four hours from now."

Pelzer eyed him in disbelief. "Is this a bad joke?" he said in disgust. "You want me to call the Fuhrer at this time of night? To tell him about the sabotage of a water processing plant—in *Norway?*"

Boyd fought back a smile. He had read that Hitler was well known for insisting he not be awakened under any circumstances, and by this time in the war, he frequently slept until noon, beset by failing health and addicted to a wide array of medications.

D-Day could well have been a disaster for the Allies, but when they crashed the shores of Normandy, the Nazis were terrified to wake Hitler, who insisted on making every key decision, so they were paralyzed for many critical hours.

If his generals wouldn't wake him for D-Day, this SS captain wouldn't begin to consider waking him for something whose significance he couldn't possibly comprehend. And Boyd wasn't about to help.

"I know it sounds odd," said Boyd. "But my powers as a seer are now *infallible*. And this is extremely important. A mystical power is telling me your High Command will want to know about this."

"Are you sure these commandos aren't just passing through the water processing section on their way to something more vital?"

"I'm sure," said Boyd. "And this is urgent. You have to trust me."

Boyd almost felt sorry for the SS captain. The top-secret plant in Norway, known only to a select few, was a vital part of Germany's effort to build an atomic bomb. The water to which Boyd was referring was called *heavy* water, and it was exceedingly difficult to make or isolate. Instead of the hydrogen atoms in this water having only a single proton, they each had a single neutron as well, doubling their atomic weight.

An atomic bomb required a chain reaction to split uncountable molecules of uranium and liberate energy. The Allied and Nazi scientists had chosen different strategies to achieve this result. The Allies focused their efforts on purifying uranium, which would make a chain reaction easier to achieve. Germany, on the other hand, used *unenriched* uranium, but bathed it in heavy water, which was also known to improve the efficiency of a chain reaction.

But according to Sage and history, a team of Allied commandos was even now on its way to sabotage the Nazi's heavy water production, dealing a major blow to their efforts.

"You're out of your mind," said Pelzer in contempt. "There is no chance I'm going to wake the Fuhrer to protect *water*. None!"

"Then wake someone *else*," insisted Boyd, counting on Pelzer not to do this, either. "Anyone else who can stop it. Go through your chain of command until it reaches the Fuhrer."

"You must have just had a strange dream, Herr Boyd, that you mistook for a vision. So I'm ending this discussion. I don't want to hear any more about it. Understood?"

Boyd opened his mouth, pretending he wanted to argue further, and then closed it again, as if reacting to the resolve on Pelzer's face. Finally, he blew out a long breath and nodded. "Understood," he said, trying to come across as both frustrated and distraught. "But don't say I didn't try."

"I won't," said the captain.

"So when will the general arrive?" asked Boyd, switching gears.

"In six hours."

"Then I'd like to take you up on your offer of a meal. And a shower and clean clothes also."

"Of course," said Pelzer graciously.

Boyd knew the captain now thought he was formidable and crazy both, the most dangerous of all combinations. "Can I assume you'll be having three men with machine guns guarding me from afar while I wash up?" he asked with a sigh.

Pelzer studied his prisoner for several long seconds. "At least three," he said with a humorless smile.

42

The Rolling Hills Mansion was private, secluded, and as magnificent as it was enormous. Boyd had seen major museums with less square footage. A connected complex of mansions rather than just one, made from stone, brick, and marble, it spread out over several acres of land, a series of single-story structures that had the height of two or even three stories, as soaring, vaulted ceilings were an architectural mainstay.

There were five main sections. The central mansion was even more ornate than the rest, with even higher ceilings, and six towering white pillars at its front entrance. Two peripheral wings extended out from the south side of the central mansion, and two more from the north, arranged in perfect symmetry, making the entire estate from above resemble a giant butterfly with an extra pair of wings tacked on. Including vast ballrooms, dining halls, libraries, kitchens, bedrooms, and others, the five connected single-story mansions contained well over a hundred separate rooms, not including closets and bathrooms.

The extensive grounds contained a series of gardens and fountains, with a wide, gray-colored brick road leading to an enormous stone roundabout driveway abutting the main residence. The roundabout, large enough to hold dozens of cars, encircled a section of land with a thirty-foot diameter, like a tire surrounding a rim. Within this spacious inner circle, a series of eight-foot-tall shrubs had been sculpted into the shape of an enormous swastika, which Boyd found as surreal as anything he had ever seen.

The American prisoner's hands were cuffed behind his back, and he was led through a series of rooms, each grander than the last, with ornate chandeliers and furniture, exquisite sculptures, and vivid oil paintings. He found himself wondering if the mansion had once belonged to prominent Jews who had been starved and then gassed to death while the Nazis stole their home, and then filled it with pilfered art. Or if the furnishings had been purchased with proceeds from a literal mountain of gold fillings pulled from the teeth of the millions they had gassed to death.

More than twenty guards patrolled both the inside and outside of the residence, about half with handguns or rifles and half with machine guns.

Boyd decided that as surreal as the giant swastika hedge had been, his trip through the mansion was even more so. It was the biggest residence he had ever been in, and it was crawling with men in crisp SS uniforms straight off a movie set, their swastika armbands so bright red they almost glowed.

For a place named *Rolling Hills*, the grounds and surroundings could not have been flatter, and Sage had no record of the mansion in her database.

Boyd was taken to the far south wing and ushered into a large inner courtyard by two uniformed SS officers, while three others of lower rank manned the only entrance back into the house. The courtyard was beautiful, with lush green ivy running up its walls, large pots filled with colorful flowers, and a large running fountain at its center.

"Sorry about the handcuffs, Herr Boyd," said one of the two SS officers in perfect English, almost solicitously. "But I have been told to extend every courtesy to you. We are preparing a bedroom for your use. In the meanwhile, I can offer the best food and wine, and will honor any further request, within reason. I'd like you to feel more an honored guest than a prisoner."

"An honored guest with his hands cuffed behind his back?"

The SS officer winced. "Again, my apologies," he said. "We're in the far south wing, as you know. My superiors believe that even if you turn out to be a dangerous spy, the fact that your wife is being held in the far *north* wing will keep you in check. The cuffs are just an added precaution that we hope won't be needed for long. In the meanwhile, is there anything I can do for you?"

"Yes, I'd like to speak with Major Kurt Hahn."

"Certainly, Herr Boyd," said the man. He and his comrade proceeded to go back inside the residence, leaving Boyd alone once again, still under the watchful eyes of the three soldiers manning the entrance.

Less than five minutes later Hahn walked into the courtyard, unrestrained in any way. His face showed pleasure at seeing the American, and he moved as if to clap him on the shoulder, but he thought better of it since the guards were watching. Boyd couldn't blame him. He had a cover to protect, at least for the time being.

Boyd motioned the German major to sit with him on the low wall of the circular central fountain, so the sound of water would drown out their voices.

"It's good to see you, Herr Boyd," said Hahn by way of greeting. "But also surprising. I was told you wouldn't be joining us for several days—at minimum. That you had to first convince an SS general of your clairvoyance and loyalty to the Reich."

The American nodded. Ironically enough, the general in question had turned out to be Magnus Becker, the same man whom Otto had written of in his journal, who had initially taken the boy from his home. "I was very efficient," said Boyd, keeping his voice low.

The American told Hahn about the intel he had provided on the plant in Norway and its significance, and that the captain he had shared it with hadn't passed it on, as he had known would be the case. Naturally, it had proven to be accurate. The commando team had made it in, sabotaged the facility, and made it out again, exactly when and how Boyd had predicted.

Just after dawn, Boyd had told Becker of his earlier vision and attempts to sound the alarm, and the general had checked and confirmed that the sabotage had indeed taken place, and had learned from the German High Command why this site was so important. This success immediately burnished Boyd's credentials, and someone above Becker in rank had been impressed enough to clear the American to move into the mansion well ahead of schedule. Boyd had met with Becker between five and six that morning and had arrived at Rolling Hills before noon.

"Brilliantly done, Herr Boyd," said the SS major when the American had finished, keeping his voice low. "But how do you know what's going to happen with such precision? Yes, you're from 2027. But I can't believe that people from eighty-four years in the future know the day-to-day history of every attack in this war—to the hour."

"They don't," replied Boyd. "I just happen to have a nearly perfect memory," he explained. *And that perfect memory is called Sage*, he thought, as the hint of a smile crossed his face.

"The important thing," continued Boyd out loud, "is that I've joined you and Kelly. Which means we can get the hell out of here tonight and make our way back to Canada."

"We can't go *now*," said Hahn in dismay. "You do know where we are, right?"

Boyd blinked in confusion. "Apparently not."

"I'm a little surprised by that," said Hahn. "This is an estate that Hitler is having converted for use as his private home. But it will also serve as a retreat for gatherings of his inner circle, and as a command center. He's decided he needs something similar to the Berghof, but on the outskirts of Berlin. It should be finished in just a few weeks."

Boyd was familiar with the infamous Berghof, Hitler's beloved mountain palace on the Bavarian-Austrian border, from which he had governed Germany and planned the invasions of multiple countries. The Nazis had evicted farmers and homeowners from the area and constructed what amounted to a Nazi village, a fortress town on the side of a mountain, with barracks for Hitler's guards, houses for key Nazi officials, parade grounds, shooting ranges, and even a cinema. In many ways it was Hitler's White House, war room, and Camp David retreat all rolled into one.

But if the complex they were in was meant to be the Berghof's second coming closer to Berlin, it was odd that Sage had found no mention of it. The Fuhrer must have decided not to follow through with it after all.

"Why isn't it finished?" asked Boyd.

"I only know bits and pieces from what I overheard," said Hahn. "But I think they're still upgrading security, and putting the finishing touches on the war room."

"War room?"

"Yes, a meeting room, map room, and telephone room all rolled into one. Apparently, a first set of telephones has been installed and activated, but they are now installing a second set."

"Does the general public know about this new Berghof?"

"Not yet," replied Hahn. "They will when it's finished. But now you know why we can't leave."

"I'm afraid I still don't," admitted Boyd. "So Satan is taking over another home for his personal use. Good for him. Why does that matter to *us*?"

"Why does that matter to *us*?" repeated Hahn in disbelief. "It matters because all the men you see are here to guard and maintain this mansion. *Hitler's* mansion. So you're the only real . . . guest. Kelly and I are just along for the ride. Which means only one thing. Your accurate vision of the heavy-water sabotage, on top of your accurate vision of the attack on the submarine base, has attracted Hitler's full attention. He no longer intends to have Himmler size you up. He wants to do it *himself*. In person."

Boyd recoiled in horror. "That's crazy," he said. "Wild speculation."

"Not at all," insisted Hahn. "Do you think you'd be at Hitler's newest residence unless he planned to meet you? I'm not clairvoyant, but I know the Third Reich, and I guarantee that this is the case."

The SS major raised his eyebrows. "So don't think of this as a prison," he added. "Think of it as Adolf Hitler's waiting room."

43

Boyd issued a soft whistle, which was drowned out by the sound of water falling into the fountain behind him, and tried to get his mind around this new state of affairs. The thought of sharing the same room with the personification of evil, with a monster who had ordered the torture and murder of millions of innocent civilians without batting an eye, was appalling, grotesque.

After he and Kelly had crash landed in 1943, all he had wanted to do was help Otto Richter get the Enigma Cube to Spokane. But his ridiculous backstory had been more effective than he thought it would be. *Too* effective. Just the thought of seeing Adolph Hitler in the flesh made his skin crawl, but the idea of actually meeting him was *psychotic*.

Justin Boyd shot the German major a nauseated expression. "When do you think he'll arrive?"

"I have no idea. He doesn't share his schedule with me. Or *anyone*. He's erratic."

"Not to mention busy with genocide and world conquest," said Boyd in disgust.

"Yes. So he could be on his way here this second, or he might not come for a month. But given his superstitions, and what you might mean for the war effort, I'd guess within the next three or four days."

"I'm afraid I'll have to disappoint him, then," said Boyd. "Because we're leaving tonight."

"What are you talking about?" protested Hahn. "This is a dream opportunity. You wanted to help us keep the Atlantis Cube out of Hitler's hands. Well, now you can do a *lot more* than that. You can cut off those same hands. And his *head* along with it."

"As tempting as that is," said Boyd, "that's not why we're here. And I believe Hitler will change his mind about meeting me, anyway, when he's had some time to think it through."

"Why?"

"I've learned the hard way that just because someone is evil and barbaric doesn't necessarily make them *stupid*. Very soon it will occur to him that I just disclosed an attack that I had to know wouldn't be taken seriously. So now I've given the Nazis intel on two attacks I knew they wouldn't act on. Hitler will come to realize I managed to establish my credentials without hurting the Allies at all.

"Once this occurs to him," continued Boyd, "he won't meet with me until I can prove myself further. Until I give up decisive intelligence that leads to a great victory. And even then, he'll conclude he can't really trust me. Not a Canadian with zero ties to Germany, who is reportedly too good at combat for his own good. He'll decide I'm still a spy. That the Allies are willing to give up as many men as necessary to get me in tight with him."

Boyd frowned. "And he'd be right," he added. "I have no doubt the Allies *would* be willing to make almost any sacrifice to position an operative inside Hitler's inner circle. I'm telling you, Major, he won't be meeting with me. We have to escape *now*, before he comes to these conclusions and becomes certain I'm a spy."

Hahn grimaced, as if he had been stabbed in the neck. "But what if you're *wrong*?" he said, almost pleading. "We'll never get a chance like this again. Isn't the possible reward worth the risk?"

"What if I'm *right*?" said Boyd. "Or what if he does meet with me, but we fail to take him out? Then we're of no use to Otto, and we risk that the fellow scientist on the team—Alex Wentz, I think it was—will unlock the cube using *Otto's* invention. And that will make Hitler truly unstoppable."

Hahn turned away in disgust, and Boyd gave him time to think it through. Finally, after more than a minute, the SS major reluctantly agreed to attempt escape on Boyd's timetable.

"I'm sorry," said the American. "I really am. I can only imagine how desperately you want to kill this monster. Because I know how much *I* do. In fact, over the next eight decades, the question of killing

Hitler will become a favorite in ethics classes. Many millions will ponder if a time machine took them to when Hitler was an infant, would they kill him? Would they put a bullet into the brain of a helpless two-year-old, who had yet to commit a single crime, knowing his destiny?"

Boyd paused. "The vast majority *would* kill him, by the way. Even as a baby. Never have so many dreamt so passionately of ending a man's life. Fantasized about it, even after he was long dead." He shook his head. "But *we* can't make the attempt. Not now. We have to be smart about this."

Hahn nodded woodenly, staring at the ground.

"Look, let's move on to other topics," said Boyd gently. "When did it get pitch-dark last night?"

The SS major mourned his fantasy of killing Hitler for just a few more seconds and then turned back to Boyd. "Around eight," he replied.

"Okay, we'll begin our escape at ten sharp."

"Do you have a plan?"

"That depends on your situation here. I'm cuffed, and multiple eyes are always on me. Can I assume you're able to roam freely around the mansion and grounds?"

"Not freely, but close enough. These men know that I'm accused of nothing more than having an unauthorized conversation with a prisoner. So I'll have one or two . . . escorts, but they'll let me get exercise and wander around."

"Perfect," said Boyd. "Then yes, I do have a plan. I need you to provide reconnaissance on the layout of this mansion, numbers and positioning of the guards, how they're armed, and so on. Right away. Along with the precise location of the war room you spoke of."

"That's a lot of wandering," said Hahn.

"I'm afraid that's only the beginning. This home is electric powered, right?"

"Yes," replied the German. "Most homes have been since the mid-thirties. And the wealthier homes for sure."

"And it gets its power from outside? From a power plant of some kind?"

"*Yes*," said Hahn. "I'm sure we aren't as advanced as you, but we aren't *primitives*."

"Right," said Boyd. "Of course. And since you aren't, your top priority will be to find the circuit breakers to the house."

"I don't know what those are."

"They're in a steel box where electricity comes into the residence from transmission lines."

"You mean the fuse box?"

"Right. Circuit breakers must not be around yet. I need you to position yourself near these fuses just before our scheduled escape. Then, at ten o'clock exactly, destroy them. Completely. Smash them up, rip out wires, whatever, but I need the electricity to never come back on."

Hahn nodded.

"Tell me more about this war room," said Boyd. "Especially about the telephones."

"I haven't seen it, but I know the type. It'll be a large room with maps covering walls and tables. There will likely be a huge conference table in the center. Perhaps ten phones will be spaced around the room's perimeter. Each phone will be connected directly to Hitler's private underground switchboard in Berlin. This is manned day and night by multiple women who connect the calls, and loyal SS soldiers making sure they don't listen in. Whenever Hitler's here, that room basically becomes the command center for the entire German army."

"You mentioned there was a second set of phones being installed," said the American. "Why would this be necessary?"

"I don't know. I'd guess as backup. But if the first set are taken out or not working, I'm not sure why the extras would be any different."

"Will the phones work if the electricity is out?"

"Yes, they don't need much power, which they get through the copper wires that connect them to the switchboard." Hahn paused. "Why?" he asked. "Do your phones require more power than the wires can deliver?"

"Less," said Boyd. "It's just that most of our phones aren't connected to wires anymore. But this is good news. So the second you kill the electricity, I need you to get to the war room as fast as possible

Douglas E. Richards

and lock it down. Kelly and I will be joining you there as soon as we can. We'll want to use a telephone, and we need to prevent the SS from using one to call in reinforcements."

"They won't," said Hahn. "First, they won't dare enter Hitler's war room unless he invites them there, and he isn't on site. Second, there are more than twenty-five men here, well-armed and highly trained. Their pride won't let them believe they could possibly need reinforcements to face a single enemy combatant. Or *two* enemy combatants if they realize I've turned. In fact, even *I* can't believe they'll need reinforcements. You really think we can win this thing?"

"I thought you were the one arguing that we shouldn't just escape, we should stop to assassinate Hitler on the way out."

"Well, when you put it that way, my thinking may have been blinded by hatred."

"I can't blame you," said Boyd. "But to answer your question, I have some tricks up my sleeve that will even the playing field. We'll have at least a fifty-fifty chance."

"Good enough for me," said Hahn. "Two unarmed men, one with his hands cuffed behind his back, against dozens of soldiers—many with machine guns. I'll gladly take fifty-fifty."

"The odds are a lot worse if you aren't able to kill the electricity."

"Why is this so vital?"

"Let's just say that I'm extremely skilled at fighting in the dark."

Hahn stared deeply into the American's eyes, taking his measure. "Okay, then," he said finally. "If you say you can fight in the dark, I'm willing to believe you. So don't worry, the lights will be out at ten sharp, even if I have to do it from the afterlife."

"I appreciate your heart, Major, but do it from this plane of existence. We need you to stay alive."

Hahn smiled. "If you insist," he said wryly, "I guess I'll have to give that a try."

* * *

The American prisoner watched as Kurt Hahn began his leisurely stroll through the mansion to collect intel, with two armed escorts in tow.

Once his German ally had vanished from sight, Boyd had one of the guards bring him a drink, which the man did with more enthusiasm than a professional butler. Never had an SS prisoner had more accommodating guards. But then again, never had an SS prisoner been slated to meet with the Fuhrer himself, with a real chance of becoming his right-hand man in the very near future.

Boyd's minders would be shot if they let him escape. But if he turned out to be Hitler's golden boy, they could also find themselves at the wrong end of an execution if they treated him with anything less than perfect respect.

Boyd sipped at his drink, took a deep breath, and asked Sage to convert his subvocalized words into his voice and transmit them to Kelly Connolly, who was now well within range.

"Kelly, it's me," he began, turning his back to the guards and gazing at the fountain. *"Don't react. Reply when you get somewhere where they can't see your mouth. Remember, the comm will amplify the faintest whisper."*

He waited for the longest fifteen seconds of his life.

"Justin, what a relief," she answered finally. *"Are you okay?"*

Boyd exhaled, unaware that he had been holding his breath. She had taken the words right out of his mouth. But *relief* wasn't a strong enough word to convey his emotions at hearing her voice, at receiving confirmation that she was alive and well.

"I'm fine," he replied quickly. *"What about you? How are they treating you?"*

"I have guards watching me, but other than that I've been treated like royalty. They offered me clothing, but I prefer the garb our Chinese friends provided. So they actually washed it and gave me clean clothes to wear while I waited. They even let me change in private. They've been feeding me anything I want, and jumping to attention when I bat an eyelash."

"Wow, I almost feel bad for you that we're going to have to blow this joint."

"Blow this joint?" said Kelly. *"Really? You do realize that's an expression from the 1990s, right?"*

"*I do,*" said Boyd in amusement. "*But I'm sure you realize that the nineties are still five decades away. So I'm way ahead of my time.*"

Kelly laughed. "*So tell me what happened after you boarded the transport plane,*" she asked.

Boyd brought her up to speed as efficiently as he could, ending with a description of how he had been vetted by Magnus Becker, the same SS general who had been referenced in her grandfather's journal.

"*So where are you now?*" she asked when he had finished.

"*In the far south wing. As far away from you as they could manage. Like you, they're treating me like a VIP in some ways. Even gave me my own bedroom.*"

"*That's great. They're trusting you a lot more than I thought they would.*"

"*Well, they do have me cuffed,*" he noted, "*and they stripped the room of anything but pillows. They even removed the cover of the water tank on the toilet, and what's really unfortunate for me, the toilet seat.*"

"*Yuck,*" said Kelly. "*So, what, you have to sit on the rim?*"

"*Okay, I really didn't need to put that thought picture in your head. Too much information.*"

Kelly laughed. "*Seriously, though, why would they do that?*"

"*They uncuff me when I use the facilities. The tank lid is made of heavy porcelain and comes right off. So I could use it as a weapon. I'm strong enough to rip off the toilet seat and do the same.*"

"*Yet another conversation I'd have bet my life I'd never have,*" said Kelly. "*And I can't believe we're actually staying at one of Hitler's residences. Talk about insane.*"

"*Insane is par for the course lately,*" he noted. "*Apparently, the impossible becomes routine when you're involved. You know what they say, it's a jolly holiday with Kelly.*"

"*More a nightmarish holiday than a jolly one,*" she replied in amusement. "*But I can't believe you managed to land a joke referencing Mary Poppins while you're a prisoner inside the home of Adolf Hitler. That's not something just any man could pull off.*"

"I guess I'm special that way," said Boyd with a grin. *"But we should get back to business. I need you to test your leash. See how far they'll let you wander around. Wherever you manage to go, whisper what you're seeing. Guards, layout, and so on. I'll have Sage convert it into a 3D map. There's no urgency, as jailbreak is more than ten hours away, so you can be very casual about your requests for exercise."*

"Roger that," she replied, and Boyd smiled at her use of the military vernacular. *"So tell me your plan."*

"I will," he said. *"But first, I need to tell you the bad news."* He blew out a long breath. *"I know you know this, Kelly, but I have to say it anyway. There's not a clean way out of here. We're looking at another bloodbath. I wish I could sugarcoat it, but I can't. I keep on putting you in these situations, and I couldn't be more sorry about it."*

She sighed. *"You haven't been putting me in these situations, Justin. You've been trying to get me out of them. But I know how sorry you are about the need to take lives. And I appreciate how sensitive you've been about what this might be doing to my psyche."*

Boyd frowned. He only wished there was something more he could do to make this easier for her. But there was not. He thought for a moment of telling her that seventy-five million people had died in this war, hoping to put the coming carnage into perspective.

But he already knew her well enough to know that this statistic wouldn't help in the slightest.

44

It was just after eight at night, and the sun had finally vanished below the horizon. Three Mercedes sedans paraded onto the brick drive of the Rolling Hills Mansion and made their way to the roundabout that abutted the central section of the residence. All three sedans were black—making them nearly invisible on this dark, cloudy night—with the one in the middle being the grandest.

When the vehicles stopped on the roundabout in front of the imposing swastika hedge and parked, eight machine-gun-wielding SS soldiers poured out of the two smaller sedans as if they were glorified clown cars. Two of them rushed to open the passenger's door of the car in the middle, standing on either side of it and delivering vigorous *Heil Hitler* salutes to Hitler himself, who absently acknowledged them, not by thrusting his arm out with a straight elbow, but by raising his forearm and pointing his hand backwards for just a moment, dismissively.

The eight SS guards surrounded their Fuhrer with ecstatic expressions, as if they had been tasked with protecting a god, while Hitler himself looked bored. He wore his standard garb, a relatively unadorned brown-orange uniform and matching tie. His demeanor was stern, his eyes dead and devoid of all empathy, and his face was unattractive, although nothing compared to the ugliness within.

Hitler surveyed the premises and then marched inside. He soon made his way to the nearly completed war room, where he contemplated several options he had been given earlier for tactical redeployment of troops.

Two of his private guards accompanied him inside the room, while six others waited outside.

Hitler turned to a large map of the world that covered an entire wall, and which showed the various fronts in the war and current

German positions. He knew he needed to take bold action once again. As bold and decisive as the initial blitzkrieg had been.

But what should that be? No easy answers presented themselves.

Still, he allowed himself a rare smile. Because what he desperately needed was the help of a clairvoyant.

And as good fortune would have it, there happened to be one in this very complex.

45

Justin Boyd had found the long wait to launch their attack agonizing. He had passed much of the time reviewing the plan in his mind, thinking about various ways things could go awry, and reading information projected onto his lenses, continuing his quest to bring himself up to speed on all things World War II.

He now sat on the edge of the bed inside the room he had been issued with his hands still cuffed behind his back. He had always preferred the future to the past, science fiction over history, but it was hard not to find much of the information fascinating.

He was reading an article on why Hitler had demanded he be addressed only as the *Fuhrer*, and about one of his favorite propaganda slogans, "*Ein Volk, ein Reich, ein Fuhrer*—one People, one Empire, one Leader," which had been endlessly repeated on posters, magazines, and radio broadcasts.

Boyd finished the short article and glanced up at a digital clock he had asked Sage to display at the edge of his field of vision. He groaned. It was still only a quarter past eight. Time seemed to be standing still.

Three sharp raps sounded at the closed door, which was thrown open before Boyd could respond. An SS Colonel named Ernst Dietrich rushed across the threshold along with three comrades, and each held a gun in their hand.

"The Fuhrer is on the premises," announced Dietrich excitedly in heavily accented English. "He wants to meet with you. I was ordered to bring you to his war room at nine—which is forty-five minutes from now."

Boyd's face froze as he fought not to show the fury he was feeling. So much for his theory that Hitler would decide not to meet with him. Maybe the man *was* as stupid as he was malevolent. Or maybe his superstition overwhelmed his reason.

Regardless, they had been so close, less than two hours away from triggering their attack. And now this, the mother of all wrenches thrown into the works.

"What a great honor," said the American finally, struggling to choke out the most disgusting words he had ever uttered.

He tilted his head, as though in thought. "Since we still have some time before the meeting, can you have one of your men get Major Hahn for me?"

"The Fuhrer wants to meet with you alone," replied the SS colonel.

"I realize that," said Boyd. "But I'd still like to speak with Major Hahn for a few minutes. I'm a little nervous about meeting your Fuhrer, and I know the major can help calm me down."

The colonel nodded. "I understand completely, Herr Boyd. Being in the presence of such a great man can unsettle anyone."

He issued orders in German, and one of the three men he had brought into the room rushed off to get Hahn.

"Thank you, Colonel," said the American.

Dietrich nodded. "Of course. But I must apologize in advance, Herr Boyd. Before you enter the war room, I'll need to cuff your ankles also. And chain you to the desk when you sit before the Fuhrer. But this way, you can have a private conversation without any guards present."

"No need to apologize," said Boyd amiably. "But since we have time," he added, gesturing toward a door at the back of the room. "I'd like to use the, ah . . . water closet. Can you remove my cuffs one more time?"

Boyd turned so his back was facing the SS colonel, not waiting for an answer. Dietrich produced a key and unlocked the cuffs while the two remaining guards trained their handguns at their VIP prisoner's head.

Boyd made a show of stretching the kinks from his arms and entered the bathroom without another word.

"Kelly, we've got a problem," he said, counting on Sage to transmit his subvocalizations once again. *"Adolf Hitler is here. He's actually*

here. Now! And he wants to meet me at nine. So we need to move up our escape plans."

"*To when?*" asked Kelly, to her credit not wasting time being surprised.

"*One minute from now,*" he replied. "*Where are you now?*"

"*In my room. The door is closed, and two guards are posted outside.*"

Boyd frowned, all out of good ideas. "*I'd advise lying low in the bathroom. With luck, they'll rush off when all hell starts to break loose. But if they spare a second to check on you and see the bathroom door closed, maybe they won't bust in. And if the action comes your way, lie down in the tub so you'll be protected from stray bullets. We'll coordinate more later, but I have to go.*"

"*Good luck, Justin,*" she said anxiously, her whispered voice heavy with emotion.

"*You too,*" he said, trying not to get choked up, himself.

Boyd flushed the toilet for his guards to hear and braced himself for what was to come. Once it began, it wouldn't end until he was dead, or every hostile on site was. Kelly had quoted from a stanza of *Horatius at the Bridge* just before they had surrendered to Shen in Pennsylvania, and this stanza was equally appropriate now.

How can a man die better, he recited to himself, *than facing fearful odds. For the ashes of his fathers, and the temples of his gods.*

Boyd decided he definitely had the *fearful odds* part of the stanza covered. He just needed to avoid the *dying* part. He needed to adhere to the wisdom of the great general George Patton, who had said, "You don't win a war by dying for your country. You win a war by making the other dumb bastard die for his."

Boyd opened the door with studied calm and exited the bathroom. "Thank you, Colonel," he said with a pleasant tone. "I feel much better," he added, turning and putting his hands behind his back once again. "I only wish I was dressed better for the meeting."

"I wouldn't worry too much," said the colonel. "The Fuhrer won't be judging you on your clothing."

He reached out to cuff the prisoner, but one moment he was moving the cuffs toward Boyd's hands, and the next Boyd had changed places with him, in a blur of motion, so that he was now *behind* the SS colonel. Before Dietrich had even registered what had happened, the prisoner grabbed his head and yanked hard, snapping the German's neck with a sharp crack like it was rotted wood.

Boyd propped up the limp body in front of him with his left arm while pulling the man's gun from its holster with his right. Both guards began firing at the American as he ducked down behind his human shield, and succeeded only in pumping bullet after bullet into their dead commander, whose body jerked about in a grisly dance from the dense barrage.

Boyd got off three shots in just over a second, and two hit their targets, blowing gaping holes through the foreheads of the SS guards, who crashed to the floor like felled trees. The American released his bloody, bullet-ridden human shield, allowing the colonel's body to quickly join his mutilated comrades on the floor, and then raced behind the open door.

Using his comm-amplified hearing, the major detected three soldiers rushing toward the room, sure to be followed by others, as the gunfire had been heard by everyone in the far south wing, perhaps in the entire residence.

The first SS guard arrived at the open door and dived across the threshold, rolling on the floor and coming up with a machine gun pointed forward, searching for a target, but Boyd's reflexes were at least twice as fast as the intruder, and he got off a clean shot, putting him down.

A second guard charged through with only a handgun, the same guard who had gone to fetch Hahn, and Boyd made quick work of him. But while this was happening, a third burst through, with his finger an instant away from depressing the trigger of a machine gun, which would spray the American with a curtain of death.

Boyd rolled to his right, but just as he was about to come up firing, the man's head exploded like a brain-and-blood-filled water balloon. The guard toppled to the ground, revealing Kurt Hahn standing behind him with a borrowed gun, one still pointed where the man's head used to be. Hahn was being brought to see the American, but the guards escorting him there had made the fatal mistake of neglecting him while they went after Boyd.

The American grabbed a machine gun from the floor and jumped to his feet, rushing over to the open door and surveying the wide-open great room beyond, using amplified hearing and vision, both.

"The coast is clear for the moment," he announced, handing Hahn the machine gun and picking up another off the floor. "There's obviously been a change of plans," he continued rapidly. "Hitler is here, and Sage says he'll have eight personal bodyguards with him. So our odds are worse than ever. They'll be storming this wing soon, and the lights are still on. I need you to get them off at all costs."

"How? There are only two ways out of this wing, one to the south, and one to the north. By now they'll be congregated at both exits, coordinating a joint attack. I'll never get through."

Boyd's mind raced, and the solution came to him almost immediately. "You're officially a prisoner here, yes, but you're only under suspicion. You may not be in uniform, but you're still an SS major. So leave the machine gun here. Pretend to be a victim. Pretend to be on *their* side. Make up a story they'll believe. And find a way to get to the fuse box."

Hahn exhaled loudly and nodded. "Good plan," he said. "I'll make it work."

"Good. Hitler's in the war room, so we can't meet there afterward as planned. Instead, once you've killed the power, meet me at the east wall of the main residence."

"I'll be there," said Hahn, surveying the mansion beyond the room. The coast continued to be clear, no doubt as the forces on either side of them gathered, only to soon draw inward like a python constricting its prey.

Hahn bent down and soaked the side of his shirt with a healthy sampling of the blood that had pooled in various locations throughout the room, while Boyd looked on approvingly.

"Who's Sage?" asked the German as he moved to the door, placing the machine gun on the ground. "You said she told you that Hitler would have eight personal bodyguards."

"If we live, I'll tell you all about her," said Boyd. "But for now, get that power off."

Boyd handed the SS major a handgun, which he shoved into his pants, concealing it from view. "Thanks," said Hahn. "You'll be in the dark before you know it," he added confidently.

Boyd knew this was nothing but false bravado, a kind gesture made to reassure a besieged ally. "I have no doubt," he said, feigning confidence of his own.

* * *

Kelly Connolly paced back and forth in the room she had been issued and tried to get her heart to stop racing. Boyd hadn't yet left the bathroom, and had ordered Sage to transmit what was happening on his end, so at least she'd be able to keep some tabs on what was going on.

Still, she was starting to panic, and desperately wished she could be by his side. He was a beast, a whirlwind, and no doubt smarter and quicker on his feet than any SS soldier here, but he was still only a human being. All it would take was a single stray shot to end his life.

She couldn't shake the seeping, hollow terror that invaded her soul at the thought of losing him now, after all they had been through together.

Suddenly, a barrage of gunshots nearly shattered her eardrums, her comm ensuring she heard them as loudly as if she were in the center of the maelstrom. These same sounds could be heard coming from outside of her head, as well, but off in the distance, muted, as they had to travel through numerous rooms and walls to reach her.

Her eyes glistened with moisture as the firefight continued, desperate to hear Boyd's voice, to learn he was still alive, but knowing better than to try to communicate and cause a distraction.

Finally, the gunfire ceased, and the only sound she heard was her own heart threatening to pump right out of her chest.

A burst of elation surged through her as Boyd's voice came over the comm.

"There's obviously been a change of plans," he was saying, although clearly not to her. *"Hitler is here, and Sage says he'll have eight personal bodyguards with him. So our odds are worse than ever. They'll be storming this wing soon, and the lights are still on. I need you to get them off at all costs."*

Kelly realized that he was talking to Kurt Hahn, which meant they had both made it through unscathed. She had known this first action would be the most perilous. Boyd had been cuffed and weaponless. As vulnerable as he would ever be. But he had obviously turned this around. He wasn't out of the woods, but surviving the first few minutes was a huge step in the right direction.

She listened carefully for any movement of the guards outside and heard at least one of them rush off to join the fray, but she had a sick feeling that the other remained. She wouldn't be surprised if he soon decided to haul her out of the room, to bring Boyd's supposed wife and only weakness into play.

She considered pretending to be using the bathroom, or hiding in the tub, as Boyd had recommended, but decided these tactics would be useless. She had fancied herself a pacifist, but that ship had recently sailed in a big way. To pretend otherwise would be akin to a woman insisting she was a virgin after sleeping with a dozen men.

She had to do whatever it took to get out of this, no matter what. Not only was her life on the line, but the life of a man she was drawn to like no other, and the fate of the entire timeline if they couldn't get back to Canada and the cube.

So she wouldn't lie low in a bathtub.

But perhaps a trip to the bathroom would prove useful, anyway.

46

Adolf Hitler studied a map of Europe that covered an entire wall of the war room. Normally, a room such as this would be filled with generals and advisors, but he wanted to consider the merits of various options in solitude, for once.

He scowled as a timid knock at the door interrupted his thoughts. All eight of his personal bodyguards were now outside of the room, and he had left strict instructions not to be disturbed.

"What is it!" he screeched.

"There has been gunfire on the premises," shouted the chief of his personal security contingent at the top of his lungs, knowing the room was well-insulated from noise.

"Enter!" shouted Hitler.

His security chief quickly entered and closed the door behind him, his expression suggesting he would rather be anywhere else, even though he tried to hide it. "Apologies, mein Fuhrer, but there has been considerable gunfire coming from the far south wing. Mansion security believes the Canadian prisoner is responsible. We'll have his wife brought here as an insurance policy. But given that there are twenty-eight men on security duty here tonight, you are in no danger, sir. We'll let them handle it and will remain with you."

Hitler screamed curses like a man whose hair was on fire. He had been counting on this clairvoyant to give him much-needed insight, and now it seemed that the man calling himself Justin Boyd was a spy after all.

Well, this Boyd would *pay* for his treachery—in ways the world had never seen. The Reich had perfected tortures that the ancient Chinese would envy, and Hitler vowed to himself that this spy would suffer worse than any man had ever suffered. First, he would make him watch as a dozen men gang-raped his wife and then tortured her to death.

And then the fun would really begin.

He would demand that Josef Mengele and others of his ilk get more creative than they had ever been, devising tortures that would make having one's skin removed with a razor blade seem like a gentle caress.

"*I want Boyd brought to me alive!*" he thundered at his security chief. "*Understood!*"

"*Jawohl, mein Fuhrer!*" responded the chief of security. He swallowed hard. "But what if he's *already* dead?"

"He had better not be!" screamed Adolf Hitler in a blind rage, his soulless eyes bulging out even more than usual. "Or members of mansion security will live to regret it."

* * *

Kurt Hahn made his way through the far south wing of the Rolling Hills Mansion and was struck by just how well lighted it was, despite the fall of darkness outside. Seemingly every lamp and chandelier were blazing, as if the mansion were showing off.

He neared the towering door leading to the outer grounds and began walking like a zombie dragging its undead carcass across the floor.

"Help!" he yelled as loudly as he could in German. "It's Hahn. I've been shot."

Hahn was dressed in civilian clothing, but everyone at Rolling Hills knew all about the SS major who had arrived in Berlin with the mysterious Canadian spy/seer, and why he was temporarily under guard.

"Help!" Hahn shouted a second time as he continued making his way to the door, cutting a pathetic, wounded figure inside the well-lighted building.

The mammoth door swung open and two men rushed over to him, one on either side, and waited for him to put an arm around their shoulders before they moved off, hoisting him across the floor and back outside. Deep darkness had fallen, but the grounds were sporadically illuminated by artificial lighting, ensuring ten to fifteen feet of eye-straining visibility.

Too many soldiers were congregated at the door for Hahn to count at one glance as he was helped over to yet another SS colonel.

The colonel fished a field dressing from a bag, a large pad of absorbent cloth with strips of fabric to tie it in place. The two men still propping him up, a lieutenant and a captain, helped him to secure it firmly over the faux wound on the side of his stomach.

"Report," said the SS officer in charge when this was finished.

Hahn made a show of wincing in pain. "It's . . . Boyd," he began. "Thought he wanted to . . . serve Reich. But went berserk. Killed at least two men," he added, minimizing the number so Boyd wouldn't sound as formidable as he was. "Tried to . . . stop him. But had no . . . weapon."

"Is he still alive?"

Hahn nodded weakly. "Yes."

"Outstanding," said the colonel, as relieved as if he were a man whose doctor had just told him his tumor was benign.

"Outstanding?" repeated Hahn in confusion.

"The Fuhrer is on site," explained the colonel, "and has been apprised of the situation. He wants Boyd alive. *Badly.* So yes, your report that he's alive is very good news. I plan to make sure that your bravery and intel on this matter is rewarded. I've seen your record, Major, and it's impressive. I believe that Colonel Zimmerman overreacted."

"Thank you . . . sir," said Hahn weakly. "But are you sure . . . Fuhrer is . . . safe?"

"*Positive,*" said the colonel. "He's angry, because this Canadian deceived us, but he couldn't be safer."

Hahn pretended to be relieved. "Great news, sir."

"We need to get you patched up properly, Major. There's an infirmary in the central mansion." He gestured to the two soldiers still on either side of Hahn. "These men will take you there."

"Thank you, Colonel. But I can . . . make it . . . on my own."

"Nonsense. I won't hear of it." The colonel glanced at his watch. "We're entering this wing in a little over a minute. There's another group that will be entering from the south at the same time. We have twelve men and they have eleven. Even given the need to take Boyd alive, this is far more than necessary, so I can spare two men."

"Thank you, sir," said Hahn.

Having escorts foisted upon him was a bad break, but the fact that all nineteen soldiers would be well inside the building when the lights went out would be ideal for Justin Boyd, assuming he was half the night-fighter he claimed to be.

The colonel made sure the captain had a flashlight, as they would be taking an outside route to the central mansion, and then the colonel and nine other Nazi soldiers opened the door and fanned out inside the far south wing.

The men on either side of Hahn continued to serve as human crutches, supporting him and moving away from the door and around an edge of the building, the darkness intensifying with every step.

After they had traveled fifteen yards, without warning, the major jerked forward wildly, pretending to convulse, and slipped his arms from around the two men helping him. He slumped to the ground and fell forward, face down on the lawn, clutching at his makeshift bandage and moaning in agony.

The captain and lieutenant worked together to gently roll Hahn onto his back, but as the roll was completed, he somehow held a gun in his hand, and suddenly seemed anything but injured.

Hahn's gun spit out four rounds, and his two helpers fell to the ground beside him, dead. Wasting no time, the SS major jumped to his feet, shoved the captain's gun into his pants so he would have a spare, and retrieved the fallen flashlight.

This done, Hahn began to sprint across the darkened grounds, making his way to the fuse box on the west wall of the central mansion as quickly as he could.

* * *

"Frau Boyd," said a Nazi soldier, knocking gently at the door. "Frau Boyd, I need to come in."

Kelly Connolly was already in position behind the closed door. One of the guards had stayed back, as she had suspected, and was now either checking on her, or ready to drag her away to use against her "husband."

She held her breath as the handle turned and the door slowly began to swing inward. She quietly backed up farther behind the door and tried to ratchet up her courage and resolve, even though her heart was now beating more wildly than ever, and her temples were throbbing.

She had turned the lights off in the room, leaving the bathroom light on and the door closed, hoping that the attention of an entering guard would be drawn there.

Sure enough, the guard crept inside, gun extended, and began to make his way to the bathroom.

Kelly turned soundlessly as the guard passed and failed to look behind the door. She held a heavy, ceramic toilet tank lid, her focus on nothing but the back of the man's skull. Still not daring to breathe, she swung the rectangular bludgeon with both arms, like a two-handed tennis backhand, and connected with a sickening *crack*.

The guard was propelled forward from the strength of her adrenaline-powered blow and collapsed in a heap, unmoving. Kelly fought back tears of relief and horror, refusing to check to see if he was still breathing, afraid of what she might learn.

"Justin," she whispered hurriedly, knowing he was in a period of calm before the storm, and would soon be facing SS soldiers coming at him from all sides. *"I knocked out my only guard with the toilet-tank lid. I guess you didn't overshare earlier after all. What now?"*

"Well done!" said Boyd. *"Get the hell out of there. Find another room as far away as possible and hide. Tell me where you are, and I'll come get you as soon as I can."*

Kelly was about to reply when two additional soldiers charged into the room, machine guns drawn, and threw on the lights, turning hope to despair in an instant.

"Hande hoch!" shouted one of the two newcomers.

"Shit!" barked Boyd, having heard this order also. *"It means hands up. I can't believe the bastards sent backup."*

Kelly raised her arms above her head as the second soldier knelt down and checked the pulse of the guard she had hit. He turned to his partner and shook his head, indicating the guard was dead.

Both of the newcomers had different markings on their uniforms than any she had seen, which she guessed meant they were with Hitler's private guard.

The guard rose from the floor and faced Kelly, a menacing look on his face. "*Komm mit uns!*" he hissed. "*Schnell!*"

"English?" she asked.

Both men shook their heads. "*Nein.*"

"Why do your two uniforms have different markings than the rest?" she asked for Boyd's benefit.

"*Got it,*" he said. "*There are two of them, and they're with Hitler's personal guard. Way to think on your feet.*"

"I learned from the best," she replied out loud, as the two Germans eyed her quizzically.

They stood behind her and gestured to the open door, making it clear that they would shove her forward violently with the butts of their guns if she didn't start moving on her own.

"*Hang in there, Kelly,*" said Boyd. "*If Hahn is able to kill the power, it will happen soon. So be ready to move. Study your surroundings carefully and try to work out a path you can navigate blind. Remember, they need you alive to use against me, so they won't shoot wildly in the dark.*"

"Roger that," said Kelly out loud, while the two Germans glanced at each other, wondering why this crazy woman continued to talk to herself.

47

Justin Boyd had wrestled with a decision for some time, only reaching one when his amplified hearing indicated that walls of SS soldiers were closing in.

He finally decided to put his faith in Kurt Hahn. To give him five more minutes to kill the lights.

If Boyd had decided the other way, concluded that Hahn had no chance, he would be handling the incoming Nazi force quite differently. He would be preparing to conduct an aggressive, scorched-earth campaign. *Literally* scorched earth.

He would force the SS to search through each room for him, one at a time, and when he saw them spread thin, which would happen before too long, he would take the path of least resistance, shooting his way through whoever was blocking his exit from the mansion while always racing forward, enacting his own personal blitzkrieg. He would rush headlong toward the outside, mowing down anyone in his path, while torching the place behind him, setting drapes, carpets, couches, and libraries aflame to protect his flank and trap as many hostiles inside as he could.

But if his German ally *was* able to kill the power, this would dictate an entirely different strategy. In this case, a raging fire would be the last thing he wanted, as this would provide enough light to level the playing field.

Boyd had busily collected weapons from the men he had downed. Now, along with the machine gun in his hands, he had another draped around his neck, two handguns shoved into two borrowed holsters, and two combat knives, one in a sheath at his side, and one in a sheath strapped to his right ankle.

He chose one of the many bedrooms and hid as nineteen Nazi soldiers spread out like scurrying cockroaches, clearing the larger rooms quickly and continuing to close in toward the middle of the wing.

What he wouldn't give for just a single dragonfly drone, but this was for another life, far away in both time and space.

Boyd checked the time on his lens and scowled. He had been hiding for three minutes and any number of hostiles were nearing the room he was in. If he was going to switch gears and enact his blitzkrieg strategy, he needed to do it *now*.

And then it happened, just like that. The power crashed. It was as if a god had snapped his fingers, and every last light, inside and out, was instantly snuffed out, plunging the mansion complex into total darkness.

Hahn, you magnificent bastard, thought Boyd, borrowing the words that Patton had used when speaking of Rommel. He activated the night vision feature of his lenses and raced from the room, knowing the enemy would be dazed, terrified, and disorganized, and not wanting to give them a chance to regroup, mentally or physically.

He rushed through the premises and picked off four soldiers before they knew what had hit them. He was a sighted man in the midst of a blind, panicked mob, gunning down Nazis with bursts of his machine gun, not because the handgun wouldn't suffice, but knowing that nothing provoked terror like automatic fire.

The survivors, spread out over several rooms and open spaces, ran into each other or walls, and struggled to produce flashlights or light matches, which only served as beacons to alert Boyd to their locations.

The American picked off three more soldiers and then dived to the ground as several of the terrorized Nazis began shooting wildly at phantoms, only succeeding in killing each other in what had become nothing but a circular firing squad.

Boyd continued to spray those left standing, and less than a minute later, all but three of the hostiles were dead. He calmly located the final three survivors and picked them off with ease, not having even begun to break a sweat.

Boyd couldn't help but feel guilty by the unfairness of the battle, but he shook it off. These were members of the *Waffen SS*, not choirboys, and feeling guilty was better than being dead.

* * *

Kelly Connolly took in her surroundings and plotted blind escape routes as she moved toward the central mansion and what she could only guess would be an encounter with Adolf Hitler himself, something she dreaded beyond reason.

All lights vanished in an instant, and the mansion became a cave. Although she had been prepared for this very moment, she hesitated for just a few seconds, as an instinctive aversion to running blind through a cluttered room kicked in.

Finally, breaking free of her brief paralysis, she began moving, but it was too late. One of the two guards dived toward where she had been, blindly, and crashed into the back of her left leg, gripping it as they both fell and pulling her toward him.

She kicked and threw both elbows, but his grip was like steel, and she knew she wasn't going anywhere as his hold on her became more and more secure.

Finally, almost ten seconds later, the man's partner located his flashlight and turned it on, and she was let up from the floor at gunpoint, her situation unimproved.

Kelly heard almost continuous bursts of machine-gun fire through her comm and knew that Boyd had once again sprung into action in the south wing. The two members of Hitler's private guard heard the fire off in the distance and glanced at each other in disbelief, as if wondering how dozens of SS soldiers assigned to this site could possibly be having such a difficult time with just one man.

The firing continued unabated for what seemed like ages and then ceased entirely.

"Did you get them?" said Kelly out loud.

"*I did*," said Boyd, and her relief at hearing his voice was once again palpable, even though she had been more confident this time that he would come out on top. Her own spell in total darkness had driven home just how helpless a blind combatant truly was.

"*Were you able to escape?*" he asked her.

"Not so much. Turns out that running while blind isn't my strong suit."

"*This is all my fault. How could I be so galactically stupid as to introduce you to Zimmerman as my wife?*"

"Everyone's allowed to have their fantasies," she replied.

"Is that an attempt at humor?" said Boyd incredulously. *"How can I possibly resist a woman who can joke under these circumstances?"*

"You clearly can't."

"No doubt," said Boyd. *"I need you to stay alert and optimistic,"* he continued. *"They can't use you as leverage until I'm close enough for them to show me they have you and issue threats. I'm on my way to meet with Hahn. I promise you, Kelly, we're going to figure out a way to get you out of this."*

"I'm going to hold you to that," she replied, as the two Germans prodding her on through the darkness shook their heads yet again, wondering just how crazy she had to be to persist in having a conversation with herself.

* * *

The American major found his German ally crouched low against the east wall of the central mansion in total darkness, his flashlight wisely switched off.

"It's Justin Boyd," he whispered as he neared, so as not to startle him. "Outstanding work, Major," he said.

"Thanks," said Hahn. "Apparently, you didn't do too badly yourself. So what now?"

"Kelly and I are wearing communication devices that you don't have in 1943," he whispered rapidly. "I can hear what she hears, and talk to her from here. Hitler's personal bodyguards have her. My guess is that they're bringing her to where Hitler is now as an insurance policy against me."

"Do you think he's still in the war room?"

"Yes," said Boyd. "But they're about to arrive, so I need to stop talking and listen in."

The German nodded his understanding.

Kelly arrived at her destination only seconds later. *"Welcome, Frau Boyd,"* said a heavily accented voice in Boyd's ear. *"Your husband has been more trouble than we thought he'd be. But don't worry, my comrades will have him here soon."*

"*Your comrades are dead,*" said Kelly in contempt. "*And my husband is just getting started.*"

"Kelly, I need to know how many soldiers are with you," said Boyd, speaking aloud for Hahn's benefit, "and if they brought you to the war room. And don't just tell me directly, since some speak English and might become suspicious."

"*Do you really need six men to keep your Fuhrer safe from a helpless woman?*" said Kelly.

"*I'm not sure the guard you killed would agree that you're helpless,*" said the male voice.

"*I heard there's a war room on site. Is that where we are now?*"

"*Yes. It's right through that door. The Fuhrer is inside, working.*"

"Well done, Kelly," said Boyd. "But keep him talking. The more he talks, the more we learn."

"*So what's he doing in there?*" she continued. "*Is he coming up with war plans by flashlight? You and your men should really go out and restore the power. I'll wait here.*"

"*We will soon. We have all the fuses we need. But we can spare a few minutes until your husband arrives.*"

"*Spare a few minutes?*" said Kelly in disgust. "*What you really mean is that you're terrified to face my husband. And why not? You only outnumber him six to one. Your cowardice is pathetic.*"

"*Watch your tongue!*" spat the SS soldier angrily. "*Don't think I won't kill you because you're a woman.*"

"*No, I know you will. Most of you SS monsters enjoy killing women and children. I'm sure your mother is very proud. But we both know that you need me. At least for now. And I'm going to make sure that your Fuhrer knows his private bodyguards left him in the dark because they didn't have the courage to change a few fuses.*"

"*He isn't in the dark!*" barked the man angrily.

"*Really?*" said Kelly. "*Then why don't I see any light under the door?*"

Boyd's forehead wrinkled in confusion. The soldier had been adamant that the room was still lighted. But if this was so, and the outside waiting area was dark, Kelly would certainly detect a glow coming from under the door.

Boyd gasped. *Of course.* Because Hitler *wasn't* in his war room. He was *underneath* it. He was in a system of rooms and tunnels that must be served by a backup generator, providing ample lighting, since the entire subterranean lair was there for emergencies. He was in a private suite of panic rooms.

That's where they were installing the second set of phones, and why the site wasn't quite finished. The mansion was ready, but the subterranean part was still being completed.

He should have guessed this sooner. Almost no one in 1943 could have done so, but he had the benefit of having just learned the history of the war.

In 1945, the Russians had laid siege to Berlin, and Hitler had been found dead inside an underground command center at his Berlin headquarters, having taken his own life. It was later discovered that the Berghof possessed an extensive subterranean bunker system, as well, consisting of numerous rooms and multi-level concrete tunnels, along with its own power, heating, and ventilation systems. If these other two command centers had been constructed with subterranean lairs, this one would be too.

"Kelly, say the following," he instructed. "'Your Fuhrer is in a bunker, isn't he? Below the war room.'"

"He's in a bunker below the war room, isn't he?" said Kelly immediately. *"Which is why he has working lights,"* she continued, taking Boyd's lead and running with it. *"Because he has a backup generator down there. I should have known he'd be cowering underground,"* she added.

"The Fuhrer is not cowering!" thundered the SS soldier. *"He's there for the lighting, not because he fears for his safety. There are two of my men with him, and we're out here. He has never been safer. He's furious, but he isn't worried in the slightest."*

"He should be worried," said Kelly ominously. *"Because he's as good as dead already. My husband will see to that. I hope you're at least calling in reinforcements to make this fair."*

The man snorted derisively. *"Reinforcements?"* he said in disgust. *"For what? Your husband is probably dead, and mansion security hasn't reported it yet because they're afraid of displeasing the Fuhrer."*

Perfect, thought Boyd. She had elicited a *yes* on the underground lair, and a *no* on reinforcements. "Brilliantly done," he said in admiration. "But I need to leave you for a minute. Be back soon."

He turned quickly to Hahn. "What do you know about the underground tunnels here?" he asked.

"Underground tunnels?" the German repeated in confusion.

"Damn," said Boyd in disappointment. "I need to think," he added hurriedly, cutting off further conversation.

The tunnels would have various entrances and exits, and he needed to find one in a hurry. But they could be *anywhere*. The problem was *daunting*.

He took a deep breath and forced himself to stay calm, to think logically.

If he was in the war room when an enemy force was approaching, what would he want to be in place? First, he'd want a hidden trapdoor that led underground. And then he'd want a tunnel that would allow him to escape by traveling right under the advancing enemy line. He'd want at least one exit that was fairly close. Possibly near a car that he could use to flee to safety.

An image of the elaborate swastika hedge flashed into his mind's eye, and his mouth fell open.

That would be the perfect spot for a tunnel exit.

Its eight-foot walls would offer absolute concealment, and it would provide immediate access to the vehicles parked on the roundabout.

"Kelly," he said excitedly, "I know how we can turn this around. A frontal assault won't work. Not when they have you. But I might have found a backdoor. I'm going to assume I have and put together a quick plan with Major Hahn. Stop talking and listen in. If I'm wrong we'll have to keep thinking, but my gut tells me I'm not."

He paused. "Cough if you understand."

"*Cough*," she said out loud.

Boyd couldn't help but smile. Kelly Connolly was nothing if not an original.

48

Justin Boyd crept along the brick and concrete tunnels with practiced quiet, having found the entrance he was looking for within the expansive hedge sculpture, hidden just below the soil at the intersection of the two hooked swastika arms.

The tunnel system was extensive, although "tunnel" was really a misnomer, as these were finished rectangular corridors, seven feet high, with electric bulbs in the ceiling every eight yards.

He passed several uninhabited rooms, both finished and unfinished, and stopped in one that appeared to be an infirmary, with stainless steel tables, scalpels, blood pressure cuffs, splints, bandages, and a whole host of other equipment, all of it brand-new. Nothing but the best for Hitler and any wounded and retreating members of the German High Command.

He carefully opened various cabinets until he came across several green rolls of tape that beckoned to him like an old friend. *Duct tape.* Incredible. He had learned the history of this miracle product during his recent cramming on the war. It had only been invented by the Allies three months earlier, and must have been taken from fallen American troops.

A mother and ordnance-factory worker had come up with the idea, and she had sent a letter to FDR explaining how such tape could be used to more reliably package ammunition boxes and save lives. Not only did FDR pass this idea on to J&J to produce—originally called *duck tape* for its duck-like resistance to water—but soldiers soon found the tape indispensable for repairing equipment and even sealing wounds.

Boyd shoved a roll in his pocket and moved back into the tunnel. He had other uses for it in mind.

He soon neared a room he estimated to be directly under the war room, and he was easily able to hear the breathing of the three men inside. He hugged a wall and inched closer until he could just see beyond the open door.

His breath caught in his throat as Adolf Hitler came into view.

Boyd's mind almost refused to accept what he was seeing. Arguably the most contemptible human the species had ever produced, he was even more repulsive than his pictures had suggested, his hair greasy and his eyes cold and dead. He was engrossed in a large map on a table, while two guards stood idly by, their backs to Boyd, here only so their Fuhrer could have working lights, and feeling more secure, more untouchable, than they ever had.

If these men were hyper-alert, hyper-vigilant, Boyd's enhanced reflexes would still win the day. But given their false sense of security, a first-year cadet could take them out.

The room looked soundproof, which would be important to the Nazis to ensure they didn't give away their presence to an invading force in the mansion above. Even so, Boyd wanted to minimize noise, and set his machine gun down gently on the ground.

He readied a handgun and burst through the door, putting holes through the skulls of both guards before they had even begun to turn.

Hitler jumped, and his eyes bulged out in shock and terror as Boyd pointed a gun at his chest. "Freeze!" he hissed through clenched teeth, fighting off an almost irresistible urge to pull the trigger.

Hitler didn't speak English, but Boyd's meaning was clear.

"*Sit*," he said subvocally, and Sage pronounced the German word in his ear, as he had instructed the AI to do before entering the room. "*Sitzen!*" he demanded, parroting his AI.

Hitler studied him with contempt, a man who had believed himself invincible for too long, but finally sat in the chair in front of him.

"*Speak and you're dead*," he said subvocally to Sage, who supplied him with the correctly pronounced German translation. "*Sprechen und du bist tot!*" he barked out loud. "*Move* and you're dead!" he added seconds later.

Hitler tested this threat, slowly moving his hand lower under the table, and Boyd shot, carving a shallow but bloody groove across the top of his shoulder.

The American proceeded to bind the prisoner's hands behind him with five revolutions of duct tape, and slapped a piece of this miracle product over his mouth, silencing a man whose poisoned discourse was as putrid as the endless discharge of gas from his flatulent body.

Boyd felt disgusted, diseased, to even be breathing the same air as this man. He would have preferred dunking his head in a vat of cockroaches to touching Hitler's oily skin. He wondered if he would ever feel clean again.

Boyd's lack of German necessitated he communicate in very short sentences. "I can kill you," he said, repeating back Sage's translation, "*Ich kann dich toten*. But I won't. I just want my wife. *Ich will nur meine Frau*. And to escape to England. So, here's the deal. First choice, we go back to your war room. You order your men to send my wife in—alone. All by herself. Then I tie and gag you. And escape through your tunnel."

The American paused. "Take this option and you stay alive. And unhurt. I give you my word. *Ich gebe dir mein Wort*. Unlike you, I'm a man of honor. So this *means* something."

"Or, second choice," hissed Boyd through clenched teeth, "*zweite Wahl*. You cross me. In that case, I shoot out your kneecaps and blind you with my knife."

He leaned in menacingly. "Your decision. *Deine Entscheidung*."

Boyd stared ferociously into Hitler's eyes with utter contempt. "I almost hope you *do* cross me," he added in halting German as he pulled a combat knife from its sheath with maniacal zeal.

"Your move, *Adolf*."

* * *

Kurt Hahn had been crouching silently behind a life-sized statue of a royal Lipizzaner stallion for almost ten minutes now, clutching a machine gun. He was growing restless. The statue was in a library just beyond the ballroom-sized outer waiting area abutting Hitler's war room, and it was still dark as a cave.

But this wasn't true of the immediate vicinity of the war-room door, which was illuminated by several flashlights to reveal six of Hitler's hand-picked guards, with Kelly Connolly out front, being used as a human shield. The men appeared more and more troubled with every passing moment. When Hahn had arrived, a single gun had been pressed into Kelly's back. But a second gun, held by a separate guard, had soon been added for good measure, and was now being held against the back of her skull.

No member of mansion security had yet arrived to report, and it was becoming clear that Justin Boyd had killed every last one of them. The question was, had he been fatally wounded in the effort? If so, he was now also lying dead in the far south wing.

If not, if he had prevailed, unscathed, then he was out there, planning, waiting patiently for an opening to free his wife.

If this latter was the case, the guards' flashlights and tight formation made them sitting ducks, which they could only mitigate by making sure that Kelly couldn't possibly survive an attack.

Hahn continued waiting for something to happen. Either Boyd would tap him on the shoulder, and he would know that the American had failed to find the tunnel entrance, or he would see evidence that the opposite was true. Either way, it would happen *soon*.

Right on cue, three short, distinct German sentences were shouted through the closed door of the war room, so loudly that even Hahn could hear them. Shouted sentences unmistakably issued by Adolf Hitler, himself, whose standard public speaking voice was little more than a shriek.

"Send the girl in here!" demanded the Fuhrer. "Alone! Now!"

Hahn's heart raced and he felt light-headed. Boyd had done it! It was hard for the SS major to believe he wasn't *dreaming*. After all this time, after so many failed attempts to assassinate Adolf Hitler, the time had come at last.

The guards wouldn't be happy about having to give up their human shield, but disobeying a direct order wasn't an option either.

"The Fuhrer would like you to join him, Frau Boyd," said the chief of security in English. "By yourself," he added, gesturing to the door.

Hahn readied himself for action, gritting his teeth in anticipation.

Kelly didn't hesitate to honor this request, well aware that Justin Boyd was behind it, and knowing that her safety and freedom were but a few feet away. She barged through the door and slammed it shut behind her the moment she could.

Hahn waited three seconds for Kelly to work her way deeper into the room and then stepped out from behind the large statue, opening fire with absolute glee. He sprayed the six guards with machine-gun rounds, moving from side to side and then back again, as though he were holding a fire hose and dousing a particularly fierce blaze.

Hahn took his finger off the trigger and marched toward the war room, making his way by the light of two fallen flashlights that hadn't been blown to bits like the others.

It was time to meet Adolf Hitler.

And to send him to the fires of hell where he belonged.

* * *

Kelly entered the war room, which Boyd was illuminating with a single flashlight, and rushed into his arms, kissing him hungrily. Both of them had initiated this at the same time, spontaneously, as if such a greeting was obvious and preordained, while the welcome sounds of machine-gun fire greeted them from outside the door.

Kurt Hahn was carrying out his part of the mission, right on cue.

Kelly reluctantly ended their kiss and almost gagged as she caught her first glimpse of the ruthless psychopath who made the worst serial killer of her day look like a harmless *kitten*. Adolf Hitler, in the bone-chilling flesh. His hands were duct taped to the back of a chair, and Boyd had re-taped the German tyrant's mouth shut the moment he had finished issuing his command.

The door opened once again, and a beaming Kurt Hahn stood before the threshold. "We did it!" he said triumphantly.

But as he took a step into the room, one of Hitler's guards, bleeding out on the ground, managed to squeeze off two shots before expiring, one piercing Hahn's stomach and another his chest.

The SS major fell forward into darkness, coughing blood.

"Nooo!" shouted Boyd in horror, rushing over to the fallen soldier and kneeling down beside him.

"You're going to be okay, Kurt," he assured him. "Hang in there. There's an infirmary underground, and I'll have you patched up in no time."

Hahn shook his head, almost imperceptibly. "Can't save me," he whispered as more blood fell from his mouth. "It's okay. Was . . . swept up in evil. Did terrible things. Tried to . . . make amends. But . . . deserve this."

He turned his head. "Show me . . . Hitler," he said faintly.

Boyd shined his flashlight on the Nazi Fuhrer tied to a chair.

Hahn managed the hint of a smile, despite being seconds away from death, and roused up the energy to spit a ball of blood in Hitler's direction. "Kill him," he pleaded. "Hurry. Before I . . . go."

"I will," said Boyd. "But you need to know you *have* made amends, *have* redeemed yourself. And we couldn't have made it without you."

Boyd quickly made his way over to the prisoner, setting a flashlight on the table so the beam was directed at Hitler's face. He then stood behind him and forced one forearm under his chin and pressed hard on the back of his head with the other.

Hitler thrashed against his bonds and screamed into his duct-tape gag, but seconds later became absolutely still.

Boyd released the monster's head and watched in satisfaction as it collapsed against his chest and lolled around lifelessly.

"He's dead," he said simply to Kurt Hahn.

A euphoric smile spread across the German's face. "Thank you," he whispered, and then, closing his eyes, he took his final breath, dying happily with the knowledge that this psychopathic scourge on Germany and the entire human race was finally gone.

49

There was a long silence in the dark war room. Kelly felt numb. In a matter of seconds, they had lost a man who had become a valued ally and put an end to Adolf Hitler before he could inflict even more damage on the world.

These were stunning developments. Far too much to digest.

Boyd caught her eye and blew out a long breath. "He isn't dead," he said in disgust.

"*Who* isn't dead?"

"Hitler. I used a choke hold—a sleeper hold—and he'll only be out for fifteen to twenty minutes."

Kelly's eyes bulged. "What?" she said in disbelief. "But you told Hahn that he was."

"I know. It was the least I could do for him in the last seconds of his life."

"Well then kill him now!" insisted Kelly. "What are you waiting for? Give me a gun and *I'll* do it."

"Aren't you the one who won't kill spiders? Who would never take a helpless life unless you *had* to."

"Are you kidding me? This isn't a spider. This is Adolf *fricking* Hitler. No one has ever deserved to die more. And we *do* have to take his life. Killing him will save millions."

Kelly couldn't believe her ears. Was Justin Boyd really hesitating? Yes, he killed only reluctantly, and only when necessary, but no case had ever been more open and shut.

"What about changing history?" said Boyd.

"Too late. You've wiped out one of Hitler's residences, killed dozens of guards, including his private team. You *kidnapped* him."

"I know. But I think this has happened before. I think we did it in a previous cycle. Maybe an infinite number of previous cycles. Sage has no record of Rolling Hills Mansion. But how can that be? It should be as famous to history as the Berghof."

"The what?" said Kelly.

"Just trust me, since it was scheduled to be one of Hitler's principal headquarters very soon, Sage should know all about it. It should have been part of *our* history. But I think our actions here are what changed that. We left Hitler alive. My guess is that he'll awaken, humiliated. He won't want the world to know how vulnerable he was. That he was at our mercy. That we killed more than thirty members of his security detail.

"So he'll hide it," continued Boyd. "He'll call one of his inner circle to come get him, and pretend this never happened. He'll pretend he was never here. I wouldn't put it past him to torch the place on his way out. But no matter what, I'm sure he'll keep these events a closely guarded secret. So closely guarded that the Rolling Hills Mansion never makes the history books."

Kelly shrank back in disgust. "Even if we *haven't* changed our future to this point," she said, "we need to now. Because this abomination *has* to die. And no amount of inertia will keep history on track with a change this huge."

"Didn't you promise the Enigma AI that you'd do your best to minimize changes?"

"This situation supersedes that promise. If there's ever a justification for changing history, this is it."

"Even if this were true, we have to let him wake up. Sage just told me she doesn't have enough of a voice sample to impersonate him with perfect accuracy."

"How can that be?"

"Hitler purposely shrieked his words out when speaking publicly. He thought it helped him project the ultimate command presence. There is only one known recording of his normal speaking voice, and this has been degraded through time."

"But you just had him all to yourself?"

"Yes, but I insisted he remain silent. I only let him speak to bark the order for you to join us. I asked Sage if she could transmit an impersonated voice through these phones when I was planning our escape, but I thought what you thought. That she'd have plenty of Hitler voice samples to go on. When I learned this wasn't the case, I planned to get him to talk once you were safe. But Hahn only had seconds to live, and he was pleading to see him dead. And we *owed* him that."

"So we're stuck here until Adolf Hitler comes to and we can get him to use his *inside* voice? Really?"

"I'm afraid so," said Boyd. "But I think we're safe here. This place doesn't get uninvited guests. When I was planning this, Hahn gave me the name of one of the Luftwaffe pilots tasked with the transport of supplies and human resources between here and the Atlantis Cube site in Canada. A Captain Warren Kruger. Kruger didn't bring either of us here, so he won't know who we are, and he speaks English. Hahn also diagrammed the placement of the tripwires in Canada and the layout of every building in the encampment, which Sage recorded."

Kelly sighed. She knew of Boyd's inspired plan to have Sage impersonate Hitler and order a pilot to take them back to Canada, but she didn't know the details. Still, it was obvious that they couldn't jeopardize their escape by having Sage use a less-than-perfect impersonation.

"You've never really walked me through the entire plan from here," she said.

"It's simple. We pick up a phone in the war room connected to Hitler's switchboard, and have 'Hitler' ask a switchboard operator to place a call to this Captain Kruger. The switchboard will know the call is originating from here and will make sure that Kruger is informed that the Fuhrer is on the line. With a perfect impersonation, he won't doubt it's really Hitler for a second."

Boyd paused. "I'll be feeding Sage her lines in real-time. I plan on having Sage/Hitler tell the captain that you and I saved the Fuhrer's life at the Rolling Hills Mansion, but that Kruger can never breathe a word of this to another soul. Ever. That we're Canadians working for the Reich who need to be reinstalled in Canada. That Hitler wants him to pick us up at the mansion's roundabout as soon as possible and fly us to wherever we want to go. That he needs to follow Justin

Boyd's every order, no matter what, as if Boyd were the Fuhrer himself. And again, Hitler will insist that not even Kruger's superiors can know that this discussion ever took place. That it's a top-secret mission that can never be disclosed to anyone."

"That should do the trick," said Kelly.

"As I said, we should be safe in this room for some time to come. But as an added precaution, we can wait in the tunnels until Kruger's expected arrival time here, and then meet him at the roundabout."

"How do we get inside the tunnels, anyway?" asked Kelly. "Trapdoor?"

Boyd shined a flashlight against the back wall, which showed shelf after shelf of military texts. "That's a sliding bookcase," he said with the hint of a smile. "There's an entrance and ramp down to the tunnels behind it."

Kelly groaned. "Wow," she said. "A sliding bookcase leading to a secret room is cliché, even in 1943."

"True, but unless you expect there to be a tunnel system, you'd never think to check."

"Okay," said Kelly, changing the subject. "I love the plan. But as soon as Sage has the Hitler voice sample she needs, you *are* going to be killing him, right?"

Boyd frowned. "Look, it's been the dream of millions to kill this bastard. Mine too. I can't tell you how hard it was not to pull the trigger when I first had him in my sights. But I've had access to Sage's database and dozens of hours of downtime to study up on this war. And it turns out that we *shouldn't* kill him. Not now."

"Are you out of your mind?"

"*Come on*, Kelly," he said, sounding hurt. "You don't think I despise him as much as you do? As much as *anyone* would? You don't think I'd give my life a hundred times over to see him dead? But hear me out."

Kelly nodded, coming back to her senses. He was right to be hurt. He had never given her a reason to doubt his judgment. So the least she could do was give him the benefit of the doubt. "Sorry, Justin," she said. "I know you must have your reasons. Go ahead."

"Look, I understand. When Hitler is involved, emotions run high, and all bets are off. But killing him now could well make the future *worse* rather than better. *Much* worse."

Kelly's eyes narrowed. Hitler's reign had been so horrific and bloody, it never crossed her mind that history might be worse if he were killed prematurely. But maybe this was so. Boyd seemed certain of it.

"The more I read about this time, and the more I thought about it," continued Boyd, "the more it seems like a miracle that things worked out as well as they did. And yes, I'm well aware that more than seventy-five million people perished in World War II. That Hitler gassed six million Jews, and exterminated, castrated, or sterilized untold others, be they Gypsies, homosexuals, the disabled, clergy, and so on. He was an equal opportunity psychopath. But even given these atrocities, it was still a miracle things didn't turn out even *worse*.

"First, a little relevant background," he added. "In 1939, Germany and Russia signed a treaty of non-aggression known as the Molotov–Ribbentrop Pact. Then, in 1940, Hitler tried to get Russia to ally with Germany and the Axis powers, and came close. If he had succeeded, Germany, Russia, Japan, and Italy would have conquered the world and divided up the spoils. Nothing could have stopped them. But the negotiations broke down, and a year later Hitler stabbed Stalin in the back, invading Russia in direct violation of their non-aggression pact."

Boyd paused. "You should also know that in a few months from now, FDR, Churchill, and Stalin secretly met for the first time in Tehran, Iran. Secretly *will* meet," he corrected.

"Keep going," said Kelly. "Don't worry about tenses, I know what you mean."

"This meeting ultimately will lead to plans for the D-Day invasion of Normandy. These were very tense and delicate discussions, which almost fell apart."

Kelly found herself hanging on Boyd's every word. She had never been a history buff. On the other hand, she was now sitting in a pitch-black room illuminated only by flashlight, giving this the feel of a spooky-story session at a campout, debating whether or not to kill Adolf Hitler, while the man in question sat ten feet away.

If this couldn't bring history to life, nothing ever could.

"I could flesh out my thesis for hours, but I'll get right to it. If we kill Hitler tonight, Nazi Germany could be dramatically weakened. His death could leave a power vacuum and spark a civil war, crippling Germany. Which you'd think would be ideal. You'd think the Allies would then go on to an easy victory. Game over."

"Why isn't that the case?" asked Kelly.

"Because this could well set the stage for *Russia* to take Hitler's place. With Germany defanged, Stalin could roll across Europe and take over very quickly. The Russian army at the end of the war had more than twice as many men and armaments as the rest of the Allies combined. And the alliance between the Allies and Russia was uneasy, at best. Both sides had plans drawn up to attack the other at the end of the war. Both sides suspected they'd be enemies in a World War III soon enough, so why not start it when their armies and equipment were already in full gear? In some ways it's a miracle that these tensions only led to a *cold* war between Russia and America after WWII, rather than a *hot* one."

Kelly shook her head. How had she not known any of this?

"So cripple Germany," continued Boyd, "and Stalin might break off from his uneasy alliance with the rest of the Allied powers and complete the world conquest that Hitler started. And Stalin was an epic, historic monster in his own right. He executed more than a million of his own citizens. Millions more died in labor camps, massacres, and famines. Many historians believe that Stalin was responsible for even more deaths than *Hitler* was. He was just as ruthless a psychopath, but in many ways he was better at it than Hitler. Shrewder."

Boyd paused to allow this to sink in. "So weaken the Nazis," he continued, "and you might find yourself with an even bigger monster to deal with. But there is another alternative, one that I think is more likely. If we kill Hitler tonight, we might make the Nazis considerably *stronger*. Strong enough to *win* the war this time.

"Not hard to imagine," he added. "Hitler was superstitious and irrational. And by 1943 his health was deteriorating quickly. Not only was he flatulent, he was often ill with stomach pains, headaches, nausea, and diarrhea, and was on a host of meds to keep him going. He slept late and demanded that he never be disturbed. He paralyzed his own forces by insisting on too much control, by not being available until eleven or noon, and by failing to heed wise advice from his best generals. For example, Rommel wanted to position tank divisions close to the French coastline to repel a D-Day style invasion, but his request was overruled by Hitler. *Will be* overruled.

"So it's easy to imagine Hitler's replacement being much more competent than he was. He surrounded himself with ruthless men who subscribed to his vision of totalitarianism. And many of these were better strategists, in better health, who would be more willing to delegate, allow themselves to be awakened in emergencies, make better decisions, and so on. And even if Himmler wasn't the one to take over, he'd remain exceedingly powerful, so the holocaust would very likely continue unabated."

Kelly considered. She couldn't argue Boyd's point. Just because Hitler had excelled at fanning zealotry, hatred, and a diseased ideology didn't make him a master war strategist.

"And what if the new, stronger Nazi leader decided to try to bury the hatchet with Russia?" continued Boyd. "To tempt Stalin to switch sides and *join* Germany and Japan, as Hitler had tried to do in 1940? The new leader could insist that Hitler was solely to blame for the collapse of the German-Soviet Axis talks, and for later stabbing them in the back. That he, the new leader, had been dead set against the invasion of Russia, and had been horrified by this development. The more competent the German leader, the more it would be in Russia's best interest to change sides. Join them rather than fight them."

"In which case the Allies would be screwed."

"Very," agreed Boyd. "But even if this *didn't* happen, a stronger Nazi leader could change Stalin's calculations. As I said, FDR had barely managed to talk him into supporting D-Day, with great difficulty. So replace Hitler now, and maybe Stalin doesn't support D-Day this time, and it never happens.

"Worse, maybe it happens, but it now becomes the ultimate disaster. The new Fuhrer might listen to Rommel and be ready for the attack this time. Or at least allow himself to be awakened in time to react properly and win the day."

Kelly felt sick to her stomach. Boyd had laid it out like a demented Goldilocks fable. Strengthen Germany and Nazi fascism might dominate the world for decades, maybe centuries to come. *Weaken* Germany, and Stalinist Russia might dominate the world, with its own form of fascism in communist clothing. But leave Hitler in power and you threaded the needle—the porridge was just right.

"So you have all these forces," continued Boyd, "balanced on a razor's edge. A delicate dynamic. Treacherously complex. Push on any side of the triangle just a little and you might end up with German domination, Russian domination, or World War III between the US and Russia.

"And this is before trying to factor in the atomic bomb, which won't be ready in the current timeline until the middle of 1945. With Hitler gone, do the Nazis make the sabotage of the Manhattan Project a top priority? Does *Russia* decide to go after it? Is America thrashed by either Germany or Russia to the point where it feels forced to drop atomic bombs on Europe once they're available? And would this even succeed? After all, if Russia or Germany controlled the skies, they could well prevent this from happening, as the bombs could only be dropped by slow-moving planes."

Kelly swallowed hard. "I had no idea things could get this complicated," she admitted.

"When Hahn told me where we were," said Boyd, "and suggested killing Hitler, I was against it, not wanting to risk everything to try it. But I changed my mind. As you said, if ever there was a justification to take risks, to change history, this was it. But before I went forward, I took it upon myself to double-check the implications."

He shook his head miserably. "No one was more shocked by what this revealed than I was. How could killing Hitler be the wrong decision? It was an insane result, one that I fought for some time. If we don't end him now, millions more will die in gas chambers. And how could I live with myself, knowing I had the chance to kill him and didn't take it?

"Besides," he added, "my analysis could be dead wrong. It's like trying to read tea leaves. Historians might be able to poke holes in my thesis the size of Texas, and ten of them could come to ten different conclusions."

Boyd sighed. "I finally realized there was only thing I could be certain of—the way things turned out in the history *we* know. In the time period we're in now, there were four fascist/totalitarian forces, led by four monsters: Adolf Hitler, Joseph Stalin, Benito Mussolini, and Hideki Tojo.

"While Stalinist Russia was technically communist rather than fascist, because of the way Stalin wielded his communism, the practical outcome was almost identical. And Tojo was just as ruthless as Hitler and Stalin. Between 1937 and 1945, the Japanese military murdered as many as six million Chinese, Koreans, and others, many of them civilians. During the infamous Nanking Massacre alone, the Japanese slaughtered hundreds of thousands of Chinese and raped thousands of women."

Boyd paused for several seconds to let this sink in.

"But despite this worldwide surge of brutal fascist tyrants," he continued, "all arising at the same time, in the history *we* know, fascism was defeated, and democracy ended up thriving. So I've concluded that even if my analysis only has a small chance of being correct, how can I take any risk that this outcome might change? How can I live with myself if Stalin ends up replacing Hitler and succeeds in turning the world fascist where Hitler failed? Or if the Nazis end up winning this time? Or if in the new timeline, the Manhattan Project bomb is sabotaged, and Tojo's Japan somehow becomes triumphant?

"This change of history could well result in the defeat of the Allies, of America. Instead of the rise of democratic, peace-loving societies around the world, which we know is what happens if Hitler lives until 1945, we could get the opposite."

Kelly shook her head in horror. WWII had been sickening on so many levels. These years were humanity's very darkest. But after the war ended, the world improved with every passing decade. Less poverty, longer life, fewer wars, more democracies. It was far from perfect, but it was almost as if the world had hit rock bottom in these years, and then vowed to avoid the future it had narrowly missed at all costs.

"Goddammit!" she said in disgust. "We're going to have to let the bastard live, aren't we? I so want this evil asshole to die, I can't even tell you."

"You don't have to. I *know*. And I don't like it any more than you do. If I could kill him as a baby, I'd do it in a heartbeat. But not in 1943, when the world's war machines are in full gear, and so many forces are in such delicate balance."

"Well, as much as I hate to say it, thanks for doing such a thorough analysis. I never imagined saying this, but killing Hitler here really could have been the biggest mistake we ever made. So what now?"

"He'll awaken any minute. We'll get a voice sample to satisfy Sage's needs, bind and gag him more securely, and knock him unconscious so he won't trouble us while we recruit Kruger and begin our flight to Canada."

"Won't Hitler find out we called this Luftwaffe captain when he comes to?"

"That's doubtful. He'll think we fled the moment we could. Which is what I told him we'd be doing. I told him that if he did as I asked, I'd leave him alive and we'd flee to England—you know, just to throw in a little misdirection. Not that he'd imagine we'd go back to Canada in a million years. Or imagine we'd impersonate his voice and call a pilot."

"So you're going to put him in another sleeper hold right before the pilot is due to pick us up?"

"Not a chance," said Boyd with a weary smile. "I need him knocked out for an *extended* period when we leave. And there won't be anything gentle about the way I do it *this* time. I can't kill this repulsive maggot of a man. But the least I can do is make sure that he wakes up in some *serious* pain."

PART 8

"Battle not with monsters,
Lest ye become a monster.
And if you gaze into the abyss,
The abyss gazes back into you."

—Friedrich Nietzsche, German philosopher

50

The never-ending roar of the transport plane's churning propellers wailed in Kelly Connolly's head, but while she had expected the journey to be long, perilous, and cramped, it turned out to be a godsend, instead, a tranquil life preserver in a stormy sea.

Boyd's plan had gone like clockwork, and Captain Kruger couldn't have been more accommodating—still pinching himself that he had actually spoken to the Fuhrer—and willing to do anything for the two people who he had been told had saved the Fuhrer's life.

Sage, in her debut role playing the most evil man in history, had ordered Kruger to take them to Canada and to follow Boyd's orders. The captain had been surprised when Boyd asked to be flown to the secret Atlantis Cube site. Even more surprised when Boyd insisted that he maintain radio silence, to the point of not even responding to Colonel Zimmerman's attempts to contact him upon arrival. Kruger would simply land, drop them off, and then take off again before the propellers even stopped spinning, never telling another soul the identities of the passengers he had flown. Or even that he had made the trip.

The Luftwaffe pilot had understandably questioned these strange orders, but Boyd had told him he wasn't free to answer, and had then reminded him they were on a secret mission that had the Fuhrer's full support. Given how convincing Sage's performance had been, Kruger didn't press any further.

The torturous flight Kelly had imagined turned out to be *amazing*. Instead of cramped seats and quarters, she and Boyd could practically luxuriate in the private cargo hold, a sizable space they had all to themselves, since they were the only passengers or cargo on board. The hold was crisscrossed with rope handholds, but the flight had been remarkably smooth, and these were rarely necessary.

Kruger had brought along four military-issue sleeping bags for them to use to get comfortable, the same design German soldiers had used to keep warm at night on the Russian front. These were large, rugged, and brownish-green in color, with canvas on the outside and soft flannel within, along with flat metal buttons, leather-reinforced buttonholes, and brass grommets. Mercifully, the bags had no military or Nazi markings. Like the vast majority of people around the world, they found the swastika repugnant, and had been drowning in these symbols since their arrival in the past.

The two American passengers both managed to get in ten hours of sound sleep on a trip that would last twenty-eight, having been more exhausted, physically *and* mentally, than they had ever been. Kruger had taken a four-hour nap during a layover on a tiny island, one of dozens spread throughout the five hundred thousand square miles that comprised the Hudson Bay. An island too small and unimportant to even show up on charts. The island was rarely used by the Nazis, for refueling purposes only, and they had been the sole inhabitants during their entire stay there.

The fact that Kelly could spread out, sleep, and relax with no immediate threats to her life, to history, or to the fate of humankind was amazing in and of itself. But the multiple sessions of lovemaking she and Justin Boyd engaged in as soon as they realized they were alone, as fast as they could tear each other's clothes off, were even *more* amazing.

The sex had been intense, passionate, *electric*. They had worked as a team, survived against incredible odds, saved each other's lives a number of times, and were highly compatible even before they were thrown together in the trenches. But in addition, she learned that having her life in constant danger, operating under intense, adrenaline-fueled fight-or-flight conditions for days, had unleashed a greater need for human contact, for intimacy, for connection, than she had ever felt before. The lovemaking was almost a religious experience for her, a desperately needed release for her body and mind.

Afterward, they would chat for hours, growing ever closer, and then fall asleep, only to awaken and repeat the entire sequence all over again. They allowed themselves to temporarily pretend they were back in 2027, having a normal existence, and speak of friends, and family, and careers, and favorite books and movies, and anything else that might be considered normal for a couple to share after having epic sex.

Kelly tried to put all worries out of her mind, but one managed to burrow its way in. If her grandfather's future was changed in the slightest, she would never be born. But Boyd would. His parents in faraway Nebraska wouldn't be affected at all.

In this case, she might be able to travel to some point in the future, possibly even back to 2027. This would depend on whether the cube was ever activated in the new timeline, since she would no longer exist to activate it herself, and time travel required an active cube on the other end.

There was no way to know if this would be the case, but if it were, she'd be able to get back to modern civilization. Boyd, on the other hand, would not be, as he would be blocked by another version of himself.

So what would she do in this case? How could she *not* travel back to her own time? She didn't belong here. She had never waxed nostalgically for life in 1943. What would she do in a scientifically primitive world, without access to a computer, or the internet, or a cell phone? There was so much she took for granted that didn't exist here.

But how could she leave Boyd behind? How could she sentence him to this same fate all alone? A fate he would never have had to face if not for her, since her theft of the cube had set everything that followed in motion.

Besides, they were great together. They weren't in love—maybe only because no adult would admit, even to themselves, that they had fallen in love so quickly—but it was only a matter of time.

The ethical dilemmas, the impossible decisions, just kept coming, and didn't get any easier. Just a week ago, her biggest decision was which type of cheese to buy. Now her decisions involved stealing the world's most powerful object, engaging in mass murder, killing Adolf Hitler, changing history, and leaving a man behind whom she was coming to love.

She realized as she thought it through that she wouldn't abandon him. That she *couldn't* abandon him. To do so was unthinkable. And she was equally sure that he wouldn't abandon her if their situations were reversed.

When they were two hours from their destination, they made love for a fourth time, which was almost as epic as the first three, and she rested her head on Boyd's chest, as content as she had ever been.

"Now *that's* the way to join the mile-high club," he said, putting his arm around her.

"Really?" replied Kelly with a grin. "You wouldn't prefer having sex inside a disgusting 737 lavatory the size of a dresser?"

"Not so much."

"Yeah, I never got the appeal. I guess people do it for the excitement, not the venue."

"Well, I prefer to be boring," said Boyd in amusement. "Our first kiss was inside the back seat of a car while hiding from Chinese commandos. Our first sex was in the cargo hold of a Nazi long-distance transport plane, more than fifty years before we were born." He grinned. "I mean, who hasn't done *that*? It's a tale as old as time. Maybe we're being *too* cliché."

Kelly laughed. "Nah, it's best to stick with the classics. And what girl *hasn't* dreamed of sleeping with a guy for the first time inside a Nazi plane?"

He rolled his eyes. "I know we've alluded to this before, but how did we get in a situation where every second brings another absurdity?"

"It wasn't easy, that's for sure," said Kelly wryly.

They laid in silence for several minutes. "I can't tell you how great I feel right now," said Boyd. "How great I feel about *you*. About *us*. But in a few minutes, I'm going to have to leave this fantasy and begin preparing for the landing—and for *after* the landing."

Kelly winced. "I know," she said, and seconds later, several tears escaped and rolled down her face, a habit she had developed lately that she couldn't seem to break.

Boyd kissed her forehead gently and remained silent, allowing her to decide if she wanted to share her feelings or keep them to herself.

"Sorry," she said softly. "But how can it be that we have yet another massacre to commit? *One* is inconceivable. But they just keep coming. It's too much. I know we've had this discussion before, but I have enough blood on my hands for a thousand lifetimes."

"I know. And it's little comfort, but all I can keep telling you is that we've made the decisions we've had to make. Horrible decisions that have been forced upon us. A train was about to hit ten people, so you switched the track to only kill one. Intellectually, you know you had no choice. But emotionally, it isn't about the math. It's easy for you, a wonderful, caring person, to lose sight of the ten lives saved, and focus on the one your actions ended."

Boyd shook his head. "Still," he continued, "you have to know you did the right thing. That it was the only possible decision. That if you hadn't had the strength to make this decision, you'd be even more haunted by the ten lives you *failed* to save."

He kissed her gently on the forehead once again and held her in silence.

"Let me try a different angle," he continued after a few minutes had passed. "You read your grandfather's journal. Read of his plans to wipe out the entire Nazi compound in Canada, which included SS soldiers, but also numerous civilian scientists. He must have done this himself the first time, before whatever loop we might be in got started. And while his journal said he didn't remember doing it, when you read it, you assumed he had, right?"

She nodded.

"And you understood *why*. To keep the cube from Hitler. Because if witnesses were left behind, Hitler would be even more interested in Otto and the cube and would galvanize every resource he had to hunt them both down."

Boyd paused. "So what did you think of Otto after you read this passage? Did you see him as a monster?"

"No," she said with a sigh. "I saw him as having to make impossible choices. But choices that were well justified. Choices he was forced into. I saw him as a hero for making sure the cube was protected first from Hitler, and then from mankind."

"Then why aren't you a hero for doing the same?"

"I get what you're saying. I did find Otto's actions justifiable. But that was when they were in the abstract, eighty-four years in the past. When I'm the one pulling the trigger, when I'm the one looking into the eyes of fellow human beings as I end their lives, I feel like the *opposite* of a hero."

"I know," said Boyd softly. "And I keep putting you in this position, over and over again. It's a nightmare that won't end. So you need to sit this one out. I've got it. Just hide near the runway and it'll be over before you know it."

Kelly was tempted to take him up on this offer, even though putting blinders on was nothing but self-delusion. Boyd likely *could* handle the situation without her. He would have the element of surprise. He possessed telephoto lenses and bionic hearing. But even better, he had made certain they would land at night, when his night-vision lenses would provide the ultimate advantage. His reflexes and strength were genetically enhanced, and his blood was so doped with respirocytes he could run for miles without taking a breath. He was smarter than they were, better trained, more experienced.

She frowned. Even if he could handle this alone, she couldn't let him. They were in this together. Anything could happen, and with her along, his task was greatly simplified. He would just need to get her to the cube, rather than battle the entire encampment himself.

Strangely, she was buoyed by what the Enigma AI had told her, that it had judged her somehow and found her to be worthy, well-intentioned. She had no idea how this judgment had been made, and against what standard. And she wasn't sure why she should care about an assessment made by an alien AI. Still, this did help her as she contemplated the unspeakable.

"Thanks, Justin," she said after a long silence, "but I can't let you shoulder this burden all on your own. Not when I can help by using an unstoppable weapon. And not with stakes as high as they are."

Kelly sighed miserably. "You know," she added, "Nietzsche once said that if you battled with monsters, you couldn't help but become one yourself. That it was inevitable."

Boyd kissed her gently on the forehead one last time. "That's only because Nietzsche never met *you*," he said earnestly.

51

The transport plane was equipped with an instrument landing system, which had become increasingly popular during the war for use when runway lighting was ill-advised, and Kruger had landed in the dark on this very runway dozens of times. His landing on this occasion was perfect, and he stopped just long enough for his passengers to exit before turning and launching the plane back into the sky.

Boyd was loaded to the gills with weapons, and Kelly clutched a large rucksack with medical supplies, food, and water. Once again, she would be carrying the bag to free Boyd's hands for the assault to come.

Boyd was fully aware that the SS soldiers on sky watch couldn't have missed the transport plane's approach and landing, even if they had been blind, as they were quite familiar with the roar of six separate propellers, three on each wing. They would be waking Zimmerman even now, reporting that an unscheduled German transport plane had mysteriously landed and taken off again while maintaining radio silence, and the colonel would send men to investigate.

Boyd had briefly considered eliminating these men as they approached the runway, but without a silencer, he would need to kill them all with a knife, and this would be challenging, even for him. If any of them got off a single shot, the entire camp would be awake and on high alert.

They both opened their comms so they could hear whatever the other heard, as they had done in the mansion. Boyd wanted all communications between them to go through Sage, with him speaking subvocally and her whispering.

But he first addressed his AI. *"You have the tripwire map Hahn gave me in Berlin,"* he said, *"but this map may be out of date. So process all visual input from my lenses from here on out, scanning for tripwires and anything else out of place in a forest. Alert me as soon as you identify anything."*

"*Understood,*" said Sage.

Boyd could detect flashlights quickly approaching, and estimated that Zimmerman was sending four men to investigate.

"*Okay, Kelly,*" he said subvocally. "*Let's get this over with.*"

There were flashlights in the bag Kelly carried, but while he hated to effectively blind her once again, any glow in the blackness would give their position away. He took her hand and guided her carefully through the woods, circling around beyond the approaching investigative force. Their pace was necessarily slow, but they made it to their destination with no trouble, as expected, easily avoiding the three tripwires that Sage identified.

As unsettling as the darkness was for Kelly, it once again proved itself to be Boyd's greatest ally.

They made their way to the edge of the encampment closest to the cube room, where Otto's journal indicated Kurt Hahn had helped him hide and retrieve his dark energy generator each morning and night. It should be inside a hollowed-out section of a large fallen tree, camouflaged by a removable moss-covered plug of dirt and roots that Hahn had found in another section of forest. Boyd found the fallen tree in question, and both he and Kelly held their breath. If Otto had moved the generator, their odds of success would plummet.

The American major removed the moss plug and reached in. It was there! Right where it was supposed to be. A device that would have been groundbreaking in 2027, but which was an absolute miracle in 1943.

"*So far, so good,*" said Boyd, placing the device gently inside Kelly's rucksack.

With this completed, he located an overgrown area of the forest floor about ten feet away, at the base of a mighty trunk, and sat Kelly down.

"*Watch carefully for any beams of light heading your direction,*" he told her. "*Roll out of their way if you can. If you can't, let me know immediately.*"

"Will do," she replied, and even though he was very close, he could only hear her faint whisper through his comm, which was reassuring.

He made his way to the building that housed the cube and was encouraged by how silent and sedate the encampment seemed to be. Based on flashlights, the four men were now making their way back from the runway, no doubt still scratching their heads, and a number of others were spread out beyond the periphery of the camp, on standard patrol.

He hated to leave Kelly alone, even for a moment, but clearing a path for her to reach the cube would be very ugly, and he wasn't about to let her witness it. Guards would be awake in the cube room. But this wouldn't be the case in the outer room, and killing soldiers in their *sleep* was a whole new level of despicable.

Once he was finished with these heinous acts, he would kill the men guarding the cube and drag them into the dark outer room to join their slain comrades. Finally, with this completed, he would guide Otto and Kelly past the grisly dead bodies, which they'd be unable to see, and into the cube room. Once Kelly unlocked the cube, she could do her thing, and it would all be over.

Boyd entered the structure with practiced quiet and took inventory. Five SS soldiers were spread out on cots, all of them sleeping.

He surveyed the room for a second time, his pulse quickening.

Where was Otto Richter?

When they had been here last, the eighteen-year-old had lost his permission to sleep with the cube, but had been relegated to the outer room. Boyd had counted on this not changing.

But it had. And while no plan survived engagement with the enemy, this was a potentially disastrous development.

"Change of plans," he said subvocally to Kelly. *"Otto isn't here. We need to find him fast. I'll conduct an interrogation and keep you posted."*

Boyd removed a combat knife from its sheath and carefully slit the first guard's throat, pressing his left hand over the soldier's mouth, pushing up to expose his jugular, and then slashing through it in a single motion with his right, taking care that the eruption of blood didn't hit him or any of the other guards. He repeated this process three more times, quickly and methodically.

With four down, he pressed his hand hard over the mouth of the fifth to suppress noise, but instead of killing him, put him in a sleeper hold. This time he cut off the man's airway for a much shorter period of time than he had done with Hitler, ensuring the soldier would only be out for a minute or two.

When Boyd felt the body go limp, he lifted the man in a fireman's carry and rushed outside and into darkness, moving through the woods for about twenty seconds to put distance between himself and the encampment.

The soldier came to less than a minute later to find himself being held from behind, with a knife pressed into his throat. "Where is Otto Richter?" whispered Boyd.

"Ich spreche kein Englisch," replied his hostage.

Boyd consulted Sage, who was down to her last few hours of power. *"Flustern oder sterben,"* he hissed, repeating the exact pronunciation provided by his AI. *Whisper or die. "Wo ist Otto Richter?"*

After two minutes of further knife-point interrogation, Boyd had his answers, and snapped the SS soldier's neck, lowering his limp body to the forest floor. He then brought Kelly up to speed. She had heard the man's words, but wasn't able to translate.

Just that morning, Otto had been caught destroying the dark energy generator that Alex Wentz had been constructing, using Otto's found notebook. Wentz must have been very near the finish line, and it was clear that Otto had decided he had no other choice but to show his hand, in what must have been an act of total desperation. An act designed to buy his granddaughter and her commando friend a few more weeks to make it back to Canada. Remarkably, Otto hadn't given up hope that they would somehow find a way.

The German prodigy was now chained once again inside the same conference room/prison in which they had first met. This was his first day of what was expected to be two weeks of solitary confinement.

And Colonel Zimmerman once again held the keys to his shackles.

Which meant that what should have been a straightforward Op had suddenly become far more complicated.

"Stay where you are," he told Kelly as he began making his way back to the encampment. *"I'll get the keys from Zimmerman, free Otto, and then get you into the cube room as planned."*

Two flashlight beams suddenly appeared, and Boyd dived into the brush a second before they swept by where he had been. He guessed they were being held by two of the men who had investigated the strange landing and takeoff, and they were getting closer in a hurry.

Boyd stayed to the side of the beams, behind a tree, and waited for them to pass.

Closer. Closer. Now!

Boyd slipped soundlessly from the shadows and fell into place behind one of the two men, snatching his head and breaking his neck with a sickening crack.

His partner jumped in surprise and turned to fire, but Boyd chopped the gun from his hand and spun him around. Before the man knew what was happening the American was behind him with a knife to his neck, just as his comrade had recently been.

"Flustern oder sterben," said Boyd in his ear, *whisper or die*, which was becoming his favorite German phrase. "Do you speak English?" he added.

"Yes," whispered the SS soldier.

"Good. Were you part of the team checking out the runway?"

"Yes."

"Have you reported your findings to Zimmerman?"

"Yes, just a few minutes ago. But there *weren't* any findings."

"So where is the colonel now?"

"I can't tell you that."

Boyd flicked his knife, and blood began to fall from a deep slash he had made under the man's chin. "Where is your colonel now?" he repeated. "Don't be a hero. I'll get the information anyway, and you'll be dead."

The soldier's chin throbbed painfully as he considered these words. "You'll let me go if I tell you?" he said, his blood continuing to water the forest floor.

"I will," said Boyd, disgusted by the necessity of having to lie, but knowing he had no choice but to kill the man, and consoling himself that the typical SS soldier was a sadistic thug with neither honor nor compassion.

"He's heading to the radio room to contact Berlin," the guard said.

Of course he was, thought Boyd. The colonel would be demanding to know who had sent a phantom transport plane. This Op should have been long over by now, and the longer it wasn't, the more complications would develop.

Boyd twisted hard, breaking the man's neck, and ordered Sage to show him the location of the radio room from the map Hahn had drawn of the compound and tripwires. He raced there as quickly as he could, abandoning caution in his haste to stop this upcoming communication from taking place.

Boyd found the surprisingly large building that housed the radio equipment and rushed inside with his gun drawn. Zimmerman was in front of a bank of equipment on the far side of the room, but he was still turning dials and had yet to make any connections.

"Freeze!" said the American forcefully, keeping his voice low.

The room was illuminated by a lantern, and the colonel stared at Boyd as if he had seen a ghost. "You!" he whispered, his eyes bulging. "How did you get back here? I was told you would never leave Berlin again."

"Don't believe everything you hear."

"Why would you come back?"

"For the boy. We heard you were treating him poorly again."

"He deserves it. Not the loyal Nazi we'd like to see."

"So I hear. But I need the keys to his shackles. Let me have them and I'll let you live."

Zimmerman shook his head. "We both know that's a lie," he said.

His eyes narrowed in thought. Suddenly, he snatched his gun from its holster, but kept it down, making sure not to point it at Boyd. "But you can't shoot me either, can you?" he added. "If you do, the entire camp comes to life. Like you've kicked an anthill. Even a man as skilled as you can't take them all on. Especially since your wife is probably nearby. You can't kill us all and protect her at the same time.

"So stay where you are and I'll keep my gun down," continued the colonel. "Take a step closer to try to kill me with a knife or other quiet method, and I'll either shoot you first, or you'll have to shoot me. Either way, the noise will attract attention you can't have."

Boyd cursed inwardly. Zimmerman continued to prove himself one of the sharpest adversaries he had ever encountered. He, on the other hand, had failed to think this action through, and now would pay the price.

"You're correct," he said calmly. "I would prefer not to wake the camp. But make no mistake, if you draw on me, or try to leave this room, I'll shoot you and take my chances."

"Looks like we have a standoff," said the German. "So here's what I propose. I agree to let you leave here, and you agree not to return. Just holster your gun and go. I won't sound the alarm for ten minutes."

"Interesting proposal," said Boyd. "Let me think about it."

"*Kelly, I assume you're hearing this,*" he said subvocally.

"*Yes! And I think he's right. If the camp is alerted, anything can happen. Especially if one of the SS finds me to use against you. The only way you'll be able to use your gun is if I turn myself from a liability into an asset. So I'm going to get control of the cube. This will free you up to kill Zimmerman and get Otto.*"

"*There are guards still in the cube room,*" protested Boyd, "*armed and awake.*"

"*I can repeat what I did on Sun Island. But if there's any gunfire, you'll spook the soldiers guarding the cube. So find a way to maintain your stalemate until I have the cube secured.*"

Boyd wanted desperately to argue with her, to insist that her plan was too dangerous, but he knew it was the right move and that every second mattered. "*I will, Kelly, good luck,*" he said quickly.

He wanted to tell her to take care of herself, that he was falling in love with her, but this would only serve to distract her. "*Deactivate your comm so you can concentrate,*" he said instead, "*and I'll do the same. Let me know when you have the cube secured.*"

"*Roger that,*" said Kelly.

Boyd had maintained eye contact with Zimmerman the entire time he was communicating with Kelly, and now frowned and shook his head. "After further consideration," he said, "I'm afraid your proposal won't work for me. We'll need to come up with another. Do you at least have the keys to Otto's shackles in your pocket?"

"I do. I forgot to add that if you agree to leave, I'll give you the keys and let you take Otto Richter with you."

"That may just do the trick," said Boyd. "I have to admit that you've impressed the hell out of me, Colonel. You outwitted me thoroughly the first time I was here, and you reasoned your way to a stalemate now. I've continued to underestimate you."

Boyd paused. "Your suspicions about Kurt Hahn were also correct," he continued. "You were able to sense he had turned traitor based on the flimsiest of evidence, even after years of what appeared to be loyal service to the Reich."

Zimmerman ignored the compliments. "Who are you really, Herr Boyd?" he said. "An American spy?"

"The cube can facilitate time travel," said Boyd, acutely aware of the need to continue stalling. "I'm from the future. And it turns out that you Nazis lose big."

The SS colonel's eyes narrowed in thought. "Or do we *win* big," he said, "and you've come back to try to change that?"

"You doubted my clairvoyance, but you're willing to accept that I'm from the future? Just like that?"

"I'm good at reading people."

"You should change sides, Colonel. We could use a man like you in the future. What do I have to do to make that happen?" he asked, frantically searching for additional ways to delay the inevitable gunshots for just a few minutes longer.

52

Kelly Connolly pulled a flashlight from her rucksack and entered the building that housed the Atlantis Cube, shining the light so it illuminated the cube room entrance at the back of the structure. She knew better than to shine it around the room she was now in, not wanting to see Boyd's earlier handiwork.

She knocked gently at the door and waited. It was thrown open to reveal four guards inside. Their faces showed absolute shock upon seeing her there. She had been the only woman they had seen in some time, and they were not about to forget her.

"Frau Boyd?" said one of them as she boldly pushed her way inside.

"Hello, gentlemen," she said pleasantly. "Do any of you speak English?"

"I do," said the shortest of the four. "What is this about?"

Kelly kept a mental note of the elapsed time. She had to be quick, because Boyd couldn't maintain his stalemate with Zimmerman for long.

"I'm here to show you how to use the cube. To turn you into heroes in the eyes of your Fuhrer."

The man shot her a look of contempt. "Sure you are," he said.

"I'll prove what I say in just a moment. Please translate for your comrades."

While he was doing this, Kelly reached carefully inside the open rucksack and removed Otto's generator, ever so slowly, making sure none of them got jumpy.

Without waiting for permission, she walked over to the cube and lifted the steel box that was covering it, releasing its brilliant, otherworldly light.

The men began to point their weapons at her, but quickly lowered them, realizing that she couldn't possibly harm or move the cube, as dozens of top scientists hadn't even managed to scratch it. She hit a switch on Otto's generator. In a single instant, the light ceased streaming from the cube's corners, and it became solid rather than a cage.

She ignored the four gasps coming from behind her and proceeded to press and hold the cube's corners, bringing up fiery glyphs, which blazed in the dark room. The mouths of all four SS guards were now open, and they were so transfixed that not one made a move to lift his gun.

She reached out and calmly pressed the glyph that called up the telepathic AI.

"Step away from the cube!" demanded the English-speaking soldier, suddenly coming to his senses.

"Of course," she said, lifting her hands in the air so they could all see them.

"Enigma AI," she thought, mentally bracing herself for what she needed to do. *"Increase the force of gravity in such a way as to break the necks of the men in this room. Please make sure they die quickly with as little suffering as possible."*

"When would you like this to happen?" said the AI's voice in her head.

"Immediately!" she thought, squeezing her eyes shut.

She heard four sharp cracks and opened her eyes to see all four SS soldiers now dead on the floor nearby. A wave of nausea overtook her, but she fought through it. *"Enigma AI,"* she thought at it, deciding that this name was too clumsy, *"from now on, please respond to the name Eeny."*

"Eeny it is," responded the AI.

Kelly tapped a finger twice just beyond her ear canal to reactivate her comm. "Justin, I have the cube and the room is secured," she reported.

* * *

Major Justin Boyd heard Kelly's voice in his ear and marveled once again at this remarkable woman. He was beginning to think that they were truly an unbeatable team.

Bruno Zimmerman was in the middle of a sentence, but Boyd no longer needed to stall. He squeezed off two quick shots, killing him instantly, and closed the distance between them, frisking the SS colonel rapidly until he found the keys he was looking for.

Every soldier in the encampment and on patrol would now be up and on full alert, with guns and flashlights at the ready. "Well done," he said to Kelly out loud. "I'll get Otto and be with you soon. How many men did you have to take out?"

"Four."

As Boyd neared the door he did the math in his head. There had been twenty-five SS in total before Hahn had left. He had killed eight and Kelly four, which meant that only twelve remained.

He exited the radio room and made his way to where Otto was being held, dodging the men who were flying around the dark woods, setting up lighting and trying to discover the origin of the two gunshots.

Boyd made it to the prison, illuminated by a single dim lantern, and entered quickly. Otto had been awakened by the gunshots as well, and was fully alert. In fact, he already had his hands and ankles positioned so the locks would be easy for Boyd to get to, having anticipated his arrival.

"Is Kelly okay?" he said by way of greeting, which brought a smile to Boyd's face as he went about unlocking his shackles.

"She's fine and in control of the cube," he replied hurriedly. "She can hear us and says hello. We need to get you back to the cube room right away."

Now free, Otto rose from the ground. "I hoped you'd be able to make it back, but I never really thought you would."

The door burst open and two men entered with guns drawn. Boyd kicked the lantern out and spun Otto to the ground in one fluid motion, coming up firing. He killed both soldiers and pulled Otto back up from the ground, the entire action taking only a few seconds.

Otto's eyes bulged, not from the near-death experience, but from the dazzling speed of Boyd's reflexes and decision-making.

"Stay behind me," said the American, rushing from the prison as three more SS soldiers approached, having heard the additional gunfire and shining flashlights on the two escapees.

Boyd dived into the darkness and made quick work of the three soldiers before continuing to make his way toward Kelly and the cube.

"Justin, talk to me," said Kelly frantically. *"Are you and Otto okay?"*

"We're both fine and on our way," he replied out loud, suddenly realizing he wasn't detecting any additional activity in or near the compound.

"Thank God!" she said. *"I've been able to kill seven more of them with the cube,"* she reported.

"Outstanding!" said Boyd. "With the five I just eliminated, that's all of them. We did it, Kelly! The hard way. We'll meet you just outside the cube building. I know Otto's eager to see you."

53

Kelly threw her arms around Otto Richter and held him close, never losing her grip on the cube in her right hand. "Thank God you're okay," she said. The adolescent returned the hug awkwardly, having little experience with affection that wasn't coming from his parents.

She then embraced Boyd, kissing him as they parted.

"Why haven't we seen any of the scientists?" she asked.

"They're lying low in their quarters," said Otto. "They aren't about to pop their heads out of a foxhole when shooting begins."

"So they're just huddling inside in a panic," said Kelly, "hoping that the soldiers handle whatever is going on?"

"Yes," said Otto.

After an extended silence, Kelly turned to Boyd and shook her head. "I can't do it," she said numbly. "I *won't*. I don't care what happens, Justin, but I've had enough. If letting these scientists live somehow turns the world fascist, or even destroys the entire planet, I'm willing to take that chance."

Boyd and Otto exchanged glances but didn't speak.

"Except for rarities like Kurt Hahn," she continued, "the SS is comprised of cruel, ruthless zealots, too brainwashed for redemption. Zealots who would have killed us without a second thought. So we killed them, instead. I get that. But *enough* already. I'm not saying these scientists are saints. Some might be as big a monster as Joseph Mengele. I'm just saying I'm done killing."

Boyd studied her and then nodded. "Okay," he said.

"Okay?" she repeated, looking surprised. She had expected an argument.

"Yes. Okay. I agree with you. It's a risk to the future, but one we need to take. Hopefully, if it is a change, it won't be a big enough one to nudge history off its course. As you said, history is more resilient than it seems. But regardless, I'm *glad* you drew the line, Kelly. You're right. Killing Nazis, killing soldiers, is one thing. But enough is enough. I knew that if anyone could battle monsters without becoming one, it would be you."

"I'm pretty sure that I am one already."

"Not even close," said Boyd. "And thank you for bringing me back from the brink."

He sighed. "But if we're going to take this risk, I have an idea for how we can minimize it."

54

Thirty-six German scientists huddled together in a large clearing in the Canadian Forest, illuminated by almost fifty lanterns and flashlights, and faced two Americans and Otto Richter, who, after collecting ample supplies for their trip to Spokane, had herded the scientists there.

The American major and young scientist stood side by side, while Kelly sat five feet behind them, concealing the cube, the *Wizard of Oz* behind the curtain, wanting the attention to be drawn to the two males.

"Are you and Otto ready?" she whispered to Boyd through his comm.

"Go for it," he replied subvocally, signaling his young companion that they were about to begin.

Kelly issued telepathic orders to Eeny, and Boyd and Otto rose gently into the air, hovering about seven feet above the forest floor. Thirty-six pairs of eyes widened, and Boyd had no doubt that he now had their full and undivided attention.

"I have eliminated all the SS soldiers stationed here," he shouted, and Otto repeated the German translation just as loudly. "But I'm willing to let *you* live. Under certain conditions."

He paused to let these words sink in. "This woman and I are not human," he said. "We're from a planet thousands of light years away. One that has mastered science and technology that you can't possibly fathom. For any of you who are still skeptical of this claim, let me demonstrate in a way that's more . . . personal."

Boyd waited for Otto to finish the translation and then thrust both arms in front of him, palms showing, and tilted his hands upward, a priest motioning for his congregation to rise.

All thirty-six scientists lurched twenty-five feet into the air, accompanied by a symphony of their own gasps and screams of terror, and were held there.

"Silence!" shouted Boyd, as they had all begun talking at once, and his meaning was so clear that Otto didn't need to translate.

When tomb-like silence returned, Boyd turned his palms face down and brought both arms toward the ground. Kelly made sure the scientists followed suit, landing softly once again on the floor of the clearing. Boyd only wished he could do the same. He was pretending that floating in midair wasn't the least bit disconcerting, but the truth was quite different.

"When we learned you had found a cube we left behind," he continued, bellowing as he imagined a god might do, "my partner and I took human form. To get a taste for what is happening on your Earth." He shook his head haughtily. "And we're not impressed. Humanity is cruel and savage. Primitive, and undeserving of our help."

When Otto was done translating, he continued. "So we're destroying the cube. You don't *deserve* to study it. And we killed your soldiers. They didn't deserve to live."

He waited again for Otto to catch up. "But *you* do," he added. "Just barely. And you *will* if you do as I say. First, collect food and supplies. Quickly. Then leave here for good. In three hours I'll destroy the cube, which will create a crater with a radius of almost a mile. If you want to live, be sure you're beyond this radius in three hours.

"You're now behind Allied lines, so you'll need to come up with a convincing story of how you got here. Perhaps the Reich was forcing you to work on an undisclosed scientific project on a desert island in the Pacific, but on your way to it you were blown off course. You mutinied after landing on Canadian shores, intent on asylum."

Boyd paused, still hovering in the air. "All of you are clever, so you'll think of something. Just think through what questions you might get asked and have answers ready. And if you volunteer your expertise in service of the Allies, this will go a long way. Do whatever you need to do to convince the Canadians or Americans not to have you executed. All I ask is that you lead productive, peaceful lives.

"But here is what you *can't* do. You can't go back to Germany until after the war, or have any contact with the Reich. Most importantly, you can't tell *anyone* about the cube. Not a word. Not orally, or in writing. If you do this, I will know it. If you have any contact with any German who isn't here now, on any subject, I will know it. And I will make sure that you're killed. You will die more painfully than any human ever has."

While Otto translated, Boyd sent a subvocal message to Kelly. *"How am I doing?"* he asked.

"You have me convinced."

"Are you and Eeny ready to give them something more to think about?"

"We're at your service."

"What you've witnessed here is not magic," bellowed Boyd. "It's advanced technology that I can access with simple gestures. But in case you doubt that I can carry out my threat, I'll give you a further demonstration."

Boyd spent the next few minutes putting on a show, pretending to control immense power that Kelly and the cube's telepathic AI were actually wielding. Kelly had the cube uproot two mammoth trees at the edge of the clearing—which shook the ground like an earthquake—and toss them through the air and out of sight, like a giant who was throwing toothpicks. She caused two other trees to splinter into tiny fragments the *size* of toothpicks. She followed this up by having the cube seize a boulder weighing at least ten tons and fly it to the center of the clearing, where it was crushed into rubble and then sand. Finally, to make the demonstration personal, she pinned all thirty-six scientists to the ground, holding them there until they almost blacked out.

"Know this," shouted Boyd when the demonstrations were complete, "we have technology that will monitor your every word, every breath. The second you write or speak about what you call the Atlantis Cube, the instant you contact a German soldier or official, we *will* find out. And you will learn how a grape feels when someone crushes it beneath their heel. Are we clear?"

This question was answered with a hearty chorus of affirmatives even before Otto finished translating, and more after.

"Good," bellowed Boyd as he floated above the ground next to his young German partner. "We're taking the one called Otto Richter with us. Since he's the youngest among you, we want to see if we can mold him."

When Otto finished his translation, Boyd delivered his final words. "Go now. Get beyond the radius of destruction. But always remember that I can kill you with the snap of my fingers, but I have so far chosen not to."

He glared down at them in contempt. "So don't do anything to make me change my mind."

55

While the German scientists packed and prepared to leave, the two Americans brought Otto up to speed on what had transpired in Berlin, and he told them of his experiences.

Otto was saddened to learn the fate of his one German ally, but celebrated that Hahn had died a hero, and had been happy and at peace at the time, believing he had witnessed the demise of Adolf Hitler.

After all the young genius had been through, when it finally hit him that he was free of the Nazis forever, he shed tears of joy, and couldn't have been more grateful to the two Americans for making it possible. They reminded him that his path to freedom would have been much easier had they never arrived, but this didn't diminish his gratitude.

When the last of the scientists left, less than an hour later, dawn was finally breaking, and the trio found themselves alone in what had become a mixture of ghost town and killing field. Boyd led them into the forest, out of sight of any bodies, and they sat on the forest floor in a triangle, facing each other.

Boyd nodded at the brilliant young German. "So what do you think, Otto?" he said, changing the subject from the events in Berlin to the events that had just transpired. "Will our little performance keep your scientists from telling Hitler what happened here? And keep the cube out of the history books?"

"Very likely, yes. Although, I think it will ultimately depend on if they're able to successfully integrate into society."

"If only they had your ability to speak perfect American English," said Kelly.

"No doubt," said Otto. "A German accent isn't ideal right now. They're going to find themselves less than welcome here or in America, no matter how convincing a story they tell."

"I think you might be surprised," said Boyd. "Scientists and doctors are needed and respected no matter what wars their countries start. America and Russia will both take in scores of German scientists just after the war, even those who were in the Nazi party."

Otto raised his eyebrows. "That surprises me," he said. "But getting back to your performance, it was smart to play to their belief in science and technology rather than their superstitions. The scientists all pretended to believe the cube was made by ancient Aryans from Atlantis, but I'm sure they all really believed the obvious—that it was alien. Also, because they've lived for so many years in such a repressive society, they're already programmed to keep their mouths closed. So that's working for us."

"What's working *against* us?" asked Boyd.

"Mostly the fact that you don't speak German," said Otto. "You portrayed yourself as all-powerful and all-knowing. And the cube helped you make a very strong case for the all-powerful part. But they will wonder why someone who is all knowing needs a translator to speak German."

"Good point," said Boyd. "To be fair," he added with a smile, "I do know some Arabic and Farsi."

Otto laughed. "You should have told them that," he said wryly. "Because, obviously, that would have made all the difference."

"Wow," said Boyd, "even given all you've been through, you're still a smart ass. I think you take after Kelly."

"I'm pretty sure she takes after *me*," said Otto in amusement.

There were smiles all around, but Boyd soon became serious once more. "You're right about my lack of German language skills. It will make them scratch their heads. But I still think they'll refrain from talking about the cube."

"I agree," said Otto. "What would be the point? If your threat was real, telling others about the cube is a death sentence. If not, they have nothing to gain by talking, anyway. Who here will believe them? Especially since one has to see the cube to believe it, and the cube won't be available for a viewing. And tales about an all-powerful alien disguised as a Canadian clairvoyant—who can float—will be even less believable."

"What about Alex Wentz?" asked Boyd. "He was close to completing the dark energy generator. Would it change history if he did?"

"Hard to imagine it would," replied Kelly. "You made sure the generator he was working on and Otto's notebook were left behind. Even if he had a photographic memory, and could get the sophisticated parts needed to complete it, no one will even know it does anything. It can unlock the cube, yes, but there's no longer any cube to unlock."

"I'm sure you're right," said Boyd. "I guess we'll find out."

Kelly shrugged. "Even if letting the scientists go does change history for the worse, I'm prepared to accept it. I'm just relieved I came to my senses in time."

"Yeah, me too," said Boyd.

"I agree with your decision," said Otto, "but I can't bring myself to agree with the one you made in Germany." He shook his head and an expression of hatred came over his face, one fiercer and more all-consuming than the young scientist had seemed capable of. "Hitler needed to die," he hissed. "I would have killed him no matter what."

"An understandable instinct," said Boyd. "No one could have blamed you."

Otto looked ill. "What's even more horrific than his existence," he added in disgust, "is that we in Germany let him come to power. Many of us were dead set against it, but not enough. The majority stood by and let him commit his atrocities. Stood by while he and others treated millions of human beings like vermin, and engaged in endless acts of inhumanity. All the while convincing themselves that they were part of some Master Race."

He shook his head. "What does that say about humanity? Worse, Hitler isn't alone. Add in Stalin, Mussolini, and Tojo, and you have an undeniable pattern. Honestly, if not for the two of you, I'd have no hope for the species at all. You're a living demonstration that fascism loses, that humanity survives for at least eighty-four more years. But please tell me society gets better. I mean orders of magnitude better."

"It does," Kelly assured him. "Orders of magnitude better."

She had little knowledge of history, but she was aware of the long-term *trajectory* of history, having read several books that used the progress humanity had made socially and technologically over the decades to extrapolate how much progress could be expected in the future.

"On average," she continued, "the quality of human life in my time is demonstrably better in every way imaginable than it is now. More democracy, more tolerance, and more freedom. Higher literacy, fewer wars, and fewer violent deaths. The list goes on and on. Right now, only a small fraction of the world's population can read and write. But in my time, over ninety percent can. In 1950, three-quarters of the world will be living in extreme poverty. In my day, the figure is less than ten percent. Life expectancy has increased substantially, and we take medical advances for granted that the people of this time would see as miracles."

They still had almost two hours before they would crater the area and leave, so Kelly brought Otto up to speed on computers, the internet, cell phones, video, and GPS. As per usual, he was breathtakingly fast on the uptake.

"So in our age," she continued after her quick tutorial, "we have access to more information, and more entertainment, than the most farsighted visionary of this time would ever dare predict. We have instant access to tens of millions of books, hundreds of thousands of movies, weather from around the globe, directions to anywhere, and a dizzying array of goods and services that can be delivered to our doors within days. We have access to billions of pages of information that can be searched in an instant. Countless goods and services that used to be scarce are now abundant. We have better clothing, better housing, and better living conditions. Every decade the cost of computing power, electricity, long-distance communication, and countless other goods and services has plummeted."

Otto listened in rapt attention.

"Socially," continued Kelly, "the world has become ever more tolerant, with all races, religions, and sexual preferences not only accepted by most, but even celebrated. Yes, there is still bigotry and persecution in the world, but compared to the level seen in the time period we're in now, it's microscopic."

Boyd chimed in, describing such advances as supersonic jets, microwave ovens, and Moon and Mars missions, completed by rocket ships capable of returning from space and setting back down gently on a landing pad, like something out of an early science fiction novel.

"Absolutely amazing," said Otto in awe when they were done, having soaked it all in like a superintelligent sponge. "You must have to keep pinching yourself so you don't think it's all a dream."

Boyd shook his head. "Actually, not so much. Things have improved dramatically, but we still have a ways to go. And never underestimate the ability of human beings to take things for granted, and find ways to be miserable. The truth is, even though we live in the best of times, most of us believe the opposite. That poverty, and literacy, and so on have gotten worse, even though they've gotten considerably better. This is actually a fairly recent phenomenon. Just in the last thirty years or so."

"Why would that be?" asked Otto.

Boyd frowned. "Turns out that in our day we're drowning in news," he explained. "Every second, every day, a weight of news that is almost inconceivable. And those providing this news know that only the most dramatic will stand out. So we're told the sky is falling a hundred times a day. And rather than discuss how far we've come, the dire problems we thought our way out of, we amplify every problem, every behavior that is less than perfect, into crisis proportions. Pessimism sells far better than optimism."

"Incredible," said Otto. "More of you need a visit to 1943 to put things in perspective."

Kelly smiled. "No doubt about it. If I ever return, I'll never take our social or technological progress for granted again."

"I'd love to hear more about your world," said Otto.

"You'll have plenty of time for that," said Boyd. "We have a long journey ahead of us." He frowned. "Made longer because Sage can't help us navigate. She's finally out of power, and not even the heat of my body and motion of my leg will be enough to spark her back to life."

"But before we set out," said Kelly, turning her gaze on Otto, "you should know that apart from anything we can say about humanity as a whole, you, personally, have a wonderful life in store. At least if our activity here *creates* your future rather than changing it.

"Every family member who knew you and my grandmother always talked about how much in love the two of you were—throughout your entire marriage. A real fairy-tale love story, one for the ages. Your journal makes this clear also. You cherished every second together, and both your journal and family lore suggest that you experienced as much happiness during your life as anyone could ever ask for."

A smile spread over Otto's face. "Thank you for that, Kelly," he said. "One decision I need to make is whether or not I want to try to keep the future exactly the same as you remember it. It's a tough call. If I repeat history, I lead a life that sounds a lot like heaven. But the downside is that you would get born again—which would block you from returning to your own time. You'd be trapped here forever."

Kelly sighed. She had already decided she wasn't leaving Boyd no matter what. "It might not be as tough a call as you think," she said. "But we can discuss that later. For now, it's time to pretend to destroy the cube and cover our tracks."

They returned to the center of the encampment and Kelly gave instructions to the telepathic AI. As soon as she was finished, the cube released a torrent of energy that was devastating on a scale that was beyond biblical, making the power required to part the Red Sea seem infinitesimal.

While they were protected within a circle with a thirty-foot radius, the area beyond was not so fortunate. All at once, in a wave that passed at the speed of light, the forest for almost a mile around them collapsed in on itself, and they were deafened by the death throes of countless trees.

Mighty oaks and lowly foliage were crushed to the forest floor and then through it, tilling the ground and bringing up virgin rock and soil that had been buried, in an astonishing and terrifying cataclysm of raw energy the likes of which had never been witnessed from so close a vantage point.

In the blink of an eye, a massive stretch of what had been thriving forest became a shallow crater, six feet deep, as if an asteroid had struck, but without any fire or other fallout. While this was occurring, the earth shook wildly beneath them, knocking them off their feet, and they were unable to comprehend even a fraction of the power that had obliterated nine square miles of forest in seconds.

They reeled from the awesome destructive power that Kelly had unleashed, but they weren't quite done. They hiked for ten minutes, lowering themselves carefully to the shallow crater floor when they reached its edge, and Kelly turned the cube back on the Nazi encampment, crushing it also, so that it blended in with the rest of the devastation.

The steel structures, equipment, bodies, and runway were crushed to an unrecognizable slurry that was then pulled under the earth, leaving no trace of its previous existence.

When it was all over, Otto turned to Kelly with a haunted look in his eyes, one shared by the two Americans. "That was just the tiniest fraction of that thing's power, wasn't it?" he whispered.

Kelly nodded. "I'm afraid so."

"I mean, to look at the cube is to know it has virtually unlimited destructive power," said Otto. "But actually seeing this power in action brings home the point in a far more visceral way. I'm more certain than ever that deactivating it and hiding it in the woods of Spokane is the right thing to do. And that you did the right thing by stealing it from your government."

Otto Richter shook his head in horror. "God help us if the wrong person ever gets control of this thing," he finished solemnly.

56

Kelly, Boyd, and Otto hiked for three days before making it to civilization, and then spent two additional days working their way south, mostly sitting in the back of pickup trucks driven by Canadians kind enough to give them a lift. They learned they were closer to Seattle than Spokane and decided to stop there to begin with.

They arrived without a single nickel between them, nor did they have lodging or identification. Not an ideal start for a group with important things to accomplish who didn't want to draw attention to themselves.

So the first thing they did in Seattle was find and rob the largest bank in the city. After all they had been through, their Bonnie and Clyde act was almost boring, with Boyd's night vision and Kelly's precision control of the most powerful object on the planet almost making it *too* easy.

They broke in at night, and Kelly had the Enigma AI crush massive steel pins, each the circumference of a baseball bat, into nonexistence, the same steel pins that were holding a steel vault door, more than two feet thick, closed. The cube managed this surgically, without affecting the rest of the door at all, leaving a mystery that would never be solved.

Inside, they found millions of dollars in cash. They took exactly a thousand.

This amount, while the equivalent of about fifteen thousand in modern times, was still such a minuscule percentage of the total that bank management was never certain they had been robbed at all. They checked and rechecked how much they were supposed to have in the vault, and kept concluding they were short by a thousand, but were half convinced it was an accounting error.

In the end, the vault-door company replaced the faulty door along with the thousand dollars stolen, horrified that their best product had failed in such a mystifying way. The police pursued the case for a few weeks, mostly looking at rival vault-door companies for the culprit, and then quickly let it go.

Boyd spent some of this stolen money to buy clothing, hotel rooms, and specialized electrical equipment that Kelly and Otto used to jerry-rig a charger for Sage.

With Sage recharged and her database back online, they bet on horse racing and other sporting events to quickly parlay their nest egg into a small fortune, almost embarrassed to be taking advantage of such an overused time-travel cliché. Still, the proceeds completed their journey from rags to riches, enabling them to purchase a car and impeccably forged IDs.

Otto became Jim Connolly from Clear Lake, Iowa. And Kelly Connolly and Justin Boyd became Kelly Connolly and Justin Boyd, except this time with birth certificates dated in the 1910s rather than the 1990s.

Then, just over two weeks after they had cratered the secret Nazi base, they pulled their green, 1941 Buick Century into Spokane, and bought a house on the outskirts of town.

The next months were almost idyllic and went a long way toward healing all three of their tortured souls, not that Kelly or Boyd could ever fully heal. Otto got his first taste of true freedom since he had been eight and Hitler had come to power, and he forged a bond with the two time travelers that couldn't be stronger. And since he was happier and eating better, he filled out, and soon became the picture of health.

Boyd and Kelly found peace and calm, and to no one's surprise, fell madly in love, breaking all speed records. Two months after their arrival in Spokane, they were married by a Justice of the Peace, with Otto serving as best man.

During their months in Spokane they also went about buying the land around which Otto would build a cabin to house the cube, making sure the purchase was untraceable. Basically, recreating history as they knew it.

When Otto learned that Kelly would be staying in this time period with Boyd, even if she *was* able to travel to the future, his decision with respect to his own future became simple. By all accounts, if history repeated itself precisely, Otto Richter, now Jim Connolly, would lead a joyous, happy, and loving life. So he dedicated himself to making this happen.

Kelly checked with the Enigma Cube AI every day, and every day Eeny confirmed that Kelly couldn't travel into the future because she already existed there. This meant that history really was unfolding just as it had before. That Otto had married the exact same woman under the exact same circumstances. That the exact same sperm had hit the exact same egg at the exact same instant to produce Kelly's father. Which meant that their presence in the past had always been factored into Otto's future, including their decision not to kill the Nazi scientists.

Once Otto had decided to repeat history, he decided to do so as meticulously as he could, down to leaving a leather-bound journal inside a zero-point energy text at some point in the future. A leather-bound journal that would contain the precise contents of the one Kelly had found, down to the comma.

Sage had uploaded a backup copy of Kelly's phone in 2027, which had contained her grandfather's journal. Each night, the AI would dictate the contents to Kelly's comm, and she would copy them to a notebook for Otto to later rewrite in his own hand. She found it endlessly frustrating that she couldn't just order Sage to print it out, but decided that recreating it by hand would be *slightly* faster than reinventing the laser printer.

Otto was delighted to read his own journal as it took form, and to use it as a blueprint. It gave few details about his personal life, which was ideal, so he wouldn't have to worry about memorizing lines and robotically trying to stay on a precise path. The journal had the name of the woman he would marry and that he loved her more than life itself, but didn't specify when, and under what circumstances, they would meet, and so on, so he was free to let events unfold organically.

Otto, being the genius he was, came to all the right conclusions about how the journal had skipped a generation and ultimately landed in Kelly's hands. He correctly assumed he had died suddenly before being able to share his knowledge with his own offspring.

Kelly had initially refused to confirm this or provide details. But Otto convinced her that he wouldn't let this foreknowledge become a sword of Damocles above his head, and that he was overjoyed to be destined to live a much longer and better life than he had ever dared hope for, despite a somewhat abrupt ending.

So Kelly told him about the heart attack, and its timing. He didn't want to change how the future would unfold, but he did drill down into the exact circumstances surrounding his death, including his last words, which would at least give him the option of potentially extending his life. If he did find a way to beat the heart attack, he could stage a fake death along the exact lines that Kelly had specified, and ensure future history remained intact. This would require him to persuade his wife to be a willing accomplice, but it wasn't beyond the realm of possibility.

Kelly and Boyd were deep in the mad, romantic stage of love, and could have been happy together in the pits of hell, as long as they had a bed and a few hours of privacy each night. Still, they were nagged by one critical piece of unfinished business. If the future unfolded as it had before, then they would be stuck in an infinite loop. One that began with their birth, led to their visit to Sun Island, and ended with them living out the rest of their lives in the past—only to repeat itself when they were born anew in the nineties once again.

But if this were the case, China would end up in possession of two Enigma Cubes, and the rest of the world would have none.

They discussed what to do about this at great length. Should they break the loop? *Could* they break the loop?

They first considered making a change that would result in Kelly not being born. But while this would disrupt the wonderful life in store for Otto, it wouldn't solve their problem. The cube would still be found, and Uru established. Boyd would still visit with Harry Salazar and suggest Haycock's dark energy generator be tried. And the Chinese would still have their cube, and still be spying on Uru, with the US none the wiser. Given the inertia of the timeline, without a dramatic kick in the teeth, the future would likely try to find a way back to its original track, with China ultimately gaining control of both cubes.

No, the only way to be sure they left the future in good hands was to find a way to alert future Kelly to the Chinese threat *after* she had joined the Enigma team. Otto would still live out the extraordinary life he was destined to have. Kelly would still find his journal as she had done before, ensuring the cube had a thoughtful and capable caretaker. And Chinese spying on their efforts would be exposed.

And none of this would have any effect on their current lives. Even though they would change the future so they would never be brought to Sun Island, and never travel to the past, it wouldn't matter. They were already in 1943 Spokane and grandfathered in. So was Otto. As long as no one went back and mucked with the past again, there was no changing what had just happened. All three would be able to move forward from here.

Still, if they were in an infinite loop, they feared that any effort to change the future and break the loop might be destined to fail.

On the other hand, Otto pointed out that this might only be their second time through. If so, their new knowledge of the first iteration of the loop might allow them to make the changes required to break free. Or maybe, after a nearly infinite number of passages through the loop, some random, quantum event would finally be disruptive enough to break them out.

Regardless, if there was any hope at all, they had to try. If they left the future as it was, they would have ensured totalitarianism was defeated in the past, while helping to seal a different variety of this in the future. A future in which billions of cameras and advanced computers were available to monitor an entire population, bringing Orwell's nightmarish vision into reality.

Eeny had become annoyingly unhelpful, refusing to answer time travel questions, or provide Kelly with any further information on the subject. The telepathic AI was only willing to confirm that she was still alive in the future, and that this had stopped being the case when she had vanished from Sun Island.

This information, while frustratingly scant, would at least tell them if they had successfully broken the loop. If so, Sun Island would never happen, and Eeny would confirm that Kelly was alive in the future beyond this time.

So when they weren't copying journals, setting up land permits and secret cabin construction, or getting married, they made almost a hundred attempts to change the future. Most of these attempts involved hiding Sage in a place that was unlikely to ever be stumbled upon, and having precision timers recharge her at a selected date and time in the far future, using a foolproof, redundant system that Otto had perfected. Upon awakening, Sage would tap the local Wi-Fi to deliver whatever warnings they wanted to send to themselves.

Yet the efforts failed every time, probably due to Eeny's intervention. The telepathic AI had made it clear it wouldn't allow two versions of a person to exist at the same time. But it had also specified that it wouldn't allow a version of a person in the past to communicate with themselves in the future.

They knew their efforts conflicted with this second rule, they just doubted Eeny could do anything about it.

Apparently, they were wrong.

Their efforts to communicate with *others* in the future also failed, even Tom Osborne. Otto believed Eeny was blocking this as well. Believed that the cube's AI had deemed that future actions the colonel would take, based on the information provided to him, would still impact the decision-making of the Kelly and Boyd who existed in the future. In this way, they would still be influencing their future selves, however indirectly.

Finally, almost four months after leaving Canada, the last in a long line of valiant attempts to change the future failed, and Boyd's frustration was greater than it had ever been. "Is there really a point to this anymore?" he asked as he and his two companions sat around a glass patio table in the backyard of their home, awaiting nightfall. "We always knew the loop might be inescapable. When do we decide that it *is*?"

"We've been over this," said Kelly. "And we aren't giving up. We *can't*. I've never been happier than I am now. But the way I left things in 2027 is driving me crazy. *Haunting* me. Because of me, the communist Chinese will have a monopoly on technology that can't be stopped or matched. I've condemned the entire world to a bleak future."

"How can you blame yourself?" said Boyd. "You had no idea this would happen."

"Doesn't matter. I'm still responsible. And even if I wasn't, I'd still be willing to move heaven and earth to do something about it."

"With the cube, you *can* move heaven and earth," pointed out Boyd. "And we have, at least metaphorically. We've tried to change the future using Sage, time capsules, journals, and hidden letters. We've tried to contact multiple people, and to intervene at multiple points on the timeline."

He grimaced. "It's not like we haven't been creative. But each time our future selves end up on Sun Island, and China gets both cubes. It's fate. Or maybe it's the inertia you've talked about. Future history actively resisting being pushed off course. Like the timeline is an elephant, and we're gnats trying to affect it."

Kelly shook her head. "My sense from what Eeny planted in my mind is that history has inertia, but not *that* much. There has to be a way to do this. The laws of physics aren't the problem. It's the laws of the cube."

"I agree," said Boyd. "But we can't change these either. Otto's the smartest person *ever*, and even his arguments for persuading Eeny to break the rules have failed."

Kelly's face fell. "I know," she said miserably. "But there's still no way I'm throwing in the towel."

She paused for several seconds in thought. Finally, she blew out a long breath. "But maybe it is time we moved away and let Otto live his life, meet his future wife, and find the happiness we know he'll find."

"How do you know you don't stay in my life here?" asked Otto.

"We can't be sure," said Kelly. "But there's a notable absence of any reference in your journal that could possibly hint at us."

The young genius nodded. "I think you're right," he said. "I just don't want you to leave."

"You guessed how this would play out from the very beginning, didn't you?" said Kelly.

"Yes. Given the rules Eeny laid out and the contents of the journal, I thought this is where we'd end up. Failing to change what happened in 2027 and staying trapped in the loop. With you and Justin concluding that you should move away to ensure my future."

Otto raised his eyebrows. "But there is one idea that I've been holding back," he said. "One that I think can circumvent the cube's rules."

"Holding back?" said Kelly in dismay. "If you think an idea might work, why would you ever hold it *back*?"

"I was waiting for us to exhaust all other possibilities."

Kelly frowned. "Which means we aren't going to like it," she said.

"I'm afraid not."

"Well, don't keep us in suspense," said Boyd. "What is it?"

"It's fairly simple, really," said the young genius.

He paused for effect. "You and Kelly have to commit suicide."

57

There were several long seconds of silence around the patio table as the sun continued inching below the horizon. "Come again," said Boyd in disbelief. "If this is a joke, it isn't funny."

"Sorry," said Otto. "I couldn't resist using the word *suicide*. Technically, you might say that my idea calls for you to commit one-tenth suicide, and nine-tenths *homicide*.

"We've discussed our failures at length," he continued. "And we've hypothesized that not only won't Eeny allow you to communicate directly with yourselves, it won't even let you communicate with others. Not as long as this communication leads to changes that provide the other versions of you with information they wouldn't have otherwise had."

"Right," said Kelly.

"The way I've come to look at it," continued Otto, "is that Eeny thinks it's cheating for a version of you in the past to influence a version of you in the future, for the future version's benefit."

"Good way to think of it," said Kelly.

"But what if the information you provide *isn't* for the benefit of future you?" continued Otto. "What if it doesn't change the thinking or behavior of future you at all? Because, afterward, future you can't engage in thinking *or* behavior? In short, what if you found a way to *kill* your future self? This wouldn't give future Kelly any forbidden knowledge, because she would no longer exist in the timeline."

"That's horrible," said Kelly.

"Which is why I didn't bring it up earlier. But not nearly as horrible as you think. And I believe it will skirt Eeny's *no communication* rule. And once future Kelly and Justin are gone, Eeny's rules will allow the two of you to journey back to your time and resume your lives. It won't allow you to go further into the future than any version of you has ever been, but that's okay, too. You just have to kill your-selves after the cube was activated, but before the time you originally traveled into the past from Sun Island."

He paused to let this sink in. "Think about it," he continued. "You'd have it all. You'd have your life back, in the proper era. You'd have your love for each other. But in addition, you'd bring your knowledge with you. Knowledge of how to call forth the cube's telepathic AI. And knowledge of what China has been up to. So you can make sure Sun Island never happens."

"Sounds perfect," said Kelly wistfully. "Other than the fact that we have to murder two more innocent people to do it. Two people I happen to *really like*."

"Yeah," said Boyd, "I'm pretty sure this would be a hundred per-cent homicide, zero percent suicide. It's like killing your identical twin. Just because you share DNA doesn't mean you aren't two com-pletely different people."

"That isn't a good analogy," said Otto. "You and your future self are more than just identical twins. You don't just look alike and have the same DNA. You have the exact same life experiences. The exact same memories. Identical down to the last neuronal trace. Imagine that the two of you spring forward and replace the versions of you in the future just as they meet for the first time. You two would still possess every last life memory they had prior to meeting. So you wouldn't be erasing them physically, emotionally, or intellectually. You'd be *adding* to them. Their very soul would be preserved in you."

Boyd and Kelly both considered his points, but still looked dis-tinctly unconvinced.

"One could argue that having *two* versions of Justin Boyd and Kelly Connolly is the real ethical transgression," continued Otto. He smiled. "I mean, the two of you are *so* awesome, having an additional set is an embarrassment of riches."

Both Americans couldn't help but laugh.

"Kelly, imagine that I snap my fingers and create an exact copy of you," the young scientist continued. "Then imagine that the instant this copy appears, I snap them again, and she is disintegrated. How is that murder? Your unique soul, body, and memories still remain in the universe."

"I get that," said Kelly. "But you've also killed someone, someone who wanted to live. Who could feel pain when you did it."

"Not if they were disintegrated instantly. And you weren't worried about possible pain when I brought them *into* existence. In one blink I summoned them from nothingness to life. In the next, I returned them back to nothingness.'

Kelly nodded thoughtfully. She had read an article about the transporter machine from *Star Trek* that had some eerily similar points to make. Scientists agreed that the transporter worked by scanning a person's pattern into a computer and then reconstituting a copy of the person on the planet below, destroying the original in an instant. This view was supported by episodes in which a crewmember's information was trapped in the pattern buffer, and there was a delay in reconstitution. Which meant that every time the transporter was used, a crewmember was copied and then killed.

Boyd turned to Otto. "But in your example," he said, "the creation and destruction of a copy occurs almost simultaneously. Which wouldn't be the case with what you're proposing. Kelly and I have diverged considerably from the versions of us we'd replace."

"So much the better," said Otto. "As I said, you'd have experienced every last instant that they did, and then you'd add to that. You'd add your love for each other. Along with memories of how that love came about, the sacrifice, heroism, trauma, and triumph that you shared. You'd be the same Kelly and Justin, just with a wealth of hard-won knowledge to bring to the table."

"You really are remarkably persuasive," said Kelly. "I've been told that grandfathers have a lot of accumulated wisdom. But I swore off killing, and I'm not about to start again on myself."

Otto shook his head. "You're missing the big picture, Kelly. If this works, it's the only way to set things back to where they were before the Chinese got the upper hand. You've made sacrifices to ensure Hitler didn't get an unstoppable weapon. You've committed possible treason to make sure your own people don't get it. Are you telling me you aren't willing to make a sacrifice to keep it from the Chinese?

My guess is that the future Kelly Connolly would be willing to die to keep the cube in safe hands. If she were here now, I know she'd be urging you to do this."

"He's right," said Boyd. "Absolutely right. We'd both be willing to die to prevent the future that will arise if China rules the world. And we've already proven it, remember? In the clearing in Pennsylvania. We were willing to surrender, believing it to be suicide, just on the off chance we could stop China from getting the cube. How can a man die better, remember?"

"How could I forget?"

"And even beyond that," he continued, "if we do this, Sun Island doesn't happen. Which means that Shen will have no reason to nuke it and kill many thousands of people. So at minimum, if Otto's idea works, those lives would all be spared. *At minimum.*"

Kelly paused in thought for almost a minute, now bathed in nothing but twilight. Finally, she nodded, looking miserable. "You and Otto are right," she said. "About all of it. I'm in. Knowing what's at stake, future me *would* be willing to sacrifice herself. She *would* urge me to do this."

She turned to face her young grandfather. "I'm sure you realize that this action could have a significant impact on your future, right?"

"I do," said Otto. "If you and Justin break out of this loop and go back to your time, where in previous loops you stayed here, this could change my thinking, my actions, and thus my future. But I don't think it will. You plan to remove yourselves from my life either way. I don't think this is a substantive enough difference to counteract history's resistance to change. I think history wants me to meet my future wife and go down the original path as much as I do, and it will find a way to return to this course."

"But we can't know for sure," said Boyd.

"I think we can," said Otto. "Imagine that your ability to break the loop and return to your time finally causes my future to change. In that case, Kelly will never get born again in the nineties. But if this is true, then she won't exist for you to kill. So you can only succeed in killing yourselves if this action *won't* end up derailing my future."

Otto sighed. "But it doesn't matter," he added. "Even if this killed me, I'd urge you to do it. Because it will save thousands of lives on Sun Island, if nothing else."

Kelly nodded. "So it seems we'd all be willing to sacrifice ourselves for the right reasons," she said. "It's ironic. I was willing to die for the cause, but less willing to *kill myself* for the cause. But none of that matters. Because we don't really have much of a choice."

"Do you have any ideas about how to go about this?" Boyd asked the young genius.

"I do. But you know your own future and any players involved a lot better than I do, so I'll leave it to you to iron this out."

Boyd frowned. "I was afraid you might say that," he replied miserably.

58

Colonel Tom Osborne sat in a black leather recliner in the middle of a stranger's living room and shook his head, thinking that the only way the unreality of the moment could be any greater was if the police stormed into the house to try to arrest him for breaking and entering.

It was just over twenty minutes until time zero. Which meant that if he was going to change his mind, he needed to do it soon.

He pressed a button to recline the chair and closed his eyes, running through the events of the past three weeks for the hundredth time, making sure he hadn't missed something. Because even after three weeks of marinating in the impossible, he still couldn't believe he was really doing what he was doing.

He would suspect he was being manipulated by a malicious magician of extraordinary skill, except for one thing: *no* magician was *that* good.

Three weeks earlier he had received an encrypted communication to his private email address that purported to be from Justin Boyd's supercomputer and AI, which the major had named Sage. The AI had all the right passwords and codes to reach him, and a simple exchange proved it also knew everything about Justin Boyd that only the real Sage would know.

The AI had insisted that its communication involved a national security emergency, and that Major Boyd not be told of it under any circumstances. It then proceeded to give Osborne its location, concealed under a floorboard in room 396 of the historic Adams Mount Hotel, less than thirty minutes distant. All the while, Osborne's central computer insisted that the supercomputer that housed Sage was still affixed by high-tech bandage firmly to Justin Boyd's leg.

Even so, despite smelling a trap, the colonel led a team to retrieve it, finding it exactly where the AI had said it was, and not running into a hint of trouble.

He laughed to himself as he remembered thinking that things couldn't possibly get any more bizarre than this. How naive he had been. At that point, the truly bizarre had yet to even *begin*.

Once in his possession, Sage had played him a video message from Justin Boyd himself, along with one of the Enigma Cube scientists, Dr. Kelly Connolly. They began by claiming they were sending the message from 1943 Spokane, and then asked him to pause the playback while he checked Sage's internal clock.

Osborne didn't believe a word of it, of course. It was preposterous.

Still, he did now have an EHO-issued supercomputer in his possession that shouldn't exist. These were as rare as they were expensive, and every one ever built was fully accounted for. Plus, the device was weathered and dirty enough for him to imagine it had been hiding in the false floorboard for a *very* long time. Sure enough, the computer's internal clock, which operated even when it was off, indicated that it had been in operation for over eighty-five years.

Not conclusive by any means, but good enough to prompt him to cancel his meetings for the day. And he was very glad he did. Because for three hours straight, Justin Boyd and Kelly Connolly absolutely blew his mind. They laid out future history, beginning with how the Enigma Cube—the immovable Enigma Cube!—would soon be stolen by Kelly Connolly. And this history was often accompanied by footage from Boyd's lenses, showing battles they had waged with Chinese forces in Pennsylvania and on Sun Island, how they had been threatened with a nuclear bomb by a Chinese commander named Shen, and how they had suddenly appeared in a dark room in Canada in 1943.

Then, just when Osborne had thought the story couldn't get any wilder, it promptly did.

Much wilder.

Boyd described such things as a telepathic AI resident in the Enigma Cube, the rules of time travel, and their travel to Berlin. And then he showed footage of Nazi Germany and Adolf Hitler.

Adolf Hitler!

Osborne was seeing actual, crystal-clear modern footage of the unconscious Nazi Fuhrer, illuminated only by flashlight, while Justin Boyd explained to Dr. Connolly why history might be better served if Hitler was left alive.

It was all so fantastic. So demented. So *extraordinary*.

When Osborne had finished viewing the lengthy video message, he had been stunned into inactivity for ten full minutes, until he decided to play the entire message once again.

And then again.

The explanations coming from Boyd and Connolly made a kind of bizarre sense. Their story seemed to hang together somehow, with enough color and detail to make it come alive, as if they had actually experienced every minute of it.

Even so, this still hadn't been enough to convince him. Extraordinary claims required extraordinary evidence, and computer clocks could be altered, video faked.

Yet Boyd and Connolly had expected this kind of skepticism, had prepared for it. They insisted that Osborne proceed normally, and not speak a word of this to the versions of themselves alive in 2027. And they explained why this was so important.

They also told him the exact date and time that Kelly would steal the cube, begging him not to prevent it, or do anything else that might influence the thoughts or actions of their future selves. Apparently, if he decided to take any such action, the cube's telepathic AI would somehow know it, and would no longer allow their message to reach him in the first place.

Finally, they provided a list of dozens of events that would happen in the near future, including the precise timing of storms and earthquakes in far-off lands, final scores of sporting events, and future prices of stocks. Osborne checked these predictions every day for five days, and marveled as each one came to pass.

He could no longer deny it. Their story was real! There was no other explanation. Faking video was one thing. Accurately predicting the future was another thing entirely.

The major and physicist claimed to have intel that was vital to national security, which they could only reveal if the current versions of themselves were dead, and gave a lengthy explanation of what they had in mind. Osborne found this part of the message extremely suspect.

Could he really kill his own people? This was madness.

Yes, they had assured him that this act would allow the versions of them in the past to return. But what if they were wrong? Or what if he was being played somehow, in a way that was too clever for him to figure out?

No matter how compelling the evidence they had provided, the cold-blooded murder of Justin Boyd and Kelly Connolly would still require the biggest leap of faith he had ever made.

He threw his eyes open with a start. It was time for the final test. He couldn't delay it any longer.

Colonel Tom Osborne tilted his head to stare at a massive Halloween spider, one that had been placed high on a rope web that had been strung from floor to ceiling in the room. Ryan and Charity Lee, whoever they were, certainly took their Halloween decorations seriously.

He pulled the five-foot spider down and set it on the floor. This would be the final proof. If he opened the spider's abdomen and there was nothing inside, he would abort.

On the other hand, if he found a cube inside, as he had been told he would, one that would produce burning glyphs when its corners were pressed for an extended period, he would go forward as planned.

He wasn't sure what he hoped would happen. Justin Boyd was like a son to him, and just the thought of ending his life made him sick to his stomach.

***

Kelly Connolly couldn't believe what was happening. How had it come to this? How was she trapped in a self-driving Lexus with no way out? The leaves of the trees that surrounded her had turned an array of spectacular colors, but she had no time to enjoy them, and she worried that she might not be alive for much longer to do so.

How had this become her life?

She never should have agreed to go to the Haycock site with Justin Boyd in the first place. She should have just come up with an excuse as to why she couldn't make it. She should have taken the cube before he brought back the generator and focused on finding a permanent hiding place for it.

Kelly was embarrassed to admit it, even to herself, but she had only traveled to Pennsylvania because she was taken with the black ops major. She tried to fight it off but couldn't. For some inexplicable reason, since meeting Boyd the week before, she hadn't been able to get him out of her head. She had known that coming to meet with him right after taking the cube was a mistake, but she had no idea just *how much* of a mistake.

And now that he had saved her from knockout gas and shown off his respirocytes, among numerous other enhancements, she found him even *more* interesting, *more* appealing. But perhaps this was simply because her emotions were heightened by the danger she was in. If they managed to get out of this alive, she was sure her interest in him would be fleeting. A flash in the pan. He seemed to be compassionate and have a good heart, but he was still a cold-blooded killer. The idea that she could fall for such a man was preposterous.

"We'll be stopping very soon," he said beside her, continuing to show an icy calm in the face of unknown danger. "When we do, leave your phone in the car, since they can trace it. I'm sure it's been backed up fairly recently, but I'll have Sage place a copy in her memory just in case."

"Uh . . . thanks," said Kelly. "I guess." She was uncomfortable that his computer would have the contents of her grandfather's journal, but she trusted him enough to delete the data after the danger had passed.

"I'm going to protect you, Kelly," he said. "I promise."

The car finally rolled to a stop. Ten men were gathered in a clearing and ordered them out. Each soldier was carrying a machine gun, a weapon she'd been sure she would never see in person.

Boyd escorted her to the front of the car as the men closed in.

"How are you even conscious?" one of the soldiers asked her companion.

"Oh, I'm full of surprises, Master Sergeant Knudson," said Boyd. "Oh, sorry. I know you prefer to be called *Dredd*. Like the judge, I guess."

"How do you know that?"

"I know *everything*," replied Boyd. "Look, you guys are in a fight that you didn't choose. I do realize that this is what mercs *do*," he added, "but this time, you're in over your heads."

"Yeah, we've heard all about you," replied the man. "Why do you think there are *ten* of us? The boss told us to expect you to be the most badass commando we've ever seen. And that if you didn't arrive unconscious, to knock your ass out right away."

Boyd laughed. "You poor shithead," he said. "You have *no idea* what you're up against here. So I'm prepared to show you mercy. Walk away with your men right now, and I'll pretend this never happened."

Dredd shook his head in disbelief. "*Who are you?*" he whispered.

They continued their exchange for several minutes. The mercenary wanted Boyd to take a knockout pill. Remarkably, the major made a plea to let Kelly go, and offered to go quietly if they agreed. It was a heroic gesture of epic proportions.

"I'd love to take you up on the offer," the merc said. "But—funny thing—we were told just this morning that *she* is our main priority. You're important, but secondary. Likely more dangerous, so we need you to go to sleep first. But, actually, if we had to choose just one of you to capture, it'd be *her*."

Kelly's eyes widened. Did they know about her and the cube? How could that be?

This was the last thought Dr. Kelly Connolly would ever have. As she was about to consider these questions further, with no warning, the entire clearing exploded into a fireball three stories tall. Kelly and the EHO major were vaporized before they even had a glimmer that this might be happening.

One moment she was a living, conscious being, and the next she had been blown apart with enough force to splatter her across fifty feet of flaming, superheated air. A force that tore the Lexus behind her into tiny bits of shrapnel and created its own non-nuclear mushroom cloud.

And thousands of miles away, Colonel Tom Osborne, sitting on a recliner in the home of a stranger, watched it all happen through a telescopic drone feed in absolute revulsion.

59

Justin Boyd placed the supercomputer gently beneath a floorboard in room 396 of the newly built Adams Mount Hotel, and then tightened it back down.

"We're all set," he told Kelly and her young grandfather, who were standing nearby. "Same as before. Sage is set to be recharged in eighty-four years, three weeks prior to our first face-off with Shen in Pennsylvania. Once she awakens, she'll immediately contact Colonel Osborne with our message."

"Let's just hope the third time is the charm," said Kelly, dropping her large purse to the bed, which held an alien cube inside.

"If it's ever going to work," said Otto, "this is the time."

"I agree," said Boyd. "This hotel is the perfect spot for it. Sage says it's still standing in 2027, with no renovations, other than to the bathrooms."

Kelly sighed. "I worry that our first two failures mean that this idea won't work either."

"I know," said Boyd. "But we need to make at least fifteen to twenty attempts to be sure."

"Of course," she mumbled. A weary smile slowly crossed her face. "I guess we always knew we'd have to *kill ourselves* to get this to work."

"Really?" said Boyd. "Gallows humor? About this?"

"Sometimes you have to laugh when it hurts too much to cry."

"In that case," said Boyd, "let's find out if it worked. The suspense is *killing me*."

Kelly frowned. "Yeah, I take it back. Let's make that the last word-play ever on the subject."

"Are you two done?" said Otto, rolling his eyes.

"Definitely," said Kelly. "Hold on, I'll find out where we stand."

She paused. *"Eeny,"* she thought at the cube in her purse, *"is there a version of me still alive in the future?"*

"Yes," replied the AI simply, having answered this same question now hundreds of times.

"And is this version still alive at the time I originally reached Sun Island?"

"She is not," said the AI, showing no sign of emotion.

Kelly gasped and reeled backwards, falling to a seated position on the bed behind her with her mouth wide open. She thought a few more questions at the telepathic AI and then turned to face her companions, who were staring at her with bated breath.

"It worked," she whispered unnecessarily. "It really worked. The future has changed. Justin and I are no longer alive after we entered the woods of Pennsylvania. Osborne did it!"

"Unbelievable," said Boyd.

Kelly's face fell. "I'm elated that it worked. But also heartbroken."

There was a long silence in the room as they all digested the implications.

"So we're really free to go back home?" said Boyd, still not quite believing it. "And Eeny confirmed it?"

"It's confirmed. We can return at any time between our death in Pennsylvania and when we originally traveled into the past."

Kelly turned to Otto. "Thank you!" she said emphatically. "You saved thousands of lives on Sun Island. And you saved the world from tyranny."

"Glad to help," said Otto awkwardly. He tried to fake a smile, but several tears escaped from his eyes and began to run down his face.

Kelly rose from the bed and held him in her arms. "I've come to love you like a younger brother over the past five months, Otto," she said as she began to spill tears of her own. "But more than that, I've come to think the world of you. And not just because you're my grandfather. Or because of your intellect. But because you're a wonderful person."

"I feel the same about you," said Otto as they separated. He turned to Boyd. "And you're pretty special yourself," he added through his tears, extending a hand.

Boyd ignored the hand and hugged the young man fondly. "To say it's been an honor doesn't even come close," he said. "Having the chance to work with and befriend a young man with your wisdom and maturity, not to mention an intellect that puts Albert Einstein to shame, has been one of the highlights of my life."

Otto grinned. "And being able to get dating advice from an American commando married to my granddaughter has been one of the highlights of mine."

Boyd laughed.

"Are you okay to drive back to Spokane on your own?" asked Kelly.

Otto nodded sadly.

"Wait a minute," said Boyd. "We don't need to make him travel back home by himself. We can travel to the future any time we want, right? And we know spending extra time with him won't derail his future, or your birth, or we would have never succeeded."

"Exactly right!" said Kelly excitedly. "I didn't expect our plan to work this time, so I wasn't really prepared. But the least we can do is stay with Otto for a few more weeks and get him settled in. And have the chance to say proper goodbyes."

The young scientist brightened. "I would *love* that," he said. "But are you sure? I thought you were dying to get back to your time." He winced as he realized what he had just said. "Sorry, I wasn't trying for gallows humor there. It was an accident."

Kelly beamed. "No need to apologize," she said. "And while I am looking forward to going back home, having the chance to spend another few weeks with you and go out in style is priceless. Besides, I'm enjoying the simple life here more than I thought I would. There's something to be said about a time without cell phones."

"Wow," said Boyd. "And I thought after all we've been through that I had heard absolutely *everything*. But apparently not."

60

Tom Osborne squeezed his eyes shut and shuddered as the fireball on his tablet computer continued to shoot skyward, taking with it the incinerated remains of the most impressive EHO operative he had ever recruited, whom he had tapped to be his successor.

And *he* had been responsible. He had personally seen to it that the clearing was laced with hidden explosives of devastating power, and he had pulled the trigger.

He had known Justin Boyd since he was a seventeen-year-old kid, and now his friend was dead.

Two loud cracks reverberated throughout the room, like snaps of a whip, and Osborne's eyes shot open. Kelly Connolly and Justin Boyd were standing on the floor next to the cube, both with tears in their eyes, and both looking woozy.

The colonel's sorrow and guilt were instantly replaced with joy—and awe.

Incredible. It had actually worked!

He rushed over to Boyd and hugged him tight. "Thank God," he said simply.

Instead of issuing a response, the major turned into dead weight, and Osborne set him gently down on the carpet, as Kelly Connolly's legs went wobbly and she fell to the carpet as well.

Just as they had predicted, time travel didn't agree with them.

Osborne laid the two time travelers on their backs in the most comfortable position he could, unable to keep himself from smiling at their appearance. It was as if they had walked off the set of a movie taking place in the forties. And why not? When in Rome, dress as the Romans dress.

Dr. Connolly was wearing her hair relatively short, and pulled back off her forehead, mirroring the style of the day. Boyd's hair was

short as usual, but also combed back to reveal as much of his forehead as possible. He wore pleated cotton slacks and a button-down
shirt, while she was wearing a simple lightweight blue dress, cinched
with a thin leather belt.

A relieved Tom Osborne returned to the recliner and waited for
them to come to, coordinating with his forces in Pennsylvania while
he did so.

He still had much to accomplish.

61

Kelly Connolly opened her eyes, but everything was blurry. She felt someone help her to her feet and coax her to a seat on a comfortable couch, but it was as though she were sleepwalking. Her vision finally swam into focus, and she watched this same person—a tall man in his fifties—help an awakening Justin Boyd to the couch beside her.

The man who had helped her and Justin retreated a few yards away to a recliner and waited patiently for them to show signs of life.

"Tom?" said Boyd faintly beside her as his faculties slowly returned.

"Justin!" said the man across from them with gusto. "Welcome back to 2027."

"Thanks, Colonel," whispered Boyd. "Glad to be here."

"Dr. Connolly," said the man, obviously Colonel Tom Osborne, "nice to finally meet you. I've heard good things. And I watched your video message, ah . . . several times."

"Thanks," she said, her voice soft but gaining strength as vitality returned. "I've heard good things about you too. How long were we out?"

"A little over an hour," replied the colonel. "Can I ask why you both arrived with tears in your eyes?"

Boyd blew out a long breath. "We were saying farewell to a good friend," he explained.

"I thought you might be mourning, you know . . . *yourselves.*"

"No. Kelly and I managed to get through the bulk of that by the end of last week."

"Even though your future selves were only killed an hour ago?"

"Two weeks ago for us," said Boyd. "Time travel can be funny that way," he added. "But tell me about the ongoing operation in Pennsylvania."

"As you specified," said Osborne, "I sent in every EHO agent available, along with dozens of standard commandos. The Op is now completed. We killed about half the men you said would be in the woods, and captured the other half. Several of these were Chinese nationals. *Enhanced* Chinese nationals. Giving us the unprecedented opportunity to learn more about the state of their EHO program."

"Did you capture Commander Shen Ning?"

Osborne nodded.

"Outstanding," said Boyd, his voice now back to full strength. "Can I assume you have your team in place here?"

"Yes. Ready to take on the wave of commandos you indicated would be breaking into this house looking for the cube in five to six hours."

Kelly winced. "So you let them shred my house?"

"You and Justin insisted that I not do anything to stop them. Not do anything to change events until I pulled the trigger on the explosives."

"I know," said Kelly miserably. "We chose the timing. But that doesn't mean I have to like it. Any wall or piece of my furniture that they *didn't* slice open?"

The colonel made a face. "Not so much."

"Okay, then," said Kelly. "But at least be sure to intercept the hostiles this time before they destroy *this* house? The Lees are close friends and neighbors. I'm just guessing, but if they get back from vacation to find their home a bullet-ridden war zone, they may not ask me to house sit again."

Osborne smiled. "Our goal will be to capture the incoming hostiles. We'll rig the place with enough gas to put Godzilla to sleep and wait for them to come inside. With any luck, there won't be any damage at all."

Kelly looked around, and the place looked fine, other than the damaged Halloween spider, which she had already planned to replace after using it as a cube storage facility.

It had been six months since she was in this house last, but it seemed like a lifetime. And in many ways, it was.

"I'll want to be part of all prisoner interrogations," said Boyd, "here and in Pennsylvania."

"Of course. But why are the Chinese after you and Dr. Connolly?"

"That's what we came back to tell you about," said Boyd. "They know all about Project Uru. And they've been spying on our research, using undetectable bugs."

"That isn't possible," said the colonel.

"That *wasn't* possible," corrected Boyd. "But they found a way. Most importantly, they have a cube of their own."

Osborne shrank back. "What? Are you *certain*?"

"I don't know where it is, but I'm sure they have one. Fortunately, they haven't managed to unlock it, so we're ahead of the game. And now that you've changed history, Colonel, we can make sure we *stay* ahead. Finding their cube has to become the intelligence community's number one priority."

"I'll see to that personally."

"Good," said Boyd. "Even though they found our cube, they had no way to steal it. Because even if they sent an overwhelming force against us, they knew they wouldn't be able to budge it a millimeter. But if we find *theirs*, that won't be the case."

The colonel turned to Kelly. "Speaking of budging the cube," he said, "how did you know how to activate it in the first place?"

"I'll be happy to go into that later," she replied. "But we're eager to hear your response to the proposal we made at the end of our message. So what do you say, Colonel Osborne? Are you ready to take this program more . . . private?"

They had spent the last fifteen minutes of their message trying to persuade the colonel to consider establishing a program even more exclusive, and more secret, than the Enigma program had been—which was really saying something, since no program had ever been more classified.

"It's a big step," said Osborne.

"You saw the devastation this thing managed in Canada," said Kelly. "And that's only the *beginning* of what it can do."

"Yes, Sage's playback showed an effortless power that was truly extraordinary. But we had already assumed the cube possessed immeasurable power. That it likely represented the most destructive force on Earth. Which is why we instituted the safeguards that we did. This is just a confirmation."

Kelly shook her head. "It's more than a confirmation," she insisted. "It's unlocked now, which makes all the difference. We were responsible for a gun inside an unbreakable safe. Now the gun's out, loaded, and cocked. So we need to be even more certain than ever it's kept in good hands rather than bad. That it's used and studied for the right reasons."

"The right reasons being in pursuit of science rather than weaponry."

"Exactly," said Kelly. "Just imagine a world with unlimited free energy. A world in which transportation, construction, and space travel—including *interstellar* space travel—are utterly transformed, along with dozens of other industries."

"But all of these individual capabilities can also be used for destructive purposes," said Osborne.

"That's true," said Kelly, "but they'll each be much less dangerous than the cube in its entirety. And our job won't just be to discover revolutionary technology, but to make this tech as childproof as possible."

"And we alone would decide how to proceed with the cube," said the colonel.

"That's right," confirmed Boyd.

"That's what troubles me," said Osborne. "Who made us gods?"

Boyd grinned. "The fact that you'd even *ask* that is what makes you qualified," he said. "You're the most ethical, decent man I've ever known. That's why I trusted you with the information we sent from the past. Why I trusted you to kill us. I've seen firsthand how careful you are when recruiting for EHO. How committed you are to making sure that only men and women of the highest moral character become involved. Why? Because you know you can't take the chance that the wrong person will wield this kind of power. Which makes you *perfect* for shepherding the cube along."

Osborne nodded but didn't respond.

"Let me ask you this," said Boyd, "did you get rich from our predictions?"

"What?"

"You heard me. Be honest. Once we proved we were right every time, did you bet on any sports? Buy any stocks that you knew for certain were going higher?"

Osborne shook his head. "No. I didn't think that would be right."

Boyd turned triumphantly to Kelly. "See," he said. "I told you he wouldn't. I'm not even sure this guy is human."

"You're the same way," said Osborne.

"No," replied Boyd, "I'm not nearly the saint you are, Colonel. For instance, Kelly and I bought a number of shares in three companies before we left: DuPont, Boeing, and Procter & Gamble. We put the stock certificates in a safe deposit box. As part of my brilliant buy and hold strategy," he added with a smile. "It's simple, really. You just have to choose companies you know won't go out of business and hold the stock for eighty-four years. Works every time."

"I didn't think you cared about money," said Osborne.

"I don't. But I wanted to be able to fund the initial steps required to set up our own cube research group if need be. If we're keeping this a secret even from black ops management, even from the Secretary of Defense and president, funding will become an issue. And I wanted us to be able to spend every waking second studying the cube."

Boyd paused. "You'd be in charge," he continued. "Kelly and I would be co-equal number twos."

"Interesting," said Osborne noncommittally. "Do you think Dr. Connolly has the experience in these matters to operate at this level? She's a brilliant physicist, but this would require additional skills."

"She's more savvy, resourceful, and courageous under fire than anyone I've ever worked with. And the cube's AI has forged a bond with her. Once it finds a boss it deems to be worthy, it sticks with them, and *only* them."

"Sounds very . . . monogamous," said Osborne with a smile. "A good quality in an alien AI."

Kelly laughed. "The AI won't tell me as much about time travel as I'd like," she said, "but I know it will tell us what every glyph controls. Which will accelerate our study of the cube substantially, and eliminate the risk we'd be taking by poking around blindly. The AI is sure to make us work out the science on our own, but it will still prove invaluable."

"Which makes Kelly the most important of all of us," said Boyd. "Not to mention we wouldn't even know how to operate the cube without her."

"Okay, I'm sold," said the colonel. He turned to Kelly with a new-found respect in his eyes. "I've never heard Justin rave about anyone this much. Sounds like *you* should be running the show instead of me."

"I wouldn't go that far," replied Kelly. "We'd want you to be responsible for finding China's cube. Once you do, I can use ours to clear a path to theirs, and to retrieve it. Other than that, we'll dedicate ourselves to pure research, for peaceful, commercial uses only. We'll bring in select members of the old Enigma team, but we'll need different skills now that it's unlocked, so not all of them will be suitable. And others won't pass the new rigorous vetting standards we'll employ."

"You've really thought this through."

"What do you say?" asked Boyd. "I suggest we wait a month and then disband Project Uru. Tell the team that despite great effort, we have no leads on what happened to the cube. Then reconnect with those on the team we decide to re-recruit, and bring in select newcomers."

"And where would you propose to house this group?"

Boyd shrugged. "That's something for further discussion. We can use the cube to excavate a new subterranean site or bore through a mountain with ease. Kelly and I can fund the rest of the necessary construction and security with our own money."

"Just how much profit will you make on these stocks of yours?"

"When we purchased the shares, Sage calculated they would be worth a little over two hundred million in 2027. So we can self-fund for years, and find a way to siphon off money from other black budgets if necessary."

Osborne sighed. "You do know that I vowed never to set up this kind of off-the-reservation program," he said.

"I do," said the major. "And I vowed that if I ever went back in time and had the chance to kill Adolf Hitler, I would do that. These are strange times, Colonel. Most importantly, Kelly also made a vow. To her grandfather. To protect the cube from any group she didn't trust with all her heart and soul. So if you want to study the cube, it's either *this* way, or *no* way."

"Her grandfather?" said Osborne in confusion.

"Long story," said Boyd.

Osborne stared into the eyes of both time travelers for several seconds. "I'll want to hear all of these *long stories*," he said, "ask a lot of questions, and check things out." He paused. "But if everything checks out, I'm in."

"Outstanding," said Boyd.

"I'm looking forward to getting to know you," said Kelly. "Justin thinks the world of you."

"And you as well, it seems, Dr. Connolly."

"First of all, call me Kelly. Second, *Connolly* isn't actually my last name anymore. I've changed it to *Connolly-Boyd*."

"What does that mean?" said Osborne, blinking in confusion. "Are you two *married*?"

Kelly grinned. "Surprise," she said. "I was thinking of changing my name to *Frau Boyd*," she added in amusement, "but thought better of it."

"Frau Boyd?" repeated Osborne.

"Another long story," said Boyd. "But I can see why this might come as a shock. After all, in this timeline, I only met Kelly last week, and we haven't even spent a full day together. But I've been with her now for almost six months."

"I'm, ah . . . very happy for you both," said Osborne. "Sorry I missed the wedding," he added wryly, "but I was busy not being in existence at the time."

Boyd laughed. "Perfectly understandable. And if it makes you feel any better, we'll be doing it again. We don't mind the 1943 marriage certificate so much. The problem is that we don't know what anniversary gifts to get each other," he added, trying to keep a straight face. "My understanding is that the first is the paper anniversary. And the sixtieth is the *diamond* anniversary. But what the hell is the *eighty-fifth* anniversary, which is coming up next year?"

"I see the dilemma," said Osborne in amusement. "I guess you really do have no choice but to remarry."

The discussion continued, and Colonel Osborne soon informed his protégé that his supercomputer was on site, and Sage was ready to reunite with him, unless he wanted a model that was less than eighty-five years old. Boyd wouldn't hear of it, as expected.

As the colonel helped affix Boyd's trusty AI companion to his leg, Kelly found herself reflecting on everything that had happened since the fateful day she had first met the EHO major, convinced that all those in the military were throwbacks to more barbaric times.

Since then, she had lived during the most barbaric time in human history, and had learned what barbarism was *really* about. And she had fallen head over heels in love with a commando, who just happened to also be the kindest, most thoughtful man she had ever known.

Even more surprising, she, herself, had been forced to become barbaric, to abandon pacifism to become a warrior, for what she deemed were the right reasons.

All of this was as unexpected, as *extraordinary* in its own way as anything else she had been through. If she had been asked before meeting Boyd which was more likely, interacting with a telepathic alien AI and traveling in time, or falling in love with a major and becoming a mass murderer, she would have chosen the former.

But, somehow, everything had worked out much better than she and her new husband could have ever hoped for. When she had removed the cube from the Uru facility—an agonizing decision— she hadn't been sure what might happen next. But after a number of even more agonizing decisions, here they were, just down the block from her home, having accomplished some truly remarkable things. They had thwarted the Chinese, maintained the timeline, and gained extraordinary insight into time travel, the capabilities of the cube, and even a glimpse of the thinking of the alien species behind it.

She also found herself trusting Colonel Osborne as much as Boyd had said she would. So after so many torturous decisions, the choice to go forward with these men and find ways to catapult human civilization to new heights couldn't have been easier. Humankind was more than a little rough around the edges. But the species had also made gargantuan strides in maturity since the 1940s, and had become self-aware enough to realize that additional improvement was sorely needed.

Her grandfather's decision to keep the cube out of human hands for eight decades had been the right one. But she was equally certain that her decision to take it out of hibernation and explore its potential, in a careful, tightly controlled and altruistic manner, was also correct.

As she thought of her grandfather, an image of young Otto Richter flashed into her mind, tall and thin and physically awkward, but mentally a giant, mature beyond his years.

Her grandfather was just as extraordinary as the powers of the cube and her personal transformation had been. She had no doubt that Otto's intellect was the most exceptional the human race had ever produced, with no other scientific luminary even coming close.

So had he found a way to beat a heart attack? Had he convinced his wife to lie to the family, to pretend he had died, to pass along his supposed last words, and to mourn him at a pretend funeral?

Even if he had managed it, there was no way he could still be alive today. He would be a hundred and two years old.

Still, Otto had invented a dark energy generator in 1943, while the vile Nazi SS was breathing down his neck. If he could do *that*, what *couldn't* he do?

Kelly considered this for another few seconds and shook her head, feeling silly. Constructing a device, no matter how advanced, was one thing, but beating a heart attack and living past a hundred was something else entirely. She decided she was letting her imagination run away with her.

Yet despite this, Kelly found herself staring at the entrance to the Lees' home, half expecting her grandfather to pull the door open and march across the threshold.

There was no way this was going to happen, of course.

Even so, she found that she couldn't take her eyes from the door.

Because if anyone could pull this off, it would be Otto Richter.

AUTHOR'S NOTES

Thanks for reading *The Enigma Cube*. I hope that you enjoyed it.

Please feel free to write to me at douglaserichards1@gmail.com, as I love hearing from readers and always respond. And if you have interest in my author bio and list of books, these appear on the very last page.

At the end of most of my novels, I include a section detailing what in the work is real, and what isn't, along with a few personal anecdotes—and these sections have been extremely well received.

So here I go again, beginning with what I hope is an entertaining passage about how I came to write this crazy novel in the first place.

As a quick rule of thumb, everything in the novel is scientifically and historically accurate with the exception of the following: Alien cubes that can control gravity, Otto Richter, Zanamine gas, The Rolling Hills Mansion, a Nazi refueling station on an island in the Hudson Bay, all Germans other than Himmler and Hitler, and Sun Island (although the Chinese do have other islands in the South China Sea as described).

With this said, I'll get right to it. I've listed the subjects I'll be covering below in order of appearance. Since research and interpretations can differ, I encourage you to explore these topics further to arrive at your own conclusions. And if you aren't interested in an early topic on this list, feel free to skip ahead to one that might interest you more.

- How this novel came to be
- Killing Adolf
- The Nazis and the occult
- The history of WWII
- Enhanced Human Operations
- Slaughterbots (HKs)

- Are UFOs real?
- Controlling gravity
- Time travel
- Things really are getting better
- Miscellaneous science
- China

How this novel came to be

When I first set out to write *The Enigma Cube*, if you would have suggested it would contain a single word about Nazis or time travel, I would have laughed hysterically and called you insane.

Just goes to show how much *I* know.

So how did this novel come to be? Well, many years ago, I wrote a series of science fiction adventures for kids nine and older (*The Prometheus Project* 1, 2, and 3) that center around an abandoned alien city discovered on Earth, packed with alien technology. A brother and sister become part of the project and, of course, soon outdo all the adults.

In the last of these novels, I introduced the Enigma Cube. I even called it that, and described it almost exactly the way I describe it in *this* novel, including its need to go on a diet. It, too, gets stolen, begging the question, how does one steal an object weighing millions of pounds?

In the kids' novel, this cube was a tangential plot element, but I always thought the idea of introducing an immovable object, and then having it promptly stolen, was a great hook, and vowed to someday expand upon this in a full-blown adult novel.

But a funny thing happened on the way to writing the first word. While I was studying up on the science I might need for the novel, I came upon an article that described a Nazi project to develop anti-gravity. I was intrigued. How in the world had they come to be attempting something like this in the *1940s*?

And then I learned of the Nazis' bizarre fascination with superweapons and the occult. With evil archaeology. I discovered that the Nazis depicted in *Raiders of the Lost Ark* and *Hellboy* were less fictional than I had imagined.

And I found it all strangely fascinating.

I've always studied the future, never the past, but it occurred to me that maybe my readers would find this as fascinating as I did.

So I introduced Otto Richter, with the idea that he would solve the cube, bury it in Spokane, and pass on his solution in a journal, allowing his granddaughter to steal the immovable cube from Project Uru.

My original plan was to keep Otto confined solely to the pages of his journal. But the more Otto scenes I wrote, and the more I studied the Nazis and WW II, the more intrigued I became by what I was learning

The Nazi soldiers were all hopped up on crystal meth? Are you kidding me?

The heinous *Heil Hitler* salute was pervasive in German society and even used by little kids in school? Really? I always thought it was for use by soldiers only, or during Hitler's speeches, and confined only to the war years.

So, gradually, the idea of connecting the two plot threads became more and more compelling to me. Especially since control of the fabric of spacetime *could* lead to time travel, which meant I could achieve this result fairly readily.

Even so, it wasn't an easy decision to make. My novel *Split Second*, which introduces a totally unique time travel premise, was my most commercially successful novel ever, having been the 27th bestselling Kindle Book of the year in 2017. Still, I had never written a traditional time travel novel, and had vowed to do so one day.

But I never imagined I'd return to time travel in *The Enigma Cube*. Or that it would involve *Nazi Germany*. Are you kidding? Nazi Germany. Can't get more uplifting than that, right? And was I really going to take the plunge and set much of my futuristic novel in *1943*?

This was a very scary prospect to someone who has never studied history. Was I pushing my luck? Would my fans think this setting was interesting? Or would they find it depressing, or boring, or a step too far?

Finally, as you know, I took the plunge. When I made the decision to link the two halves of the story in the past, I had no idea what the plot would be from there. What in the world would Kelly and Justin do with themselves in 1943? My own plot going forward had become its own enigma.

I found the scenes in the past to be among the most challenging of any I've ever done. I never felt comfortable, because I have so little knowledge of what things were really like back then, and don't even watch movies based in this time.

I did many hours of research, but I found myself having to Google constantly. When was the washing machine invented? Zippers? Sleeping bags? Did homes have electricity? Would 1943 phones work with the power out? When were fuses invented? Could they land planes at night back then? When was *1984* written? *The Time Machine* by H.G. Wells? How far could long-range transport planes fly? And so on.

Still, while these scenes took more work than they would have for most other people, and often had me pulling out my hair, I'd like to think I got them more or less correct.

So that's the story of this story. How I ended up writing the novel that you just read.

The fact that *The Enigma Cube* ended up the way it did surprised me more than anyone, and it turned out to be the most difficult novel I've ever written, requiring the most research.

But all in all, I'm happy with how it turned out.

I can only hope that my readers feel the same.

Killing Adolf

One can't write a time travel novel set in 1943 without thinking of the possibility of killing Adolf Hitler. And I did. Just for the record, I would love to write a scene in which this psychopathic monster gets the agonizing death he so richly deserves.

Still, I would never have actually written this scene, because the idea of going back in time to kill Hitler has been a mainstay in our cultural zeitgeist for so long, doing this would be the height of unoriginality.

But then a funny thing happened. The more I learned of the history of the time, the more I realized that killing Hitler, at least in 1943, might actually have been a bad idea. I realized a strong case could be made that, while this abomination didn't deserve to live another second, humanity might be better served by locking in the future that came after the war, rather than risking a new one that might be considerably worse.

And then I agonized over whether I should actually play out this possible insight in the novel. No one in history evokes stronger emotions than Adolf Hitler. Did I really want to be the author who has a protagonist argue that the Hitler of 1943 should be spared?

In the end, as you know, I decided to go forward. I'm not a historian, and might have missed huge counterarguments that would blow my thesis out of the water, but I believe that my analysis was strong enough to raise at least a possibility that killing him in 1943 would have been a mistake.

So having decided to go in, I decided to go *all in*. I had an idea that would have been even more agonizing for my protagonists than what I ended up writing. They wouldn't just fail to kill the most despicable man in history. They would be forced to actively prevent *good* men from killing him.

Yikes!

It turns out that there were more than two dozen attempts by Germans to kill their psychopathic leader, but all of them failed. So I thought, what if the presence of Kelly and Justin changes things, such that an assassination attempt that had historically failed would now succeed? And what if they then realized, to their absolute *horror*, that they had to actively *stop* it? How tough of a decision would *that* be? Talk about brutal. Talk about gut-wrenching.

So I spent any number of hours reading about the various failed assassination attempts. In fact, there is an entire book on the subject, by Paddy Ashdown, entitled *Nein: Standing up to Hitler 1935-1944*.

But after reading this, and after straining my brain for more hours than I care to admit, I came up completely empty. I just couldn't get it to work no matter how often I beat my forehead against my desk. I couldn't figure out how to squeeze my characters, and my narrative needs, into an actual historical situation. How to put Kelly and Justin in the right place at the right time.

In the end, I think this turned out for the best. Forcing my characters to make the horrifying decision to stop good men from killing Hitler, despite being more dramatic, would have been a bridge too far, unjustifiable no matter how strong an argument they could have mustered.

The Nazis and the occult

Everything in the novel about Hitler's and Himmler's belief in the supernatural is accurate, including the Ahnenerbe, archaeological expeditions, World Ice Theory, the Aryans of Atlantis, and so on. Erik Jan Hanussen really was a supposed clairvoyant who played a vital role in Hitler's rise to power.

Eric Kurlander wrote a book detailing these absurd beliefs in 2017, entitled, *Hitler's Monsters: A Supernatural History of the Third Reich*. According to Kurlander, "To many Nazis, the Aryan race descended from Nordic "God Men" who came straight down from Heaven and created the lost civilization of Atlantis."

Here is an excerpt from the description of this book on Amazon:

EXCERPT: The Nazi fascination with the occult is legendary, yet today it is often dismissed as Himmler's personal obsession or wildly overstated for its novelty. Preposterous though it was, however, supernatural thinking was inextricable from the Nazi project. The regime enlisted astrology and the paranormal, paganism, Indo-Aryan mythology, witchcraft, miracle weapons, and the lost kingdom of Atlantis in reimagining German politics and society, and recasting German science and religion.

Himmler's library, as described in the novel, was also real. As Kelly recounted, in 2016, a collection of 13,000 occult and witchcraft texts were found in the National Library of the Czech Republic in Prague, which had belonged to the SS leader. Many of the books in the collection were quite rare, and had been gathered by the Ahnenerbe, an organization created to research the archaeological and historical roots of the Aryan race. The Ahnenerbe also conducted experiments and expeditions to prove that Aryans were the ancestors of the

Nordic population that had once ruled the world. Heinrich Himmler believed that the power of the old occult masters could help the Nazis do the same.

I'll leave this section with just a sampling of articles that I read during the writing of *The Enigma Cube,* and encourage you to read these and others if you have further interest.

- The Nazis' search for Atlantis and the Holy Grail: a new TV documentary reveals the truth about Hitler's archaeological quest to rediscover the lost Aryan race and retrieve its forgotten secrets. (Express, UK, 2013)
- Heinrich Himmler Thought Germans Were Descended From Nordic Gods—So He Tried to Prove It (All That's Interesting, 2019)
- A Song of Ice and Fire: World Ice Theory and the supernatural imaginings of the Third Reich. (Lapham's Quarterly, 2017)
- Why Hitler and other Nazis thought the world was really made of ice. (BigThink 2018)
- Hitler's Obsession With the Occult (Yale University Press, 2017)
- Did Hitler's obsession with the occult lose him the war? (The Spectator, 2017)
- What did the Nazis have to do with archaeology? (How Things Work, 2016)

The history of WWII

World War II was horrible beyond compare. But also complex, bizarre, and utterly fascinating. Who knew?

Almost everything I wrote in *The Enigma Cube* about this era, with a few obvious exceptions, was as accurate as I could make it, with the understanding that historians often disagree on details. For example, all historians agree that Stalin took millions of lives, but estimates as to the exact number vary wildly.

Wewelsburg Castle, where Otto first meets Himmler, is real. Spandau Prison is real. And the Berghof, Hitler's mountain retreat, is also real, complete with extensive underground tunnels.

The superweapons programs described in the text, including the space-based sun gun, sonic emitters, and five-story-tall, three-million-pound cannons, were real as well.

The Allied attacks on the submarine base in Italy, and the heavy water plant in Norway, also happened, although their spacing wasn't close enough to match what is depicted in the novel.

Hitler did cultivate a shrieking voice when speaking publicly, one that he designed and rehearsed, and which many Germans at the time found hypnotic—so there really is only one known recording of his normal speaking voice.

The passages that describe the geopolitics of the era, and how they might have changed if Hitler was killed in 1943, were also as accurate as I could make them. I found it breathtaking how little I knew about this age. I had no idea that Nazi Germany and Stalinist Russia had signed a non-aggression treaty, or that Russia had been in talks to join the Axis Powers. I'm sure that most of you knew a lot more about this era than I did when I began this project. Still, I'd like to think my self-guided crash course in the subject (the same crash course that Justin Boyd took in the novel) brought me up to speed enough to be able to introduce at least some novel information.

It really is stunning that Stalin, Hitler, and Tojo were all active at the same time, each responsible for the deaths of millions of innocents. Talk about your axis of evil.

On a lighter note, the passage on the origins of duct tape is accurate, and I thought I'd expand upon it here just a bit (because there's nothing more awesome than duct tape).

Its inventor was a woman named Vesta Stoudt, who had two sons in the Navy, and who worked at the Green River Ordnance Plant, inspecting and packing cartridges used to launch rifle grenades. The cartridges were packed in boxes taped shut and waxed to make them waterproof. The problem was that the quick-release tabs on the tape often tore off when soldiers were in desperate need of ammo, leaving them scrambling to pry the boxes open while under fire. This cost numerous lives, which could one day include Vesta's sons. So Vesta proposed sealing the boxes with a strong, cloth-based waterproof tape instead. Voilà!

Naturally, her idea was shot down at the plant. Fortunately for the world, Vesta was far too stubborn to let that stop her. She ended up writing a letter to the president, himself, and the rest is history. If you'd like to read more of this history, or see a copy of her actual letter to FDR, you can Google, "The Woman Who Invented Duct Tape."

As I mentioned earlier, the two findings that most fascinated me were the prolonged and saturated usage of the *Heil Hitler* salute in German society, and the use of crystal meth and others drugs in this era. I had no idea crystal meth even existed back then. But not only did it exist, it played a huge role in the war. Again, who knew?

Apparently, Norman Ohler did, since he came out with a book on the subject in 2017, with perhaps the most perfect title of any book I've ever seen. *Blitzed*. The subtitle of the book is good, too—*Drugs in the Third Reich*. But nothing can compare to *Blitzed*, a book about getting *blitzed* to wage a *blitzkrieg*

Here is an excerpt from the book's back cover:

EXCERPT: The Third Reich was saturated with drugs. On the eve of World War II, Germany was a pharmaceutical powerhouse, and companies such as Merck and Bayer cooked up cocaine, opiates, and, most of all, methamphetamines, to be consumed by everyone from factory workers to housewives to millions of German soldiers. In fact, troops regularly took rations of a form of crystal meth, and the elevated energy and feelings of invincibility associated with the high even help to explain certain German military victories.

Enhanced Human Operations

I've used EHO commandos in two other novels, because I have no doubt these are quickly becoming real. The race to create supersoldiers has been on for some time, but we now have better and better tools to do the job.

The two excerpts about enhanced soldiers that I provided at the start of Part 3 of the novel are real. As a reminder, the first was from *Popular Mechanics* and quoted then Deputy Defense Secretary Bob Work about the need for America to catch up to its rivals on the world stage with respect to enhancements. The second was from the

San Diego Union-Tribune, my hometown paper, which indicated that EHO programs had become all but inevitable.

In short, I didn't borrow the EHO concept from science fiction, I borrowed it from present-day reality.

Before I leave this section, I'll go through some of the enhancements described in the novel. If you've read my other novels with EHO characters, most of this will sound very familiar, so I would encourage you to skip it.

SMART CONTACT LENSES: These are being worked on now, and I've begun to use them in many of my novels. Why? Because I find their potential breathtaking.

I have provided a brief excerpt below from an article that appeared in the May 2016 edition of *Computerworld*, entitled, "Why a Smart Contact Lens is the Ultimate Wearable." This article also describes the possibility of night vision. Before I read this, I never would have had the audacity to think night vision capabilities could be embedded in a contact lens, even in a futuristic novel—so this is an example in which reality was ahead of my imagination.

EXCERPT: Smart contact lenses sound like science fiction. But there's already a race to develop technology for the contact lenses of the future—ones that will give you superhuman vision and will offer heads-up displays, video cameras, medical sensors, and much more. In fact, these products are already being developed.

Sounds unreal, right? But it turns out that eyeballs are the perfect place to put technology.

Contact lenses sit on the eye, and so can enhance vision. They're exposed to both light and the mechanical movement of blinking, so they can harvest energy.

University of Michigan scientists are building a contact lens that can give soldiers and others the ability to see in the dark using thermal imaging. The technology uses graphene, a single layer of carbon atoms, to pick up the full spectrum of light, including ultraviolet light.

Sony applied for a patent for a smart contact lens that can record video. You control it by blinking your eyes. According to Sony's patent, sensors in the lens can tell the difference between voluntary and involuntary blinks.

SAGE (and subvocal communication): I could fill hundreds of pages detailing the various advances in both hardware and software that make the creation of something like Sage almost inevitable, but I'll spare you. There is just too much, and I suspect that no reader doubts that an AI of this size, and with these capabilities, is just around the corner.

Computers that can recognize human thoughts and engage in a sort of telepathy are being developed now, and prosthetic limbs and video games, among other items, can now be controlled using thoughts alone. I could have used this as the means of communication between EHO agents and their AIs, but chose subvocal communication instead.

So before I leave this section, I'll share an excerpt from a 2014 article from *New Scientist,* entitled, "NASA develops 'mind-reading' system." (Despite the title, this is about subvocal communication.)

EXCERPT: A computer program that can read silently spoken words by analyzing nerve signals in our mouths and throats has been developed by NASA. Preliminary results show that using button-sized sensors, which attach under the chin and on the side of the Adam's apple, it is possible to pick up and recognize nerve signals and patterns from the tongue and vocal cords that correspond to specific words.

"Biological signals arise when reading or using silent, sub-auditory speech, with or without actual lip or facial movement," says Chuck Jorgensen, a neuro-engineer at NASA. Just the slightest movements in the voice box and tongue is all it needs to work.

The sensors have already been used to do simple web searches. In everyday life, they could even be used to communicate on the sly—people could use them on crowded buses without being overheard, say the NASA scientists.

RESPIROCYTES: The concept behind the respirocyte is real, although the reality is many years away. The theoretical underpinnings of this engineering marvel were introduced by Robert Freitas, a nanotechnology researcher, in a paper entitled, "A Mechanical Artificial Red Blood Cell: Exploratory Design in Medical Nanotechnology."

Here is a fascinating excerpt from an article in *The Nano Age.com*, entitled, "Respirocytes—Improving Upon Nature's Design."

EXCERPT: A respirocyte is a theoretical engineering design for an artificial red blood cell. Respirocytes are micron-scale spherical robotic red blood cells containing an internal pressure of 1000 atmospheres of compressed oxygen and carbon dioxide. At this intense pressure, a respirocyte could hold 236 times more oxygen and carbon dioxide than our natural red blood cells. Respirocytes are an elegantly simplistic design, powered by glucose in the blood and able to manage carbonic acidity via an onboard internal nanocomputer and a multitude of chemical/pressure sensors. 3D nanoscale fabrication will allow respirocytes to be manufactured in practically unlimited supply very inexpensively.

An injection of such nanotechnological devices would enable a person to run at top speed for 15 minutes or remain underwater for four hours on a single breath.

BRAIN STIMULATION: The use of transcranial electrical brain stimulation to enhance performance has not only been studied, it has been used in the field, as was mentioned in the novel. Here is an excerpt from a 2017 article that appeared in *Military.com* entitled, "Super SEALs: Elite Units Pursue Brain-Stimulating Technologies."

EXCERPT: "In experiments, the concentration levels of people watching these screens would fall off in about 20 minutes," Szymanski said. "But they did studies whereby a little bit of electrical stimulation was applied, and they were able to maintain the same peak performance for 20 *hours*."

Transcranial electrical stimulation was one of the technologies touted by then-Defense Secretary Ash Carter in July 2016 as part of his Defense Innovation Unit Initiative. Since then, multiple SEAL units have begun actively testing the effectiveness of the technology, officials with Naval Special Warfare Command told *Military.com*.

"Early results show promising signs," he said. "Based on this, we are encouraged to continue and are moving forward with our studies."

ELECTROACTIVE BODY SUIT: Powered exoskeletons have been in the public eye since before the first *Iron Man* movie, for use by soldiers, the disabled, and even the average man or woman. I chose to use a less bulky version of a powered suit for *The Enigma Cube* that has been in development since 2017. The idea is to create exoskeletons that can double as clothing, and which work by expansion and contraction of fibers, just as human muscles do.

Slaughterbots (HKs)

The slaughterbots depicted in the novel aren't real—yet.

But we should be very afraid.

I first learned about these killers from several fans who alerted me to this technology and sent a link to the *Slaughterbots* video, which you can easily find by conducting a simple online search. My fans thought that this technology was terrifying, and that I might be able to use it in a novel. They were right on both counts. I encourage you to see the video, as nothing demonstrates the horrific potential of the technology any better.

The video, produced with almost Hollywood-level special effects, shows a future in which swarms of microdrones are used to kill political enemies, and was made to highlight the dangers of the development of lethal, autonomous weapons, which most knowledgeable sources suggest are right around the corner.

Are UFOs real?

There is no question that UFO sightings by well-trained observers have become increasingly common. What to make of it all? My instincts say that advanced alien visitors would either want to stay completely off our radar, or would want to announce their presence.

So this in-between state, where they don't announce their presence but are sloppy enough to be detected with great frequency, doesn't make sense to me. On the other hand, there is nothing to say that the motives of an alien species *have* to make sense to me.

I'll leave this section with an excerpt from a May 2019 article in the *New York Post*, entitled "UFOs have come out of the fringe and into the mainstream."

EXCERPT: You'd have to be living on another planet not to have heard one of the biggest news stories in recent times: After years of denial, it turns out that the US government has a secret program, researching and investigating UFOs.

Details were released of multiple events where UFOs have been tracked on radar and chased by military jets. Videos of three of these spectacular midair encounters have been made public, though many more have yet to be released. Also last year, the Defense Intelligence Agency (DIA) briefed Congress on this work. In a January 9, 2018, letter to key members of Congress, the DIA disclosed that they had researched anti-gravity, warp drives, wormholes, and other theoretical physics concepts needed for interstellar travel, as part of an effort to understand what they termed "foreign advanced aerospace weapon threats."

Controlling gravity

Everything written in the novel about what a device like the Enigma Cube might be able to do is scientifically accurate. Possibilities such as using gravity control to crush objects and float train cars are fairly obvious. But using gravity control to tap into higher dimensions, create wormholes, and power a warp drive are not as well known.

Anti-gravity has quickly become the Holy Grail of interstellar travel. The Defense Intelligence Agency (DIA) really did declassify research into these exotic means of traversing the galaxy recently (see above), and the excerpts from the reports that Sage read from in the novel are real. I printed out three such reports (which took a lot of paper, I can tell you), and they conclude that the physics is ready—all that is missing is the anti-gravity source.

Here are the titles of the DIA reports that I downloaded, if you have interest in doing so yourself.

- Warp Drive, Dark Energy, and the Manipulation of Extra Dimensions
- Traversable Wormholes, Stargates, and Negative Energy
- Advanced Space Propulsion Based on Vacuum (Spacetime Metric) Engineering

As always, one has to wonder if humanity will ever be mature enough to handle such capabilities, but I, for one, have always been optimistic, and believe that one day our descendants really will spread throughout the galaxy.

Time travel

Science suggests that time travel could well be possible someday. I presented my own time travel logic in the novel, but it's anyone's guess as to how this might actually work.

It goes without saying that time travel can get treacherously complicated in a hurry. I worked very hard to keep it all straight, and logically consistent with the rules I laid out. I believe I succeeded, but, of course, all I can guarantee is that I did my best.

Things really are getting better

I'm optimistic by nature, and I find it depressing how so many of us have become convinced that world is worse off than it's ever been, when just the opposite is true. So in several of my recent novels, I've thrown in discussions that correct the record.

For those of you who would like to read more about this subject, I highly recommend the following two books. They are both well written and extremely eye-opening.

1. *The Rational Optimist: How Prosperity Evolves*, by Matt Ridley
2. *Factfulness: Ten Reasons We're Wrong About the World—and Why Things Are Better Than You Think*, by Hans Rosling.

Just to give you a sense of content, here is an excerpt from FACTFULNESS:

EXCERPT: I have tested audiences from all around the world [asking if things are getting better or worse when it comes to poverty, democracy, violence, and so on], including medical students, teachers, scientists, journalists, activists, and even senior political decision makers. It is not a question of intelligence, but most of them—a stunning majority of them—get most of the answers devastatingly wrong. [So wrong that a chimpanzee choosing answers at random will consistently outguess any group of humans.]

What's more, the chimps' errors would be random, whereas the human errors _all tend to be in one direction._ Every group of people I ask thinks the world is _more_ frightening, _more_ violent, and _more_ hopeless—in short, more dramatic—than it really is.

This book is my very last battle in a lifelong mission to fight devastating global ignorance. It is my last attempt to make an impact on the world: to change people's ways of thinking, calm their irrational fears, and redirect their energies into constructive activities.

Miscellaneous Science

The information in the novel on the butterfly effect, chaos theory, zero-point energy, and how neutron stars are formed is all accurate. I thought using a mini-EMP gun would be cool, but I had no idea these were real. I thought they required a nuclear pulse. Imagine my surprise when I found DIY videos and instructions for making one in your own home. Who knew?

I'll leave you with an interesting zero-point field conjecture that solves a riddle presented by the creation story in the Bible. One that I explored in the novel, but ended up cutting.

According to the Bible, God said, "Let there be light," and there was light. But the Bible also makes it clear that this occurred on the very first day of creation. Fascinating, since the sun and stars weren't created until the _fourth_ day.

So either the creation passage needs some serious proofing, or it wasn't a mistake at all. Biblical scholars have long debated how there could be light without any stars. The Kabbalah, often called Jewish mysticism, explains this discrepancy by claiming that the light created on the first day was *different* than the light produced by stars. Not the kind of light we can see.

It turns out that this would fit the zero-point field perfectly, which is thought to have existed before the rest of creation. Electromagnetic particles that pop into and out of the zero-point field include infrared light, ultraviolet light, microwaves, and gamma-rays. All of these are forms of light, and all are carried on photons.

So before stars ever came on the scene, the entire universe was a zero-point field full of light, even though only some of it was in the visible spectrum. Perhaps this was what the Creator was calling forth on that very first day by commanding the universe to, "Let there be light."

China

The Chinese government does a great job of projecting a friendly, benign face to the world, but, alas, this government is increasingly clamping down on the civil rights of its wonderful population. I recommend that you read an article in *Time Magazine* entitled, "Five Ways China Has Become More Repressive Under President Xi Jinping," which has China ranked 176 out of 180 countries on a world index of press freedom, and calls them, "The world's worst jailer of the press."

The Chinese government oversees one of the strictest online censorship regimes in the world, and exerts strong ideological control over education and mass media. They restrict religious freedom, persecute human rights activists, and, according to the World Economic Forum, ranked 100 out of 144 countries for gender parity in 2017. Women and girls in China confront sexual abuse and harassment, employment discrimination, and domestic violence. China is also imprisoning over one million Muslims in what they officially call an effort to prevent terrorism, extremism, and separatism.

Finally, China is racing to implement a pervasive system of algorithmic surveillance that will turn China's leaders into a high-tech Big Brother. In 2015, China's Ministry of Public Safety called for the creation of an "omnipresent, completely connected, always on and fully controllable" national video surveillance network. One estimate puts the number of cameras in China at over two hundred million, with a plan to have four hundred million installed in just a few years. One hundred percent of Beijing is now blanketed by surveillance cameras.

All in all, while the Chinese regime is not even a fraction as troubling as the Nazis, it isn't the kind of regime one would want to be in sole possession of one or more Enigma Cubes.

So this concludes *The Enigma Cube* author notes section. I hope that you found it interesting. Now, as promised, I will provide my author bio and list of books.

ABOUT THE AUTHOR

Douglas E. Richards is the *New York Times* and *USA Today* bestselling author of *WIRED* and numerous other novels (see list below). A former biotech executive, Richards earned a BS in microbiology from the Ohio State University, a master's degree in genetic engineering from the University of Wisconsin (where he engineered mutant viruses now named after him), and an MBA from the University of Chicago.

In recognition of his work, Richards was selected to be a "special guest" at San Diego Comic-Con International, along with such icons as Stan Lee and Ray Bradbury. His essays have been featured in *National Geographic*, the *BBC*, *the Australian Broadcasting Corporation*, *Earth & Sky*, *Today's Parent*, and many others.

The author has two children and currently lives with his wife and dog in San Diego, California.

You can friend Richards on Facebook at Douglas E. Richards Author, visit his website at douglaserichards.com, and write to him at douglaserichards1@gmail.com

Near Future Science Fiction Thrillers by Douglas E. Richards
WIRED (Wired 1)
AMPED (Wired 2)

MIND'S EYE (Nick Hall 1)
BRAINWEB (Nick Hall 2)
MIND WAR (Nick Hall 3)

SPLIT SECOND (Split Second 1)
TIME FRAME (Split Second 2)

QUANTUM LENS
GAME CHANGER
INFINITY BORN
SEEKER
VERACITY
ORACLE
THE ENIGMA CUBE

Kids Science Fiction Thrillers (9 and up, enjoyed by kids and adults alike)
TRAPPED (Prometheus Project 1)
CAPTURED (Prometheus Project 2)
STRANDED (Prometheus Project 3)
OUT OF THIS WORLD
THE DEVIL'S SWORD